THE
BOURNE
SANCTION

ROBERT LUDLUM'S™
THE BOURNE SANCTION

A New Jason Bourne Novel by
Eric Van Lustbader

First published in Great Britain in 2008 by Orion Books,
an imprint of The Orion Publishing Group Ltd
Orion House, 5 Upper Saint Martin's Lane
London WC2H 9EA

An Hachette Livre UK Company

3 5 7 9 10 8 6 4

A CIP catalogue record for this book is available
from the British Library.

ISBN (hardback): 978 1 4091 0048 5
ISBN (Export Trade Paperback): 978 1 4091 0049 2

Printed and bound in Great Britain by
Clays Ltd, St Ives plc

The Orion Publishing Group's policy is to use papers that are natural,
renewable and recyclable products and made from wood grown in
sustainable forests. The logging and manufacturing processes are
expected to conform to the environmental regulations of the country of origin.

www.orionbooks.co.uk

For Dan and Linda Jariabka,
with thanks and love.

My thanks to:

The intrepid reporters at *The Exile*.
Bourne's adventures in Moscow
and Arkadin's history in Nizhny Tagil
would not have existed without their help.

Gregg Winter for turning me on to
the logistics of transporting LNG.

Henry Morrison for clutch
ideating at all hours.

A note to my readers:

I try to be as factual as possible in my novels,
but this is, after all, a work of fiction.
In order to make the story as exciting as possible,
I've inevitably taken artistic license
here and there, with places, objects, and,
possibly, even time.
I trust readers will overlook these small anomalies
and enjoy the ride.

Prologue

High Security Prison Colony 13, Nizhny Tagil, Russia/ Campione d'Italia, Switzerland

WHILE THE FOUR inmates waited for Borya Maks to appear, they lounged against filthy stone walls whose cold no longer affected them. Out in the prison yard where they smoked expensive black-market cigarettes made from harsh black Turkish tobacco, they talked among themselves as if they had nothing better to do than to suck the acrid smoke into their lungs, expel it in puffs that seemed to harden in the freezing air. Above their heads was a cloudless sky whose glittering starlight turned it into a depthless enamel shell. Ursa Major, Lynx, Canes Venatici, Perseus—these same constellations burned the heavens above Moscow, six hundred miles to the southwest, but how different life was here from the gaudy, overheated clubs of Trehgorny val and Sadovnicheskaya street.

By day the inmates of Colony 13 manufactured parts for the T-90, Russia's formidable battle tank. But at night what do men without conscience or emotion talk to one another about? Strangely, family. There was a stability to coming home to a wife and children that defined their previous lives like the massive walls of High Security Colony 13 defined their present ones. What they did to earn money—lie, cheat, steal, extort, blackmail, torture, and kill—was all they knew. That they did these things well was a given, otherwise they would have been dead. Theirs was a life outside civilization as most people knew it. Returning to the warmth of a familiar woman, to the homey smells of sweet beets, boiled cabbage, stewed meat, the fire of peppery vodka, was a comfort that made them all nostalgic. The nostalgia bound them as securely as the tattoos of their shadowy profession.

A soft whistle cut through the frosty night air, evaporated their reminiscences like turpentine on oil paint. The night lost all its imagined color, returned to blue and black as Borya Maks appeared. Maks was a big man—a man who lifted weights for an hour, followed by ninety minutes of skipping rope every single day he'd been inside. As a contract killer for Kazanskaya, a branch of the Russian *grupperovka* trafficking in drugs and black-market cars, he held a certain status among the fifteen hundred inmates of Colony 13. The guards feared and despised him. His reputation preceded him like a shadow at sunset. He was not unlike the eye of a hurricane, around which swirled the howling winds of violence and death. The latest being the fifth man in the group that was now four. Kazanskaya or no Kazanskaya, Maks had to be punished, otherwise all of them knew their days in Colony 13 were numbered.

They smiled at Maks. One of them offered him a cigarette, another lit it for him as he bent forward, cupping a hand to keep the tiny flame alive in the wind. The other two men each grabbed one of Maks's steelbanded arms, while the man who had offered the cigarette drove a makeshift knife he'd painstakingly honed in the prison factory toward Maks's solar plexus. At the last instant Maks slapped it away with a superbly attuned flick of his hand. Immediately the man with the burned match delivered a vicious uppercut to the point of Maks's chin.

Maks staggered back into the chests of the two men holding his arms. But at the same time, he stomped the heel of his left boot onto the instep of one of the men holding him. Shaking his left arm free, he swung his body in a sharp arc, driving his cocked elbow into the rib cage of the man holding his right arm. Free for the moment, he put his back against the wall deep in shadow. The four closed ranks, moving in for the kill. The one with the knife stepped to the fore, another slipped a curved scrap of metal over his knuckles.

The fight began in earnest with grunts of pain and effort, showers of sweat, smears of blood. Maks was powerful and canny; his reputation was well deserved, but though he delivered as good as he got, he was facing four determined enemies. When Maks drove one to his knees another would take his place, so that there were always two of them beating at him while the others regrouped and repaired themselves as best they could. The four had had no illusions about the task ahead of them. They knew they'd never overcome Maks at the first or even the second attack. Their plan was to wear him down in shifts; while they took breaks, they allowed him none.

And it appeared to be working. Bloody and bruised, they continued their relentless assault, until Maks drove the edge of his hand into the throat of one of the four—the one with the homemade knife—crushing his cricoid cartilage. As the man staggered back into the arms of his compatriots, gasping like a hooked fish, Maks grabbed the knife out of his hand. Then his eyes rolled up and he became a deadweight. Blinded by rage and bloodlust, the remaining three charged Maks.

Their rush almost succeeded in getting inside Maks's defenses, but he dealt with them calmly and efficiently. Muscles popped along his arms as he turned, presenting his left side to them, giving them a smaller target, even as he used the knife in short, flicking thrusts and stabs to inflict a picket line of wounds that, though not deep, produced a welter of blood. This was deliberate, Maks's counter to their tactic of trying to wear him out. Fatigue was one thing, loss of blood quite another.

One of his assailants lunged forward, slipped on his own blood, and Maks hammered him down. This created an opening, and the one with the makeshift knuckle-duster moved in, slamming the metal into the side of Maks's neck. Maks at once lost breath and strength. The remaining men beat an unholy tattoo on him and were on the verge of plowing him under when a guard emerged out of the murk to drive them methodically back with a solid wood truncheon whose force was far more devastating than any piece of scrap metal could be.

A shoulder separated, then cracked under the expertly wielded truncheon; another man had the side of his skull staved in. The third, turning to flee, was struck flush on his third sacral vertebra, which shattered on impact, breaking his back.

"What are you doing?" Maks said to the guard between attempts to regain control of his breathing. "I assumed these bastards bribed all the guards."

"They did." The guard grabbed Maks's elbow. "This way," he indicated with the glistening end of the truncheon.

Maks's eyes narrowed. "That's not the way back to the cells."

"Do you want to get out of here or not?" the guard said.

Maks nodded his conditional assent, and the two men loped across the deserted yard. The guard kept his body pressed against the wall, and Maks followed suit. They moved at a deliberate pace, he saw, that kept them out of the beams of the roving spotlights. He would have wondered who this guard was, but there was no time. Besides, in the back of his mind he'd been expecting something like this. He knew his boss, the head of the Kazanskaya, wasn't going to let him rot in Colony 13 for the rest of his life, if only because he was too valuable an asset to let rot. Who could possibly replace the great Borya Maks? Only one, perhaps: Leonid Arkadin. But Arkadin—whoever he was; no one Maks knew had ever met him or seen his face—wouldn't work for Kazanskaya, or any of the families; he was a freelancer, the last of a dying breed. If he existed at all, which, frankly, Maks doubted. He'd grown up with stories of bogeymen with all manner of unbelievable powers— for some perverse reason Russians delighted in trying to scare their children. But the fact was, Maks never believed in bogeymen, was never scared. He had no reason to be scared of the specter of Leonid Arkadin, either.

By this time the guard had pulled open a door midway along the wall. They ducked in just as a searchlight beam crawled across the stones against which, moments before, they had been pressed.

After several turnings, he found himself in the corridor that led to the communal men's shower, beyond which, he knew, was one of the two entries to the wing of the prison. How this guard meant to get them through the checkpoints was anyone's guess, but Maks wasted no energy trying to second-guess him. Up to now he'd known just what to do and how to do it. Why should this be any different? The man was clearly a professional. He'd researched the prison thoroughly, he obviously had major juice behind him: first, to have gotten in here, second, to have the apparent run of the place. That was Maks's boss all over.

As they moved down the corridor toward the opening to the showers, Maks said, "Who are you?"

"My name is unimportant," the guard said. "Who sent me is not."

Maks absorbed everything in the unnatural stillness of the prison night. The guard's Russian was flawless, but to Maks's practiced eye he didn't look Russian, or Georgian, Chechen, Ukrainian, or Azerbaijani, for that matter. He was small by Maks's standards, but then almost everyone was small by his standards. His body was toned, though, its responses finely honed. He possessed the preternatural stillness of properly harnessed energy. He made no move unless he needed to and then used only the amount of energy required, no more. Maks himself was like this, so it was easy for him to spot the subtle signs others would miss. The guard's eyes were pale, his expression grim, almost detached, like a surgeon in the OR. His light hair thick on top, spiked in a style that would have been unfamiliar to Maks had he not been an aficionado of international magazines and foreign films. In fact, if Maks didn't know better he'd say the guard was American. But that was impossible. Maks's boss didn't employ Americans; he co-opted them.

"So Maslov sent you," Maks said. Dimitri Maslov was the head of Kazanskaya. "It's about fucking time, let me tell you. Fifteen months in this place feels like fifteen years."

At that moment, as they came abreast of the showers, the guard, without turning fully around, swung the truncheon into the side of Maks's head. Maks, taken completely by surprise, staggered onto the bare concrete floor of the shower room, which reeked of mildew, disinfectant, and men lacking proper hygiene.

The guard came after him as nonchalantly as if he were out for the evening with a girl on his arm. He swung the truncheon almost lazily. He struck Maks on his left biceps, just hard enough to herd him backward toward the line of showerheads protruding from the moist rear wall. But Maks refused to be herded, by this guard or by anyone else. As the truncheon whistled down from the apex of its arc, he stepped forward, broke the trajectory of the blow with his tensed forearm. Now, inside the guard's line of defense, he could go to work in the way that suited the situation best.

The homemade knife was in his left hand. He thrust it point-first. When the guard moved to block it, he slashed upward, ripping the edge of the blade against flesh. He'd aimed for the underside of the guard's wrist, the nexus of veins that, if severed, would render the hand useless. The guard's reflexes were as fast as his own, though, and instead the blade scored the arm of the leather jacket. But it did not penetrate the leather as it should have. Maks only had time to register that the jacket must be lined with Kevlar or some other impenetrable material before the callused edge of the guard's hand struck the knife from his grip.

Another blow sent him reeling back. He tripped over one of the drain holes, his heel sinking into it, and the guard smashed the sole of his boot into the side of Maks's knee. There was an awful sound, the grinding of bone against bone as Maks's right leg collapsed.

As the guard closed in he said, "It wasn't Dimitri Maslov who sent me. It was Pyotr Zilber."

Maks struggled to extricate his heel, which he could no longer feel, from the drain hole. "I don't know who you're talking about."

The guard grabbed his shirtfront. "You killed his brother, Aleksei. One shot to the back of the head. They found him facedown in the Moskva River."

"It was business," Maks said. "Just business."

"Yes, well, this is personal," the guard said as he drove his knee into Maks's crotch.

Maks doubled over. When the guard bent to haul him upright, he slammed the top of his head against the point of the guard's chin. Blood spurted from between the guard's lips as his teeth cut into his tongue.

Maks used this advantage to drive his fist into the guard's side just over his kidney. The guard's eyes opened wide—the only indication that he felt pain—and he kicked Maks's ruined knee. Maks went down and stayed down. Agony flowed in a river through him. As he struggled to compartmentalize it, the guard kicked again. He felt his ribs give way, his cheek kissed the stinking concrete floor. He lay dazed, unable to rise.

The guard squatted down beside him. Seeing the grimace the guard made gave Maks a measure of satisfaction, but that was all he was destined to receive in the way of solace.

"I have money," Maks gasped weakly. "It's buried in a safe place where no one will find it. If you get me out of here, I'll lead you to it. You can have half. That's over half a million American dollars."

This only made the guard angry. He struck Maks hard on his ear, making sparks fly behind his eyes. His head rang with a pain that in anyone else would have been unendurable. "Do you think I'm like you? That I have no loyalty?" He spat into Maks's face.

"Poor Maks, you made a grave error killing this boy. People like Pyotr Zilber never forget. And they have the means to move heaven and earth to get what they want."

"All right," Maks whispered, "you can have it all. More than a million dollars."

"Pyotr Zilber wants you dead, Maks. I came here to tell you that. And to kill you." His expression changed subtly. "But first."

He extended Maks's left arm, trod on the wrist, pinning it securely against the rough concrete. He then produced a pair of thick-bladed pruning shears.

This procedure roused Maks from his pain-induced lethargy. "What are you doing?"

The guard grasped Maks's thumb, on the back of which was a tattoo of a skull, mirroring the larger one on his chest. It was a symbol of Maks's exalted status in his murderous profession.

"Besides wanting you to know the identity of the man who ordered your death, Pyotr Zilber requires proof of your demise, Maks."

The guard settled the shears at the base of Maks's thumb, then he squeezed the handles together. Maks made a gurgling sound, not unlike that of a baby.

As a butcher would, the guard wrapped the thumb in a square of waxed paper, snapped a rubber band around it, then sealed it in a plastic bag.

"Who are you?" Maks managed to get out.

"My name is Arkadin," the guard said. He opened his shirt, revealing a pair of candlestick tattoos on his chest. "Or, in your case, Death."

With a movement full of grace Arkadin broke Maks's neck.

Crisp Alpine sunlight lit up Campione d'Italia, a tiny exquisite Italian enclave of two-thirds of a square mile nestled within the clockwork-perfect setting of Switzerland. Owing to its prime position on the eastern edge of Lake Lugano, it was both stupendously picturesque and an excellent place to be domiciled. Like Monaco, it was a tax haven for wealthy individuals who owned magnificent villas and gambled away idle hours at the Casino di Campione. Money and valuables could be stored in Swiss banks, with their justly famous reputation for discreet service, completely shielded from international law enforcement's prying eyes.

It was this little-known, idyllic setting that Pyotr Zilber chose for the first face-to-face meeting with Leonid Arkadin. He had contacted Arkadin through an intermediary, for various security reasons opting not to contact the contract killer directly. From an early age Pyotr had learned that there was no such thing as being too security-minded. There was a heavy burden of responsibility being born into a family with secrets.

From his lofty perch on the overlook just off Via Totone, Pyotr had a breathtaking panorama of the red-brown tile roofs of the chalets and apartment houses, the palm-lined squares of the town, the cerulean waters of the lake, the mountains, their shoulders mantled with capes of mist. The distant drone of powerboats, leaving frothy scimitars of white wake, came to him intermittently while he sat in his gray BMW. In truth, part of his mind was already on his imminent trip. Having gotten the stolen document, he had sent it on the long journey along his network to its ultimate end.

Being here excited him in the most extraordinary way. His anticipation of what was to come, of the accolades he would receive, especially from his father, sent an electric charge through him. He was on the brink of an unimaginable victory. Arkadin had called him from the Moscow airport to tell him that the operation had been successful, that he had in his possession the physical proof Pyotr required.

He had taken a risk going after Maks, but the man had murdered Pyotr's brother. Was he supposed to turn his cheek and forget the affront? He knew better than anyone his father's stern dictum to keep to the shadows, to remain hidden, but he thought this one act of vengeance was worth the risk. Besides, he'd handled the matter via intermediaries, the way he knew his father would have.

Hearing the deep growl of a car engine, he turned, saw a dark blue Mercedes come up the rise toward the overlook.

The only real risk he was taking was going to happen right now, and that, he knew, couldn't be helped. If Leonid Arkadin was able to infiltrate Colony 13 in Nizhny Tagil and kill Borya Maks, he was the man for the next job Pyotr had in mind. One his father should have taken care of years ago. Now he had a chance to finish what his father was too timid to attempt. To the bold belonged the spoils. The document he'd procured was proof positive that the time for caution was at an end.

The Mercedes drew to a stop beside his BMW, a man with light hair and even lighter eyes emerging with the fluidity of a tiger. He was not a particularly large man, he wasn't overmuscled like many of the Russian *grupperovka* personnel; nevertheless something inside him radiated a quiet menace Pyotr found impressive. From a very young age Pyotr had been exposed to dangerous men. At the age of eleven he had killed a man who had threatened his mother. He hadn't hesitated in the slightest. If he had, his mother would have died that afternoon in the Azerbaijani bazaar at the hands of the knife-wielding assassin. That assassin, as well as others over the years, had been sent by Semion Icoupov, Pyotr's father's implacable nemesis, the man who at this moment was safely ensconced in his villa on Viale Marco Campione, not a mile from where Pyotr and Leonid Arkadin now stood.

The two men did not greet each other, did not address each other by name. Arkadin took out the stainless-steel briefcase Pyotr had sent him. Pyotr reached for its twin inside the BMW. The exchange was made on the hood of the Mercedes. The men put the cases down side by side, unlocked them. Arkadin's contained Maks's severed thumb, wrapped and bagged. Pyotr's contained thirty thousand dollars in diamonds, the only currency Arkadin accepted as payment.

Arkadin waited patiently. As Pyotr unwrapped the thumb he stared out at the lake, perhaps wishing he were on one of the powerboats slicing a path away from land. Maks's thumb had withered slightly on the journey from Russia. A certain odor emanated from it, which was not unfamiliar to Pyotr Zilber. He'd buried his share of family and compatriots. He turned so the sunlight struck the tattoo, produced a small magnifying glass through which he peered at the marking.

At length, he put the glass away. "Did he prove difficult?"

Arkadin turned back to face him. For a moment he stared implacably into Pyotr's eyes. "Not especially."

Pyotr nodded. He threw the thumb over the side of the overlook, tossed the empty case after it. Arkadin, taking this to be the conclusion of their deal, reached for the packet filled with diamonds. Opening it, he took out a jeweler's loupe, plucked a diamond at random, examined it with an expert's aplomb.

When he nodded, satisfied as to the clarity and color, Pyotr said, "How would you like to make three times what I paid you for this assignment?"

"I'm a very busy man," Arkadin said, revealing nothing.

Pyotr inclined his head deferentially. "I have no doubt."

"I only take assignments that interest me."

"Would Semion Icoupov interest you?"

Arkadin stood very still. Two sports cars passed, heading up the road as if it were Le Mans. In the echo of their throaty exhausts, Arkadin said, "How convenient that we happen to be in the tiny principality where Semion Icoupov lives."

"You see?" Pyotr grinned. "I know precisely how busy you are."

"Two hundred thousand," Arkadin said. "The usual terms."

Pyotr, who had anticipated Arkadin's fee, nodded his agreement. "Conditional on immediate delivery."

"Agreed."

Pyotr popped the trunk of the BMW. Inside were two more cases. From one, he transferred a hundred thousand in diamonds to the case on the Mercedes's hood. From the other, he handed Arkadin a packet of documents, including a satellite map, indicating the precise location of Icoupov's villa, a list of his bodyguards, and a set of architectural blueprints of the villa, including the electrical circuits, the separate power supply, and details of the security devices in place.

"Icoupov is in residence now," Pyotr said. "How you make your way inside is up to you."

"I'll be in touch." After paging through the documents, asking a question here and there, Arkadin placed them in the case on top of the diamonds, snapped the lid shut, slung the case into the passenger's seat of the Mercedes as easily as if it were filled with balloons.

"Tomorrow, same time, right here," Pyotr said as Arkadin slid behind the wheel.

The Mercedes started up, its engine purring. Then Arkadin put it in gear. As he slid out onto the road, Pyotr turned to walk to the front of the BMW. He heard the squeal of brakes, the slewing of a car, and turned to see the Mercedes heading directly toward him. He was paralyzed for a moment. *What the hell is he doing?* he asked himself. Belatedly, he began to run. But the Mercedes was already on top of him, its front grille slammed into him, pinned him to the side of the BMW.

Through a haze of agony he saw Arkadin get out of his car, walk toward him. Then something gave out inside him and he passed into oblivion.

He regained consciousness in a paneled study, gleaming with polished brass fixtures, lush with jewel-toned Isfahan carpets. A walnut desk and chair were within his field of vision, as was an enormous window that looked out on the sparkling water of Lake Lugano and the veiled mountains behind it. The sun was low in the west, sending long shadows the color of a fresh bruise over the water, up the whitewashed walls of Campione d'Italia.

He was bound to a plain wooden chair that seemed to be as out of place in the surroundings of wealth and power as he was. He tried to take a deep breath, winced with shocking pain. Looking down, he saw bandages wrapped tightly around his chest, realized that he must have at least one cracked rib.

"At last you have returned from the land of the dead. For a while there you had me worried."

It was painful for Pyotr to turn his head. Every muscle in his body felt as if it were on fire. But his curiosity would not be denied, so he bit his lip, kept turning his head until a man came into view. He was rather small, stoop-shouldered. Glasses with round lenses were fitted over large, watery eyes. His bronzed scalp, lined and furrowed as pastureland, was without a single hair, but as if to make up for his bald pate his eyebrows were astonishingly thick, arching up over the skin above his eye sockets. He looked like one of those wily Turkish traders from the Levant.

"Semion Icoupov," Pyotr said. He coughed. His mouth felt stiff, as if it were stuffed with cotton. He could taste the salt-copper of his own blood, and swallowed heavily.

Icoupov could have moved so that Pyotr didn't have to twist his neck so far in order to keep him in view, but he didn't. Instead he dropped his gaze to the sheet of heavy paper he'd unrolled. "You know, these architectural plans of my villa are so complete I'm learning things about the building I never knew before. For instance, there is a sub-basement below the cellar." He ran his stubby forefinger along the surface of the plan. "I suppose it would take some doing to break into it now, but who knows, it might prove worthwhile."

His head snapped up and he fixed Pyotr with his gaze. "For in-stance, it would make a perfect place for your incarceration. I'd be as-sured that not even my closest neighbor would hear you scream." He smiled, a cue for a terrible focusing of his energies. "And you *will* scream, Pyotr, this I promise you." His head swiveled, the beacons of his eyes searching out someone else. "Won't he, Leonid?"

Now Arkadin came into Pyotr's field of view. At once he grabbed Pyotr's head with one hand, dug into the hinge of his jaw with the other. Pyotr had no choice but to open his mouth. Arkadin checked his teeth one by one. Pyotr knew that he was looking for a false tooth filled with liquid cyanide. A death pill.

"All his," Arkadin said as he let go of Pyotr.

"I'm curious," Icoupov said. "How in the world did you procure these plans, Pyotr?"

Pyotr, waiting for the proverbial shoe to drop, said nothing. But all at once he began to shiver so violently his teeth chattered.

Icoupov signaled to Arkadin, who swaddled Pyotr's upper body in a thick blanket. Icoupov brought a carved cherry chair to a position facing Pyotr, sat down on it.

He continued just as if he hadn't expected an answer. "I must admit that shows a fair amount of initiative on your part. So the clever boy has grown into a clever young man." Icoupov shrugged. "I'm hardly sur-prised. But listen to me now, I know who you really are—did you think you could fool me by continually changing your name? The truth of the matter is you've prodded open a wasp's nest, so *you* shouldn't be sur-prised to get stung. And stung and stung and stung."

He inclined his upper body toward Pyotr. "However much your fa-ther and I despise each other, we grew up together; once we were as close as brothers. So. Out of respect for him, I won't lie to you, Pyotr. This bold foray of yours won't end well. In fact, it was doomed from the start. And d'you want to know why? You needn't answer; of course you do. Your earthly needs betrayed you, Pyotr. That delicious girl you've been bedding for the past six months belongs to me. I know you're thinking that's not possible. I know you vetted her thoroughly; that's your MO. I anticipated all your inquiries; I made certain you received the answers you needed to hear."

Pyotr, staring into Icoupov's face, found his teeth chattering again, no matter how tightly he clamped his jaw.

"Tea, please, Philippe," Icoupov said to an unseen person. Moments later, a slender young man set an English silver tea service onto a low table at Icoupov's right hand. Like a favorite uncle, Icoupov went about pouring and sugaring the tea. He put the porcelain cup to Pyotr's bluish lips, said, "Please drink, Pyotr. It's for your own good."

Pyotr stared implacably at him until Icoupov said, "Ah, yes, I see." He sipped the tea from the cup himself to assure Pyotr it was only tea, then offered it again. The rim chattered against Pyotr's teeth, but eventually Pyotr drank, slowly at first, then more avidly. When the tea was drained, Icoupov set the cup back on its matching saucer. By this time Pyotr's shivering had subsided.

"Feeling better?"

"I'll feel better," Pyotr said, "when I get out of here."

"Ah, well, I'm afraid that won't be for some time," Icoupov said. "If ever. Unless you tell me what I want to know."

He hitched his chair closer; the benign uncle's expression was now nowhere to be found. "You stole something that belongs to me," he said. "I want it back."

"It never belonged to you; you stole it first."

Pyotr replied with such venom that Icoupov said, "You hate me as much as you love your father, this is your basic problem, Pyotr. You never learned that hate and love are essentially the same in that the person who loves is as easily manipulated as the person who hates."

Pyotr screwed up his mouth, as if Icoupov's words left a bitter taste in his mouth. "Anyway, it's too late. The document is already on its way."

Instantly, there was a change in Icoupov's demeanor. His face became as closed as a fist. A certain tension lent his entire small body the aspect of a weapon about to be launched. "Where did you send it?"

Pyotr shrugged, but said nothing more.

Icoupov's face turned dark with momentary rage. "Do you think I know nothing about the information and matériel pipeline you have been refining for the past three years? It's how you send information you stole from me back to your father, wherever he is."

For the first time since he'd regained consciousness, Pyotr smiled. "If you knew anything important about the pipeline, you'd have rolled it up by now."

At this Icoupov regained the icy control over his emotions.

"I told you talking to him would be useless," Arkadin said from his position directly behind Pyotr's chair.

"Nevertheless," Icoupov said, "there are certain protocols that must be acknowledged. I'm not an animal."

Pyotr snorted.

Icoupov eyed his prisoner. Sitting back, he fastidiously pulled up his trouser leg, crossed one leg over the other, laced his stubby fingers on his lower belly.

"I give you one last chance to continue this conversation."

It was not until the silence was drawn out into an almost intolerable length that Icoupov raised his gaze to Arkadin.

"Pyotr, why are you doing this to me?" he said with a resigned tone. And then to Arkadin, "Begin."

Though it cost him in pain and breath, Pyotr twisted as far as he was able, but he couldn't see what Arkadin was doing. He heard the sound of implements on a metal cart being rolled across the carpet.

Pyotr turned back. "You don't frighten me."

"I don't mean to frighten you, Pyotr," Icoupov said. "I mean to hurt you, very, very badly."

* * *

With a painful convulsion, Pyotr's world contracted to the pinpoint
of a star in the night sky. He was locked within the confines of his mind,
but despite all his training, all his courage, he could not compartmentalize the pain. There was a hood over his head, drawn tight around his
neck. This confinement magnified the pain a hundredfold because,
despite his fearlessness, Pyotr was subject to claustrophobia. For someone who never went into caves, small spaces, or even underwater, the
hood was the worst of all possible worlds. His senses could tell him
that, in fact, he wasn't confined at all, but his mind wouldn't accept that
input—it was in the full flight of panic. The pain Arkadin was inflicting
on him was one thing, its magnification was quite another. Pyotr's mind
was spinning out of control. He felt a wildness enter him—the wolf
caught in a trap that begins to frantically gnaw its leg off. But the mind
was not a limb; he couldn't gnaw it off.

Dimly, he heard someone asking him a question to which he knew
the answer. He didn't want to give the answer, but he knew he would
because the voice told him the hood would come off if he answered.
His crazed mind only knew it needed the hood off; it could no longer
distinguish right from wrong, good from evil, lies from truth. It reacted
to only one imperative: the need to survive. He tried to move his fingers,
but in bending over him his interrogator must have been pressing down
on them with the heels of his hands.

Pyotr couldn't hang on any longer. He answered the question.

The hood didn't come off. He howled in indignation and terror. *Of
course it didn't come off*, he thought in a tiny instant of lucidity. If it did,
he'd have no incentive to answer the next question and the next and
the next.

And he would answer them—all of them. He knew this with a bone-
chilling certainty. Even though part of him suspected that the hood
might never come off, his trapped mind would take the chance. It had
no other choice.

But now that he could move his fingers, there was another choice.

Just before the whirlwind of panicked madness overtook him again, Pyotr made that choice. There was one way out and, saying a silent prayer to Allah, he took it.

Icoupov and Arkadin stood over Pyotr's body. Pyotr's head lay on one side; his lips were very blue, and a faint but distinct foam emanated from his half-open mouth. Icoupov bent down, sniffed the scent of bitter almonds.

"I didn't want him dead, Leonid, I was very clear on the point." Icoupov was vexed. "How did he get hold of cyanide?"

"They used a variation I've never encountered." Arkadin did not look happy himself. "He was fitted with a false fingernail."

"He would have talked."

"Of course he would have talked," Arkadin said. "He'd already begun."

"So he took it upon himself to shut his own mouth, forever." Icoupov shook his head in distaste. "This will have significant fallout. He's got dangerous friends."

"I'll find them," Arkadin said. "I'll kill them."

Icoupov shook his head. "Even you can't kill them all in time."

"I can contact Mischa."

"And risk losing everything? No. I understand your connection with him—closest friend, mentor. I understand the urge to talk to him, to see him. But you can't, not until this is finished and Mischa comes home. That's final."

"I understand."

Icoupov walked over the window, stood with his hand behind his back contemplating the fall of darkness. Lights sparkled along the edges of the lake, up the hillside of Campione d'Italia. There ensued a long silence while he contemplated the face of the altered landscape. "We'll have to move up the timetable, that's all there is to it. And you'll take Sevastopol as a starting point. Use the one name you got out of Pyotr before he committed suicide."

He turned around to face Arkadin. "Everything now rides on you, Leonid. This attack has been in the planning stages for three years. It has been designed to cripple the American economy. Now there are barely two weeks left before it becomes a reality." He walked noiselessly across the carpet. "Philippe will provide you with money, documents, weaponry that will escape electronic detection, anything you need. Find this man in Sevastopol. Retrieve the document, and when you do, follow the pipeline back and shut it down so that it will never again be used to threaten our plans."

Book One

One

WHO IS DAVID Webb?"

Moira Trevor, standing in front of his desk at Georgetown University, asked the question so seriously that Jason Bourne felt obliged to answer.

"Strange," he said, "no one's ever asked me that before. David Webb is a linguistics expert, a man with two children who are living happily with their grandparents"—Marie's parents—"on a ranch in Canada."

Moira frowned. "Don't you miss them?"

"I miss them terribly," Bourne said, "but the truth is they're far better off where they are. What kind of life could I offer them? And then there's the constant danger from my Bourne identity. Marie was kidnapped and threatened in order to force me to do something I had no intention of doing. I won't make that mistake again."

"But surely you see them from time to time."

"As often as I can, but it's difficult. I can't afford to have anyone following me back to them."

"My heart goes out to you," Moira said, meaning it. She smiled. "I

must say it's odd seeing you here, on a university campus, behind a desk."
She laughed. "Shall I buy you a pipe and a jacket with elbow patches?"

Bourne smiled. "I'm content here, Moira. Really I am."

"I'm happy for you. Martin's death was difficult for both of us. My anodyne is going back to work full-bore. Yours is obviously here, in a new life."

"An old life, really." Bourne looked around the office. "Marie was happiest when I was teaching, when she could count on me being home every night in time to have dinner with her and the kids."

"What about you?" Moira asked. "Were you happiest here?"

A cloud passed across Bourne's face. "I was happy being with Marie." He turned to her. "I can't imagine being able to say that to anyone else but you."

"A rare compliment from you, Jason."

"Are my compliments so rare?"

"Like Martin, you're a master at keeping secrets," she said. "But I have doubts about how healthy that is."

"I'm sure it's not healthy at all," Bourne said. "But it's the life we chose."

"Speaking of which." She sat down on a chair opposite him. "I came early for our dinner date to talk to you about a work situation, but now, seeing how content you are here, I don't know whether to continue."

Bourne recalled the first time he had seen her, a slim, shapely figure in the mist, dark hair swirling about her face. She was standing at the parapet in the Cloisters, overlooking the Hudson River. The two of them had come there to say good-bye to their mutual friend Martin Lindros, whom Bourne had valiantly tried to save, only to fail.

Today Moira was dressed in a wool suit, a silk blouse open at the throat. Her face was strong, with a prominent nose, deep brown eyes wide apart, intelligent, curved slightly at their outer corners. Her hair fell to her shoulders in luxuriant waves. There was an uncommon serenity about her, a woman who knew what she was about, who wouldn't be intimidated or bullied by anyone, woman or man.

Perhaps this last was what Bourne liked best about her. In that, though in no other way, she was like Marie. He had never pried into her relationship with Martin, but he assumed it had been romantic, since Martin had given Bourne standing orders to send her a dozen red roses should he ever die. This Bourne had done, with a sadness whose depth surprised even him.

Settled in her chair, one long, shapely leg crossed over her knee, she looked the model of a European businesswoman. She had told him that she was half French, half English, but her genes still carried the imprint of ancient Venetian and Turkish ancestors. She was proud of the fire in her mixed blood, the result of wars, invasions, fierce love.

"Go on." He leaned forward, elbows on his desk. "I want to hear what you have to say."

She nodded. "All right. As I've told you, NextGen Energy Solutions has completed our new liquid natural gas terminal in Long Beach. Our first shipment is due in two weeks. I had this idea, which now seems utterly crazy, but here goes. I'd like you to head up the security procedures. My bosses are worried the terminal would make an awfully tempting target for any terrorist group, and I agree. Frankly, I can't think of anyone who'd make it more secure than you."

"I'm flattered, Moira. But I have obligations here. As you know, Professor Specter has installed me as the head of the Comparative Linguistics Department. I don't want to disappoint him."

"I like Dominic Specter, Jason, really I do. You've made it clear that he's your mentor. Actually, he's David Webb's mentor, right? But it's Jason Bourne I first met, it feels like it's Jason Bourne I've been coming to know these last few months. Who is Jason Bourne's mentor?"

Bourne's face darkened, as it had at the mention of Marie. "Alex Conklin's dead."

Moira shifted in her chair. "If you come work with me there's no baggage attached to it. Think about it. It's a chance to leave your past lives behind—both David Webb's and Jason Bourne's. I'm flying to Munich shortly because a key element of the terminal is being manufactured there. I need an expert opinion on it when I check the specs."

"Moira, there are any number of experts you can use."

"But none whose opinion I trust as much as yours. This is crucial stuff, Jason. More than half the goods shipped into the United States come through the port at Long Beach, so our security measures have to be something special. The US government has already shown it has neither the time nor the inclination to secure commercial traffic, so we're forced to police it ourselves. The danger to this terminal is real and it's serious. I know how expert you are at bypassing even the most arcane security systems. You're the perfect candidate to put nonconventional measures into place."

Bourne stood. "Moira, listen to me. Marie was David Webb's biggest cheerleader. Since her death, I've let go of him completely. But he's not dead, he's not an invalid. He lives on inside me. When I fall asleep I dream of his life as if it was someone else's, and I wake up in a sweat. I feel as if a part of me has been sliced off. I don't want to feel that way anymore. It's time to give David Webb his due."

Veronica Hart's step was light and virtually carefree as she was admitted past checkpoint after checkpoint on her way into the bunker that was the West Wing of the White House. The job she was about to be handed—director of Central Intelligence—was a formidable one, especially in the aftermath of last year's twin debacles of murder and gross breach of security. Nevertheless, she had never been happier. Having a sense of purpose was vital to her; being singled out for daunting responsibility was the ultimate validation of all the arduous work, setbacks, and threats she'd had to endure because of her gender.

There was also the matter of her age. At forty-six she was the youngest DCI in recent memory. Being the youngest at something was nothing new to her. Her astonishing intelligence combined with her fierce determination to ensure that she was the youngest to graduate from her college, youngest to be appointed to military intelligence, to central army command, to a highly lucrative Black River private intelligence position in Afghanistan and the Horn of Africa where, to this day, not even the heads of the seven directorates within CI knew precisely where she had been posted, whom she commanded, or what her mission had been.

Now, at last, she was steps away from the apex, the top of the intelligence heap. She'd successfully leapt all the hurdles, sidestepped every trap, negotiated every maze, learned who to befriend and who to show her back to. She had endured relentless sexual innuendo, rumors of conduct unbecoming, stories of her reliance on her male inferiors who supposedly did her thinking for her. In each case she had triumphed, emphatically putting a stake through the heart of the lies and, in some instances, taking down their instigators.

She was, at this stage of her life, a force to be reckoned with, a fact in which she justifiably reveled. So it was with a light heart that she approached her meeting with the president. In her briefcase was a thick file detailing the changes she proposed to make in CI to clean up the unholy mess left behind by Karim al-Jamil and the subsequent murder of her predecessor. Not surprisingly, CI was in total disarray, morale had never been lower, and of course there was resentment across the board from the all-male directorate heads, each of whom felt he should have been elevated to DCI.

The chaos and low morale were about to change, and she had a raft of initiatives to ensure it. She was absolutely certain that the president would be delighted not only with her plans but also with the speed with which she would implement them. An intelligence organization as important and vital as CI could not long endure the despair into which it had sunk. Only the anti-terrorist black ops, Typhon, brainchild of Martin Lindros, was running normally, and for that she had its new director, Soraya Moore, to thank. Soraya's assumption of command had been seamless. Her operatives loved her, would follow her into the fires of Hades should she ask it of them. As for the rest of CI, it was for herself to heal, energize, and give a refocused sense of purpose.

She was surprised—perhaps *shocked* wasn't too strong a word—to find the Oval Office occupied not only by the president but also by Luther LaValle, the Pentagon's intelligence czar, and his deputy, General

Richard P. Kendall. Ignoring the others, she walked across the plush American blue carpet to shake the president's hand. She was tall, long-necked, and slender. Her ash-blond hair was cut in a stylish fashion that fell short of being masculine but lent her a business-like air. She wore a midnight-blue suit, low-heeled pumps, small gold earrings, and a minimum of makeup. Her nails were cut square across.

"Please have a seat, Veronica," the president said. "You know Luther LaValle and General Kendall."

"Yes." Veronica inclined her head fractionally. "Gentlemen, a pleasure to see you." Though nothing could be farther from the truth.

She hated LaValle. In many ways he was the most dangerous man in American intelligence, not the least because he was backed by the immensely powerful E. R. "Bud" Halliday, the secretary of defense. LaValle was a power-hungry egotist who believed that he and his people should be running American intelligence, period. He fed on war the way other people fed on meat and potatoes. And though she had never been able to prove it, she suspected that he was behind several of the more lurid rumors that had circulated about her. He enjoyed ruining other people's reputations, savored standing impudently on the skulls of his enemies.

Ever since Afghanistan and, subsequently, Iraq, LaValle had seized the initiative—under the typically wide-ranging and murky Pentagon rubric of "preparing the battlefield" for the troops to come—to expand the purview of the Pentagon's intelligence-gathering initiatives until now they encroached uncomfortably on those of CI. It was an open secret within American intelligence circles that he coveted CI's operatives and its long-established international networks. Now, with the Old Man and his anointed successor dead, it would fit LaValle's MO to try to make a land grab in the most aggressive manner possible. This was why his presence and that of his lapdog set off the most serious warning bells inside Veronica's mind.

There were three chairs ranged in a rough semicircle in front of the president's desk. Two of them were, of course, filled. Veronica took the third chair, acutely aware that she was flanked by the two men, doubtless by design. She laughed inwardly. If these two thought to intimidate her by making her feel surrounded, they were sorely mistaken. But then as the president began to talk she hoped to God her laugh wouldn't echo hollowly in her mind an hour from now.

Dominic Specter hurried around the corner as Bourne was locking the door to his office. The deep frown that creased his high forehead vanished the moment he saw Bourne.

"David, I'm so glad I caught you before you left!" he said with great enthusiasm. Then, turning his charm on Bourne's companion, he added, "And with the magnificent Moira, no less." As always the perfect gentleman, he bowed to her in the Old World European fashion.

He returned his attention to Bourne. He was a short man full of unbridled energy despite his seventy-odd years. His head seemed perfectly round, surmounted by a halo of hair that wound from ear to ear. His eyes were dark and inquisitive, his skin a deep bronze. His generous mouth made him look vaguely and amusingly like a frog about to spring from one lily pad to another. "A matter of some concern has come up and I need your opinion." He smiled. "I see that this evening is out of the question. Would dinner tomorrow be inconvenient?"

Bourne discerned something behind Specter's smile that gave him pause; something was troubling his old mentor. "Why don't we meet for breakfast?"

"Are you certain I'm not putting you out, David?" But he couldn't hide the relief that flooded his face.

"Actually, breakfast is better for me," Bourne lied, to make things easier for Specter. "Eight o'clock?"

"Splendid! I look forward to it." With a nod in Moira's direction he was off.

"A firecracker," Moira said. "If only I'd had professors like him."

Bourne looked at her. "Your college years must've been hell."

She laughed. "Not quite as bad as all that, but then I only had two years of it before I fled to Berlin."

"If you'd had professors like Dominic Specter, your experience would have been far different, believe me." They sidestepped several knots of students gathered to gossip or to trade questions about their last classes.

They strode along the corridor, out the doors, descended the steps to the quad. He and Moira walked briskly across campus in the direction of the restaurant where they would have dinner. Students streamed past them, hurrying down the paths between trees and lawns. Somewhere a band was playing in the stolid, almost plodding rhythm endemic to colleges and universities. The sky was steeped in clouds, scudding overhead like clipper ships on the high seas. A dank winter wind came streaming in off the Potomac.

"There was a time when I was plunged deep in depression. I knew it but I wouldn't accept it—you know what I mean. Professor Specter was the one who connected with me, who was able to crack the shell I was using to protect myself. To this day I have no idea how he did it or even why he persevered. He said he saw something of himself in me. In any event, he wanted to help."

They passed the ivy-covered building where Specter, who was now the president of the School of International Studies at Georgetown, had his office. Men in tweed coats and corduroy jackets passed in and out of the doors, frowns of deep concentration on their faces.

"Professor Specter gave me a job teaching linguistics. It was like a life preserver to a drowning man. What I needed most then was a sense of order and stability. I honestly don't know what would have happened to me if not for him. He alone understood that immersing myself in language makes me happy. No matter who I've been, the one constant is my proficiency with languages. Learning languages is like learning history from the inside out. It encompasses the battles of ethnicity, religion, compromise, politics. So much can be learned from language because it's been shaped by history."

By this time they had left campus and were walking down 36th Street, NW, toward 1789, a favorite restaurant of Moira's, which was housed in a Federal town house. When they arrived, they were shown to a window table on the second floor in a dim, paneled, old-fashioned room with candles burning brightly on tables set with fine china and sparkling stemware. They sat down facing each other and ordered drinks.

Bourne leaned across the table, said in a low voice,"Listen to me, Moira, because I'm going to tell you something very few people know. The Bourne identity continues to haunt me. Marie used to worry that the decisions I was forced to make, the actions I had to take as Jason Bourne would eventually drain me of all feeling, that one day I'd come back to her and David Webb would be gone for good. I can't let that happen."

"Jason, you and I have spent quite a bit of time with each other since we met to scatter Martin's ashes. I've never seen a hint that you've lost any part of your humanity."

Both sat back, silent as the waiter set the drinks in front of them, handed them menus. As soon as he left, Bourne said, "That's reassuring, believe me. In the short time I've known you I've come to value your opinions. You're not like anyone else I've ever met."

Moira took a sip of her drink, set it down, all without taking her eyes from his. "Thank you. Coming from you that's quite a compliment, particularly because I know how special Marie was to you."

Bourne stared down at his drink.

Moira reached across the starched white linen for his hand. "I'm sorry, now you're drifting away."

He glanced at her hand over his but didn't pull away. When he looked up, he said, "I relied on her for many things. But I find now that those things are slipping away from me."

"Is that a bad thing, or a good thing?"

"That's just it," he said. "I don't know."

Moira saw the anguish in his face, and her heart went out to him. It was only months ago that she'd seen him standing by the parapet in the Cloisters. He was clutching the bronze urn holding Martin's ashes as if he never wanted to let it go. She'd known then, even if Martin hadn't told her, what they'd meant to each other.

"Martin was your friend," she said now. "You put yourself in terrible jeopardy to save him. Don't tell me you didn't feel anything for him. Besides, by your own admission, you're not Jason Bourne now. You're David Webb."

He smiled. "You have me there."

Her face clouded over. "I want to ask you a question, but I don't know whether I have the right."

At once, he responded to the seriousness of her expression. "Of course you can ask, Moira. Go on."

She took a deep breath, let it go. "Jason, I know you've said that you're content at the university, and if that's so, fine. But I also know you blame yourself for not being able to save Martin. You must understand, though, if you couldn't save him, no one could. You did your best; he knew that, I'm sure. And now I find myself wondering if you believe you failed him—that you're not up to being Jason Bourne anymore. I wonder if you've ever considered the idea that you accepted Professor Specter's offer at the university in order to turn away from Jason Bourne's life."

"Of course I've considered it." After Martin's death he'd once again decided to turn his back on Jason Bourne's life, on the running, the deaths, a river that seemed to have as many bodies as the Ganges. Always, for him, memories lurked. The sad ones he remembered. The others, the shadowed ones that filled the halls of his mind, seemed to have shape until he neared them, when they flowed away like a tide at ebb. And what was left behind were the bleached bones of all those he'd killed or had been killed because of who he was. But he knew just as surely that as long as he drew breath, the Bourne identity wouldn't die.

There was a tormented look in his eyes. "You have to understand how difficult it is having two personalities, always at war with each other. I wish with every fiber of my being that I could cut one of them out of me."

Moira said, "Which one would it be?"

"That's the damnable part," Bourne said. "Every time I think I know, I realize that I don't."

Two

LUTHER LAVALLE WAS as telegenic as the president and two-thirds his age. He had straw-colored hair slicked back like a movie idol of the 1930s or 1940s and restless hands. By contrast, General Kendall was square-jawed and beady-eyed, the very essence of a ramrod officer. He was big and beefy; perhaps he'd been a fullback at Wisconsin or Ohio State. He looked to LaValle the way a running back looks to his quarterback for instructions.

"Luther," the president said, "seeing as how you requested this meeting I think it appropriate that you begin."

LaValle nodded, as if the president deferring to him was a fait accompli. "After the recent debacle of CI being infiltrated at its highest level, culminating with the murder of the former DCI, firmer security and controls need to be set in place. Only the Pentagon can do that."

Veronica felt compelled to jump in before LaValle got too much of a head start. "I beg to differ, sir," she said, aiming her remarks at the president. "Human intelligence gathering has always been the province of CI. Our on-the-ground networks are unparalleled, as are our armies of contacts, who have been cultivated for decades. The Pentagon's expertise has always been in electronic surveillance. The two are separate, requiring altogether different methodologies and mind-sets."

LaValle smiled as winningly as he did when appearing on Fox TV or *Larry King Live*. "I'd be remiss if I didn't point out that the landscape of intelligence has changed radically since 2001. We're at war. In my opinion this state of affairs is likely to last indefinitely, which is why the Pentagon has recently expanded its field of expertise, creating teams of clandestine DIA personnel and special-ops forces who are conducting successful counterintelligence ops in Iraq and Afghanistan."

"With all due respect, Mr. LaValle and his military machine are eager to fill any perceived vacuum or create one, if necessary. Mr. La-Valle and General Kendall need us to believe that we're in a perpetual state of war whether or not it's the truth." From her briefcase Veronica produced a file, which she opened and read from. "As this evidence makes clear, they have systematically directed the expansion of their human intelligence-gathering squads, outside of Afghanistan and Iraq, into other territories—CI's territories—often with disastrous results. They've corrupted informers and, in at least one instance, they've jeopardized an ongoing CI deep-cover operation."

After the president glanced at the pages Veronica handed him, he said, "While this is compelling, Veronica, Congress seems to be on Luther's side. It has provided him with twenty-five million dollars a year to pay informants on the ground and to recruit mercenaries."

"That's part of the problem, not the solution," Veronica said emphatically. "Theirs is a failed methodology, the same one they've used all the way back to the OSS in Berlin after World War Two. Our paid informants have had a history of turning on us—working for the other side, feeding us disinformation. As for the mercenaries we recruited—like the Taliban or various other Muslim insurgent groups—they, to a man, eventually turned against us to become our implacable enemies."

"She's got a point," the president said.

"The past is the past," General Kendall said angrily. His face had been darkening with every word Veronica had said. "There's no evidence whatsoever that either our new informants or our mercenaries, both of which are vital to our victory in the Middle East, would ever turn on us. On the contrary, the intel they've provided has been of great help to our men on the field of battle."

"Mercenaries, by definition, owe their allegiance to whoever pays them the most," Veronica said. "Centuries of history from Roman times forward have proved this point over and over."

"All this back-and-forth is of little moment." LaValle shifted in his seat uncomfortably. Clearly he hadn't counted on such a spirited defense. Kendall handed him a dossier, which he presented to the president. "General Kendall and I have spent the better part of two weeks putting together this proposal for how to restructure CI going forward. The Pentagon is prepared to implement this plan the moment we get your approval, Mr. President."

To Veronica's horror, the president looked over the proposal, then turned it over to her. "What do you say to this?"

Veronica felt suffused with rage. She was already being undermined. On the other hand, she observed, this was a good object lesson for her. Trust no one, not even seeming allies. Up until this moment she'd thought she had the full support of the president. The fact that LaValle, who was, after all, basically the mouthpiece for Defense Secretary Halliday, had the muscle to call this meeting shouldn't have surprised her. But that the president was asking her to consider a takeover from the Pentagon was outrageous and, quite frankly, frightening.

Without even glancing at the toxic papers, she squared her shoulders. "Sir, this proposal is irrelevant, at best. I resent Mr. LaValle's flagrant attempt to expand his intelligence empire at CI's expense. For one thing, as I've detailed, the Pentagon is ill suited to direct, let alone win the trust of our vast array of agents in the field. For another, this coup would set a dangerous precedent for the entire intelligence community. Being under the control of the armed forces will not benefit our intelligence-gathering potential. On the contrary, the Pentagon's history of flagrant disregard for human life, its legacy of illegal operations combined with well-documented fiscal profligacy, makes it an extremely poor candidate to poach on anyone else's territory, especially CI's."

Only the presence of the president forced LaValle to keep his ire in check. "Sir, CI is in total disarray. It needs to be turned around ASAP. As I said, our plan can be implemented today."

Veronica drew out the thick file detailing her plans for CI. She rose, placed it in the president's hands. "Sir, I feel duty-bound to reiterate one of the main points of our last discussion. Though I've served in the military, I come from the private sector. CI is in need not only of a clean sweep but of a fresh perspective untainted by the monolithic thinking that got us into this insupportable situation in the first place."

Jason Bourne smiled. "To be honest, tonight I don't know who I am." He leaned forward and said very softly, "Listen to me. I want you to take your cell phone out of your handbag without anyone seeing. I want you to call me. Can you do that?"

Moira kept her eyes on his as she found her cell in her handbag, hit the appropriate speed-dial key. His cell phone chimed. He sat back, answered the call. He spoke into the phone as if someone was on the other end of the line. Then he closed the phone, said, "I have to go. It's an emergency. I'm sorry."

She continued to stare at him. "Could you act even the least bit upset?" she whispered.

His mouth turned down.

"Do you really have to go?" she said in a normal tone of voice. "Now?"

"Now." Bourne threw some bills on the table. "I'll be in touch."

She nodded a bit quizzically, wondering what he'd seen or heard.

Bourne went down the stairs and out of the restaurant. Immediately he turned right, walked a quarter block, then entered a store selling handmade ceramics. Positioning himself so that he had a view of the street through the plate-glass window, he pretended to look at bowls and serving dishes.

Outside, people passed by—a young couple, an elderly man with a cane, three young women, laughing. But the man who'd been seated in the back corner of their room precisely ninety seconds after they sat down did not appear. Bourne had marked him the moment he'd come in, and when he'd asked for a table in back facing them, he'd had no doubt: Someone was following him. All of a sudden he'd felt that old anxiety that had roiled him when Marie and Martin had been threatened. He'd lost Martin, he wasn't about to lose Moira as well.

Bourne, whose interior radar had swept the second-floor dining room every few minutes or so, hadn't picked up anyone else of a suspicious nature, so he waited now inside the ceramics shop for the tail to amble by. When this didn't occur after five minutes, Bourne went out the door and immediately strode across the street. Using streetlights and the reflective surfaces of windows and car mirrors, he spent another few minutes scrutinizing the area for any sign of the man at the table in back. After ascertaining he was nowhere to be found, Bourne returned to the restaurant.

He went up the stairs to the second floor, but paused in the dark hallway between the staircase and the dining room. There was the man at his rear table. To any casual observer he seemed to be reading the current issue of *The Washingtonian,* like any good tourist, but every once in a while his gaze flicked upward for a fraction of a second, focused on Moira.

Bourne felt a little chill go through him. This man wasn't following him; he was following Moira.

As Veronica Hart emerged through the outermost checkpoint to the West Wing, Luther LaValle emerged from the shadows, fell into step beside her.

"Nicely done," he said icily. "Next time I'll be better prepared."

"There won't be a next time," Veronica said.

"Secretary Halliday is confident there will be. So am I."

They had reached the hushed vestibule with its dome and columns.

Busy presidential aides strode purposefully past them in either direction. Like surgeons, they exuded an air of supreme confidence and exclusivity, as if theirs was a club you desperately wanted to belong to, but never would.

"Where's your personal pit bull?" Veronica asked. "Sniffing out crotches, I shouldn't wonder."

"You're terribly flip for someone whose job is hanging by a thread."

"It's foolish—not to mention dangerous, Mr. LaValle—to confuse confidence with being flip."

They pushed through the doors, went down the steps to the grounds proper. Floodlights pushed back the darkness to the edges of the premises. Beyond, streetlights glittered.

"Of course, you're right," LaValle said. "I apologize."

Veronica eyed him with no little skepticism.

LaValle gave her a small smile. "I sincerely regret that we've gotten off on the wrong foot."

What he really regrets, Veronica thought, *is my pulling him and Kendall to pieces in front of the president. Understandable, really.*

As she buttoned her coat, he said, "Perhaps both of us have been coming at this situation from the wrong angle."

Veronica knotted her scarf at her throat outside her collar. "What situation?"

"The collapse of CI."

In the near distance, beyond the flotilla of heavy reinforced concrete anti-terrorist barriers, tourists strolled by, chatting animatedly, paused briefly to take snapshots, then went on to their dinners at McDonald's or Burger King.

"It seems to me that more can be gained by us joining forces than by being antagonists."

Veronica turned to him. "Listen, buddy, you take care of your shop and I'll take care of mine. I've been given a job to do and I'm going to do it without interference from you or Secretary Halliday. Personally, I'm sick and tired of you people extending the line in the sand farther and farther so your empire can grow bigger. CI is off limits to you now and forever, got it?"

LaValle made a face as if he were about to whistle. Then he said, very quietly, "I'd be a bit more careful if I were you. You're walking across a knife-edge. One false step, one hesitation, and when you fall no one's going to be there to catch you."

Her voice turned steely. "I've had my fill of your threats, too, Mr. LaValle."

He turned up his collar against the wind. "When you get to know me better, Veronica, you'll realize I don't make threats. I make predictions."

Three

THE VIOLENCE of the Black Sea fit Leonid Arkadin down to his steel-tipped shoes. In a tumultuous rain, he drove into Sevastopol from Belbek Aerodrome. Sevastopol inhabited a coveted bit of territory on the southwestern edge of the Crimean peninsula of Ukraine. Because the area was blessed with subtropical weather, its seas never froze. From the time of its founding by Greek traders as Chersonesus in 422 BC, Sevastopol was a vital commercial and military outpost for fishing fleets and naval armadas alike. Following the decline of Chersonesus—"peninsula," in Greek—the area fell into ruin until the modern-day Sevastopol was founded in 1783 as a naval base and fortress on the southern boundaries of the Russian Empire. Most of the city's history was linked to its military glory—the name *Sevastopol* translated from Greek means "august, glorious." The name seemed justified: The city survived two bloody sieges during the Crimean War of 1854–1855 and World War Two, when it withstood Axis bombing for 250 days. Although the city was destroyed on two different occasions, it had risen from the ashes both times. As a result, the inhabitants were tough, no-nonsense people. They despised the Cold War era, dating to roughly

1960 when, because of its naval base, the USSR ordered Sevastopol off limits to visitors of all kinds. In 1997 the Russians agreed to return the city to the Ukrainians, who opened it again.

It was late afternoon when Arkadin arrived on Primorskiy Boulevard. The sky was black, except for a thin red line along the western horizon. The port bulged with round-hulled fishing ships and sleek steel-hulled naval vessels. An angry sea lashed the *Monument to Scuttled Ships,* commemorating the 1855 last-ditch defense of the city against the combined forces of the British, French, Turks, and Sardinians. It rose from a bed of rough granite blocks in a Corinthian column three yards high, crowned by an eagle with wings spread wide, its proud head bent, a laurel wreath gripped in its beak. Facing it, embedded in the thick seawall, were the anchors of the Russian ships that were deliberately sunk to block the harbor from the invading enemy.

Arkadin checked into the Hotel Oblast where everything, including the walls, seemed to be made of paper. The furniture was covered in fabric of hideous patterns whose colors clashed like enemies on a battlefield. The place seemed a likely candidate to go up like a torch. He made a mental note not to smoke in bed.

Downstairs, in the space that passed for a lobby, he asked the rodent-like clerk for a recommendation for a hot meal, then requested a telephone book. Taking it, he retired to an understuffed upholstered chair by a window that overlooked Admiral Nakhimov Square. And there he was on a magnificent plinth, the hero of the first defense of Sevastopol, staring stonily at Arkadin, as if aware of what was to come. This was a city, like so many in the former Soviet Union, filled with monuments to the past.

With a last glance at slope-shouldered pedestrians hurrying through the driving rain, Arkadin turned his attention to the phone book. The name that Pyotr Zilber had given up just before he'd committed suicide was Oleg Shumenko. Arkadin dearly would have loved to have gotten more out of Zilber. Now Arkadin had to page through the phone book looking for Shumenko, assuming the man had a landline, which was

always problematic outside Moscow or St. Petersburg. He made note
of the five Oleg Shumenkos listed, handed the book back to the clerk,
and went out into the windy false dusk.

The first three Oleg Shumenkos were of no help. Arkadin, posing as a
close friend of Pyotr Zilber's, told each of them that he had a message
from Pyotr so urgent it had to be transmitted in person. They looked at
him blankly, shook their heads. He could see in their eyes they had no
idea who Pyotr Zilber was.

The fourth Shumenko worked at Yugreftransflot, which maintained
the largest fleet of refrigerated ships in Ukraine. Since Yugreftransflot
was a public corporation, it took Arkadin some time just to get in to see
Shumenko, who was a transport manager. Like everywhere in the former USSR, the red tape was enough to grind all work to a near halt.
How anything got done in the public sector was beyond Arkadin.

At length, Shumenko appeared, led Arkadin to his tiny office,
apologizing for the delay. He was a small man with very dark hair and
the small ears and low forehead of a Neanderthal. When Arkadin introduced himself, Shumenko said, "Obviously, you have the wrong man. I
don't know a Pyotr Zilber."

Arkadin consulted his list. "I only have one more Oleg Shumenko
left."

"Let me see." Shumenko consulted the list. "Pity you didn't come
to me first. These three are my cousins. And the fifth, the one you
haven't seen yet, won't be of any use to you. He's dead. Fishing accident six months ago." He handed back the list. "But all isn't lost.
There's one other Oleg Shumenko. Though we're not related, people
are always getting us confused because we have the same patronymic,
Ivanovich. He doesn't have a landline, which is why I'm constantly
getting his calls."

"Do you know where I can find him?"

Oleg Ivanovich Shumenko checked his watch. "At this hour, yes,
he'd be at work. He's a winemaker, you see. Champagne. I understand

the French say you're not allowed to use that term for any wine not produced in their Champagne region." He chuckled. "Still, the Sevastopol Winery turns out quite a fine champagne."

He led Arkadin from his office out through dull corridors into the enormous main vestibule. "Are you familiar with the city, *gospadin* Arkadin? Sevastopol is divided into five districts. We're in the Gagarinskiy district, named after the world's first astronaut, Yuri Alexeevich Gagarin. This is the western section of the city. To the north is the Nakhimovskiy district, which is where the mammoth dry docks are. Perhaps you've heard of them. No? No matter. In the eastern section, away from the water, is the rural area of the city—pasturelands and vineyards, magnificent even at this time of the year."

He crossed the marble floor to a long banc behind which sat half a dozen functionaries looking as if they'd had little to do in the past year. From one of them Shumenko received a city map, which he drew on. Then he handed it to Arkadin, pointing at a star he'd marked.

"There's the winery." He glanced outside. "The sky's clearing. Who knows, by the time you get there, you may even see some sun."

Bourne walked the streets of Georgetown securely hidden within the crowds of college and university kids prowling the cobbles, looking for beer, girls, and guys. He was discreetly shadowing the man in the restaurant, who was, in turn, following Moira.

Once he had determined that the man was her tail, he'd backed away and returned to the street, where he'd called Moira.

"Can you think of anyone who wants to keep tabs on you?"

"I guess several," she said. "My own company, for one. I told you they've become paranoid ever since we started to build the LNG station in Long Beach. NoHold Energy might be another. They've been waving a vice president's job at me for six months. I could see them wanting to know more about me so they can sweeten their offer."

"Other than those two?"

"No."

He'd told her what he wanted her to do, and now in the George-town night she was doing it. They always had habits, these watchers in the shadows, little peculiarities built up from all the boring hours spent at their lonely jobs. This one liked to be on the inside of the sidewalk so he could duck quickly into a doorway if need be.

Once he had the shadow's idiosyncracies down, it was time to take him out. But as Bourne worked his way through the crowds, moving closer to the shadow, he saw something else. The man wasn't alone. A second tail had taken up a parallel position on the opposite side of the street, which made sense. If Moira decided to cross the street in this throng, the first shadow might run into some difficulty keeping her in sight. These people, whoever they were, were leaving little to chance.

Bourne melted back, matching his pace to that of the crowd's. At the same time, he called Moira. She'd put in her Bluetooth earpiece so she could take his call without being conspicuous. Bourne gave her detailed instructions, then broke off following her shadows.

Moira, the back of her neck tingling as if she were in the crosshairs of an assassin's rifle, crossed the street, walked over to M Street. The main thing for her to keep in mind, Jason said, was to move at a normal pace, neither fast nor slow. Jason had alarmed her with the news that she was being followed. She had merely maintained the illusion of being calm. There were many people from both present and past who might be fol-lowing her—a number of whom she hadn't mentioned when Jason had asked. Still, so close to the opening of the LNG terminal it was an ominous sign. She had desperately wanted to share with Jason the intel that had come to her today about the possibility of the terminal being a terrorist target, not in theory, but in reality. However, she couldn't—not unless he was an employee of the company. She was bound by her ironclad contract not to tell anyone outside the firm any confidential information.

At 31st Street NW, she turned south, walking toward the Canal Towpath. A third of the way down the block, on her side, was a discreet

plaque on which the word JEWEL was etched. She opened the ruby-
colored door, entered the high-priced new restaurant. This was the kind
of place where dishes were accessorized with kaffir lime foam, freeze-
dried ginger, and ruby grapefruit pearls.

Smiling sweetly at the manager, she told him that she was looking
for a friend. Before he could check his reservation book, she said her
friend was with a man whose name she didn't know. She'd been here
several times, once with Jason, so she knew the layout. At the rear of the
second room was a short corridor. Against the right-hand wall were two
unisex bathrooms. If you kept on going, which she did, you came to the
kitchen, all bright lights, stainless-steel pans, copper pots, huge stovetops
raging at high heat. Young men and women moved around the room in
what seemed to her like military precision—sous-chefs, line cooks, expediters, the pastry chef and her staff, all performing under the stern
commands of the chef de cuisine.

They were all too concentrated on their respective tasks to give
Moira much notice. By the time her figure did register she'd already
disappeared out the rear door. In a back alley filled with Dumpsters, a
White Top cab was waiting, its engine purring. She climbed in and the
cab took off.

Arkadin drove through the hills of rural Nakhimovskiy district, lush
even in winter. He passed checkered farmland, bounded by low for-
ested areas. The sky was lightening, the dark, rain-laden clouds already
disappearing, replaced by high cumulus that glowed like embers in the
sunlight that broke through everywhere. A golden sheen covered the
acres of vineyards as he approached the Sevastopol Winery. At this time
of year there were no leaves or fruit, of course, but the twisted, stunted
boles, like the trunks of elephants, bore a life of their own that gave the
vineyard a certain mystery, a mythic aspect, as if these sleeping vines
needed only the spell of a wizard to come awake.

A burly woman named Yetnikova introduced herself as Oleg Ivanovich
Shumenko's immediate supervisor—there was, apparently, no end to the

tiers of supervisors in the winery. She had shoulders as wide as Arkadin's, a red, round, vodka face with features as curiously small as those of a doll. She wore her hair tied up in a peasant babushka, but she was all bristling business.

When she demanded to know Arkadin's business, he whipped out one of many false credentials he carried. This one identified him as a colonel in the SBU, the Security Service of Ukraine. Upon seeing the SBU card, Yetnikova wilted like an unwatered plant and showed him where to find Shumenko.

Arkadin, following her direction, went down corridor after corridor. He opened each door he came to, peering inside offices, utility closets, storerooms, and the like, apologizing to the occupants as he did so.

Shumenko was working in the fermentation room when Arkadin found him. He was a reed-thin man, much younger than Arkadin had imagined—no more than thirty or so. He had thick hair the color of goldenrod that stood up from his scalp like a series of cockscombs. Music spilled out from a portable player—a British band, the Cure. Arkadin had heard the song many times in Moscow clubs, but it seemed startling here in the hind end of the Crimea.

Shumenko stood on a catwalk four yards in the air, bent over a stainless-steel apparatus as large as a blue whale. He seemed to be sniffing something, possibly the latest batch of champagne he was concocting. Rather than turn down the music, Shumenko gestured for Arkadin to join him.

Without hesitation Arkadin mounted the vertical ladder, climbed swiftly up to the catwalk. The yeasty, slightly sweet odors of fermentation tickled his nostrils, causing him to rub the end of his nose vigorously to stave off a sneezing fit. His practiced gaze swept the immediate vicinity taking in every last detail, no matter how minute.

"Oleg Ivanovich Shumenko?"

The reedy young man put aside a clipboard on which he was taking notes. "At your service." He wore a badly fitting suit. He placed the pen he had been using in his breast pocket, where it joined a line of others. "And you would be?"

"A friend of Pyotr Zilber's."

"Never heard of him."

But his eyes had already betrayed him. Arkadin reached out, turned up the music. "He's heard of you, Oleg Ivanovich. In fact, you're quite important to him."

Shumenko plastered a simulated smile on his face. "I have no idea what you're talking about."

"There was a grave mistake made. He needs the document back."

Shumenko, smiling still, jammed his hands in his pockets. "Once again, I must tell you—"

Arkadin made a grab for him, but Shumenko's right hand reappeared, gripping a GSh-18 semi-automatic that was pointed at Arkadin's heart.

"Hmm. The sights are acceptable at best," Arkadin said.

"Please don't move. Whoever you are—and don't bother to give me a name that in any case will be false—you're no friend of Pyotr's. He must be dead. Perhaps even by your hand."

"But the trigger pull is relatively heavy," Arkadin continued, as if he hadn't been listening, "so that'll give me an extra tenth of a second."

"A tenth of a second is nothing."

"It's all I need."

Shumenko backed up, as Arkadin wanted him to, toward the curved side of a container to keep a safer distance. "Even while I mourn Pyotr's death I will defend our network with my life."

He backed up farther as Arkadin took another step toward him.

"It's a long fall from here so I suggest you turn around, climb back down the ladder, and disappear into whatever sewer you crawled out of."

As Shumenko retreated, his right foot skidded on a bit of yeast paste Arkadin had noted earlier. Shumenko's right knee went out from under him, the hand holding the GSh-18 raised in an instinctive gesture to help keep him from falling.

In one long stride Arkadin was inside the perimeter of his defense. He made a grab for the gun, missed. His fist struck Shumenko on the right cheek, sending the reedy man lurching back into the side of the container in the space between two protruding levers. Shumenko slashed his arm in a horizontal arc, the sight on the barrel of the GSh-18 raking across the bridge of Arkadin's nose, drawing blood.

Arkadin made another lunge at the semi-automatic and, bent back against the curved sheet of stainless steel, the two men grappled. Shumenko was surprisingly strong for a thin man, and he was proficient in hand-to-hand combat. He had the proper counter for every attack Arkadin threw at him. They were very close now, not a hand's span separating them. Their limbs worked quickly, hands, elbows, forearms, even shoulders used to produce pain or, in blocking, minimize it.

Gradually, Arkadin seemed to be getting the better of his adversary, but with a double feint Shumenko managed to get the butt of the GSh-18 lodged against Arkadin's throat. He pressed in, using leverage in an attempt to crush Arkadin's windpipe. One of Arkadin's hands was trapped between their bodies. With the other, he pounded Shumenko's side, but he lacked Shumenko's leverage, and his blows did no damage. When he tried for Shumenko's kidney, the other man twisted his hips away, so his hand glanced off the hip bone.

Shumenko pressed his advantage, bending Arkadin over the railing, trying with the butt of his gun and his upper body to shove Arkadin off the catwalk. Ribbons of darkness flowed across Arkadin's vision, a sign that his brain was becoming oxygen-starved. He had underestimated Shumenko, and now he was about to pay the price.

He coughed, then gagged, trying to breathe. Then he moved his free hand up against the front of Shumenko's jacket. It would seem to Shumenko—concentrating on killing the interloper—as if Arkadin was making one last futile attempt to free his trapped hand. He was taken completely off guard when Arkadin slipped a pen out of his breast pocket, stabbed it into his left eye.

Immediately Shumenko reared back. Arkadin caught the GSh-18 as it dropped from the stricken man's nerveless hand. As Shumenko slid to the catwalk, Arkadin grabbed him by the shirtfront, knelt to be on the same level with him.

"The document," he said. And when Shumenko's head began to loll, "Oleg Ivanovich, listen to me. Where is the document?"

The man's good eye glistened, running with tears. His mouth worked. Arkadin shook him until he moaned with pain.

"Where?"

"Gone."

Arkadin had to bend his head to hear Shumenko's whisper over the loud music. The Cure had been replaced by Siouxsie and the Banshees.

"What d'you mean gone?"

"Down the pipeline." Shumenko's mouth curled in the semblance of a smile. "Not what you wanted to hear, 'friend of Pyotr Zilber,' is it?" He blinked tears out of his good eye. "Since this is the end of the line for you, bend closer and I'll tell you a secret." He licked his lips as Arkadin complied, then lunged forward and bit into the lobe of Arkadin's right ear.

Arkadin reacted without thinking. He jammed the muzzle of the GSh-18 into Shumenko's mouth, pulled the trigger. Almost at the same instant, he realized his mistake, said "Shit!" in six different languages.

Four

BOURNE, sunk deep into the shadows opposite the restaurant Jewel, saw the two men emerge. By the annoyed expressions on their faces he knew they'd lost Moira. He kept them in sight as they moved off together. One of them began to speak into a cell phone. He paused for a moment to ask his colleague a question, then returned to his conversation on the phone. By this time the two had reached M Street, NW. Finished with his call, the man put his cell phone away. They waited on the corner, watching the nubile young girls slipping by. They didn't slouch, Bourne noted, but stood ramrod-straight, their hands in view, at their sides. It appeared that they were waiting to be picked up; a good call on a night like this when parking was at a premium and traffic on M Street, as thick as molasses.

Bourne, without a vehicle, looked around, saw a bicyclist coming up 31st Street, NW, from the towpath. He was cycling along the gutter to avoid the traffic. Bourne walked smartly toward him and stepped in front of him. The cyclist stopped short, uttering a sharp exclamation.

"I need your bike," Bourne said.

"Well, you bloody well can't have it, mate," the cyclist said with a heavy British accent.

At the corner of 31st and M, a black GMC SUV was pulling into the curb in front of the two men.

Bourne pressed four hundred dollars into the cyclist's hand. "Like I said, right now."

The young man stared down at the money for a moment. Then he swung off, said, "Be my guest."

As Bourne mounted up, he handed over his helmet. "You'll be wanting this, mate."

The two men had already vanished into the GMC's interior, the SUV was pulling out into the thick traffic flow. Bourne took off, leaving the cyclist to shrug behind him as he climbed onto the sidewalk.

Reaching the corner, Bourne turned right onto M Street. The GMC was three cars ahead of him. Bourne wove his way around the traffic, moving into position to keep up with the SUV. At 30th Street, NW, they all hit a red light. Bourne was forced to put one foot down, which was why he got a late start when the GMC jumped the light just before it turned green. The SUV roared ahead of the other vehicles, and Bourne launched himself forward. A white Toyota was coming from 30th into the intersection, heading right for him at a ninety-degree angle. Bourne put on a burst of speed, swerved up onto the corner sidewalk, backing a clutch of pedestrians into those behind them, to a round of curses. The Toyota, horn blaring angrily, just missed him as it jounced across M Street.

Bourne was able to make good headway, as the GMC had been slowed by the sludgy traffic up ahead, splitting off where M Street and Pennsylvania Avenue, NW, intersected at 29th Street. Just as he neared the light he saw the GMC take off and knew he had been spotted. The problem with a bicycle, especially one that had caused a minor uproar lunging through a red light, was that the cyclist became conspicuous, exactly the opposite of what was intended.

Making the best of a worsening situation, Bourne threw caution to the wind, following the accelerating GMC into the fork as it took Pennsylvania Avenue. The good news was that the congestion prevented the GMC from keeping up speed. More good news: Another red light loomed. This time Bourne was ready for the GMC to plow right through.

Swerving in and out between vehicles, he put on another burst of speed, running the red light with the big SUV. But just as he was coming abreast of the far crosswalk, a gaggle of drunk teenagers stumbled off the curb on their way across the avenue. They closed off the lane behind the GMC and were so raucous they either didn't hear Bourne's warning shout or didn't care. He was forced to swerve sharply to the right. His front tire struck the curb, the bike lifted up. People scattered out of its way as it became, in effect, a missile. Bourne was able to keep it going after it landed, but there was simply nowhere for him to steer it without plowing into another group of kids. He applied the brakes without enough effect. Leaning to the right, he forced the bike down on its side, ripping his right trouser leg as it skidded along the cement.

"Are you all right?"

"What were you trying to do?"

"Didn't you see the red light?"

"You could have killed yourself—or someone else!"

A welter of voices as pedestrians surrounded him, trying to help him out from under the bicycle. Bourne thanked them as he scrambled to his feet. He ran several hundred yards down the avenue, but as he feared the GMC was long gone.

Expelling a string of bawdily colorful curses, Arkadin rummaged through the pockets of Oleg Ivanovich Shumenko, who lay twitching in the blood-stained catwalk deep inside the Sevastopol Winery. As he did so, he wondered how he could have been such a fool. He'd done precisely what Shumenko had wanted him to do, which was to kill him. He'd rather have died than divulge the name of the next man in Pyotr Zilber's network.

Still, there was a chance that something he had on his person would lead Arkadin farther along. Arkadin had already made a small pile of coins, bills, toothpicks, and the like. He unfolded each scrap of paper he came across, but none of them contained either a name or an address, just lists of chemicals, presumably those the winery required for fermentation or the periodic cleaning of its vats.

Shumenko's wallet was a sad affair—sliver-thin, containing a faded photo of an older couple smiling into the sun and the camera Arkadin took to be Shumenko's parents, a condom in a worn foil pouch, a driver's license, car registration, ID badge for a sailing club, an IOU chit for ten thousand hryvnia—just under two thousand American dollars—two receipts, one for a restaurant, the other for a nightclub, an old photo of a young girl smiling into the camera.

In pocketing the receipts, the only reasonable leads he'd found, he inadvertently flipped over the IOU. On the reverse was the name DEVRA, written in a sharp, spiky feminine hand. Arkadin wanted to look for more, but he heard an electronic squawk, then the bawl of Yetnikova's voice. He looked around, saw an old-fashioned walkie-talkie hanging by its strap from the railing. Stuffing the papers into his pocket, he hurried along the catwalk, slid down the ladder, made his way out of the champagne fermentation room.

Shumenko's boss, Yetnikova, marched toward him down the labyrinthine corridors as if she were in the forefront of the Red Army entering Warsaw. Even at this distance, he could see the scowl on her face. Unlike his Russian credentials, his Ukrainian ones were paper-thin. They'd pass a cursory test, but after any kind of checking he'd be busted.

"I called the SBU office in Kiev. They did some digging on you, Colonel." Yetnikova's voice had turned from servile to hostile. "Or whoever you are." She puffed herself up like a porcupine about to do battle. "They never heard of—"

She gave a little squeak as he jammed one hand over her mouth while he punched her hard in the solar plexus. She collapsed into his arms like a rag doll, and he dragged her along the corridor until he came to the utility closet. Opening the door, he shoved her in, went in after her.

Sprawled on the floor, Yetnikova slowly came to her senses. Immediately she began her bluster—cursing and promising dire consequences for the outrages perpetrated on her person. Arkadin didn't hear her; he didn't even see her. He attempted to block out the past, but as always the memories flattened him. They took possession of him, taking him out of himself, producing like a drug a dream-like state that over the years had become as familiar as a twin brother.

Kneeling over Yetnikova, he dodged her kicks, the snapping of her jaws. He withdrew a switchblade from a sheath strapped to the side of his right calf. When he *snikk*ed open its long, thin blade, fear finally twisted Yetnikova's face. Her eyes opened wide and she gasped, raising her hands instinctively.

"Why are you doing this?" she cried. "Why?"

"Because of what you've done."

"What? What did I do? I don't even know you!"

"But I know you." Slapping her hands aside, Arkadin went to work on her.

When, moments later, he was done, his vision came back into focus. He took a long, shuddering breath as if shaking off the effects of an anesthetic. He stared down at the headless corpse. Then, remembering, he kicked the head into a corner filled with filthy rags. For a moment, it rocked like a ship on the ocean. The eyes seemed to him gray with age, but they were only filmed with dust, and the release he sought eluded him once again.

Who were they?" Moira asked.

"That's the difficulty," Bourne told her. "I wasn't able to find out. It would help if you could tell me why they're following you."

Moira frowned. "I have to assume it has something to do with the security on the LNG terminal."

They were sitting side by side in Moira's living room, a small, cozy space in a Georgetown town house of red-brown brick on Cambridge Place, NW, near Dumbarton Oaks. A fire was crackling and licking in the brick hearth; espresso and brandy sat on the coffee table in front of them. The chenille-covered sofa was deep enough for Moira to curl up on. It had big roll arms and a neck-high back.

"One thing I can tell you," Bourne said, "these people are professionals."

"Makes sense," she said. "Any rival of my firm would hire the best people available. That doesn't necessarily mean I'm in any danger."

Nevertheless, Bourne felt another sharp pang at the loss of Marie, then carefully, almost reverently, put the feeling aside.

"More espresso?" Moira asked.

"Please."

Bourne handed her his cup. As she bent forward, the light V-neck sweater revealed the tops of her firm breasts. At that moment, she raised her gaze to his. There was a mischievous glint in her eyes.

"What are you thinking about?"

"Probably the same thing you are." He rose, looked around for his coat. "I think I'd better go."

"Jason . . ."

He paused. Lamplight gave her face a golden glow. "Don't," she said. "Stay. Please."

He shook his head. "You and I both know that's not a good idea."

"Just for tonight. I don't want to be alone, not after what you discovered." She gave a little shiver. "I was being brave before, but I'm not you. Being followed gives me the willies."

She offered the cup of espresso. "If it makes you feel any better, I'd prefer you sleep out here. This sofa's quite comfortable."

Bourne looked around at the warm chestnut walls, the dark wooden blinds, the jewel-toned accents here and there in the form of vases and bowls of flowers. An agate box with gold legs sat on a mahogany sideboard. A small brass ship's clock ticked away beside it. The photos of the French countryside in summer and autumn made him feel both mournful and nostalgic. For precisely what, he couldn't say. Though his mind fished for memories, none surfaced. His past was a lake of black ice. "Yes, it is." He took the cup, sat down beside her.

She pulled a pillow against her breast. "Shall we talk about what we've been avoiding saying all evening?"

"I'm not big on talking."

Her wide lips curved in a smile. "Which one of you isn't big on talking, David Webb or Jason Bourne?"

Bourne laughed, sipped his espresso. "What if I said both of us?"

"I'd have to call you a liar."

"We can't have that, can we?"

"It wouldn't be my choice." She rested one cheek on her hand, waiting. When he said nothing further, she continued. "Please, Jason. Just talk to me."

The old fear of getting close to someone reared its head again, but at the same time he felt a kind of melting inside him, as if his frozen heart were beginning to thaw. For some years, he'd made it an ironclad rule to keep his distance from other people. Alex Conklin had been murdered, Marie had died, Martin Lindros hadn't made it out of Miran Shah. All gone, his only friends and first love. With a start, he realized that he hadn't felt attracted to anyone except Marie. He hadn't allowed himself to feel, but now he couldn't help himself. Was that a function of the David Webb personality or of Moira herself? She was strong, self-assured. In her he recognized a kindred spirit, someone who viewed the world as he did—as an outsider.

He looked into her face, said what was in his mind. "Everyone I get close to dies."

She sighed, put a hand briefly over his. "I'm not going to die." Her dark brown eyes glimmered in the lamplight. "Anyway, it's not your job to protect me."

This was another reason he was drawn to her. She was fierce, a warrior, in her own way.

"Tell me the truth, then. Are you really happy at the university?"

Bourne thought a moment, the conflict inside him becoming an unholy din. "I think I am." After a slight pause, he added: "I thought I was."

There'd been a golden glow to his life with Marie, but Marie was gone, that life was in the past. With her gone, he was forced to confront the terrifying question: What was David Webb without her? He was no longer a family man. He'd been able to raise his children, he saw now, only with her love and help. And for the first time he realized what his retreat into the university really meant. He'd been trying to regain that golden life he'd had with Marie. It wasn't only Professor Specter he didn't want to disappoint, it was Marie.

"What are you thinking?" Moira said softly.

"Nothing," he said. "Nothing at all."

She studied him for a moment. Then she nodded. "All right, then." She rose, leaned over, kissed him on the cheek. "I'll make up the sofa."

"That's all right, just tell me where the linen closet is."

She pointed. "Over there."

He nodded.

"Good night, Jason."

"See you in the morning. But early. I've got—"

"I know. Breakfast with Dominic Specter."

Bourne lay on his back, one arm behind his head. He was tired; he was sure he'd fall asleep immediately. But an hour after he'd turned off the lights, sleep seemed a thousand miles away. Now and again, the red-and-black remnants of the fire snapped and softly fell in on themselves. He stared at the stripes of light seeping in through the wide wooden blinds, hoping they'd take him to far-off places, which, in his case, meant his past. In some ways he was like an amputee who still felt his arm even though it had been sawed off. The sense of memories just beyond his ability to recall was maddening, an itch he couldn't scratch. He often wished he would remember nothing at all, which was one reason Moira's offer was so compelling. The thought of starting fresh, without the baggage of sadness and loss, was a powerful draw. This conflict was always with him, a major part of his life, whether he was David Webb or Jason Bourne. And yet, whether he liked it or not, his past was there, waiting for him like a wolf at night, if only he could reach through the mysterious barrier his brain had raised. Not for the first time, he wondered what other terrible traumas had befallen him in the past to cause his mind to protect itself from it. The fact that the answer lurked within his own mind turned his blood cold because it represented his own personal demon.

"Jason?"

The door to Moira's bedroom was open. Despite the dimness, his keen eyes could make out her form moving slowly toward him on bare feet.

"I couldn't sleep," she said in a throaty voice. She stopped several paces from where he lay. She was wearing a silk paisley bathrobe, belted at the waist. The lush curves of her body were unmistakable.

For a moment, they remained in silence.

"I lied to you before," she said quietly. "I don't want you to sleep out here."

Bourne rose on one elbow. "I lied, too. I was thinking about what I once had and how I've been desperate to hang on to it. But it's gone, Moira. All gone forever." He drew up one leg. "I don't want to lose you."

She moved minutely, and a bar of light picked out the glitter of tears in her eyes. "You won't, Jason. I promise."

Another silence engulfed them, this one so profound they seemed to be the only two people left in the world.

At last, he held out his hand, and she came toward him. He rose from the sofa, took her in his arms. She smelled of lime and geranium. He ran his hands through her thick hair, grabbed it. Her face tilted up to him and their lips came together, and his heart shivered off another coating of ice. After a long time, he felt her hands at her waist and he stepped back.

She undid the belt and the robe parted, slid off her shoulders. Her naked flesh shone a dusky gold. She had wide hips and a deep navel; there seemed nothing about her body he didn't love. Now it was she who took his hand, leading him to her bed, where they fell upon each other like half-starved animals.

Bourne dreamed he was standing at the window of Moira's bedroom, peering through the wooden blinds. The streetlight fell across the sidewalk and street, casting long, oblique shadows. As he watched, one of the shadows rose up from the cobbles, walked directly toward him as if it were alive and could somehow see him through the wide wooden slats.

Bourne opened his eyes, the demarcation between sleep and consciousness instantaneous and complete. His mind was filled with the dream; he could feel his heart working in his chest harder than it should have been at this moment.

Moira's arm was draped over his hip. He moved it to her side, rolled silently out of bed. Naked, he padded into the living room. Ashes lay in a cold, gray heap in the hearth. The ship's clock ticked toward the fourth hour of the night. He went straight toward the bars of streetlight, peered out just as he had in his dream. As in his dream the light cast oblique shadows across the sidewalk and street. No traffic passed. All was quiet and still. It took a minute or two, but he found the movement, minute, fleeting, as if someone standing had begun to shift from one foot to the other, then changed his mind. He waited to see if the movement would continue. Instead a small puff of exhaled breath flared into the light, then almost immediately vanished.

He dressed quickly. Bypassing both the front and rear doors, he slipped out of the house via a side window. It was very cold. He held his breath so it wouldn't steam up and betray his presence, as it had the watcher.

He stopped just before he reached the corner of the building, peered cautiously around the brick wall. He could see the curve of a shoulder, but it was at the wrong height, so low Bourne might have taken the watcher for a child. In any event, he hadn't moved. Melting back into the shadows, he went down 30th Street, NW, turned left onto Dent Place, which paralleled Cambridge Place. When he reached the end of the block, he turned left onto Cambridge, on Moira's block. Now he could see just where the watcher was situated, crouched between two parked cars almost directly across the street from Moira's house.

A gust of humid wind caused the watcher to huddle down, sink his head between his shoulders, like a turtle. Bourne seized the moment to cross the street to the watcher's side. Without pausing, he advanced down the block swiftly and silently. The watcher became aware of him far too late. He was still turning his head when Bourne grabbed him by the back of his jacket, slammed him back across the hood of the parked car.

This threw him into the light. Bourne saw his black face, recognized the features all in a split second. At once he hauled the young man up, hustled him back into the shadows, where he was certain they wouldn't be seen by other prying eyes.

"Jesus Christ, Tyrone," he said, "what the hell are you doing here?"

"Can't say." Tyrone was sullen, possibly from having been discovered.

"What d'you mean, you can't say?"

"I signed a confidentiality agreement is why."

Bourne frowned. "Deron wouldn't make you sign something like that." Deron was the art forger Bourne used for all his documents and, sometimes, unique new technologies or weapons Deron was experimenting with.

"Doan work fo Deron no more."

"Who made you sign the agreement, Tyrone?" Bourne grabbed him by his jacket front. "Who are you working for? I don't have time to play games with you. Answer me!"

"Can't." Tyrone could be damn stubborn when he wanted to be, a by-product of growing up on the streets of the northeast Washington slums. "But, okay, I guess I can take yo where yo can see fo yoself."

He led Bourne around to the unnamed alley behind Moira's house, stopped at an anonymous-looking black Chevy. Leaving Bourne, he used his knuckle to knock on the driver's window. The window lowered. As he bent down to speak to whoever was inside, Bourne came up, pulled him aside so he could look in. What he saw astonished even him. The person sitting behind the wheel was Soraya Moore.

Five

WE'VE BEEN SURVEILLING her for close to ten days now," Soraya said.

"CI?" Bourne said. "Why?"

They were sitting in the Chevy. Soraya had turned on the engine to get some heat up. She'd sent Tyrone home, even though it was clear he wanted to be her protector. According to Soraya, he was now working for her in a strictly off-the-record capacity—a kind of personal black-ops unit of one.

"You know I can't tell you that."

"No, Tyrone can't tell me. You can."

Bourne had worked with Soraya when he'd put together his mission to rescue Martin Lindros, the founder and director of Typhon. She was one of the few people with whom he'd worked in the field, both times in Odessa.

"I suppose I could," Soraya admitted, "but I won't, because it appears that you and Moira Trevor are intimate."

She sat staring out the window at the blank sheen of the street. Her large, deep blue eyes and her aggressive nose were the centerpieces of a bold Arabian face the color of cinnamon.

When she turned back, Bourne could see that she wasn't happy at being forced to reveal CI intel.

"There's a new sheriff in town," Soraya said. "Her name is Veronica Hart."

"You ever hear of her?"

"No, and neither have any of the others." She shrugged. "I'm quite sure that was the point. She comes from the private sector: Black River. The president decided on a new broom to sweep out the hash we'd all made of the events leading up to the Old Man's murder."

"What's she like?"

"Too soon to tell, but one thing I'm willing to bet on: She's going to be a whole helluva lot better than the alternative."

"Which is?"

"Secretary of Defense Halliday has been trying to expand his domain for years now. He's moving through Luther LaValle, the Pentagon's intel czar. Rumor has it that LaValle tried to pry away the DCI job from Veronica Hart."

"And she won." Bourne nodded. "That says something about her."

Soraya produced a packet of Lambert & Butler cigarettes, knocked one out, lit up.

"When did that begin?" Bourne said.

Soraya rolled down her window partway, blew the smoke into the waning night. "The day I was promoted to director of Typhon."

"Congratulations." He sat back, impressed. "But now we have even more of a mystery. Why is the director of Typhon on a surveillance team at four in the morning? I would've thought that would be a job for someone farther down the CI food chain."

"It would be, in other circumstances." Soraya inhaled, blew smoke out the window again. What was left of the cigarette followed. Then she turned her body toward Bourne. "My new boss told me to handle this myself. That's what I'm doing."

"What does all this clandestine work have to do with Moira? She's a civilian."

"Maybe she is," Soraya said, "and maybe she isn't." Her large eyes studied Bourne's for a reaction. "I've been digging through the masses of interoffice e-mails and cell phone records going back over the last two years. I came upon some irregularities and handed them over to the new DCI." She paused for a moment, as if unsure whether to continue. "The thing is, the irregularities concern Martin's private communications with Moira."

"You mean he told her CI classified secrets?"

"Frankly, we're not sure. The communications weren't intact; they had to be pieced together and enhanced electronically. Some words were garbled, others were out of order. It was clear, however, that they were collaborating on something that bypassed the normal CI channels." She sighed. "It's possible he was merely helping her with security issues for NextGen Energy Solutions. But especially after the multiple security breaches CI recently suffered, Hart has make it clear that we can't afford to overlook the possibility that she's working clandestinely for some other entity Martin knew nothing about."

"You mean she was milking him for intel. I find that hard to believe."

"Right. Now you know why I didn't want to tell you about it."

"I'd like to see these communications for myself."

"For that you'll have to see the DCI, which, quite honestly, I wouldn't recommend. There are still high-level operatives in CI who blame you for the Old Man's death."

"That's absurd," Bourne said. "I had nothing to do with his death."

Soraya ran a hand through her thick hair. "It was you who brought Karim al-Jamil back to CI thinking he was Martin Lindros."

"He looked exactly like Martin, spoke exactly like him."

"You vouched for him."

"So did a phalanx of CI shrinks."

"You're an easy target around CI. Rob Batt, who's just been promoted to deputy director, is the ringleader of a group who are convinced you're a schizophrenic, unreliable rogue agent. I'm just saying."

Bourne closed his eyes for a moment. He'd heard these allegations leveled against him time and again. "You've left off another reason why

I'm an easy target. I'm a legacy left over from the Alex Conklin era. He had the Old Man's confidence but hardly anyone else's, mainly because no one knew what he was doing, especially with the program that created me."

"All the more reason for you to stay in the shadows."

Bourne glanced out the window. "I've got an early breakfast meeting."

As he was about to get out of the car, Soraya put a hand on his arm. "Stay out of this, Jason. That's my advice."

"And I appreciate the concern." He leaned toward her, kissed her lightly on the cheek. Then he was crossing the street. A moment later he'd vanished into shadow.

As soon as he was out of her sight, Bourne flipped open the cell phone he'd lifted from her when he'd leaned in to kiss her. Quickly he scrolled through to Veronica Hart's number, connected with it. He wondered if he'd be pulling her out of sleep, but when she answered she sounded wide awake.

"How's the surveillance going?" She had a rich, mellow voice.

"That's what I want to talk with you about."

There was the briefest of silences before she answered. "Who is this?"

"Jason Bourne."

"Where is Soraya Moore?"

"Soraya is fine, Director. I simply needed a way to contact you once I'd broken the surveillance, and I was quite certain Soraya wouldn't give it to me willingly."

"So you stole her phone."

"I want to meet with you," Bourne said. He didn't have much time. At any moment, Soraya might reach for her phone, would know he'd hijacked it and come after him. "I want to see the evidence that led you to order the surveillance on Moira Trevor."

"I don't take kindly to being told what to do, especially by a rogue agent."

"But you will meet with me, Director, because I'm the only one with access to Moira. I'm your fast track to finding out if she's really rotten or whether you're on a wild goose chase."

I think I'll stick to the proven way." Veronica Hart, sitting in her new office with Rob Batt, mouthed the words *Jason Bourne* to her DDCI.

"But you can't," Bourne said in her ear. "Now that I've broken the surveillance I can ensure that Moira vanishes off your grid."

Hart stood up. "I also don't respond well to threats."

"I have no need to threaten you, Director. I'm simply telling you the facts."

Batt studied her expression as well as her responses, trying to get a reading of the conversation. They had been working nonstop since she'd returned from her meeting with the president. He was exhausted, on the point of leaving, but this call interested him intensely.

"Look," Bourne said, "Martin was my friend. He was a hero. I don't want his reputation tarnished."

"All right," Hart said, "come to my office later this morning, say around eleven."

"I'm not setting foot inside CI headquarters," Bourne said. "We'll meet this evening at five at the entrance to the Freer Gallery."

"What if I—?"

But Bourne had already severed the connection.

Moira was up, clad in her paisley robe, when Bourne returned. She was in the kitchen, making fresh coffee. She glanced at him without comment. She had more sense than to ask about his comings and goings.

Bourne took off his coat. "Just checking the area for tails."

She paused. "And did you find any?"

"Quiet as the grave." He didn't believe that Moira had been pumping Martin for CI intel, but the inordinate sense of security—of secretiveness—instilled in him by Conklin warned him not to tell her the truth.

She relaxed visibly. "That's a relief." Setting the pot on the flame, she said, "Do we have time for a cup together?"

Gray light filtered through the blinds, brightening by the minute. An engine coughed, traffic started up on the street. Voices rose briefly, and a dog barked. The morning had begun.

They stood side by side in the kitchen. Between them on the wall was a Kit-Cat Klock, its raffish kitty eyes and tail moving back and forth as time passed.

"Jason, tell me it wasn't just mutual loneliness and sorrow that motivated us."

When he took her in his arms he felt a tiny shiver work its way through her. "One-night stands are not in my vocabulary, Moira."

She put her head against his chest.

He pulled her hair back from her cheek. "I don't feel like coffee right now."

She moved against him. "Neither do I."

Professor Dominic Specter was stirring sugar into the strong Turkish tea he always carried with him when David Webb walked into the Wonderlake diner on 36th Street, NW. The place was lined with wooden boards, the tables reclaimed wooden slabs, the mismatched chairs found objects. Photographs of loggers and Pacific Northwest vistas were ranged around the walls, interspersed with real logging tools: peaveys, cant hooks, pulp hooks, and timberjacks. The place was a perennial student favorite because of its hours, the inexpensive food, and the inescapable associations with Monty Python's "The Lumberjack Song."

Bourne ordered coffee as soon as he sat down.

"Good morning, David." Specter cocked his head like a bird on a wire. "You look like you haven't slept."

The coffee was just the way Bourne liked it: strong, black, sugar-less. "I had a lot to think about."

Specter cocked his head. "David, what is it? Anything I can help with? My door is always open."

"I appreciate that. I always have."

"I can see something's troubling you. Whatever it is, together we can work it out."

The waiter, dressed in red-checked flannel shirt, jeans, and Timberland boots, set the menus down on the table and left.

"It's about my job."

"Is it wrong for you?" The professor spread his hands. "You miss teaching, I imagine. All right, we'll put you back in the classroom."

"I'm afraid it's more serious than that."

When he didn't continue, Professor Specter cleared his throat. "I've noticed a certain restlessness in you over the past few weeks. Could it have anything to do with that?"

Bourne nodded. "I've think I've been trying to recapture something that can't be caught."

"Are you worried about disappointing me, my boy?" Specter rubbed his chin. "You know, years ago when you told me about the Bourne identity, I counseled you to seek professional help. Such a serious mental schism inevitably builds up pressure in the individual."

"I've had help before. So I know how to handle the pressure."

"I'm not questioning that, David." Specter paused. "Or should I be calling you Jason?"

Bourne continued to sip his coffee, said nothing.

"I'd love you to stay, Jason, but only if it's the right thing for you."

Specter's cell phone buzzed but he ignored it. "Understand, I only want what's best for you. But your life's been in upheaval. First, Marie's death, then the demise of your best friends." His phone buzzed again. "I thought you needed sanctuary, which you always have here. But if you've made up your mind to leave . . ." He looked at the number lit up on his phone. "Excuse me a moment."

He took the call, listening.

"The deal can't be closed without it?"

He nodded, held the phone, away from his ear, said to Bourne. "I need to get something from my car. Please order for me. Scrambled eggs and dark toast."

He rose, went out of the restaurant. His Honda was parked directly across 36th Street. He was in the middle of the street when two men came out of nowhere. One grabbed him while the other struck him several times about the head. As a black Cadillac screeched to a halt beside the three men, Bourne was up and running. The man struck Specter again, yanked open the rear door of the car.

Bourne grabbed a pulp hook off the wall, sprinted out of the restaurant. The man bundled Specter into the backseat of the Cadillac and jumped in beside him, while the first man ducked into the front passenger's seat. The Cadillac took off just as Bourne reached it. He barely had time to swing the pulp hook into the car before he was jerked off his feet. He'd been aiming for the roof, but the Cadillac's sudden acceleration had caused it to pierce the rear window instead. The pointed end managed to embed itself in the top of the backseat. Bourne swung his trailing legs onto the trunk.

The rear pane of safety glass was completely crazed, but the thin film of plastic sandwiched between the glass layers kept it basically intact. As the car began to swerve insanely back and forth, the driver trying to dislodge him, chips of the safety glass came away, giving Bourne an increasingly tenuous hold on the Cadillac.

The car accelerated ever more dangerously through building traffic. Then, so abruptly it took his breath away, it whipped around a corner and he slid off the trunk, his body now banging against the driver's-side fender. His shoes struck the tarmac with such force, one of them was ripped off. Sock and skin were flayed off his heel before he could regain a semblance of balance. Using the fulcrum of the pulp hook's turned wooden handle, he levered his legs back up onto the trunk, only to have the driver slew the Cadillac so that he was almost thrown completely clear of the car. His feet struck a trash can, sending it barreling down the sidewalk as shocked pedestrians scattered helter-skelter. Pain shot through him and he might have been finished, but the driver could not keep the Cadillac in its spin any longer. Traffic forced him to straighten out the car's trajectory. Bourne took advantage to swing himself back up onto the trunk. His right fist plunged through the shattered rear window, seeking a second, more secure hold. The car was accelerating again as it bypassed the last of the bunched-up local traffic, gained the ramp onto Whitehurst Freeway. Bourne tucked his legs up under him, braced on his knees.

As they passed into shadow beneath the Francis Scott Key Bridge the man who had shoved Specter into the backseat thrust a Taurus PT140 through the gap in the broken glass. The handgun's muzzle turned toward Bourne as the man prepared to fire. Bourne let go with his right hand, gripped the man's wrist, and jerked hard, bringing the entire forearm into the open air. The motion pushed back the sleeve of the man's coat and shirt. He saw a peculiar tattoo on the inside of the forearm: three horses' heads joined by a central skull. He slammed his right knee into the inside of the man's elbow, at the same time pushed it back against the frame of the car. With a satisfying crack, it broke, the hand opened, the Taurus fell away. Bourne made a grab for it, but missed.

The Cadillac swerved into the left lane and the pulp hook, ripping through the fabric of the backseat, was forced out of Bourne's hand. He gripped the gunman's broken arm with both hands, used it to lever himself through the ruined rear window feetfirst.

He landed between the man with the broken arm and Specter, who was huddled against the left-hand door. The man in the front passenger's seat was kneeling on the seat, turned toward him. He also had a Taurus, which he aimed at Bourne. Bourne grabbed the body of the man beside him, shifted him so that the shot plowed into the man's chest, killing him instantly. At once Bourne heaved the corpse against the gunman in the front bench seat. The gunman swiped the corpse in the shoulder in an attempt to move him away, but this only brought the corpse in contact with the driver, who had put on a burst of speed and who seemed to be focused solely on weaving in and out of the traffic.

Bourne punched the gunman in the nose. Blood spattered as the gunman was thrown off his knees, jolted back against the dashboard. As Bourne moved to follow up his advantage, the gunman aimed the Taurus at Specter.

"Get back," he shouted, "or I'll kill him."

Bourne judged the moment. If the men had wanted to kill Specter they'd have gunned him down in the street. Since they grabbed him, they must need him alive.

"All right." Unseen by the gunman, his right hand scraped along the cushion of the backseat. As he raised his hands, he flicked a palmful of glass chips into the gunman's face. As the man's hands instinctively went up, Bourne chopped him twice with the edge of his hand. The gunman drew out a push dagger, the wicked-looking blade protruding from between his second and third knuckles. He jabbed it directly at Bourne's face. Bourne ducked; the blade followed him, moving closer until Bourne slammed his fist into the side of the gunman's head, which snapped back against the rear doorpost. Bourne heard the crack as his neck broke. The gunman's eyes rolled up and he slumped against the door.

Bourne locked his crooked arm around the driver's neck, pulled back hard. The driver began to choke. He whipped his head back and forth, trying to free himself. As he did so, the car swerved from one lane to another. The car began to swerve dangerously as he lost consciousness. Bourne climbed over the seat, pushing the driver off, down into the passenger's-side foot well, so that he could slide behind the wheel. The trouble was though Bourne could steer, the driver's body was blocking the pedals.

The Cadillac was now out of control. It hit a car in the left lane, bounced off to the right. Instead of fighting against the resulting spin, Bourne turned into it. At the same time, he shifted the car into neutral. Instantly the transmission disengaged; the engine was no longer being fed gas. Now its immediate momentum was the issue. Bourne, struggling to gain control, found his foot blocked from the brake by part of a leg. He steered right, jouncing over the divider and into an enormous parking lot that lay between the freeway and the Potomac.

The Cadillac sideswiped a parked SUV, careened farther to the right toward the water. Bourne kicked the unconscious driver's inert body with his bare left foot, at last finding the brake pedal. The car finally slowed, but not enough—they were still heading toward the Potomac. Whipping the wheel hard to the right caused the Cadillac's tires to shriek as Bourne tried to turn the car away from the low barrier that separated the lot from the water. As the front end of the Cadillac went up over the barrier, Bourne jammed the brake pedal to the floor, and the car came to a halt partway over the side. It teetered precariously back and forth. Specter, still huddled in the backseat behind Bourne, moaned a little, the right sleeve of his Harris Tweed jacket spattered with blood from his captor's broken nose.

Bourne, trying to keep the Cadillac out of the Potomac, sensed that the front wheels were still on the top of the barrier. He threw the car into reverse. The Cadillac shot backward, slamming into another parked car before Bourne had a chance to shift back into neutral.

From far away he could hear the seesaw wail of sirens.

"Professor, are you all right?"

Specter groaned, but at least his voice was more distinct. "We have to get out of here."

Bourne was freeing the pedals from the strangled man's legs. "That tattoo I saw on the gunman's arm—"

"No police," Specter managed to croak. "There's a place we can go. I'll tell you."

Bourne got out of the Caddy, then helped Specter out. Limping over to another car, Bourne smashed the window with his elbow. The police sirens were coming closer. Bourne got in, hot-wired the ignition, and the car's engine coughed to life. He unlocked the doors. The instant the professor slid into the passenger's seat Bourne took off, heading east on the freeway. As quickly as he could he moved into the left-hand lane. Then he turned abruptly to his left. The car jumped the central divider and he accelerated, heading west now, in the opposite direction the sirens were coming from.

Six

ARKADIN TOOK his evening meal at Tractir on Bolshaya Morse-kay, halfway up the steep hill, a typically unlovely place with roughly varnished wooden tables and chairs. Almost one entire wall was taken up by a painting of three-masted ships in Sevastopol harbor circa 1900. The food was unremarkable, but that wasn't why Arkadin was here. Tractir was the restaurant whose name he'd found in Oleg Ivanovich Shumenko's wallet. No one here knew anyone named Devra, so after the borscht and the blini, he moved on.

Along the coast was a section called Omega, filled with cafés and restaurants. As the hub of the city's nightlife culture, it featured every variety of club one could want. Calla was a club a short stroll from the open-air car park. The night was clear and brisk. Pinpoints dotted the Black Sea as well as the sky, making for a dizzying vista. Sea and sky seemed to be virtually interchangeable.

Calla was several steps down from the sidewalk, a place filled with the sweet scent of marijuana and an unearthly din. A roughly square room was divided between a jam-packed dance floor and a raised sec-tion filled with minuscule round tables and metal café chairs. A grid of colored lights pulsed in time with the house music the straw-thin female DJ was spinning. She stood behind a small stand on which was set an iPod hooked up to a number of digital mixing machines.

The dance floor was packed with men and women. Bumping hips and elbows was part of the scene. Arkadin picked his way over to the bar, which ran along the front of the right wall. Twice he was intercepted by young, busty blondes who wanted his attention and, he assumed, his money. He brushed past them, made a beeline for the harried bartender. Three tiers of glass shelves filled with liquor bottles were attached to a mirror on the wall behind the bar so patrons could check out the action or admire themselves while getting polluted.

Arkadin was obliged to wade through a phalanx of revelers before he could order a Stoli on the rocks. When, some time later, the bartender returned with his drink, Arkadin asked him if he knew a Devra.

"Yah, sure. Over there," he said, nodding in the direction of the straw-thin DJ.

It was 1 AM before Devra took a break. There were other people waiting for her to finish—fans, Arkadin presumed. He intended to get to her first. He used the force of his personality rather than his false credentials. Not that the rabble here would challenge them, but after the incident at the winery, he didn't want to leave any trail for the real SBU to follow. The state police alias he'd used there was now dangerous to him.

Devra was blond, almost as tall as he was. He couldn't believe how thin her arms were. They had no definition at all. Her hips were no wider than a young boy's, and he could see the bones of her scapulae when she moved. She had large eyes and dead-white skin, as if she rarely saw the light of day. Her black jumpsuit with its white skull and crossbones across the stomach was drenched in sweat. Perhaps because of her DJing, her hands were in constant motion even if the rest of her stayed relatively still.

She eyed him up and down while he introduced himself. "You don't look like a friend of Oleg's," she said.

But when he dangled the IOU in front of her face her skepticism evaporated. *Thus is it ever,* Arkadin thought as she led him backstage. *The venality of the human race cannot be overestimated.*

The green room where she relaxed between sets was better off left to the wharf rats that were no doubt shuttered behind the walls, but right now that couldn't be helped. He tried not to think of the rats; he wouldn't be here long anyway. There were no windows; the walls and ceiling were painted black, no doubt to cover up a multitude of sins.

Devra turned on a lamp with a mean forty-watt bulb and sat down on a wooden chair damaged by knife scars and cigarette burns. The difference between the green room and an interrogation cell was negligible. There were no other chairs or furniture, save for a narrow wooden table against one wall on which was a jumble of makeup, CDs, cigarettes, matches, gloves, and other piles of debris Arkadin didn't bother to identify.

Devra leaned back, lit a cigarette she nimbly swiped from the table without offering him one. "So you're here to pay off Oleg's debt."

"In a sense."

Her eyes narrowed, making her look a lot like a stoat Arkadin had once shot outside St. Petersburg.

"Meaning what, exactly?"

Arkadin produced the bills. "I have the money he owes you right here." As she reached out for it, he pulled it away. "In return I'd like some information."

Devra laughed. "What do I look like, the phone operator?"

Arkadin hit her hard with the back of his hand, so that she crashed into the table. Tubes of lipstick and mascara went rolling and tumbling. Devra put a hand out to steady herself, fingers clutching through the morass.

When she pulled out a small handgun Arkadin was ready. His fist hammered her delicate wrist and he plucked the handgun from her numb fingers.

"Now," he said, setting her back on the chair, "are you ready to continue?"

Devra looked at him sullenly. "I knew this was too good to be true." She spat. "Shit! No good deed goes unpunished."

Arkadin took a moment to process what she was really saying. Then he said, "Why did Shumenko need the ten thousand hryvnia?"

"So I was right. You're not a friend of his."

"Does it matter?" Arkadin emptied the handgun, broke it down without taking his eyes off her, tossed the pieces onto the table. "This is between you and me now."

"I think not," a deep male voice said from behind him.

"Filya," Devra breathed. "What took you so long?"

Arkadin did not turn around. He'd heard the click of the switch-blade, knew what he was up against. He eyeballed the mess on the table, and when he saw the double half-moon grips of scissors peeping out from under a small pyramid of CD cases, he fixed their location in his mind, then turned around.

As if startled by the big man with heavily pocked cheeks and new hair plugs, he retreated up against the edge of the table.

"Who the hell're you? This is a private discussion." Arkadin spoke more to distract Filya from his left hand moving behind him along the tabletop.

"Devra is mine." Filya brandished the long, cruel blade of the hand-made switchblade. "No one talks to her without my permission."

Arkadin smiled thinly. "I wasn't talking to her so much as threatening her."

The idea was to antagonize Filya to the point that he'd do something precipitous and, therefore, stupid, and Arkadin succeeded admirably. With a growl, Filya rushed him, knife blade extended, tilted slightly upward.

With only one shot at a surprise maneuver, Arkadin had to make the most of it. The fingers of his left hand had gripped the scissors. They were small, which was just as well; he had no intention of again killing someone who might provide useful information. He lifted them, calculating their weight. Then as he brought the scissors around the side of his body, he flicked his wrist, a deceptively small gesture that was nevertheless all power. Released from his grip, the scissors flew through the air, embedding in the soft spot just below Filya's sternum.

Filya's eyes opened wide as his headlong rush faltered two paces from Arkadin, then he resumed his advance, brandishing the knife. Arkadin ducked away from the sweeping arc of the blade. He grappled with Filya, wanting only to wear him out, let the wound in his chest sap his strength, but Filya wasn't having any. Being stabbed had only enraged him. With superhuman strength he broke Arkadin's grip on the wrist that held the switchblade, swung it from a low point upward, breaking through Arkadin's defense. The point of the blade blurred toward Arkadin's face. Too late to stop the attack, Arkadin reacted instinctively, managing to deflect the stab at the last instant, so that the point drove through Filya's own throat.

An arcing veil of blood caused Devra to scream. As she stumbled backward, Arkadin reached for her. Clamping one hand over her mouth, he shook his head. Her ashen cheeks and forehead were spattered with blood. Arkadin supported Filya in the crook of one arm. The man was dying. Arkadin had never meant this to happen. First Shumenko, now Filya. If he had believed in such things, he would have said that the assignment was cursed.

"Filya!" He slapped the man, whose eyes had turned glassy. Blood leaked out of the side of Filya's slack mouth. "The package. Where is it?"

For a moment, Filya's eyes focused on him. When Arkadin repeated his question a curious smile took Filya down into death. Arkadin held him for a moment more before propping him up against a wall.

As he returned his attention to Devra he saw a rat glowering from a corner, and his gorge rose. It took all his willpower not to abandon the girl to go after it, rip it limb from limb.

"Now," he said, "it's just you and me."

* * *

Making certain he wasn't being followed, Rob Batt pulled into the parking lot adjacent to the Tysons Corner Baptist Church. He sat waiting in his car. From time to time, he checked his watch.

Under the late DCI, he had been chief of operations, the most influential of CI's seven directorate heads. He was of the Beltway old school with connections that ran directly back to Yale's legendary Skull & Bones Club, of which he'd been an officer during his college days. Just how many Skull & Bones men had been recruited into America's clandestine services was one of those secrets its keepers would kill to protect. Suffice it to say it was many, and Batt was one of them. It was particularly galling for him to play second fiddle to an outsider—and a female, at that. The Old Man would never have tolerated such an outrage, but the Old Man was gone, murdered in his own home reportedly by his traitorous assistant, Anne Held. Though Batt—and others of his brethren—had his doubts about that.

What a difference three months made. Had the Old Man still been alive he'd never have considered even consenting to this meet. Batt was a loyal man, but his loyalty, he realized, extended to the man who had reached out to him in grad school, recruited him to CI. Those were the old days, though. The new order was in place, and it wasn't fair. He hadn't been part of the problem caused by Martin Lindros and Jason Bourne—he'd been part of the solution. He'd even been suspicious of the man who'd turned out to be an impostor. He would have exposed him had Bourne not interfered. That coup, Batt knew, would have scored him the inside track with the Old Man.

But with the Old Man gone, his lobbying for the directorship had been to no avail. Instead, the president had opted for Veronica Hart. God alone knew why. It was such a colossal mistake; she'd just run CI into the ground. A woman wasn't constructed to make the kinds of decisions necessary to captain the CI ship. The priorities and ways of approaching problems were different with women. The hounds of the

NSA were circling CI, and he couldn't bear watching this woman turn them all, the entire company, into carrion for the feast. At least Batt could join the people who would inevitably take over when Hart fucked up. Even so, it pained him to be here, to embark upon this unknown sea.

At 10:30 AM the doors to the church swung open, the parishioners came down the stairs, stood in the wan sunshine, turning their heads up like sunflowers at dawn. The ministers appeared, walking side by side with Luther LaValle. LaValle was accompanied by his wife and teenage son. The two men stood chatting while the family grouped loosely around. LaValle's wife seemed interested in the conversation, but the son was busy ogling a girl more or less his age who was prancing down the stairs. She was a beauty, Batt had to admit. Then, with a start, he realized that she was one of General Kendall's three daughters, because here Kendall was with his arm around his stubby wife. How the two of them could have produced a trio of such handsome girls was anyone's guess. Even Darwin couldn't have figured it out, Batt thought.

The two families—the LaValles and the Kendalls—gathered in a loose huddle as if they were a football team. Then the kids went their own ways, some in cars, others on bicycles because the church wasn't far from their homes. The two wives chastely kissed their husbands, piled into a Cadillac Escalade, and took off.

That left the two men, who stood for a moment in front of the church before coming around to the parking lot. Not a word had been exchanged between them. Batt heard a heavyweight engine cough to life.

A long black armored limousine came cruising down the aisle like a sleek shark. It stopped briefly while LaValle and Kendall climbed inside. Its engine, idling, sent small puffs of exhaust into the cool, crisp air. Batt counted to thirty and, as he'd been instructed, got out of his car. As he did so, the rear door of the limo popped open. Ducking his head, he climbed into the dim, plush interior. The door closed behind him.

"Gentlemen," he said, folding himself onto the bench seat oppo-

site them. The two men sat side by side in the limo's backseat: Luther
LaValle, the Pentagon's intel czar, and his second, General Richard P.
Kendall.

"So kind of you to join us," LaValle said.

Kindness had nothing to do with it, Batt thought. A convergence of
objectives did.

"The pleasure's all mine, gentlemen. I'm flattered and, if I may be
frank, grateful that you reached out to me."

"We're here," General Kendall said, "to speak frankly."

"We've opposed the appointment of Veronica Hart from the start,"
LaValle said. "The secretary of defense made his opinion quite clear to
the president. However, others, including the national security adviser
and the secretary of state—who, as you know, is a personal friend of
the president—both lobbied for an outsider from the private security
sector."

"Bad enough," Batt said. "And a woman."

"Precisely." General Kendall nodded. "It's madness."

LaValle stirred. "It's the clearest sign yet of the deterioration of our
defense grid that Secretary Halliday has been warning against for several years now."

"When we start listening to Congress and the people of the country
all hope is lost," Kendall said. "A mulligan stew of amateurs all with
petty axes to grind and absolutely no idea of how to maintain security
or run the intelligence services."

LaValle gave off an icy smile. "That's why the secretary of defense
has labored mightily to keep the workings clandestine."

"The more they know, the less they understand," General Kendall
said, "and the more inclined they are to interfere by means of their
congressional hearings and threats of budgets cuts."

"Oversight is a bitch," LaValle agreed. "Which is why areas of the
Pentagon under my control are working without it." He paused for a moment, studying Batt. "How does that sound to you, Deputy Director?"

"Like manna from heaven."

* * *

Oleg had screwed up big time," Devra said.

Arkadin took a stab. "He got in over his head with loan sharks?"

She shook her head. "That was last year. It had to do with Pyotr Zilber."

Arkadin's ears pricked up. "What about him?"

"I don't know." Her eyes opened wide as Arkadin raised his fist. "I swear it."

"But you're part of Zilber's network."

She turned her head away from him, as if she couldn't stand herself. "A minor part. I shuffle things from here to there."

"Within the past week Shumenko gave you a document."

"He gave me a package, I don't know what was in it," Devra said. "It was sealed."

"Compartmentalization."

"What?" She looked up at him. Blood beads on her face looked like freckles. Tears had caused her mascara to run, giving her dark half circles under her eyes.

"The first principle of putting together a cadre." Arkadin nodded. "Go on."

She shrugged. "That's all I know."

"What about the package?"

"I passed it on, as I was instructed to do."

Arkadin bent over her. "Who did you give it to?"

She glanced at the crumpled form on the floor. "I gave it to Filya."

LaValle had paused a moment to reflect. "We never knew each other at Yale."

"You were two years ahead of me," Batt said. "But in Skull and Bones you were notorious."

LaValle laughed. "Now you flatter me."

"Hardly." Batt unbuttoned his overcoat. "The stories I heard."

LaValle frowned. "Are never to be repeated."

General Kendall let loose with a guffaw that filled the compartment. "Should I leave you two girls alone? Better not; one of you could wind up pregnant."

The comment was meant as a joke, of course, but there was a nasty undercurrent to it. Did the military man resent his exclusion from the elite club, or the connection the other two had through Skull & Bones? Possibly it was a bit of both. In any event, Batt noted the second's tone of voice, tucked the possible implications into a place where he could examine them later.

"What d'you have in mind, Mr. LaValle?"

"I'm looking for a way to convince the president that his more immoderate advisers made a mistake in recommending Veronica Hart for DCI." LaValle pursed his lips. "Any ideas?"

"Off the top of my head, plenty," Batt said. "What's in it for me?"

As if on cue LaValle produced another smile. "We're going to require a new DCI when we can Hart's ass out of the District. Who would be your first choice?"

"The current deputy director seems the logical one," Batt said. "That would be me."

LaValle nodded. "Our thought precisely."

Batt tapped his fingertips against his knee. "If you two are serious."

"We are, I assure you."

Batt's mind worked furiously. "It seems to me unwise at this early juncture to have attacked Hart directly."

"How about you don't tell us our business," Kendall said.

LaValle held up a hand. "Let's hear what the man has to say, Richard." To Batt, he added, "However, let me make something crystal clear. We want Hart out as soon as possible."

"We all do, but you don't want suspicion thrown back at you—or at the defense secretary."

LaValle and General Kendall exchanged a quick and knowing look. They were like twins, able to communicate with each other without uttering a word. "Indeed not," LaValle said.

"She told me how you ambushed her at that meeting with the president—and the threats you made to her outside the White House."

"Women are more easily intimidated than men," Kendall pointed out. "It's a well-known fact."

Batt ignored the military man. "You put her on notice. She took your threats very personally. She had a killer's rep in Black River. I checked through my sources."

LaValle seemed thoughtful. "How would you have handled her?"

"I would have made nice, welcomed her to the fold, let her know you're there for her whenever she needs your help."

"She'd never have bought it," LaValle said. "She knows my agenda."

"It doesn't matter. The idea is not to antagonize her. You don't want her knives out when you come for her."

LaValle nodded, as if he saw the wisdom in this approach. "So how do you suggest we proceed from here?"

"Give me some time," Batt said. "Hart's just getting started at CI, and because I'm her deputy I know everything she does, every decision she makes. But when she's out of the office, shadow her, see where she goes, who she meets. Using parabolic mikes you can listen in to her conversations. Between us, we'll have her covered twenty-four/seven."

"Sounds pretty vanilla to me," Kendall said skeptically.

"Keep it simple, especially when there's so much at stake, that's my advice," Batt said.

"What if she cottons on to the surveillance?" Kendall said.

Batt smiled. "So much the better. It'll only bolster the CI mantra that the NSA is run by incompetents."

LaValle laughed. "Batt, I like the way you think."

Batt nodded, acknowledging the compliment. "Coming from the private sector Hart's not used to government procedure. She doesn't have the leeway she enjoyed at Black River. I can already see that, to her, rules and regs are meant to be bent, sidestepped, even, on occasion, broken. Mark my words, sooner rather than later, Director Hart is going to give us the ammunition we need to kick her butt out of CI."

Seven

HOW IS your foot, Jason?"

Bourne looked up at Professor Specter, whose face was swollen and discolored. His left eye was half closed, dark as a storm cloud.

"Yes," Specter said, "after what just happened I'm compelled to call you by what seems like your rightful name."

"My heel is fine," Bourne said. "It's me who should be asking about you."

Specter put fingertips gingerly against his cheek. "In my life I've endured worse beatings."

The two men were seated in a high-ceilinged library filled with a large, magnificent Isfahan carpet, ox-blood leather furniture. Three walls were fitted floor-to-ceiling with books neatly arrayed on mahogany shelves. The fourth wall was pierced by a large leaded-glass window overlooking stands of stately firs on a knoll, which sloped down to a pond guarded by a weeping willow, shivering in the wind.

Specter's personal physician had been summoned, but the professor had insisted the doctor tend to Bourne's flayed heel first.

"I'm sure we can find you a pair of shoes somewhere," Specter said, sending one of the half a dozen men in residence scurrying off with Bourne's remaining shoe.

This rather large stone-and-slate house deep in the Virginia countryside to which Specter had directed Bourne was a far cry from the modest apartment the professor maintained near the university. Bourne had been to the apartment numerous times over the years, but never here. Then there was the matter of the staff, which Bourne noted with interest as well as surprise.

"I imagine you're wondering about all this," Specter said, as if reading Bourne's mind. "All in good time, my friend." He smiled. "First, I must thank you for rescuing me."

"Who were those men?" Bourne said. "Why did they try to kidnap you?"

The doctor applied an antibiotic ointment, placed a gauze pad over the heel, taped it in place. Then he wrapped the heel in cohesive bandage.

"It's a long story," Specter said. The doctor, finished with Bourne, now rose to examine the professor. "One I propose to tell you over the breakfast we were unable to enjoy earlier." He winced as the doctor palpated areas of his body.

"Contusions, bruises," the doctor intoned colorlessly, "but no broken bones or fractures."

He was a small swarthy man with a mustache and dark slicked-back hair. Bourne made him as Turkish. In fact, all the staff seemed of Turkish origin.

He gave Specter a small packet. "You may need these painkillers, but only for the next forty-eight hours." He'd already left a tube of the antibiotic cream, along with instructions, for Bourne.

While Specter was being examined, Bourne used his cell phone to call Deron, the art forger whom he used for all his travel documents. Bourne recited the license tag of the black Cadillac he'd commandeered from the professor's would-be kidnappers.

"I need a registration report ASAP."

"You okay, Jason?" Deron said in his sonorous London-accented

voice. Deron had been Bourne's backup through many hair-raising mis-
sions. He always asked the same question.

"I'm fine," Bourne said, "but that's more than I can say for the car's
original occupants."

"Brilliant."

Bourne pictured him in his lab in the northeast section of DC, a
tall, vibrant black man with the mind of a conjuror.

When the doctor departed, Bourne and Specter were left alone.

"I already know who came after me," Specter said.

"I don't like loose ends," Bourne replied. "The Cadillac's registration
will tell us something, perhaps something even you don't know."

The professor nodded, clearly impressed.

Bourne sat on the leather sofa with his leg up on the coffee table.
Specter eased himself into a facing chair. Clouds chased each other across
the windblown sky, setting patterns shifting across the Persian carpet.
Bourne saw a different kind of shadow pass across Specter's face.

"Professor, what is it?"

Specter shook his head. "I owe you a most sincere and abject apology, Jason. I'm afraid I had an ulterior motive in asking you to return to
university life." His eyes were filled with regret. "I thought it would be
good for you, yes, that's true enough, absolutely. But also I wanted you
near me because . . ." He waved a hand as if to clear the air of deceit.
"Because I was fearful that what happened this morning would happen.
Now, because of my selfishness, I'm very much afraid that I've put your
life in jeopardy."

Turkish tea, strong and intensely aromatic, was served along with eggs,
smoked fish, coarse bread, butter, deep yellow and fragrant.

Bourne and Specter sat at a long table covered with a white hand-
finished linen cloth. The china and silverware were of the highest qual-
ity. Again, an oddity in an academic's household. They remained mute
while a young man, slim and sleek, served their perfectly cooked, ele-
gantly presented breakfast.

When Bourne began to ask a question, Specter cut him off. "First we must fill our stomachs, regain our strength, ensure our minds are working at full capacity."

The two men did not speak again until they were finished, the plates and cutlery were cleared, and a fresh pot of tea had been poured. A small bowl of gigantic Medjool dates and halved fresh pomegranates lay between them.

When they were again alone in the dining room, Specter said without preamble, "The night before last I received word that a former student of mine whose father was a close friend was dead. Murdered in a most despicable fashion. This young man, Pyotr Zilber, was special. Besides being a former student he ran an information network that spanned several countries. After a number of difficult and perilous months of subterfuge and negotiation he had managed to obtain for me a vital document. He was found out, with the inevitable consequences. This is the incident I've been dreading. It may sound melodramatic, but I assure you it's the truth: The war I've been engaged in for close to twenty years has reached its final stage."

"What sort of a war, Professor?" Bourne said. "Against whom?"

"I'll get to that in a moment." Specter leaned forward. "I imagine you're curious, shocked even, that a university professor should be involved in matters that are more the province of Jason Bourne." He lifted both arms briefly to encompass the house. "But as you've no doubt noted there is more to me than meets the eye." He smiled rather sadly. "This makes two of us, yes?

"As someone who also leads a double life I understand you better than most others. I need one personality when I step onto campus, but here I'm someone else entirely." He tapped a stubby forefinger against the side of his nose. "I pay attention. I saw something familiar in you the moment I met you—how your eyes took in every detail of the people and things around you."

Bourne's cell buzzed. He flipped it open, listened to what Deron had to say, then put the phone away.

"The Cadillac was reported stolen a hour before it appeared in front of the restaurant."

"That is entirely unsurprising."

"Who tried to kidnap you, Professor?"

"I know you're impatient for the facts, Jason. I would be, too, in your place. But I promise they won't have meaning without some background first. When I said there's more to me than meets the eye, this is what I meant: I'm a terrorist hunter. For many years, from the camouflage and sanctuary my position at the university affords me, I have built up a network of people who gather intelligence just like your own CI. However, the intelligence that interests me is highly specific. There are people who took my wife from me. In the dead of night, while I was away, they snatched her from our house, tortured her, killed her, then dumped her on my doorstep. As a warning, you see."

Bourne felt a prickling at the back of his neck. He knew what it felt like to be driven by revenge. When Martin died all Bourne could think about was destroying the men who'd tortured him. He felt a new, more intimate connection with Specter, even as the Bourne identity rose inside him, riding a cresting wave of pure adrenaline. All at once the idea of him working at the university struck him as absurd. Moira was right: He was already chafing at the confinement. How would he feel after months of the academic life, bereft of adventure, stripped of the adrenaline rush for which Bourne lived?

"My father was taken because he was plotting to overthrow the head of an organization. They call themselves the Eastern Brotherhood."

"Doesn't the EB espouse a peaceful integration of Muslims into Western society?"

"That's their public stance, certainly, and their literature would have you believe it's so." Specter put down his cup. "In fact, nothing could be farther from the truth. I know them as the Black Legion."

"Then the Black Legion has finally decided to come after you."

"If only it were as simple as that." He halted at a discreet knock on the door. "Enter."

The young man he'd sent on the errand strode in carrying a shoe box, which he set down in front of Bourne.

Specter gestured. "Please."

Taking his foot off the table, Bourne opened the box. Inside were a pair of very fine Italian loafers, along with a pair of socks.

"The left one is half a size larger to accommodate the pad that will protect your heel," the young man said in German.

Bourne pulled on the socks, slipped on the loafers. They fit perfectly. Seeing this, Specter nodded to the young man, who turned and, without another word, left the room.

"Does he speak English?" Bourne asked.

"Oh, yes. Whenever the need arises." Specter's face was wreathed in a mischievous smile. "And now, my dear Jason, you're asking yourself why he's speaking German if he's a Turk?"

"I assume it's because your network spans many countries including Germany, which is, like England, a hotbed of Muslim terrorist activity."

Specter's smile deepened. "You're like a rock. I can always count on you." He raised a forefinger. "But there is yet another reason. It has to do with the Black Legion. Come. I've something to show you."

Filya Petrovich, Pyotr's Sevastopol courier, lived in an anonymous block of crumbling housing left over from the days the Soviets had reshaped the city into a vast barracks housing its largest naval contingent. The apartment, frozen in time since the 1970s, had all the charm of a meat locker.

Arkadin opened the door with the key he'd found on Filya. He pushed Devra over the threshold, stepped in. Turning on the lights, he closed the door behind him. She hadn't wanted to come, but she had no say in the matter, just as she'd had no say in helping him drag Filya's corpse out the nightclub's back door. They set him down at the end of the filthy alley, propped up against a wall damp with unknown fluids. Arkadin poured the contents of a half-empty bottle of cheap vodka over him, then pressed the man's fingers around the bottle's neck. Filya became one drunk among many other drunks in the city. His death would be swept away on an inefficient and overworked bureaucratic tide.

"What're you looking for?" Devra stood in the middle of the living room, watching Arkadin's methodical search. "What d'you think you'll find? The document?" Her laugh was a kind of shrill catcall. "It's gone."

Arkadin glanced up from the mess his switchblade had made of the sofa cushions. "Where?"

"Far out of your reach, that's for sure."

Closing his knife, Arkadin crossed the space between the two of them in one long stride. "Do you think this is a joke, or a game we're playing here?"

Devra's upper lip curled. "Are you going to hurt me now? Believe me, nothing you could do would be worse than what's already been done to me."

Arkadin, the blood pounding in his veins, held himself in check to consider her words. What she said was probably the truth. Under the Soviet boot, God had forsaken many Ukrainians, especially the young attractive females. He needed to take another tack entirely.

"I'm not going to hurt you, even though you're with the wrong people." He turned on his heel, sat down on a wood-framed chair. Leaning back, he ran his fingers through his hair. "I've seen a lot of shit—I've done two stints in prison. I can imagine the systematic brutalization you've been through."

"Me and my mother, God rest her soul."

The headlights of passing cars shone briefly through the windows, then dwindled away. A dog barked in an alleyway, its melancholy voice echoing. A couple passing by outside argued vehemently. Inside the shabby apartment the patchy light cast by the lamps, their shades either torn or askew, caused Devra to look terribly vulnerable, like a wisp of a child. Arkadin rose, stretched mightily, strolled over to the window, looked out onto the street. His eyes picked out every bit of shadow, every flare of light no matter how brief or tiny. Sooner or later Pyotr's people were going to come after him; it was an inevitability that he and Icoupov had discussed before he left the villa. Icoupov had offered to send a couple of hard men to lie low in Sevastopol in the event they were needed, but Arkadin refused, saying he preferred to work alone.

Having assured himself that the street was for the moment clear, he turned away from the window, back to the room. "My mother died badly," he said. "She was murdered, brutally beaten, left in a closet for the rats to gnaw on. At least that's what the coroner told me."

"Where was your father?"

Arkadin shrugged. "Who knows? By that time, the sonovabitch could've been in Shanghai, or he could've been dead. My mother told me he was a merchant marine, but I seriously doubt it. She was ashamed of having been knocked up by a perfect stranger."

Devra, who had sat down on the ripped-apart arm of the sofa during this recitation, said, "It sucks not knowing where you came from, doesn't it? Like always being adrift at sea. You'll never recognize home even if you come upon it."

"Home," Arkadin said heavily. "I never think of it."

Devra caught something in his tone. "But you'd like to, wouldn't you?"

His expression went sour. He checked the street again with his usual thoroughness. "What would be the point?"

"Because knowing where we come from allows us know who we are." She beat softly at her chest with a fist. "Our past is part of us."

Arkadin felt as if she'd pricked him with a needle. Venom squirted through his veins. "My past is an island I've sailed away from long ago."

"Nevertheless, it's still with you, even if you're not aware of it," she said with the force of having mulled the question over and over in her own mind. "We can't outrun our past, no matter how hard we try."

Unlike him, she seemed eager to talk about her past. He found this curious. Did she think this subject was common ground? If so, he needed to stay with it, to keep the connection with her going.

"What about your father?"

"I was born here, grew up here." She stared down at her hands. "My father was a naval engineer. He was thrown out of the shipyards when the Russians took it over. Then one night they came for him, said he was spying on them, delivering technical information on their ships to the Americans. I never saw him again. But the Russian security officer in charge took a liking to my mother. When he'd used her up, he started on me."

Arkadin could just imagine. "How did it end?"

"An American killed him." She looked up at him. "Fucking ironic, because this American was a spy sent to photograph the Russian fleet. When the American had completed his assignment he should've gone back home. Instead he stayed. He took care of me, nursed me back to health."

"Naturally you fell in love with him."

She laughed. "If I was a character in a novel, sure. But he was so kind to me; I was like a daughter to him. I cried when he left."

Arkadin found that he was embarrassed by her confession. To distract himself, he looked around the ruined apartment one more time.

Devra watched him warily. "Hey. I'm dying for something to eat."

Arkadin laughed. "Aren't we all?"

His hawk-like gaze took in the street once more. This time the hairs on the back of his neck stirred as he stepped to the side of the window. A car he'd heard approaching had pulled up in front of the building. Devra, alerted by the sudden tension in his body, moved to the window behind him. What caught his attention was that though its engine was still running, all its lights had been extinguished. Three men exited the car, headed for the building entrance. It was past time to leave.

He turned away from the window. "We're going. Now."

"Pyotr's people. It was inevitable they'd find us."

Much to Arkadin's surprise she made no protest when he hustled her out of the apartment. The hallway was already reverberating with the tribal beat of heavy shoes on the concrete floor.

Bourne found walking unpleasant but hardly intolerable. He'd put up with a lot worse than a flayed heel in his time. As he followed the professor down a metal staircase into the basement, he reflected that this was proof again that there were no absolutes when it came to people. He had assumed that Specter's life was neat, tidy, dull, and quiet, restricted by the dimensions of the university campus. Nothing could be farther from the truth.

Halfway down, the staircase changed to stone treads, worn by decades of use. Their way was guided by plenty of light from below. They entered a finished basement made up of movable walls that separated what looked like office cubicles outfitted with laptop computers attached to high-speed modems. All of them were staffed.

Specter stopped at the last cubicle, where a young man appeared to be decoding text that scrolled across his computer screen. The young man, becoming aware of Specter, pulled a sheet of paper out of the printer hopper, handed it to him. As soon as the professor read it a change came over his demeanor. Though he kept his expression neutral, a certain tension stiffened his frame.

"Good work." He gave the young man a nod before he led Bourne into a room that appeared to be a small library. Specter crossed to one section of the shelves, touched the spine of a compilation of haiku by the master poet Matsuo Bashō. A square section of the books opened to reveal a set of drawers. From one of these Specter pulled out what looked like a photo album. All the pages were old, each one wrapped in archival plastic to preserve them. He showed one of them to Bourne.

At the top was the familiar war eagle, gripping a swastika in its beak, the symbol of Germany's Third Reich. The text was in German. Just below was the word OSTLEGIONEN, accompanied by a color photo of a woven oval, obviously a uniform insignia, of a swastika encircled by laurel leaves. Around the central symbol were the words TREU, TAPIR, GEHORSAM, which Bourne translated as "loyal, brave, steadfast." Below that was another color photo of a woven rampant wolf's head, under which was the designation: OSTMANISCHE SS-DIVISION.

Bourne noted the date on the page: 14 December 1941.

"I never heard of the Eastern Legions," Bourne said. "Who were they?"

Specter turned the page and there, pinned to it, was a square of olive fabric. On it had been sewn a blue shield with a black border. Across the top was the word BERGKAUKASIEN—Caucasus Mountains. Directly beneath it in bright yellow was the emblem of three horses' heads joined to what Bourne now knew was a death's head, the symbol of the Nazi Schutzstaffel, the Protective Squadron, known colloquially as the SS. It was exactly the same as the tattoo on the gunman's arm.

"Not were, *are*." Specter's eyes glittered. "They're the people who tried to kidnap me, Jason. They want to interrogate me and kill me. Now that they've become aware of you, they'll want to do the same to you."

Eight

"THE ROOF or the basement?" Arkadin said.

"The roof," she said at once. "There's only one way in and out of the basement itself."

They ran as fast as they could to the stairway, then took the steps two at a time. Arkadin's heart pounded, his blood raced, the adrenaline pumped into him with every leap upward. He could hear his pursuers laboring up below him. The noose was tightening around him. Racing to the far end of the narrow hallway, he reached up with his right hand, pulled down the metal ladder that led to the roof. Soviet structures of this era were notorious for their flimsy doors. He knew he'd have no trouble breaking out onto the roof. From there, it was a short jump to the next building and the next, then down to the streets, where it would be easy to elude the enemy.

Boosting Devra's body through the square hole in the ceiling, he clambered up. Behind him, the shouted calls of the three men: Filya's apartment had been searched. All of them were coming after him. Gaining the tiny landing, he now faced the door to the roof, but when he tried to push against the horizontal metal bar nothing happened. He pushed harder, with the same result. Fishing a ring of slender metal picks out of his pocket, he inserted one after another into the lock, fiddling it up and down, getting nowhere. Looking more closely, he could see why: The interior of the cheap lock was rusted shut. It wouldn't open.

He turned back, staring down the ladder. Here came his pursuers. He had nowhere to go.

On June 22, 1941, Germany invaded Soviet Russia," Professor Specter said. "As they did so they came upon thousands upon thousands of enemy soldiers who either surrendered without a fight or were flat-out deserting. By August of that year the invading army had interned half a million Soviet prisoners of war. Many of them were Muslims—Tatars from the Caucasus, Turks, Azerbaijani, Uzbek, Kazakhs, others from the tribes in the Ural Mountains, Turkestan, Crimea. The one thing all these Muslims had in common was their hatred of the Soviets, Stalin in particular. To make a very long story short, these Muslims, taken as prisoners of war, offered their services to the Nazis to fight alongside them on the Eastern Front, where they could do the most damage both by infiltration and by decoding Soviet intelligence transmissions. The Führer was elated; the Ostlegionen became the particular interest of Reichsführer SS Heinrich Himmler, who saw Islam as a masculine, war-like religion that featured certain key qualities in common with his SS philosophy, mainly blind obedience, the willingness for self-sacrifice, a total lack of compassion for the enemy."

Bourne was absorbing every word, every detail of the photos. "Didn't his embrace of Islam fly in the face of the Nazi racial order?"

"You know humans better than most, Jason. They have an infinite capacity for rationalizing reality to fit their personal ideas. So it was with Himmler, who had convinced himself that the Slavs and the Jews were subhuman. The Asian element in the Russian nation made those people who were descended from the great warriors Attila, Genghis Khan, Tamerlane fit his criteria of superiority. Himmler embraced the Muslims from that area, descendants of the Mongols.

"These men became the core of the Nazi Ostlegionen, but the cream of the crop Himmler reserved for himself, training them in secret with his best SS leaders, honing their skills not simply as soldiers, but as the elite warriors, spies, and assassins it was widely known he'd yearned to command. He called this unit the Black Legion. You see, I've made an exhaustive study of the Nazis and their Ostlegionen." Specter pointed to the shield of three horses' heads joined by the death's head. "This is their emblem. From 1943 on it became more feared than even the SS's own twin lightning bolts, or the symbol of its adjunct, the Gestapo."

"It's a little late in the day for Nazis to be a serious threat," Bourne said, "don't you think?"

"The Black Legion's Nazi affiliation has long since vanished. It's now the most powerful and influential Islamic terrorist network no one has heard of. Its anonymity is deliberate. It is funded through the legitimate front, the Eastern Brotherhood."

Specter took out another album. This one was filled with newspaper clippings of terrorist attacks all over the world: London, Madrid, Karachi, Fallujah, Afghanistan, Russia. As Bourne paged through the album, the list grew.

"As you can see, other, known terrorist networks claimed responsibility for some of these attacks. For others, no claim was made, no terrorists were ever linked to them. But I know through my sources that all were perpetrated by the Black Legion," Specter said. "And now they're planning their biggest, most spectacular attack. Jason, we think that they're targeting New York. I told you Pyotr Zilber, the young man the Black Legion murdered, was special. He was a magician. He'd somehow managed to steal the plans for the target of the Legion's attack. Normally, of course, the planning would all be oral. But apparently the target of this attack is so complex, the Black Legion had to obtain the actual plans of the structure. That's why I believe it to be a large building in a major metropolitan area. It's absolutely imperative that we find that document. It's the only way we'll know where the Black Legion intends to strike."

* * *

Arkadin sat on the floor of the small landing, his legs on either side of the opening down to the top residential floor.

"Shout to them," he whispered. Now that he was situated on the high ground, so to speak, he wanted to draw them to him. "Go on. Let them know where you are."

Devra screamed.

Now Arkadin heard the hollow ring of someone climbing the metal ladder. When a head popped up, along with a hand holding a gun, Arkadin slammed his ankles into the man's ears. As his eyes began to roll up, Arkadin snatched the gun from his hand, braced himself, and broke the man's neck.

The moment he let go the man vanished, clattering back down the ladder. Predictably, a hail of gunfire shot through the square opening, the bullets embedding themselves in the ceiling. The moment that abated, Arkadin shoved Devra through the opening, followed her, sliding down with the insides of his shoes against the outside of the ladder.

As Arkadin had hoped, the remaining two men were stunned by the fall of their compatriot and held their fire. Arkadin shot one through the right eye. The other retreated around a corner as Arkadin fired at him. Arkadin gathered the girl, bruised but otherwise fine, ran to the first door, and pounded on it. Hearing a querulous man's voice raised in protest, he pounded on the opposite door. No answer. Firing his gun at the lock, he crashed open the door.

The apartment was unoccupied, and from the looks of the piles of dust and filth no one had been in residence in quite some time. Arkadin ran to the window. As he did so, he heard familiar squeals. He stepped on a pile of rubbish and out leapt a rat, then another and another. They were all over the place. Arkadin shot the first one, then got hold of himself and slid the window up as far as it would go. Icy rain struck him, sluiced down the side of the building.

Holding Devra in front of him, he straddled the sash. At that moment he heard the third man calling for reinforcements, and fired three shots through the ruined door. He manhandled her out onto the narrow fire escape and edged them to his left, toward the vertical ladder bolted to the concrete that led to the roof.

Save for one or two security lights, the Sevastopol night was darker than Hades itself. The rain slanted in needled sheets, beating against his face and arms. He was close enough to reach out for the ladder when the wrought-iron slats on which he was walking gave way.

Devra shrieked as the two of them plummeted, landing against the railing of the fire escape below. Almost immediately this rickety affair gave way beneath their weight and they toppled over the end. Arkadin reached out, grabbed a rung of the ladder with his left hand. He held on to Devra with his right. They dangled in the air, the ground too far for him to risk letting go. Plus there was no convenient fully loaded Dumpster to break their fall.

He began to lose his grip on her hand.

"Draw yourself up," he said. "Put your legs around me."

"What?"

He bellowed the command at her and, flinching, she did as he ordered.

"Now lock your ankles tight around my waist."

This time she didn't hesitate.

"All right," Arkadin said, "now reach up, you can just make the lowest rung—no, hold on to it with both hands."

The rain made the metal slippery, and on the first attempt Devra lost her grip.

"Again," Arkadin shouted. "And this time don't let go."

Clearly terrified, Devra closed her fingers around the rung, held on so tightly her knuckles turned white. As for Arkadin, his left arm was being slowly dislocated from its socket. If he didn't change his position soon, he'd be done for.

"Now what?" Devra said.

"Once your grip on the rung is secure, uncross your ankles and pull yourself up the ladder until you can stand on a rung."

"I don't know if I have the strength."

He lifted himself up until he'd wedged the rung in his right armpit. His left arm was numb. He worked his fingers, and bolts of pain shot up into his throbbing shoulder. "Go ahead," he said, pushing her up. He couldn't let her see how much pain he was in. His left arm was in agony, but he kept pushing her.

Finally, she stood on the ladder above him. She looked down. "Now you."

His entire left side was numb; the rest of him was on fire.

Devra reached down toward him. "Come on."

"I've got nothing much to live for, I died a long time ago."

"Screw you." She crouched down so when she reached down again she grabbed onto his arm. As she did so, her foot slipped off the rung, slid downward and against him with such force she almost dislodged them both.

"Christ, I'm going to fall!" she screamed.

"Wrap your legs back around my waist," he shouted. "That's right. Now let go of the ladder one hand at a time. Hold on to me instead."

When she'd done as he said, he commenced to climb up the ladder. Once he was high enough to get his shoes onto the rungs the going was easier. He ignored the fire burning up his left shoulder; he needed both hands to ascend.

They made the roof at last, rolling over the stone parapet, lying breathless on tar streaming with water. That was when Arkadin realized the rain was no longer hitting his face. He looked up, saw a man—the third of the trio—standing over him, a gun aimed at his face.

The man grinned. "Time to die, bastard."

Professor Specter put the albums away. Before he closed the drawer, however, he took out a pair of photos. Bourne studied the faces of two men. The one in the first photo was approximately the same age as the professor. Glasses almost comically magnified large, watery eyes, above which lay remarkably thick eyebrows. Otherwise, his head was bald.

"Semion Icoupov," Specter said, "leader of the Black Legion."

He took Bourne out of the basement library, up the steps, out the back of the house into the fresh air. A formal English garden lay before them, defined by low boxwood hedges. The sky was an airy blue, high and rich, full of the promise of an early spring. A bird fluttered between the bare branches of the willow, unsure where to alight.

"Jason, we need to stop the Black Legion. The only way to do that is to kill Semion Icoupov. I've already lost three good men to that end. I need someone better. I need you."

"I'm not a contract killer."

"Jason, please don't take offense. I need your help to stop this attack. Icoupov knows where the plans are."

"All right. I'll find him and the plans." Bourne shook his head. "But he doesn't have to be killed."

The professor shook his head sadly. "A noble sentiment, but you don't know Semion Icoupov like I do. If you don't kill him, he'll surely kill you. Believe me when I tell you I've tried to take him alive. None of my men has returned from that assignment."

He stared out across the pond. "There's no one else I can turn to, no one else who has the expertise to find Icoupov and end this madness once and for all. Pyotr's murder signals the beginning of the endgame between me and the Black Legion. Either we stop them here or they will be successful in their attack on this target."

"If what you say is true—"

"It is, Jason. I swear to you."

"Where is Icoupov?"

"We don't know. For the last forty-eight hours we've been trying to track him, but everything's turned up a blank. He was in his villa in Campione d'Italia, Switzerland. That's where we believe Pyotr was killed. But he's not there now."

Bourne stared down at the two photos he held in his hand. "Who's the younger man?"

"Leonid Danilovich Arkadin. Up until a few days ago we believed he was an independent assassin for hire among the families of the Russian *grupperovka.*" Specter tapped a forefinger between Arkadin's eyes. "He's the man who brought Pyotr to Icoupov. Somehow—we're still trying to establish how—Icoupov discovered that it was Pyotr who had stolen his plans. In any event, it was Arkadin who, along with Icoupov, interrogated Pyotr and killed him."

"Sounds as if you've got a traitor in your organization, Professor."

Specter nodded. "I've reluctantly come to the same conclusion."

Something that had been bothering Bourne now rose to the surface of his mind. "Professor, who called you when we were having breakfast?"

"One of my people. He needed verification of information. I had it in my car. Why?"

"Because it was that call that drew you out into the street just as the black Cadillac came by. That wasn't a coincidence."

A frown creased Specter's brow. "No, I don't suppose it could have been."

"Give me his name and address," Bourne said, "and we'll find out for certain."

The man on the rooftop had a mole on his cheek, black as sin. Arkadin concentrated on it as the man pulled Devra off the tar, away from Arkadin.

"Did you tell him anything?" he said without taking his eyes off Arkadin.

"Of course not," Devra shot back. "What d'you take me for?"

"A weak link," Mole-man said. "I told Pyotr not to use you. Now, because of you, Filya is dead."

"Filya was an idiot!"

Mole-man took his eyes off Arkadin to sneer at Devra. "He was your fucking responsibility, bitch."

Arkadin scissored his legs between Mole-man's, throwing him off balance. Arkadin, quick as a cat, leapt on him, pummeling him. Mole-man fought back as best he could. Arkadin tried not to show the pain in his left shoulder, but it was already dislocated and it wouldn't work correctly. Seeing this, Mole-man struck a blow as hard as he could flush into the shoulder.

All the breath went out of Arkadin. He sat back, dazed, almost blacked out with pain. Mole-man scrabbled for his gun, found Arkadin's instead, and swung it up. He was about to pull the trigger when Devra shot him in the back of the head with his own gun.

Without a word, he pitched over onto his face. She stood, wide-legged, in the classic shooter's stance, one hand supporting the other around the grips. Arkadin, on his knees, for the moment paralyzed with agony, watched her swing the gun around, point it at him. There was something in her eyes he couldn't identify, let alone understand.

Then, all at once, she let out the long breath she'd been holding inside, her arms relaxed, and the gun came down.

"Why?" Arkadin said. "Why did you shoot him?"

"He was a fool. Fuck me, I hate them all."

The rain beat down on them, drummed against the rooftop. The sky, utterly dark, muffled the world around them. They could have been standing on a mountaintop on the roof of the world. Arkadin watched her approach him. She put one foot in front of the other, walking stiff-legged. She seemed like a wild animal—angry, bitter, out of her element in the civilized world. Like him. He was tied to her, but he didn't understand her, he couldn't trust her.

When she held out her hand to him he took it.

Nine

I HAVE this recurring nightmare," Defense Secretary Ervin Reynolds "Bud" Halliday said. "I'm sitting right here at Aushak in Bethesda, when in comes Jason Bourne and in the style of *The Godfather Part II* shoots me in the throat and then between my eyes."

Halliday was seated at a table in the rear of the restaurant, along with Luther LaValle and Rob Batt. Aushak, more or less midway between the National Naval Medical Center and the Chevy Chase Country Club, was a favorite meeting place of his. Because it was in Bethesda and, especially, because it was Afghani, no one he knew or wanted to keep secrets from came here. The defense secretary felt most comfortable in off-the-beaten-path places. He was a man who despised Congress, despised even more its oversight committees, which were always mucking about in matters that didn't concern them and for which they had no understanding, let alone expertise.

The three men had ordered the dish after which the restaurant was named: sheets of pasta, filled with scallions, drenched in a savory meat-infused tomato sauce, the whole crowned by rich Middle Eastern yogurt in which flowered tiny bits of mint. The aushak, they all agreed, was a perfect winter meal.

"We'll soon have that particular nightmare laid to rest, sir," LaValle said with the kind of obsequiousness that set Batt's teeth on edge. "Isn't that so, Rob?"

Batt nodded emphatically. "Quite right. I have a plan that's virtually foolproof."

Perhaps that wasn't the correct thing to say. Halliday frowned,."No plan is foolproof, Mr. Batt, especially when it involves Jason Bourne."

"I assure you, no one knows that better than I do, Mr. Secretary."

Batt, as the seniormost of the seven directorate heads, did not care for being contradicted. He was a linebacker of a man with plenty of experience beating back pretenders to his crown. Still, he was aware that he was treading terra incognita, where a power struggle was raging, the outcome unknown.

He pushed his plate away. In dealing with these people he knew he was making a calculated gamble; on the other hand, he felt the spark that emanated from Secretary Halliday. Batt had entered the nation's true power grid, a place he'd secretly longed to be, and a powerful sense of elation shot through him.

"Because the plan revolves around DCI Hart," Batt said now, "my hope is that we'll be able to bring down two clay pigeons with one shot."

"Not another word"—Halliday held up his hand—"to either of us. Luther and I must maintain plausible deniability. We can't afford this operation coming back to bite us on the ass. Is that clear, Mr. Batt?"

"Perfectly clear, sir. This is my operation, pure and simple."

Halliday grinned. "Son, those words are music to these big ol' Texan ears." He tugged at the lobe of his ear. "Now, I assume Luther here told you about Typhon."

Batt looked from the secretary to LaValle and back again. A frown formed on his face. "No, sir, he didn't."

"An oversight," LaValle said smoothly.

"Well, no time like the present." A smile continued to light Halliday's expression.

"We believe that one of CI's problems is Typhon," LaValle said. "It's become too much for the director to properly rehabilitate and manage CI, *and* keep tabs on Typhon. As such, responsibility for Typhon will be taken off your shoulders. That section will be controlled directly by me."

The entire topic had been handled smoothly, but Batt knew he'd been deliberately sandbagged. These people had wanted control of Typhon from the beginning. "Typhon is home-grown CI," he said. "It's Martin Lindros's brainchild."

"Martin Lindros is dead," LaValle pointed out needlessly. "Another female is the director of Typhon now. That needs to be addressed, along with many other decisions that will affect Typhon's future. You will also need to be making crucial decisions, Rob, about all of CI. You don't want more on your plate than you can handle, do you." It wasn't a question.

Batt felt himself losing traction on a slippery slope. "Typhon is part of CI," he said as a last, feeble attempt to win back control.

"Mr. Batt," Halliday interjected. "We have made our determination. Are you with us or shall we recruit someone else for DCI?"

The man whose call had drawn Professor Specter out into the street was Mikhail Tarkanian. Bourne suggested the National Zoo as a place to meet, and the professor had called Tarkanian. The professor then contacted his secretary at the university to tell her that he and Professor Webb were each taking a personal day. They got in Specter's car, which had been driven to the estate by one of his men, and headed toward the zoo.

"Your problem, Jason, is that you need an ideology," Specter said. "An ideology grounds you. It's the backbone of commitment."

Bourne, who was driving, shook his head. "As far back as I can remember I've been manipulated by ideologues. So far as I can tell, all ideology does is give you tunnel vision. Everything that doesn't fit within your self-imposed limits is either ignored or destroyed."

"Now I know I'm truly speaking to Jason Bourne," Specter said, "because I tried my best to instill in David Webb a sense of purpose he lost somewhere in his past. When you came to me you weren't just cast adrift, you were severely maimed. I sought to help heal you by helping you turn away from whatever it was that hurt you so deeply. But now I see I was wrong—"

"You weren't wrong, Professor."

"No, let me finish. You're always quick to defend me, to believe I'm always right. Don't think I don't appreciate how you feel about me. I wouldn't want anything to change that. But occasionally I do make mistakes, and this was one of them. I don't know what went into the making of the Bourne identity, and believe me when I tell you that I don't want to know.

"What seems clear to me, however, is that however much you don't want to believe it, something inside you, something innate and connected with the Bourne identity, sets you apart from everyone else."

Bourne felt troubled by the direction of the conversation. "Do you mean that I'm Jason Bourne through and through—that David Webb would have become him no matter what?"

"No, not at all. But I do think from what you've shared with me that if there had been no intervention, if there had been no Bourne identity, then David Webb would have been a very unhappy man."

This idea was not a new one to Bourne. But he'd always assumed the thought occurred to him because he knew so damnably little about who he'd been. David Webb was more of an enigma to him than Jason Bourne. That realization itself haunted Bourne, as if Webb were a ghost, a shadowing armature into which the Bourne identity had been hung, fleshed out, given life by Alex Conklin.

Bourne, driving up Connecticut Avenue, NW, crossed Cathedral Avenue. The entrance to the zoo appeared up ahead. "The truth is, I don't think David Webb would have lasted to the end of the school year."

"Then I'm pleased I decided to involve you in my real passion."

Something seemed to have been settled inside Specter. "It's not often a man gets a chance to rectify his mistakes."

The day was mild enough that the gorilla family had been let out. Schoolchildren clustered noisily at the end of the area where the patriarch sat, surrounded by his brood. The silverback did his level best to ignore them, but when their incessant chatter became too much for him, he walked to the other end of the compound, trailed by his family. There he sat while the same annoyances spiraled out of control. Then he plodded back to the spot where Bourne had first seen him.

Mikhail Tarkanian was waiting for them beside the silverback gorilla area. He looked Specter up and down, clucking over his black eye. Then he took him in his arms, kissed him on both cheeks. "Allah is good, my friend. You are alive and well."

"Thanks to Jason here. He rescued me. I owe him my life." Specter introduced the two men.

Tarkanian kissed Bourne on both cheeks, thanking him effusively.

There came a shuffling of the gorilla family as some grooming got under way.

"Damn sad life." Tarkanian hooked his thumb at the silverback.

Bourne noted that his English was heavily accented in the manner of the tough Sokolniki slum of northeast Moscow.

"Look at the poor bastard," Tarkanian said.

The gorilla's expression was glum—resigned rather than defiant.

Specter said, "Jason's here on a bit of a fact-finding mission."

"Is he now?" Tarkanian was fleshy in the way of ex-athletes—neck like a bull, wary eyes sunk in yellow flesh. He kept his shoulders up around his ears, as if to ward off an expected blow. Enough hard knocks in Sokolniki to last a lifetime.

"I want you to answer his questions," Specter said.

"Of course. Anything I can do."

"I need your help," Bourne said. "Tell me about Pyotr Zilber."

Tarkanian, appearing somewhat taken aback, glanced at Specter, who had retreated a pace in order to center his man's full attention on Bourne. Then he shrugged. "Sure. What d'you want to know?"

"How did you find out he'd been killed?"

"The usual way. Through one of our contacts." Tarkanian shook his head. "I was devastated. Pyotr was a key man for us. He was also a friend."

"How d'you figure he was found out?"

A gaggle of schoolgirls pranced by. When they had passed out of earshot, Tarkanian said, "I wish I knew. He wasn't easy to get to, I'll tell you that."

Bourne said casually, "Did Pyotr have friends?"

"Of course he had friends. But none of them would betray him, if that's what you're asking." Tarkanian pushed his lips out. "On the other hand . . ." His words trailed off.

Bourne found his eyes, held them.

"Pyotr was seeing this woman. Gala Nematova. He was head-over-heels about her."

"I assume she was properly vetted," Bourne said.

"Of course. But, well, Pyotr was a bit, um, headstrong when it came to women."

"Was that widely known?"

"I seriously doubt it," Tarkanian said.

That was a mistake, Bourne thought. The habits and proclivities of the enemy were always for sale if you were clever and persistent enough. Tarkanian should have said, *I don't know. Possibly*. As neutral an answer as possible, and closer to the truth.

"Women can be a weak link." Bourne thought briefly of Moira and the cloud of uncertainty that hovered over her from the CI investigation. The idea that Martin could have been seduced into revealing CI secrets was a bitter pill to swallow. He hoped when he read the communication between her and Martin that Soraya had unearthed, he could lay the question to rest.

"We're all sick about Pyotr's death," Tarkanian offered. Again the glance at Specter.

"No question." Bourne smiled rather vaguely. "Murder's a serious matter, especially in this case. I'm talking to everyone, that's all."

"Of course. I understand."

"You've been extremely helpful." Bourne smiled, shook Tarkanian's hand. As he did so, he said in a sharp tone of voice, "By the way, how much did Icoupov's people pay you to call the professor's cell this morning?"

Instead of freezing Tarkanian seemed to relax. "What the hell kind of question is that? I'm loyal, I always have been."

After a moment, he tried to extricate his hand, but Bourne's grip tightened. Tarkanian's eyes met Bourne's, held them.

Behind them, the silverback made a noise, growing restive. The sound was low, like the sudden ripple of wind disturbing a field of wheat. The message from the gorilla was so subtle, Bourne was the only one who picked up on it. He registered movement at the extreme edge of his peripheral vision, tracked for several seconds. He leaned back to Specter, said in a low, urgent voice. "Leave now. Go straight through the Small Mammal House, then turn left. A hundred yards on will be a small food kiosk. Ask for help getting to your car. Go back to your house and stay there until you hear from me."

As the professor walked swiftly away, Bourne grabbed Tarkanian, pushed him in the opposite direction. They joined a Home Sweet Habitat scavenger hunt comprising a score of rowdy kids and their parents. The two men Bourne was tracking hurried toward them. It was this pair and their rushed anxiety that had aroused the suspicion of the silverback, alerting Bourne.

"Where are we going?" Tarkanian said. "Why did you leave the professor unprotected?"

A good question. Bourne's decision had been instantaneous, instinct-driven. The men headed toward Tarkanian, not the professor. Now, as the group moved down Olmsted Walk, Bourne dragged Tarkanian into the Reptile Discovery Center. The lights were low here. They hurried past glass cases that held dozing alligators, slit-eyed crocodiles, lumbering tortoises, evil-looking vipers, and pebble-skinned lizards of all sizes, shapes, and dispositions. Up ahead, Bourne could see the snake cases. At one of them, a handler opened a door, prepared to set out a feast of rodents for the green tree pythons, which, in their hunger, had emerged from their stupor, slithering along the case's fake tree branches. These snakes used infrared heat sensors to target their prey.

Behind them, the two men wove their way through the crowd of children. They were swarthy but otherwise unremarkable in feature. They had their hands plunged into the pockets of their wool overcoats, surely gripping some form of weapon. They weren't hurrying now. There was no point in alarming the visitors.

Passing the European glass lizard, Bourne hauled Tarkanian into the snake section. It was at that moment that Tarkanian chose to make a move. Twisting away as he lunged back toward the approaching men, he dragged Bourne for a step, until Bourne struck him a dizzying blow to the side of the head.

A workman knelt with his toolbox in front of an empty case. He was fiddling with the ventilation grille at the base. Bourne swiped a short length of stiff wire from the box.

"The cavalry's not going to save you today," Bourne said as he dragged Tarkanian toward a door set flush in the wall between cases that led to the work area hidden from the public. One of the pursuers was closing in when Bourne jimmied the lock with the bit of wire. He opened the door, stepped through. He slammed it shut behind him, set the lock.

The door began to shudder on its hinges as the men pounded on it. Bourne found himself in a narrow utility corridor, lit by long fluorescent tubes, that ran behind the cases. Doors and, in the cases of the venomous snakes, feeding windows appeared at regular intervals along the right-hand wall.

Bourne heard a soft *phutt!* and the lock popped out of the door. The men were armed with small-caliber handguns fitted with suppressors. He pushed the stumbling Tarkanian ahead of him as one of the men stepped through. Where was the other one? Bourne thought he knew, and he turned his attention to the far end of the corridor, where any moment now he expected the second man to appear.

Tarkanian, sensing Bourne's momentary shift of attention, spun, slamming the side of his body into Bourne's. Thrown off balance, Bourne skidded through the open doorway into the tree python case. With a harsh bark of laughter, Tarkanian rushed on.

A herpetologist in the case to check on the python was already protesting Bourne's appearance. Bourne ignored him, reached up, unwound one of the hungry pythons from the branch nearest him. As the snake, sensing his heat, wrapped itself around his outstretched arm, Bourne turned and burst out into the corridor just in time to drive a fist into the gunman's solar plexus. When the man doubled over, Bourne slid his arm out of the python's coils, wrapped its body around the gunman's chest. Seeing the python, the man screamed. It began to tighten its coils around him.

Bourne snatched the handgun with its suppressor from his hand, took off after Tarkanian. The gun was a Glock, not a Taurus. As Bourne suspected, these two weren't part of the same team that had abducted the professor. Who were they then? Members of the Black Legion, sent to extract Tarkanian? But if that was the case, how had they known he'd been blown? No time for answers: The second man had appeared at the far end of the corridor. He was in a crouch, motioning to Tarkanian, who squeezed himself against the side of the corridor.

As the gunman took aim at him Bourne covered his face with his folded forearms, dived headfirst through one of the feeding windows. Glass shattered. Bourne looked up to see that he was face-to-face with a Gaboon viper, the species with the longest fangs and highest venom yield of any snake. It was black and ocher. Its ugly, triangular head rose, its tongue flicked out, sensing, trying to determine if the creature sprawled in front of it was a threat.

Bourne lay still as stone. The viper began to hiss, a steady rhythm that flattened its head with each fierce exhalation. The small horns beside its nostrils quivered. Bourne had definitely disturbed it. Having traveled extensively in Africa, he knew something of this creature's habits. It was not prone to bite unless severely provoked. On the other hand, he couldn't risk moving his body at all at this point.

Aware that he was vulnerable from behind as well as in front, he slowly raised his left hand. The hissing's steady rhythm didn't change. Keeping his eyes on the snake's head, he moved his hand until it was over the snake. He'd read about a technique meant to calm this kind of snake but had no idea whether it would work. He touched the snake on the top of its head with a fingertip. The hissing stopped. It did work!

He grasped it at its neck. Letting go of the gun, he supported the viper's body with his other hand. The creature didn't struggle. Walking gingerly across the case to the far end, he set it carefully down in a corner. A group of kids were staring, openmouthed, from the other side of the glass. Bourne backed away from the viper, never taking his eyes from it. Near the shattered feeding window he knelt down, grasped the Glock.

A voice behind him said, "Leave the gun where it is and turn around slowly."

The damn thing's dislocated," Arkadin said.

Devra stared at his deformed shoulder.

"You'll have to reset it for me."

Drenched to the bone, they were sitting in a late-night café on the other side of Sevastopol, warming themselves as best they could. The gas heater in the café hissed and hiccuped alarmingly, as if it were coming down with pneumonia. Glasses of steaming tea sat before them, half empty. It was barely an hour after their hair's-breadth escape, and both of them were exhausted.

"You're kidding," she said.

"Absolutely, you will," he said. "I can't go to a proper doctor."

Arkadin ordered food. Devra ate like an animal, shoving dripping pieces of stew into her mouth with her fingertips. She looked as if she hadn't eaten in days. Perhaps she hadn't. Seeing how she laid waste to the food, Arkadin ordered more. He ate slowly and deliberately, conscious of everything he put into his mouth. Killing did that to him: All his senses were working overtime. Colors were brighter, smells stronger, everything tasted rich and complex. He could hear the acrid political argument going on in the opposite corner between two old men. His own fingertips on his cheek felt like sandpaper. He was acutely aware of his own heartbeat, the blood rushing behind his ears. He was, in short, a walking, talking exposed nerve.

He both loved and hated being in this state. The feeling was a form of ecstasy. He remembered coming across a dog-eared paperback copy of *The Teachings of Don Juan* by Carlos Castaneda, had learned to read English from it, a long, torturous path. The concept of ecstasy had never occurred to him before reading this book. Later, in emulation of Castaneda, he thought of trying peyote—if he could find it—but the idea of a drug, any drug, set his teeth on edge. He was already lost quite enough. He held no desire to find a place from which he could never return.

Meanwhile the ecstasy he was in was a burden as well as a revelation, but he knew he couldn't long stand being that exposed nerve. Everything from a car backfiring to the chirrup of a cricket crashed against him, as painful as if he'd been turned inside out.

He studied Devra with an almost obsessive concentration. He noticed something he hadn't seen before—likely, with her gesticulating, she'd distracted him from noticing. But now she'd let down her guard. Perhaps she was just exhausted or had relaxed with him. She had a tremor in her hands, a nerve that had gone awry. Clandestinely, he watched the tremor, thinking it made her seem even more vulnerable.

"I don't get you," he told her now. "Why have you turned against your own people?"

"You think Pyotr Zilber, Oleg Shumenko, and Filya were my own people?"

"You're a cog in Zilber's network. What else would I think?"

"You heard how that pig talked to me up on the roof. Shit, they were all like that." She wiped grease off her lips and chin. "I never liked Shumenko. First it was gambling debts I had to bail him out of, then it was drugs."

Arkadin's voice was offhand when he said, "You told me you didn't know what the last loan was for."

"I lied."

"Did you tell Pyotr?"

"You're joking. Pyotr was the worst of the lot."

"Talented little bugger, though."

Devra nodded. "So I thought when I was in his bed. He got away with an awful lot of shit because he was the boss—drinking, partying, and, Jesus, the girls! Sometimes two and three a night. I got thoroughly sick of him and asked to be reassigned back home."

So she'd been Pyotr's squeeze for a short time, Arkadin thought. "The partying was part of his job, though, forging contacts, ensuring they came back for more."

"Sure. Trouble was he liked it all too much. And inevitably, that attitude infected those who were close to him. Where d'you think Shumenko learned to live like that? From Pyotr, that's who."

"And Filya?"

"Filya thought he owned me, like chattel. When we'd go out together he'd act as if he was my pimp. I hated his guts."

"Why didn't you get rid of him?"

"He was the one supplying Shumenko with coke."

Quick as a cat, Arkadin leaned across the table, looming. "Listen, *lapochka*, I don't give a fuck who you like or don't like. But lying to me, that's another story."

"What did you expect?" she said. "You blew in like a fucking whirlwind."

Arkadin laughed then, breaking a tension that was stretched to the breaking point. This girl had a sense of humor, which meant she was clever as well as smart. His mind had made a connection between her and a woman who'd once been important to him.

"I still don't understand you." He shook his head. "We're on different sides of this conflict."

"That's where you're wrong. I was never part of this conflict. I didn't like it; I only pretended I did. At first it was a goal I set for myself: whether I could fool Pyotr, and then the others. When I did, it just seemed easier to keep going. I got paid well, I learned quicker than most, I got perks I never would have gotten from being a DJ."

"You could've left anytime."

"Could I?" She cocked her head. "They would've come after me like they're coming after you."

"But now you've made up your mind to leave them." He cocked his head. "Don't tell me it's because of me."

"Why not? I like sitting next to a whirlwind. It's comforting."

Arkadin grunted, embarrassed again.

"Besides, the last straw came when I found out what they're planning."

"You thought of your American savior."

"Maybe you can't understand that one person can make a difference in your life."

"Oh, but I can," Arkadin said, thinking of Semion Icoupov. "In that, you and I are the same."

She gestured. "You look so uncomfortable."

"Come on," he said, standing. He led her back past the kitchen, poked his head in for a moment, then took her into the men's room.

"Get out," he ordered a man at the sink.

He checked the stall to make sure they were alone. "I'll tell you how to fix this damnable shoulder."

When he gave her the instructions, she said, "Is it going to hurt?"

In answer, he put the handle of the wooden spoon he'd swiped from the kitchen between his teeth.

With great reluctance Bourne turned his back on the Gaboon viper. Many things flitted through his mind, not the least of which was Mikhail Tarkanian. He was the mole inside the professor's organization. Who knew how much intel he had about Specter's network; Bourne couldn't afford to let him get away.

The man before him now was flat-faced, his skin slightly greasy. He had a two-day growth of beard and bad teeth. His breath stank from cigarettes and rotting food. He pointed his suppressed Glock directly at Bourne's chest.

"Come out of there," he said softly.

"It won't matter whether or not I comply," Bourne answered. "The herpetologist down the corridor has surely phoned security. We're all about to be put into custody."

"Out. Now."

The man made a fatal error of gesturing with the Glock. Bourne used his left forearm to knock the elongated barrel aside. Slamming the gunman back against the opposite wall of the corridor, Bourne drove a knee into his groin. As the gunman gagged, Bourne chopped the gun out of his hand, grabbed him by his overcoat, flung him headlong into the Gaboon viper's case with such force that he skidded along the floor toward the corner where the viper lay coiled.

Bourne, imitating the viper, made a rhythmic hissing sound, and the snake raised its head. At the same moment it heard the hissing of a rival snake, it sensed something living thrust into its territory. It struck out at the terrified gunman.

Bourne was already pounding down the corridor. The door at the far end gaped open. He burst out into daylight. Tarkanian was waiting for him, in case he escaped the two gunmen; he had no stomach to prolong the pursuit. He drove a fist into Bourne's cheek, followed that up with a vicious kick. But Bourne caught his shoe in his hands, twisted his foot violently, spinning him off his feet.

Bourne could hear shouts, the slap and squeak of cheap soles against concrete. Security was on its way, though he couldn't see them yet.

"Tarkanian," he said, and coldcocked him.

Tarkanian went down heavily. Bourne knelt beside him and was giving him mouth-to-mouth when three security guards rounded the corner, came pounding up to him.

"My friend collapsed just as we saw the men with the guns." Bourne gave an accurate description of the two gunmen, pointed toward the open door to the Reptile Discovery Center. "Can you get help? My friend is allergic to mustard. I think there must have been some in the potato salad we had for lunch."

One of the security guards called 911, while the other two, guns drawn, vanished into the doorway. The guard stayed with Bourne until the paramedics arrived. They took Tarkanian's vitals, loaded him onto the gurney. Bourne walked at Tarkanian's side as they made their way through the gawking crowds to the ambulance waiting on Connecticut Avenue. He told them about Tarkanian's allergic reaction, also that in this state he was hypersensitive to light. He climbed into the back of the ambulance. One of the paramedics closed the doors behind him while the other prepared the IV drip of phenothiazine. The vehicle took off, siren wailing.

Tears streamed down Arkadin's face, but he made no noise. The pain was excruciating, but at least the arm was back in its socket. He could move the fingers of his left hand, just barely. The good news was that the numbness was giving way to a peculiar tingling, as if his blood had turned to champagne.

Devra held the wooden spoon in her hand. "Shit, you almost bit this in two. It must've hurt like a bitch."

Arkadin, dizzy and nauseous, grimaced in pain. "I could never get food down now."

Devra tossed aside the spoon as they left the men's room. Arkadin paid their check, and they went out of the café. The rain had stopped, leaving the streets with that slick, just-washed look so familiar to him from old American films from the 1940s and 1950s.

"We can go to my place," Devra offered. "It's not far from here."

Arkadin shook his head. "I think not."

They walked, seemingly aimlessly, until they came to a small hotel. Arkadin booked a room. The flyblown night clerk barely looked at them. He was only interested in taking their money.

The room was mean, barely furnished with a bed, a hard-backed chair, and a dresser with three legs and a pile of books propping up the fourth corner. A circular threadbare carpet covered the center of the room. It was stained, pocked with cigarette burns. What appeared to be a closet was the toilet. The shower and sink were down the hall.

Arkadin went to the window. He'd asked for a room in front, know-ing it would be noisier, but would afford him a bird's-eye view of anyone coming. The street was deserted, not a car in sight. Sevastopol glowed in a slow, cold pulse.

"Time," he said, turning back into the room, "to get some things straight."

"Now? Can't this wait?" Devra was lying crosswise on the bed, her feet still on the floor. "I'm dead on my feet."

Arkadin considered a moment. It was deep into the night. He was exhausted but not yet ready for sleep. He kicked off his shoes, lay down on the bed. Devra had to sit up to make room for him, but instead of lying down parallel to him, she resumed her position, head on his belly. She closed her eyes.

"I want to come with you," she said softly, almost as if in sleep.

He was instantly alert. "Why?" he said. "Why would you want to come with me?"

She said nothing in reply; she was asleep.

For a time, he lay listening to her steady breathing. He didn't know what to do with her, but she was all he had left of this end of Pyotr's network. He spent some time digesting what she had told him about Shumenko, Filya, and Pyotr, looking for holes. It seemed improbable to him that Pyotr could be so undisciplined, but then again he'd been betrayed by his girlfriend of the moment, who worked for Icoupov. That spoke of a man out of control, whose habits could indeed filter down to his subordinates. He had no idea if Pyotr had daddy issues, but given who his daddy was it certainly wasn't out of the question.

This girl was strange. On the surface she was so much like other young girls he'd come across: hard-edged, cynical, desperate, and de-spairing. But this one was different. He could see beneath her armor plating to the little lost girl she once had been and perhaps still was. He put his hand on the side of her neck, felt the slow pulse of her life. He could be wrong, of course. It could all be a performance put on for his benefit. But for the life of him he'd couldn't figure out what her angle might be.

And there was something else about her, connected to her fragility, her deliberate vulnerability. She needed something, he thought, as, in the end, we all did, even those who fooled themselves into thinking they didn't. He knew what he needed; it was simply that he chose not to think about it. She needed a father, that was clear enough. He couldn't help suspecting there was something about her he was missing, something she hadn't told him but wanted him to find. The answer was already inside him, dancing like a firefly. But every time he reached out to capture it, it just danced farther away. The feeling was maddening, as if he'd had sex with a woman without reaching an orgasm.

And then she stirred, and in stirring said his name. It was like a bolt of lightning illuminating the room. He was back on the rainy rooftop, with Mole-man standing over him, listening to the conversation between him and Devra.

"He was your responsibility," Mole-man said, referring to Filya.

Arkadin's heart beat faster. *Your responsibility.* Why would Mole-man say that if Filya was the courier in Sevastopol? As if of their own accord, his fingertips stroked the velvet flesh of Devra's neck. The crafty little bitch! Filya was a soldier, a guard. *She* was the courier in Sevastopol. She'd handed the document off to the next link. She knew where he had to go next.

Holding her tightly, Arkadin at last let go of the night, the room, the present. On a tide of elation, he drifted into sleep, into the blood-soaked clutches of his past.

Arkadin would have killed himself, this was certain, had it not been for the intervention of Semion Icoupov. Arkadin's best and only friend, Mischa Tarkanian, concerned for his life, had appealed to the man he worked for. Arkadin remembered with an eerie clarity the day Icoupov had come to see him. He had walked in, and Arkadin, half crazed with a will to die, had put a Makarov PM to his head—the same gun he was going to use to blow his own brains out.

Icoupov, to his credit, didn't make a move. He stood in the ruins of

Arkadin's Moscow apartment, not looking at Arkadin at all. Arkadin, in the grip of his sulfurous past, was unable to make sense of anything. Much later, he understood. In the same way you didn't look a bear in the eye, lest he charge you, Icoupov had kept his gaze focused on other things—the broken picture frames, the smashed crystal, the overturned chairs, the ashes of the fetishistic fire Arkadin had lit to burn his clothes.

"Mischa tells me you're having a difficult time."

"Mischa should keep his mouth shut."

Icoupov spread his hands. "Someone has to save your life."

"What d'you know about it?" Arkadin said harshly.

"Actually, I know nothing about what's happened to you," Icoupov said.

Arkadin, digging the muzzle of the Makarov into Icoupov's temple, stepped closer. "Then shut the fuck up."

"What I am concerned about is the here and now." Icoupov didn't blink an eye; he didn't move a muscle, either. "For fuck's sake, son, look at you. If you won't pull back from the brink for yourself, do it for Mischa, who loves you better than any brother would."

Arkadin let out a ragged breath, as if he were expelling a dollop of poison. He took the Makarov from Icoupov's head.

Icoupov held out his hand. When Arkadin hesitated, he said with great gentleness, "This isn't Nizhny Tagil. There is no one here worth hurting, Leonid Danilovich."

Arkadin gave a curt nod, let go of the gun. Icoupov called out, handed it to one of two very large men who came down the hallway from the far end where they had been stationed, not making a sound. Arkadin tensed, angry at himself for not sensing them. Clearly, they were body-guards. In his current condition, they could have taken Arkadin anytime. He looked at Icoupov, who nodded, and an unspoken connection sprang up between them.

"There is only one path for you now," Icoupov said.

Icoupov moved to sit on the sofa in Arkadin's trashed apartment, then gestured, and the bodyguard who had taken possession of Arkadin's Makarov held it out to him.

"Here, now, you will have witnesses to your last spasm of nihilism. If you wish it."

Arkadin for once in his life ignored the gun, stared implacably at Icoupov.

"No?" Icoupov shrugged. "Do you know what I think, Leonid Danilovich? I think it gives you a measure of comfort to believe that your life has no meaning. Most times you revel in this belief; it's what fuels you. But there are times, like now, when it takes you by the throat and shakes you till your teeth rattle in your skull." He was dressed in dark slacks, an oyster-gray shirt, a long black leather coat that made him look somewhat sinister, like a German SS-Stürmbannführer. "But I believe to the contrary that you are searching for the meaning of your life." His dark skin shone like polished bronze. He gave the appearance of a man who knew what he was doing, someone, above all, not to be trifled with.

"What path?" Arkadin said dully, taking a seat on the sofa.

Icoupov gestured with both hands, encompassing the self-inflicted whirlwind that had torn apart the rooms. "The past for you is dead, Leonid Danilovich, do you not agree?"

"God has punished me. God has abandoned me," Arkadin said, regurgitating by rote a lament of his mother's.

Icoupov smiled a perfectly innocent smile, one that could not possibly be misinterpreted. He had an uncanny ability to engage others one-on-one. "And what God is that?"

Arkadin had no answer because this God he spoke of was his mother's God, the God of his childhood, the God that had remained an enigma to him, a shadow, a God of bile, of rage, of split bone and spilt blood.

"But no," he said, "God, like heaven, is a word on a page. Hell is the here and now."

Icoupov shook his head. "You have never known God, Leonid Danilovich. Put yourself in my hands. With me, you will find God, and learn the future he has planned for you."

"I cannot be alone." Arkadin realized that this was the truest thing he'd ever said.

"Nor shall you be."

Icoupov turned to accept a tray from one of the bodyguards. While they had been talking, he'd made tea. Icoupov poured two glasses full, added sugar, handed one to Arkadin.

"Drink with me now, Leonid Danilovich," he said as he lifted his steaming glass. "To your recovery, to your health, to the future, which will be as bright for you as you wish to make it."

The two men sipped their tea, which the bodyguard had astutely fortified with a considerable amount of vodka.

"To never being alone again," said Leonid Danilovich Arkadin.

That was a long time ago, at a way station on a river that had turned to blood. Was he much changed from the near-insane man who had put the muzzle of a gun to Semion Icoupov's head? Who could say? But on days of heavy rain, ominous thunder, and twilight at noon, when the world looked as bleak as he knew it to be, thoughts of his past surfaced like corpses in a river, regurgitated by his memory. And he would be alone again.

Tarkanian was coming around, but the phenothiazine that had been administered to him was doing its job, sedating him mildly and impairing his mental functioning enough so that when Bourne bent over him and said in Russian, "Bourne's dead, we're in the process of extracting you," Tarkanian dazedly thought he was one of the men at the reptile house.

"Icoupov sent you." Tarkanian lifted a hand, felt the bandage the paramedics had used to keep light out of his eyes. "Why can't I see?"

"Lie still," Bourne said softly. "There are civilians around. Paramedics. That's how we're extracting you. You'll be safe in the hospital for a few hours while we arrange the rest of your travel."

Tarkanian nodded.

"Icoupov is on the move," Bourne whispered. "Do you know where?"

"No."

"He wants you to be most comfortable during your debriefing. Where should we take you?"

"Moscow, of course." Tarkanian licked his lips. "It's been years since I've been home. I have an apartment on the Frunzenskaya embankment." More and more he seemed to be speaking to himself. "From my living room window you can see the pedestrian bridge to Gorky Park. Such a peaceful setting. I haven't seen it in so long."

They arrived at the hospital before Bourne had a chance to continue the interrogation. Then everything happened very quickly. The doors banged open and the paramedic leapt into action, getting the gurney down, rushing it through the automatic glass doors into a corridor leading to the ER. The place was packed with patients. One of the paramedics was talking to a harried overworked intern, who directed him to a small room, one of many off the corridor. Bourne saw that the other rooms were filled.

The two paramedics rolled Tarkanian into the room, checked the IV, took his vitals again, unhooked him.

"He'll come around in a minute," one of them said. "Someone will be in shortly to see to him." He produced a practiced smile that was not unlikable. "Don't worry, your friend's going to be fine."

After they'd left, Bourne went back to Tarkanian, said, "Mikhail, I know the Frunzenskaya embankment well. Where exactly is your apartment?"

"He's not going to tell you."

Bourne whirled just as the first gunman—the one he'd wrapped the python around—threw himself on top of him. Bourne staggered back, bounced hard against the wall. He struck at the gunman's face. The gunman blocked it, punched Bourne hard on the point of his sternum. Bourne grunted, and the gunman followed up with a short chop to Bourne's side.

Down on one knee, Bourne saw him pull out a knife, swipe the blade at him. Bourne shrank back. The gunman attacked with the knife point-first. Bourne landed a hard right flush on his face, heard the satisfying crack of the cheekbone fracturing. Enraged, the gunman closed, the blade swinging through Bourne's shirt, bringing out an arc of blood like beads on a string.

Bourne hit him so hard he staggered back, struck the gurney on which Tarkanian was stirring out of his drugged stupor. The man took out his handgun with the suppressor. Bourne closed with him, grabbing him tightly, depriving him of space to aim the gun.

Tarkanian ripped off the bandage the paramedics had used to keep light out of his eyes, blinked heavily, looking around. "What the hell's going on?" he said drowsily to the gunman. "You told me Bourne was dead."

The man was too busy fending off Bourne's attack to answer. Seeing his firearm was of no use to him he dropped it, kicked it along the floor. He tried to get the knife blade inside Bourne's defense, but Bourne broke the attacks, not fooled by the feints the gunman used to distract him.

Tarkanian sat up, slid off the gurney. He found it difficult to talk, so he slipped to his knees, crawled across the cool linoleum to where the gun lay.

The gunman, one hand gripping Bourne's neck, was working the knife free, prepared to stab downward into Bourne's stomach.

"Move away from him." Tarkanian was aiming the gun at the two men. "I'll have a clear shot."

The gunman heard him, shoved the heel of his hand into Bourne's Adam's apple, choking him. Then he moved his upper body to one side.

Just as Tarkanian was about to squeeze the trigger Bourne rabbit-punched the gunman in the kidney. He groaned and Bourne hauled him between himself and Tarkanian. A coughing sound announced the bullet plowing into the gunman's chest.

Tarkanian cursed, moved to get Bourne back in his sights. As he did so, Bourne wrested the knife away from the gunman's limp hand, threw it with deadly accuracy. The force of it lifted Tarkanian backward off his feet. Bourne pushed the gunman away from him, crossed the room to where Tarkanian lay in a pool of his own blood. The knife was buried to the hilt in his chest. By its position, Bourne knew it had pierced a lung. Within moments Tarkanian would drown in his own blood.

Tarkanian stared up at Bourne. He laughed even as he said, "Now you're a dead man."

Ten

ROB BATT made his arrangements through General Kendall, La-Valle's second in command. Through him, Batt was able to access certain black-ops assets in the NSA. No congressional oversight, no fuss, no muss. As far as the federal government was concerned, these people didn't exist, except as auxiliary staff seconded to the Pentagon; they were thought to be pushing papers in a windowless office somewhere in the bowels of the building.

Now, this is the way the clandestine services should run, Batt said to himself as he laid out the operation for the eight young men ranged in a semicircle in a Pentagon briefing room Kendall had provided for him. No supervision, no snooping congressional committees to report to.

The plan was simple, as all his plans tended to be. Other people might like bells and whistles, but not Batt. Vanilla, Kendall had called it. But the more that was involved, the more that could go wrong was how he looked at it. Also, no one fucked up simple plans; they could be put together and executed in a matter of hours, if need be, even with new personnel. But the fact was he liked these NSA agents, perhaps because they were military men. They were quick to catch on, quicker even to learn. He never had to repeat himself. To a man, they seemed to memorize everything as it was presented to them.

Better still, because of their military background, they obeyed orders unquestioningly, unlike agents in CI—Soraya Moore a case in point—who always thought they knew a better way to get things done. Plus, these bad boys weren't afraid of rendition; they weren't afraid to pull the trigger. If given the appropriate order they'd kill a target without either question or regret.

Batt felt a certain exhilaration at the knowledge that no one was looking over his shoulder, that he wouldn't have to explain himself to anyone—not even the new DCI. He'd entered an altogether different arena, one all his own, where he could make decisions of great moment, devise field operations, and carry them out with the confidence that he would be backed to the hilt, that no operation would ever boomerang on him, bring him face-to-face with a congressional committee and disgrace. As he wrapped up the pre-mission briefing, his cheeks were flushed, his pulse accelerated. There was a heat building inside him that could almost be called arousal.

He tried not to think of his conversation with the defense secretary, tried not to think of Luther LaValle heading up Typhon while he looked helplessly on. He desperately didn't want to give up control of such a powerful weapon against terrorism, but Halliday hadn't given him a choice.

One step at a time. If there was a way to foil Halliday and LaValle, he was confident he'd find it. But for the moment, he returned his attention to the job at hand. No one was going to fuck up his plan to capture Jason Bourne. He knew this absolutely. Within hours Bourne would be in custody, down so deep even a Houdini like him would never get out.

Soraya Moore made her way to Veronica Hart's office. Two men were emerging: Dick Symes, the chief of intelligence, and Rodney Feir, chief of field support. Symes was a short, round man whose red face appeared to have been applied directly to his shoulders. Feir, several years

Symes's junior, was fair-haired, with an athletic body, an expression as closed as a bank vault.

Both men greeted her cordially, but there was a repellent condescension to Symes's smile.

"Bearding the lioness in her den?" Feir said.

"Is she in a bad mood?" Soraya asked.

Feir shrugged. "Too soon to tell."

"We're waiting to see if she can carry the weight of the world on those delicate shoulders," Symes said. "Just like with you, *Director*."

Soraya forced a smile though her clenched jaws. "You gentlemen are too kind."

Feir laughed. "Ready, willing, and able to oblige, ma'am."

Soraya watched them leave, two peas in a pod. Then she poked her head into the DCI's inner sanctum. Unlike her predecessor, Veronica Hart maintained an open-door policy when it came to her upper-echelon staff. It engendered a sense of trust and camaraderie that—as she'd told Soraya—had been sorely lacking at CI in the past. In fact, from the vast amount of electronic data she'd pored over the last couple of days it was becoming increasing clear to her that the previous DCI's bunker mentality had led to an atmosphere of cynicism and alienation among the directorate heads. The Old Man came from the school of letting the Seven vie with one another, complete with duplicity, backstabbing, and, so far as she was concerned, outright objectionable behavior.

Hart was a product of a new era, where the primary watchword was cooperation. The events of 2001 had proved that when it came to the intelligence services, competition was deadly. So far as Soraya was concerned that was all to the good.

"How long have you been at this?" Soraya asked.

Hart glanced out the window. "It's morning already? I ordered Rob home hours ago."

"Way past morning." Soraya smiled. "How about lunch? You definitely need to get out of this office."

She spread her hands to indicate the queue of dossiers loaded onto her computer. "Too much work—"

"It won't get done if you pass out from hunger and dehydration."

"Okay, the canteen—"

"It's such a fine day, I was thinking of walking to a favorite restaurant of mine."

Hearing a warning note in Soraya's otherwise light voice, Hart looked up. Yes, there was definitely something her director of Typhon wanted to talk to her about outside the confines of the CI building.

Hart nodded. "All right. I'll get my coat."

Soraya took out her new cell, which she'd picked up at CI this morning. She'd found her old one in the gutter by her car at the Moira Trevor surveillance site, had disposed of it at the office. Now she texted a message.

A moment later Hart's cell buzzed. The text from Soraya read: VAN X ST. Van across the street.

Hart folded her cell away and launched into a long story at the end of which both women laughed. Then they talked about shoes versus boots, leather versus suede, and which Jimmy Choos they'd buy if they were ever paid enough.

Both women kept an eye on the van without seeming to look at it. Soraya directed them down a side street where the van couldn't go for fear of becoming conspicuous. They were moving out of the range of its electronics.

"You came from the private sector," Soraya said. "What I don't understand is why you'd give up that payday to become DCI. It's such a thankless job."

"Why did you agree to be director of Typhon?" Hart asked.

"It was a huge step up for me, both in prestige and in pay."

"But that's not really why you accepted it, was it?"

Soraya shook her head. "No. I felt a strong sense of obligation to Martin Lindros. I was in at the beginning. Because I'm half Arab, Martin sought out my input both in the creation of Typhon and in its recruitment. He meant Typhon to be a very different intelligence-gathering organization, staffed with people who understood both the Arab and the Muslim mind-set. He felt—and I wholeheartedly agree—that the only way to successfully combat the wide array of extremist terrorist cells was to understand what motivates them. Once you were in sync with their motivation, you could begin to anticipate their actions."

Hart nodded, her long face in a neutral set as she sank deeper in thought. "My own motivations were similar to yours. I grew sick of the cynical attitude of the private security firms. All of them, not just Black River where I worked, were focused on how much money they could milk out of the mess in the Middle East. In times of war, the government is a mighty cash cow, throwing newly minted money at every situation, as if that alone will make a difference. But the fact is, everyone involved has a license to plunder and steal to their heart's content. What happens in Iraq stays in Iraq. No one's going prosecute them. They're indemnified against retribution for profiting from other people's misery."

Soraya took them into a clothes store, where they made a pretense of checking out camisoles to cover the seriousness of the conversation.

"I came to CI because I couldn't change Black River, but I felt I could make a difference here. The president gave me a mandate to change an organization that was in disarray, that long ago had lost its way."

They went out the back, across the street, hurrying now, down the block, turning left for a block, then right for two blocks, left again. They went into a large restaurant boiling with people. Perfect. The high level of ambient noise, the multiple crosscurrents of conversations would make their own conversation undetectable.

At Hart's request they were seated at a table near the rear where they had excellent sight lines of the interior as well as the front door. Everyone who came in would be visually vetted by them.

"Well executed," Hart said when they were seated. "I see you've done this before."

"There were times—especially when I was working with Jason Bourne —when I was obliged to lose a CI tail or two."

Hart scanned the large menu. "Do you think that was a CI van?"

"No."

Hart looked at Soraya over the menu. "Neither do I."

They ordered brook trout, Caesar salads to start, mineral water to drink. They took turns checking out the people who came into the restaurant.

Halfway through the salads Soraya said, "We've intercepted some unconventional chatter in the last couple of days. I don't think *alarming* would be a too strong a word."

Hart put down her fork. "How so?"

"It seems possible that a new attack on American soil is in its final stages."

Hart's demeanor changed instantly. She was clearly shaken. "What the hell are we doing here?" she said angrily. "Why aren't we in the office where I can mobilize the forces?"

"Wait until you hear the whole story." Soraya said. "Remember that the lines and frequencies Typhon monitors are almost all overseas, so unlike the chatter other intelligence agencies scan, ours is more concentrated, but from what I've seen it's also far more accurate. As you know, there's always an enormous amount of disinformation in the regular chatter. Not so with the terrorists we keep an ear on. Of course, we're checking and rechecking the accuracy of this intel, but until proven otherwise we're going on the assumption that it's real. We have two problems, however, which is why mobilizing CI now isn't the wisest course."

Three women came in, chatting animatedly. The manager greeted them like old friends, showed them to a round table near the window, where they settled in.

"First, we have an immediate time frame, that is to say within a week, ten days at the outside. However, we have almost nothing on the target, except from the intercepts we know it's large and complex, so we're thinking a building. Again, because of our Muslim expertise we believe it will be a structure of both economic and symbolic importance."

"But no specific location?"

"East Coast, most probably New York."

"Nothing's crossed my desk, which means none of our sister agencies has a clue about this intel."

"That's what I'm telling you," Soraya said. "This is ours alone. Typhon's. This is why we were created."

"You haven't yet told me why I shouldn't inform Homeland Security and mobilize CI."

"Because the source of this intel is entirely new. Do you seriously think HS or NSA would take our intel at its face value? They'd need corroboration—and A, they wouldn't get it from their own sources, and, B, their mucking about in the bush would jeopardize the inroads we've made."

"You're right about that," Hart said. "They're about as subtle as an elephant in Manhattan."

Soraya hunched forward. "The point is the group planning the attack is unknown to us. That means we don't know their motivation, their mind-set, their methodology."

Two men came in, one after the other. They were dressed as civilians, but their military bearing gave them away. They were seated at separate tables on opposite sides of the restaurant.

"NSA," Hart said.

Soraya frowned. "Why would NSA be shadowing us?"

"I'll tell you in a minute. Let's continue with what's most immediately pressing. You mean we're dealing with a complete unknown, an unaffiliated terrorist organization that is capable of planning a large-scale attack? That sounds far-fetched."

"Imagine how it'll sound to your directorate heads. Plus, our operatives have determined that keeping our information secret is the only way to get more intel. The moment this group catches wind of our mobilizing they'll postpone the operation for another time."

"Assuming the current time frame is correct, could they abort or postpone at this late stage?"

"*We* couldn't, that's for sure." Soraya gave her a sardonic smile. "But terrorist networks have no infrastructure or bureaucracy to slow them down, so who knows? Part of the difficulty in locating them and taking them down is their infinite flexibility. This superior methodology is what Martin wanted for Typhon. That's my mandate."

The waiter took their half-eaten salads away. A moment later, their main courses arrived. Hart asked for another bottle of mineral water. Her mouth was dry. Now she had NSA on one side, an off-the-grid terrorist organization about to carry out an attack on a large East Coast building on the other. Scylla and Charybdis. Either one could wreck her career at CI before it even began. She couldn't allow that to happen. She wouldn't.

"Excuse me a moment," she said, getting up.

Soraya scanned the restaurant, but kept at least one of the agents in her peripheral vision. She saw him tense when the DCI went off to the ladies' room. He had risen and was making his way toward the rear when Hart returned. He reversed course, sat back down.

When the DCI had settled herself in her chair she looked Soraya in the eye. "Since you decided to deliver this intel here instead of the office I assume you have a specific idea as to how to proceed."

"Listen," Soraya said, "we have a red-hot situation, and we don't have enough intel to mobilize, let alone act. We have less than a week to find out everything on this terrorist organization based God only knows where with who knows how many members.

"This isn't the time or place for the usual protocols. They're not going to avail us anything." She glanced down at her fish as if it were the last thing she wanted to put in her mouth. When her gaze rose again, she said, "We need Jason Bourne to find this terrorist group. We'll take care of the rest."

Hart looked at her as if she were out of her mind. "Out of the question."

"Given the urgency of the mission," Soraya said, "he's the only one who has a chance of finding them and stopping them."

"I wouldn't last a day in the job once it got out that I was using Jason Bourne."

"On the other hand," Soraya said, "if you don't follow through on this intel, if this group executes their attack, you'll be out of CI before you can catch your breath."

Hart sat back, produced a short laugh. "You really are a piece of work. You want me to authorize the use of a rogue agent—a man who's unstable at best, who many powerful people in this organization feel is dangerous to CI in particular—for a mission that could have dire consequences for this country, for the continuation of CI as you and I know it?"

A jolt of anxiety ran down Soraya's spine. "Wait a minute, back that up. What do you mean the continuation of CI as we know it?"

Hart glanced from one of the NSA agents to the other. Then she expelled a deep breath and told Soraya everything that had happened from the moment she'd been summoned into the Oval Office to meet with the president and had found herself confronting Luther LaValle and General Kendall.

"After I managed to prevail with the president, LaValle accosted me outside for a chat," Hart concluded. "He told me that if I didn't play nice with him he'd come after me with everything he has. He wants to take over CI, Soraya, wants it as part of his ever-enlarging intelligence services domain. But it isn't just LaValle we're fighting, it's his boss, the secretary of defense. The plan is Bud Halliday's through and through. Black River had some dealings with him when I was there, none of them pleasant. If he succeeds in bringing CI into the Pentagon fold, you can be sure the military will come in, ruin everything with their usual war-like mentality."

"Then there's even more reason to let me bring Jason in for this." Soraya's voice had taken on added urgency. "He'll get the job done where a company of agents can't. Believe me, I've worked with him in the field twice. Whatever's said about him within CI is totally false. Sure, lifers like Rob Batt hate his guts, why wouldn't they? Bourne's got a freedom they wish they had. Plus, he's got abilities they never dreamed of."

"Soraya, it's been implied in several evaluations that you once had an affair with Bourne. Please tell me the truth—I need to know if you're being swayed by anything other than what you think will be best for the country and for CI."

Soraya knew this was coming and was prepared. "I thought Martin had laid that office scuttlebutt to rest. There's absolutely no truth to it. We became friends when I was chief of station in Odessa. That was a long time ago; he doesn't remember. When he came back last year to rescue Martin he had no idea who I was."

"Last year you were in the field with him again."

"We work well together. That's all," Soraya said firmly.

Hart was still clandestinely watching the NSA agents. "Even if I thought what you were proposing would work, he'd never consent. From everything I've read and heard since coming to CI, he hates the organization."

"True enough," Soraya said. "But once he understands the nature of the threat I think I can convince him to sign on one more time."

Hart shook her head. "I don't know. Even talking to him is a damn huge gamble, one I'm not sure I'm willing to take."

"Director, if you don't seize this opportunity, you'll never be able to. It'll be too late."

Still, Hart was unsure which direction to take: the tried and true or the unorthodox. *No*, she thought, *not unorthodox, insane.*

"I think this place has outlived its usefulness," she said abruptly. She signaled the waiter. "Soraya, I believe you have to powder your nose. And while you're there, please call the Metro DC Police. Use the pay phone; it's in working order, I checked. Tell Metro that there are two armed men at this restaurant. Then come right back to the table and be ready to move quickly."

Soraya gave her a small conspiratorial smile, then rose, threading her way back to the ladies' room. The waiter approached the table, frowning.

"Is there something wrong with the brook trout, ma'am?"

"It's fine," Hart said.

As the waiter gathered up the plates Hart took out five twenty-dollar bills, slipped them in his pocket. "You see that man over there, the one with the wide face and football player's shoulders?"

"Yes, ma'am."

"How about you trip when you get to his table."

"If I do that," the waiter said, "I'm liable to dump these brook trouts in his lap."

"Precisely," Hart said with a winning smile.

"But it could mean my job."

"Don't worry." Hart took out her ID, showed it to him. "I'll square things with your boss."

The waiter nodded, turned away. Soraya reappeared, made her way to the table. Hart threw some bills onto their table but didn't stand up until the waiter bumped into a busboy. He staggered, the plates tipped. As the NSA shadow leapt up, Hart rose. Together she and Soraya walked to the door. The NSA shadow was berating the waiter, who was brushing him down with several napkins; everyone was looking, gesticulating. A couple of people closest to the accident were shouting their versions of what happened. Amid the escalating chaos, the second NSA shadow had gotten up to come to his compatriot's aid, but when he saw his target heading toward him he changed his mind.

Hart and Soraya had reached the door, were stepping out into the street. The second NSA shadow began to follow them, but a pair of burly Metro cops burst into the restaurant detaining him. "Hey! What about them!" he shouted at the two women.

Two more patrol cars screeched to a halt, cops raced out. Hart and Soraya already had their IDs out. The cops checked them.

"We're late for a meeting," Hart said briskly and authoritatively. "National security."

The phrase was like *open sesame*. The cops waved them on.

"Sweet," Soraya said, impressed.

Hart nodded her head in acknowledgment, but her expression was grim. Winning such a small skirmish meant nothing to her, save a bit of immediate gratification. It was the war she had her gaze set on.

When they were several blocks away and had determined that they were clean of LaValle's tags, Soraya said, "At least let me set up a meet with Bourne so we can pick his brain."

"I very much doubt this will work."

"Jason trusts me. He'll do the right thing," Soraya said with absolute conviction. "He always does."

Hart considered for some time. Scylla and Charybdis still loomed large in her thought process. Death by water or fire, which was it to be? But even now she didn't regret taking the director's position. If there was anything she was up for at this stage in her life it was a challenge. She couldn't imagine a bigger one than this.

"As you no doubt know," she said, "Bourne wants to see the files on the conversations between Lindros and Moira Trevor." She paused in order to judge Soraya's reaction to the woman Bourne was now linked with. "I agreed." There wasn't even a tremor in Soraya's face. "I'm meeting him this evening at five," she said slowly, as if still chewing the idea over. Then, all at once, she nodded decisively. "Join me. We'll hear his take on your intel then."

Eleven

SPLENDIDLY DONE," Specter said to Bourne. "I can't tell you how impressed I am with how you handled the situations at the zoo and at the hospital."

"Mikhail Tarkanian is dead," Bourne said. "I never meant that to happen."

"Nevertheless it did." Specter's black eye wasn't quite as swollen, but it was beginning to turn lurid colors. "Once again I'm deeply in your debt, my dear Jason. Tarkanian was quite clearly the traitor. If not for you, he would have been the instigator of my torture and eventual death. You'll pardon me if I don't grieve for him."

The professor clapped Bourne on the back as the two men walked down to the weeping willow on Specter's property. Out of the corner of his eye, Bourne could see several young men, armed with assault rifles, flanking them. Following the events of today, Bourne didn't begrudge the professor his armed guards. In fact, they made him feel better about leaving Specter's side.

Under the nebula of delicate yellow branches the two men gazed out at the pond, its surface as perfectly flat as if it were a sheet of steel.

A brace of skittish grackles lifted up from the willow, cawing angrily. Their feathers gleamed in brief rainbow hues as they banked away from the swiftly lowering sun.

"How well do you know Moscow?" Specter asked. Bourne had told him what Tarkanian had said, and they'd agreed that Bourne should start there in his search for Pyotr's killer.

"Well enough. I've been there several times."

"Still and all, I'll have a friend, Lev Baronov, meet you at Shereme-tyevo. Whatever you require, he'll provide. Including weapons."

"I work alone," Bourne said. "I don't want or need a partner."

Specter nodded understandingly. "Lev will be there for support only, I promise he won't be a hindrance."

The professor paused a moment. "What worries me, Jason, is your relationship with Ms. Trevor." Turning so that he faced away from the house, he spoke more softly. "I have no intention of prying into your personal life, but if you're going overseas—"

"We both are. She's off to Munich this evening," Bourne said. "I appreciate your concern, but she's as tough a woman as I've come across. She can take care of herself."

Specter nodded, clearly relieved. "All right, then. There's just the matter of the information on Icoupov." He drew out a packet. "In here are your plane tickets to Moscow, along with the documentation you'll need. There's money waiting for you. Lev has the details as to which bank, the account number attached to the safe-deposit box, and a false identity. The account has been established in that name, not in yours."

"This took some planning."

"I had it done last night, in the hope that you'd agree to go," Spec-ter said. "All that remains is for us to take a picture of you for the passport."

"And if I'd said no?"

"Someone else had already volunteered." Specter smiled. "But I had faith, Jason. And my faith was rewarded."

They turned back and were heading for the house when the profes-sor paused.

"One more thing," he said. "The situation in Moscow vis-à-vis the *grupperovka*—the criminal families—is at one of its periodic boiling points. The Kazanskaya and the Azeri are vying for sole control of the drug trade. The stakes are extraordinarily high—in the billions of dollars. So don't get in their way. If there is any contact with you, I beg you not to engage them. Instead, turn the other cheek. It's the only way to survive there."

"I'll remember that," Bourne said, just as one of Specter's men came hurrying out of the back of the house.

"A woman, Moira Trevor, is here to see Mr. Bourne," he said in German-inflected Turkish.

Specter turned to Bourne, his eyebrows raised in either surprise or concern, if not both.

"I had no other choice," Bourne said. "I need to see her before she leaves, and after what happened today I wasn't about to leave you until the last moment."

Specter's face cleared. "I appreciate that, Jason. Indeed, I do." His hand swept up and away. "Go see your lady friend, and then we'll make our last preparations."

I'm on my way to the airport," Moira said when Bourne met her in the hallway. "The plane takes off in two hours." She gave him all the pertinent information.

"I'm on another flight," he said. "I have some work to do for the professor."

A flicker of disappointment crossed her face before vanishing in a smile. "You have to do what you think is best for you."

Bourne heard the slight distance in her voice, as if a glass partition had come down between them. "I'm out of the university. You were right about that."

"Another bit of good news."

"Moira, I don't want my decision to cause any problems between us."

"That could never happen, Jason, I promise you." She kissed him on the cheek. "I have some interviews lined up when I get to Munich, security people I've been able to contact through back channels—two Germans, an Israeli, and a German Muslim, who may be the most promising of the lot."

As two of Specter's young men came through the door, Bourne took Moira into one of the two sitting rooms. A ship's brass clock on the marble mantel chimed the change in watch.

"Quite a grand palace for the head of a university."

"The professor comes from money," Bourne lied. "But he's private about it."

"My lips are sealed," Moira said. "By the way, where's he sending you?"

"Moscow. Some friends of his have gotten into a bit of trouble."

"The Russian mob?"

"Something like that."

Best that she believe the simplest explanation, Bourne thought. He watched the play of lamplight reveal her expression. He was certainly no stranger to duplicity, but his heart constricted at the thought that Moira might be playing him as she was suspected of playing Martin. Several times today he had considered bypassing the meet with the new DCI, but he had to admit to himself that seeing the questioned communication between her and Martin had become important to him. Once he saw the evidence he'd know how to proceed with Moira. He owed it to Martin to discover the truth about his relationship with her. Besides, it was no use fooling himself: He now had a personal stake in the situation. His newly revealed feelings for her complicated matters for everyone, not the least himself. Why was there was a price to pay for every pleasure? he wondered bitterly. But now he stood committed; there was no turning back, either from Moscow or from discovering who Moira really was.

Moira, moving closer to him, put a hand on his arm. "Jason, what is it? You look so troubled."

Bourne tried not to look alarmed. Like Marie, she had the uncanny ability to sense what he was feeling, though with everyone else he was adept at keeping his expression neutral. The important thing now was not to lie to her; she'd pick that up in a heartbeat.

"The mission is extremely delicate. Professor Specter has already warned me that I'm jumping into the middle of a blood feud between two Moscow *grupperovka* families."

Her grip on him tightened briefly. "Your loyalty to the professor is admirable. And after all, your loyalty is what Martin admired most about you." She checked her watch. "I've got to go."

She lifted her face to his, her lips soft as melting butter, and they kissed for what seemed a long time.

She laughed softly. "Dear Jason, don't worry. I'm not one of those people who ask about when I'll see you again."

Then she turned and, walking into the foyer, saw herself out. A moment later Bourne heard the cough of a car starting up, the crunch of its tires as it performed a quarter circle back down the gravel drive to the road.

Arkadin awoke grimy and stiff. His shirt was still damp with sweat from his nightmare. Gray light sifted in through the skewed blinds on the window. Stretching his neck by rolling his head in a circle, he thought what he needed most was a good long soak, but the hotel had only a shower in the hallway bathroom.

He rolled over to find that he was alone in the room; Devra had gone. Sitting up, he slid out of the damp, rumpled bed, scrubbed his rough face with the heels of his hands. His shoulder throbbed. It was swollen and hot.

He was reaching for the doorknob when the door opened. Devra stood on the threshold, a paper bag in one hand.

"Did you miss me?" she said with a sardonic smile. "I can see it in your face. You thought I'd skipped out."

She came inside, kicked the door shut. Her eyes, unblinking, met his. She put her free arm up. Her hand squeezed his left shoulder, gently but firmly enough to cause him pain.

"I brought us coffee and fresh rolls," she said evenly. "Don't manhandle me."

Arkadin glared at her for a moment. The pain meant nothing to him, but her defiance did. He was right. There was much more to her than what she presented on the surface.

He let go and so did she.

"I know who you are," he said. "Filya wasn't Pyotr's courier. You are."

That sardonic smile returned. "I was wondering how long it would take you to figure it out." She crossed to the dresser, lined up the paper cups of coffee, set the rolls on the flattened bag. She took out a small bag of ice and tossed it to him.

"They're still warm." She bit into one, chewed thoughtfully.

Arkadin placed the ice on his left shoulder, sighed inwardly at the relief. He wolfed down his roll in three bites. Then he poured the scalding coffee down his throat.

"Next I suppose you're going to hold your palm over an open flame." Devra shook her head. "Men."

"Why are you still here?" Arkadin said. "You could've just run off."

"And go where? I shot one of Pyotr's own men."

"You must have friends."

"None I can trust."

Which implied she trusted him. He had an instinct she wasn't lying about this. She'd washed off the heavy mascara that had run and smudged last night. Oddly, this made her eyes seem even larger. And her cheeks held a blush now that she'd scrubbed off what had to be white theatrical makeup.

"I'll take you to Turkey," she said. "A small town called Eskişehir. That's where I sent the document."

Given what he knew, Turkey—the ancient gateway between East and West—made perfect sense.

The bag of ice slipped off as Arkadin grabbed the front of her shirt, crossed to the window, threw it wide open. Though the action cost him in pain to his shoulder, he hardly cared. The early-morning sounds of the street rose up to him like the smell of baking bread. He bent her backward so her head and torso were out the window. "What did I tell you about lying to me?"

"You might as well kill me now," she said in her little-girl voice. "I won't tolerate your abuse anymore."

Arkadin pulled her back inside the room, let go of her. "What are you going to do," he said with a smirk, "jump out the window?"

No sooner had the words come out of his mouth than she walked calmly to the window and sat on the sash, staring at him all the time. Then she tipped herself backward, through the open window. Arkadin grabbed her around the legs and hauled her up from the brink.

They stood glaring at each other, breathing fast, hearts pumping with excess adrenaline.

"Yesterday, while we were on the ladder, told me that you had nothing much to live for," Devra said. "That pretty much goes for me, too. So here we both are, brothers under the skin, with nothing but each other."

"How do I know the next link in the network is Turkey?"

She drew her hair back from her face. "I'm tired of lying to you," she said. "It's like lying to myself. What's the point?"

"Talk is cheap," he said.

"Then I'll prove it to you. When we get to Turkey I'll take you to the document."

Arkadin, trying not to think too much about what she said, nodded his acknowledgment of their uneasy truce. "I won't lay a hand on you again."

Except to kill you, he thought.

Twelve

THE FREER GALLERY of Art stood on the south side of the Mall, bounded on the west by the Washington Monument and on the east by the Reflecting Pool, gateway to the immense Capitol building. It was situated on the corner of Jefferson Drive and 12th Street, SW, near the western edge of the Mall.

The building, a Florentine Renaissance palazzo faced with Stony Creek granite imported from Connecticut, had been commissioned by Charles Freer to house his enormous collection of Near East and East Asian art. The main entrance on the north side of the building where the meet was to take place consisted of three arches accented by Doric pilasters surrounding a central loggia. Because its architecture looked inward, many critics felt it was a rather forbidding facade, especially when compared with the nearby exuberance of the National Gallery of Art.

Nevertheless, the Freer was the preeminent museum of its kind in the country, and Soraya loved it not only for the depth of art it housed but also for the elegant lines of the palazzo itself. She especially loved the contained open space at its entrance, and the fact that even, as now, when the Mall was agitated with hordes of tourists heading to and from the Smithsonian Metro rail stop on 12th Street, the Freer itself was an oasis of calm and tranquility. When things boiled over in the office during the day, it was to the Freer she came to decompress. Ten minutes with Sung dynasty jades and lacquers acted like a soothing balm to her soul.

Approaching the north side of the Mall, she searched past the crowds outside the entrance to the Freer and thought she saw—among the sturdy men with their hard, clipped Midwestern accents, the scampering children and their laughing mothers, the vacant-eyed teenagers plugged into their iPods—Veronica Hart's long, elegant figure walking past the entrance, then doubling back.

She stepped off the curb, but the blare of a horn from an oncoming car startled her back onto the sidewalk. It was at that moment that her cell phone buzzed.

"What exactly do you think you're doing?" Bourne said in her ear.

"Jason?"

"Why are you coming to this meet?"

Foolishly, she looked around; she'd never be able to spot him, and she knew it.

"Hart invited me. I need to talk to you. The DCI and I both do."

"About what?"

Soraya took a deep breath. "Typhon's listening posts have picked up a series of disturbing communications pointing to an imminent terrorist attack on an East Coast city. The trouble is, that's all we have. Worse, the communications are between two cadres of a group about which we have no intel whatsoever. It was my idea to recruit you to find them and stop the attack."

"Not much to go on," Bourne said. "Doesn't matter. The group's name is the Black Legion."

"In grad school I studied the link between a branch of Muslim extremism and the Third Reich. But this can't be the same Black Legion. They were either killed or disbanded when Nazi Germany fell."

"It can and it is," Bourne said. "I don't know how it managed to survive, but it did. Three of their members tried to kidnap Professor Specter this morning. I saw their device tattooed on the gunman's arm."

"The three horses' heads joined by the death's head?"

"Yes." Bourne described the incident in detail. "Check the body at the morgue."

"I'll do that," Soraya said. "But how could the Black Legion remain so far underground all this time without being detected?"

"They have a powerful international front," Bourne said. "The Eastern Brotherhood."

"That sounds far-fetched," Soraya said. "The Eastern Brotherhood is in the forefront of Islamic–Western relations."

"Nevertheless, my source is unimpeachable."

"God in heaven, what've you been doing while you've been away from CI?"

"I was never in CI," Bourne said brusquely, "and here's just one reason why. You say you want to talk with me but I doubt you need half a dozen agents to do that."

Soraya froze. "Agents?" She was on the Mall itself now, and she had to restrain herself from looking around again. "There are no CI agents here."

"How d'you know that?"

"Hart would've told me—"

"Why should she tell you anything? We go way back, you and I."

"That's true enough." She kept walking. "But something happened earlier today that makes me believe the agents you've spotted are NSA." She described the way she and Hart had been shadowed from CI HQ to the restaurant. She told him about Secretary Halliday and Luther LaValle, both of whom were gunning to make CI a part of the Pentagon clandestine service.

"That might make sense," Bourne said, "if there were only two of them. But six? No, there's another agenda, one neither of us knows about."

"Such as?"

"The agents are vectored perfectly, triangulated on the entrance to the Freer," Bourne said. "This means that they must have had foreknowledge of the meet. It also means the six weren't sent to shadow

Veronica Hart. If they aren't here for her, they must have been sent for me. This is Hart's doing."

Soraya felt a chill crawl down her spine. What if the DCI was lying to her? What if she meant all along to lead Bourne into a trap? It would make sense for one of her first official acts as DCI to be the capture of Jason Bourne. It certainly would put her in solidly with Rob Batt and the others who despised and feared Bourne, and who resented her. Plus, capturing Jason would score her big points with the president and prevent Secretary Halliday from building on his already considerable influence. Still, why would Hart have allowed Soraya to possibly muck up her first field op by coming along? No, she had to believe this was an NSA initiative.

"I don't believe that," she said emphatically.

"Let's say you're right. The other possibility is just as dire. If Hart didn't set the trap, then there's someone highly placed in CI who did. I went to Hart directly with the request."

"Yes," she said, "using my cell, thank you very much."

"Did you find it? You're on a new one now."

"It was in the gutter where you tossed it."

"Then stop complaining," Bourne said, not unkindly. "I can't imagine Hart told too many people about this meet, but one of them is working against her, and if that's the case chances are he's been recruited by LaValle."

If Bourne was right . . . But of course he was. "You're the grand prize, Jason. If LaValle can take you down when no one in CI could, he'll be a hero. Taking over CI will be a cakewalk for him after that." Soraya felt perspiration break out at her hairline. "Under the circumstances," she continued, "I think you ought to withdraw."

"I need to see the correspondence between Martin and Moira. And if Hart is instigating this trap, then she'll never give me access to the files at another time. I'll have to take my chances, but not until you're certain Hart has the material."

Soraya, who was almost at the entrance, expelled a long breath. "Jason, I found the conversations. I can tell you what's in them."

"Do you think you could quote them to me verbatim?" he said. "Anyway, it's not that simple. Karim al-Jamil doctored hundreds of files before he left. I know the method he used to alter them. I have to see them myself."

"I see there's no way I can talk you out of this."

"Right," Bourne said. "When you've made sure the material is genuine, beep my cell once. Then I need you to move Hart into the loggia, away from the entrance proper."

"Why?" she said. "That'll only make it more difficult for you to—Jason?"

But Bourne had already disconnected.

From his vantage point on the roof of the Forrestal Building on Independence Avenue, Bourne tracked his high-powered night-vision glasses from Soraya as she moved toward the DCI, past clots of tourists hurrying about, to the agents in place around the west end of the Mall. Two lounged, chatting, at the northeast corner of the Department of Agriculture North Building. Another, hands in the pockets of his trench coat, was crossing diagonally southwest from Madison Drive toward the Smithsonian. A fourth was behind the wheel of an illegally parked car on Constitution Avenue. In fact, he was the one who'd given the game away. Bourne had spotted the car illegally parked just before a Metro police cruiser stopped parallel to it. Windows were rolled down, a conversation ensued. ID was briefly flashed by the driver of the illegally parked car. The cruiser rolled on.

The fifth and sixth agents were east of the Freer, one approximately midway between Madison and Jefferson drives, the other in front of the Arts Industries Building. He knew there had to be at least one more.

It was almost five o'clock. A short winter twilight had descended, aided by the twinkling lights wound festively around lampposts. With the location of each agent memorized Bourne returned to the ground, using the window ledges for hands and feet.

The moment he showed himself the agents would start moving.

Estimating the distance they were from where the DCI and Soraya stood, he calculated he'd have no more than two minutes with Hart to get the files.

Hidden in shadows, waiting for Soraya's signal, he strained to pick out the remaining agents. They couldn't afford to leave Independence Avenue unguarded. If Hart didn't in fact have the files, then he'd do as Soraya first suggested and get out of the area without being spotted.

He imagined her at the entrance to the Freer, talking with the DCI. There would be the first nervous moment of acknowledgment, then Soraya would have to direct the conversation around to the files. She'd have to find a way for Hart to show them to her, to make sure they were authentic.

His phone beeped once and was still. The files were authentic.

He accessed the Internet, navigating to the DC Metro site, checked the up-to-the-minute transit schedules, checking his options. This procedure took longer than he would have liked. The very real and immediate danger was that one of the six agents was in contact with home base—either CI or the Pentagon—whose sophisticated electronic telemetry could pinpoint his phone and, worse, spy on what he was pulling up from the Net. Couldn't be helped, however. Access had to be made on site and at the immediate moment in case of unforeseen transit delays. He put the worry out of his head, concentrated on what he'd have to do. The next five minutes were crucial.

Time to go.

Moments after Soraya secretly contacted Bourne she said to Veronica Hart, "I'm afraid we may have a problem."

The DCI's head whipped around. She'd been scanning the area for any sign of Bourne's presence. The crowds around the Freer had thickened as many made their way to the Smithsonian Metro station around the corner, returning to their hotels to prepare for dinner.

"What kind of problem?"

"I think I saw one of the NSA shadows we picked up at lunch."

"Hell, I don't want LaValle knowing I'm meeting with Bourne. He'll have a fit, go running to the president." She turned. "I think we ought to leave before Bourne gets here."

"What about my intel?" Soraya said. "What chance are we going to have without him? I say let's stay and talk to him. Showing him the material will go a long way toward winning his trust."

The DCI was clearly on edge. "I don't like any of this."

"Time is of the essence." Soraya took her by the elbow. "Let's move back here," she said, indicating the loggia. "We'll be out of the shadow's line of sight."

Hart reluctantly walked into the open space. The loggia was especially crowded with people milling about, discussing the art they'd just seen, their plans for dinner and the next day. The gallery closed at five thirty, so the building was starting to clear out.

"Where the hell is he, anyway?" Hart said testily.

"He'll be here," Soraya assured her. "He wants the material."

"Of course he wants it. The material concerns his friend."

"Clearing Martin's name is extremely important to him."

"I was speaking of Moira Trevor," the DCI said.

Before Soraya could form a reply, a group of people spewed out of the front doors. Bourne was in the middle of them. Soraya could see him, but he was shielded from anyone across the street.

"Here he is," she muttered as Bourne came quickly and silently up behind them. He must have somehow gotten into the Independence Avenue entrance at the south side of the building, closed to the public, made his way through the galleries to the front.

The DCI turned, impaling Bourne with a penetrating gaze. "So you came after all."

"I said I would."

He didn't blink, didn't move at all. Soraya thought that he was at his most terrifying then, the sheer force of his will at its peak.

"You have something for me."

"I said you could read it." The DCI held out a small manila envelope.

Bourne took it. "I regret I haven't the time to do that here."

He whirled, snaking through the crowd, vanishing inside the Freer.

"Wait!" Hart cried. "Wait!"

But it was too late, and in any event three NSA agents came walking rapidly through the entrance. Their progress was slowed by the people exiting the gallery, but they pushed many of them aside. They trotted past the DCI and Soraya as if they didn't exist. A third agent appeared, took up position just inside the loggia. He stared at them and smiled thinly.

Bourne moved as quickly as he thought prudent through the interior. Having memorized it from the visitors' brochure and come through it once already, he did not waste a step. But one thing worried him. He hadn't seen any agents on his way in. That meant, more than likely, he'd have to deal with them on the way out.

Near the rear entrance, a guard was checking galleries just before closing time. Bourne was obliged to detour around a corner with an outcropping of a fire call box and extinguisher. He could hear the guard's soft voice as he herded a family toward the exit in front. Bourne was about to slip out when he heard other voices sharper, clipped. Moving into shadow, he saw a pair of slim, white-haired Chinese scholars in pin-striped suits and shiny brogues arguing the merits of a Tang porcelain vase. Their voices faded along with their footsteps as they headed toward Jefferson Drive.

Without losing another instant Bourne checked the bypass he'd made on the alarm system. So far it showed everything as normal. He pushed out the door. Night wind struck his face as he saw two agents, sidearms drawn, hurrying up the granite stairs. He had just enough time to register the oddness of the guns before he ducked back inside, went directly to the fire call box.

They came through the door. The leading one got a face full of fire-smothering foam. Bourne ducked a wild shot from the second agent. There was virtually no noise, but something pinged off the Tennessee white marble wall near his shoulder, then clattered to the floor. He hurled the fire extinguisher at the shooter. It struck him on the temple and he went down. Bourne broke the call box's glass, pulled hard on the red metal handle. Instantly the fire alarm sounded, piercing every corner of the gallery.

Out the door, Bourne ran diagonally down the steps, heading west, directly for 12th Street, SW. He expected to find more agents at the southwest corner of the building, but as he turned off Independence Avenue onto 12th Street he encountered a flood of people drawn to the building by the alarm. Already the sirens of fire trucks could be heard floating through the rising chatter of the crowd.

He hurried along the street toward the entrance down to the Smithsonian Metro stop. As he did so, he accessed the Internet through his cell. It took longer than he would have liked, but at last he pressed the FAVORITES icon, was returned to the Metro site. Navigating to the Smithsonian station, he scrolled down to the hyperlink to the next train arrival, which was refreshed every thirty seconds. Three minutes to the Orange line 6 train to Vienna/Fairfax. Quickly he composed a text mail "FB," sent it to a number he'd prearranged with Professor Specter.

The Metro entrance, clogged with people stopped on the stairs to watch the unfolding scenario, was a mere fifty yards away. Bourne heard police sirens now, saw a number of unmarked cars heading down 12th Street toward Jefferson. They turned east when they got to the junction— all except one, which headed due south.

Bourne tried to run, but he was hampered by the press of people. He broke free, into a small area blessedly empty of the gigantic jostle, when the driver's window of a cruising car slid down. A burly man with a grim face and a nearly bald head aimed another one of those strange-looking handguns at him.

Bourne twisted, putting one of the Metro entrance posts between himself and the gunman. He heard nothing, no sound at all—just as he hadn't back inside the Freer—and something bit into his left calf. He looked down, saw the metal of a mini dart lying on the street. It had grazed him, but that was all. With a controlled swing, Bourne went around the post, down the stairs, pushing his way through the gawkers into the Metro. He had just under two minutes to make the Orange 6 to Vienna. The next train didn't leave for four minutes after that—too much time in the platform, waiting for the NSA agents to find him. He had to make the first train.

He bought his ticket, went through. The crowds thinned and thickened like waves rushing to shore. He began to sweat. His left foot slipped. Rebalancing himself, he guessed that whatever was in that mini dart must be having an effect despite only grazing him. Looking up at the electronic signs, he had to work to focus in order to find the correct platform. He kept pushing forward, not trusting himself to rest, though part of him seemed hell-bent on doing just that. *Sit down, close your eyes, sink into sleep*. Turning to a vending machine, he fished in his pockets for change, bought every chocolate bar he could. Then he entered the line for the escalator.

Partway down he stumbled, missed the riser, crashed into the couple ahead of him. He'd blacked out for an instant. Gaining the platform, he felt both shaky and sluggish. The concrete-paneled ceiling arched overhead, deadening the sounds of the hundreds crowding the platform.

Less than a minute to go. He could feel the vibration of the oncoming train, the wind it pushed ahead of it.

He'd gobbled down one chocolate bar and was starting on the second when the train pulled into the station. He stepped in, allowing the surge of the crowd to take him. Just as the doors were closing, a tall man with broad shoulders and a black trench coat sprinted into the other end of Bourne's car. The doors closed and the train lurched forward.

Thirteen

AS HE SAW the man in the black trench making his way toward him from the end of the train car, Bourne felt an unpleasant form of claustrophobia. Until they reached the next station, he was trapped in this finite space, Moreover, despite the initial chocolate hit, he was starting to feel a lassitude creeping up from his left leg as the serum entered his bloodstream. He tore off the wrapping on another chocolate bar, wolfed it down. The faster he could get the sugar and the caffeine into his system, the better able his body would be to fight off the effects of the drug. But that effect would only be temporary, and then his blood sugar would plummet, draining the adrenaline out of him.

The train reached Federal Triangle and the doors slid open. A mass of people got off, another mass got on. Black Trench used the brief slackening of passengers to make headway toward where Bourne stood, hands clasped around a chromium pole. The doors closed, the train accelerated. Black Trench was blocked by a huge man with tattoos on the backs of his hands. He tried to push by, but the tattooed man glared at him, refusing to budge. Black Trench could have used his federal ID to move people out of the way, but he didn't, no doubt so as not to cause a panic. But whether he was NSA or CI was still a mystery. Bourne, struggling to stop his mind from going in and out of focus, stared into the face of his newest adversary, looking for clues to his affiliation. Black Trench's face was blocky, bland, but with the particular dry cruelty the military demanded in its clandestine agents. He must be NSA, Bourne decided. Through the fog in his brain, he knew he had to deal with Black Trench before the rendezvous point at Foggy Bottom.

Two children swung into Bourne as the train lurched around a bend. He held them upright, returning them to their place beside their mother, who smiled her thanks at him, put a protecting arm around their narrow shoulders. The train rolled into Metro Center. Bourne saw a brief glare of temporary spotlights where a work crew was busy fixing an escalator. On the other side of him a young blonde with earbuds leading to an MP3 player pressed her shoulder against his, took out a cheap plastic compact, checked the state of her makeup. Pursing her lips, she slid the compact back in her bag, dug out flavored lip gloss. While she was applying it, Bourne lifted the compact, palming it immediately. He replaced it with a twenty-dollar bill.

The doors opened and Bourne stepped out within a small whirlwind of people. Black Trench, caught between doors, rushed down the car, made it onto the platform just in time. Weaving his way through the hurrying throngs, he followed Bourne toward the elevator. The majority of people headed for the stairs.

Bourne checked the position of the temporary spotlights. He made for them, but not at too fast a pace. He wanted Black Trench to make up some of the distance between them. He had to assume that Black Trench was also armed with a dart gun. If a dart struck Bourne anywhere, even in an extremity, it would mean the end. Caffeine or no caffeine, he'd pass out, and NSA would have him.

There was a wall of elderly and disabled people, some of them in wheelchairs, waiting for the elevator. The door opened. Bourne sprinted ahead as if making for the elevator, but the moment he reached the glare of the spotlights, he turned and aimed the mirror inside the compact at an angle that reflected the dazzle into Black Trench's face.

Momentarily blinded, Black Trench halted, put up his hand palm-outward. Bourne was at him in a heartbeat. He drove his hand into the main nerve bundle beneath Black Trench's right ear, wrested the dart gun out of his hand, fired it into his side.

As the man listed to one side, staggering, Bourne caught him, dragged him to a wall. Several people turned their heads to gape, but no one stopped. The pace of the crowd hurrying by barely flickered before returning to full force.

Bourne left Black Trench there, eeled his way through the almost solid curtain of people back to the Orange line. Four minutes later, he'd eaten through two more chocolate bars. Another Orange 6 to Vienna rolled in and, with a last glance thrown over his shoulder, he got on. His head didn't feel any deeper in the mist, but he knew what he needed most now was water, as much as he could get down his throat, to flush the chemical out of his system as quickly as possible.

Two stops later, he exited at Foggy Bottom. He waited at the rear of the platform until no more passengers got off. Then he followed them up, taking the stairs two at a time in an attempt to further clear his head.

His first breath of cool evening air was a deep and exhilarating one. Except for a slight nausea, perhaps caused by a continuing vertigo, he felt better. As he emerged from the Metro exit a nearby engine coughed to life; the headlights of a dark blue Audi came on. He walked briskly to the car, opened the passenger's-side door, slid in.

"How did it go?" Professor Specter nosed the Audi out into the heavy traffic.

"I got more than I bargained for," Bourne said, leaning his head against the seat rest. "And there's been a change of plan. People are sure to be looking for me at the airport. I'm going with Moira, at least as far as Munich."

A look of deep concern crossed the professor's face. "Do you think that's wise?"

Bourne turned his head, stared out the window at the passing city. "It doesn't matter." His thoughts were of Martin, and of Moira. "I passed wise some time ago."

Book Two

Fourteen

IT'S AMAZING," Moira said.

Bourne looked up from the files he'd snatched from Veronica Hart. "What's amazing?"

"You sitting here opposite me in this opulent corporate jet." Moira was wearing a sleek black suit of nubbly wool, shoes with sensible heels. A thin gold chain was around her neck. "Weren't you supposed to be on your way to Moscow tonight?"

Bourne drank water from the bottle on his side tray table, closed the file. He needed more time to ascertain whether Karim al-Jamil had doctored these conversations, but he had his suspicions. He knew Martin was far too canny to tell her anything that was classified—which covered just about everything that happened at CI.

"I couldn't stay away from you." He watched a small smile curl Moira's wide lips. Then he dropped the bomb. "Also, the NSA is after me."

It was as if a light went out in her face. "Say again?"

"The NSA. Luther LaValle has decided to make me a target." He waved a hand to forestall her questions. "It's political. If he can bag me when the CI hierarchy can't, he'll prove to the powers that be that his thesis that CI should come under his jurisdiction makes sense, especially after the turmoil CI has been in since Martin's death."

Moira pursed her lips. "So Martin was right. He was the only one left who believed in you."

Bourne almost added Soraya's name, then thought better of it. "It doesn't matter now."

"It matters to me," she said fiercely.

"Because you loved him."

"We both loved him." Her head tilted to one side. "Wait a minute, are you saying there's something wrong in that?"

"We live on the outskirts of society, in a world of secrets." He deliberately included her. "For people like us there's always a price to pay for loving someone."

"Like what?"

"We've spoken about it," Bourne said. "Love is a weakness your enemies can exploit."

"And I've said that's a horrid way to live one's life."

Bourne turned to stare out the Perspex window at the darkness rushing by. "It's the only one I know."

"I don't believe that." Moira leaned forward until their knees touched. "Surely you see you're more than that, Jason. You loved your wife; you love your children."

"What kind of a father can I be to them? I'm a memory. And I'm a danger to them. Soon enough I'll be a ghost."

"You can do something about that. And what kind of friend were you to Martin? The best kind. The only kind that matters." She tried to get him to turn back to her. "Sometimes I'm convinced you're looking for answers to questions that have none."

"What does that mean?"

"That no matter what you've done in the past, no matter what you'll do in the future, you'll never lose your humanity." She watched his eyes engage hers slowly, enigmatically. "That's the one thing that frightens you, isn't it?"

* * *

"What's the matter with you?" Devra asked.

Arkadin, behind the wheel of a rental car they had picked up in Istanbul, grunted irritably. "What're you talking about?"

"How long is it going to take you to fuck me?"

There being no flights from Sevastopol to Turkey, they'd spent a long night in a cramped cabin of the *Heroes of Sevastopol*, being transported southwest across the Black Sea from Ukraine to Turkey.

"Why would I want to do that?" Arkadin said as he headed off a lumbering truck on the highway.

"Every man I meet wants to fuck me. Why should you be any different?" Devra ran her hands through her hair. Her raised arms lifted her small breasts invitingly. "Like I said. What's the matter with you?" A smirk played at the corners of her mouth. "Maybe you're not a real man. Is that it?"

Arkadin laughed. "You're so transparent." He glanced at her briefly. "What's your game? Why are you trying to provoke me?"

"I like to extract reactions in my men. How else will I get to know them?"

"I'm not your man," he growled.

Now Devra laughed. She wrapped slender fingers around his arm, rubbing back and forth. "If your shoulder's bothering you I'll drive."

He saw the familiar symbol on the inside of her wrist, all the more fearsome for being tattooed on the porcelain skin. "When did you get that?"

"Does it matter?"

"Not really. What matters is *why* you got it." Faced with open highway, he put on speed. "How else will I get to know you?"

She scratched the tattoo as if it had moved beneath her skin. "Pyotr made me get it. He said it was part of the initiation. He said he wouldn't go to bed with me until I got it."

"And you wanted to go to bed with him."

"Not as much as I want to go to bed with you."

She turned away then, stared out the side window, as if she was suddenly embarrassed by her confession. Perhaps she actually was, Arkadin thought as he signaled, moving right through two lanes as a sign for a rest stop appeared. He turned off the highway, parked at the far end of the rest stop, away from the two vehicles that occupied parking slots. He got out, walked to the edge, and, with his back to her, took a long satisfying pee.

The day was bright and warmer than it had been in Sevastopol. The breeze coming off the water was laden with moisture that lay on his skin like sweat. On the way back to the car he rolled up his sleeves. His coat was slung with hers across the car's backseat.

"We'd better enjoy this warmth while we can," Devra said. "Once we get onto the Anatolian Plateau, the mountains will block this temperate weather. It'll be colder than a witch's teat."

It was as if she'd never made the intimate statement. But she'd caught his attention, all right. It seemed to him now that he understood something important about her—or, more accurately, about himself. It went through Gala, as well, now that he thought of it. He seemed to have a certain power over women. He knew Gala loved him with every fiber of her being, and she wasn't the first one. Now this slim tomboyish *dyevochka*, hard-bitten, downright nasty when she needed to be, had fallen under his spell. Which meant he had the handle on her he was searching for.

"How many times have you been to Eskişehir?" he asked.

"Enough to know what to expect."

He sat back. "Where did you learn to answer questions without revealing a thing?"

"If I'm bad, I learned it at my mother's breast."

Arkadin looked away. He seemed to have trouble breathing. Without a word, he opened the door, bolted outside, stalking in small circles like a lion in the zoo.

I cannot be alone," Arkadin had said to Semion Icoupov, and Icoupov had taken him at his word. At Icoupov's villa where Arkadin was installed, his host provided a young man. But when, a week later, Arkadin had beaten his companion nearly into a coma, Icoupov switched tactics. He spent hours with Arkadin, trying to determine the root of his outbursts of fury. This failed utterly, as Arkadin seemed at a loss to remember, let alone explain these frightening episodes.

"I don't know what to do with you," Icoupov said. "I don't want to incarcerate you, but I need to protect myself."

"I would never harm you," Arkadin said.

"Not knowingly, perhaps," the older man said ruminatively.

The following week a stoop-shouldered man with a formal goatee and colorless lips spent every afternoon with Arkadin. He sat in a plush upholstered chair, one leg crossed over the other, writing in a neat, crabbed hand in a tablet notebook he protected as if it were his child. For his part, Arkadin lay on his host's favorite chaise longue, a roll pillow behind his head. He answered questions. He spoke at length about many things, but the things that shadowed his mind he kept tucked away in a black corner of the deepest depths of his mind, never to be spoken of. That door was closed forever.

At the end of three weeks, the psychiatrist handed in his report to Icoupov and vanished as quickly as he had appeared. No matter. Arkadin's nightmares continued to haunt him in the dead of night when, upon awakening with a gasp and a start, he was convinced he heard rats scuttling, red eyes burning in the darkness. At those moments, the fact that Icoupov's villa was completely vermin-free was of no solace to him. The rats lived inside him squirming, shrieking, feeding.

The next person Icoupov employed to burrow into Arkadin's past in an attempt to cure him of his fits of rage was a woman whose sensuality and lush figure he felt would keep her safe from Arkadin's outbursts of fury. Marlene was adept at handling men of all kinds and kinks. She possessed an uncanny ability to sense the specific thing a man desired from her, and provide it.

At first Arkadin didn't trust Marlene. Why should he? He couldn't trust the psychiatrist. Wasn't she just another form of analyst sent to coax out the secrets of his past? Marlene of course noted this aversion in him and set about countering it. The way she saw it, Arkadin was living under a spell, self-induced or otherwise. It was up to her to concoct an antidote.

"This won't be a short process," she told Icoupov at the end of her first week with Arkadin, and he believed her.

Arkadin observed Marlene walking on little cat feet. He suspected she was smart enough to know that even the slightest misstep on her part might strike him as a seismic shift, and then all the progress she'd made in gaining his trust would evaporate like alcohol over a flame. She seemed to him wary, acutely aware that at any moment he could turn on her. She acted as if she were in a cage with a bear. Day by day you could track the training of it, but that didn't mean it wouldn't unexpectedly rip your face off.

Arkadin had to laugh at that, the care with which she was treating every aspect of him. But gradually something else began to creep into his consciousness. He suspected that she was coming to feel something genuine for him.

Devra watched Arkadin through the windshield. Then she kicked open her door, went after him. She shaded her eyes against a white sun plastered to a high, pale sky.

"What is it?" she said when she'd caught up to him. "What did I say?"

Arkadin turned a murderous look her way. He appeared to be in a towering rage, just barely holding himself together. Devra found herself wondering what would happen if he let himself go, but she also didn't want to be in his way when it happened.

She felt an urge to touch him, to speak soothingly until he returned to a calmer state of mind, but she sensed that would only inflame him further. So she went back to the car to wait patiently for him to return.

Eventually he did, sitting sideways on the seat, his shoes on the ground as if he might bolt again.

"I'm not going to fuck you," he said, "but that doesn't mean I don't want to."

She felt he wanted to say something else, but couldn't, that whatever it was was too bound up in what had happened to him a long time ago.

"It was a joke," she said softly. "I was making a stupid joke."

"There was a time when I would've thought nothing of it," he said, as if talking to himself. "Sex is unimportant."

She sensed that he was speaking about something else, something only he knew, and she glimpsed just how alone he was. She suspected that even in a crowd, even with friends—if he had any—he'd feel alone. It seemed to her that he'd walled himself off from sexual melding because it would underscore the depth of his apartness. He seemed to her to be a moonless planet with no sun to revolve around. Just emptiness everywhere as far as he could see. In that moment she realized that she loved him.

How long has he been in there?" Luther LaValle asked.

"Six days," General Kendall replied. He was in his shirtsleeves, which were turned up. That precaution hadn't been enough to protect them from spatters of blood. "But I guarantee that to him it feels like six months. He's as disoriented as it's possible for a human being to be."

LaValle grunted, peering at the bearded Arab through the one-way mirror. The man looked like a raw piece of meat. LaValle didn't know or care whether he was Sunni or Shi'a. They were the same to him— terrorists bent on destroying his way of life. He took these matters very personally.

"What's he given up?"

"Enough that we know the copies of the Typhon intercepts Batt has given us are disinformation."

"Still," LaValle said, "it comes straight from Typhon."

"This man's very highly placed, there's no question whatsoever of his identity, and he knows of no plans moving into their final stages to hit a major New York building."

"That in itself could be disinformation," LaValle said. "These bastards are masters of that kind of shit."

"Right." Kendall wiped his hands on a towel he'd thrown over his shoulder like a chef at the stove. "They love nothing better than to see us running around in circles, chasing our tails, which is what we'll be doing if we put out an alert."

LaValle nodded, as if to himself. "I want our best people to follow up on it. Confirm the Typhon intercepts."

"We'll do our best, but I feel it my duty to report that the prisoner laughed in my face when I asked him about this terrorist group."

LaValle snapped his fingers several times. "What are they called again?"

"The Black Lesion, the Black Legion, something like that."

"Nothing in our database about this group?"

"No, or at any of our sister agencies, either." Kendall threw the soiled towel into a basket whose contents were incinerated every twelve hours. "It doesn't exist."

"I tend to agree," LaValle said, "but I'd like to be certain."

He turned from the window, and the two men went out of the viewing room. They walked down a rough concrete corridor painted an institutional green, the buzzing fluorescent tubes that hurled purple shadows on the linoleum floor as they passed. He waited patiently outside the locker room for Kendall to change his clothes; then they proceeded down the corridor. At the end of it they climbed a flight of stairs to a reinforced metal door.

LaValle pressed his forefinger onto a fingerprint reader. He was rewarded by the clicking of bolts being shot, not unlike a bank vault opening.

They found themselves in another corridor, the polar opposite of the one they were leaving. This one was paneled in polished mahogany; wall sconces produced a soft, buttery glow between paintings of historical naval engagements, phalanxes of Roman legions, Prussian Hussars, and English light cavalry.

The first door on the left brought them into a room straight out of a high-toned men's club, replete with hunter-green walls, cream moldings, leather furniture, antique breakfronts, and a wooden bar from an old English pub. The sofas and chairs were well spaced, the better to allow occupants to speak of private matters. Flames cracked and sparked comfortingly in a large fireplace.

A liveried butler met them before they'd taken three steps on the thick, sound-deadening carpet. He guided them to their accustomed spot, in a discreet corner where two high-backed leather chairs were arranged on either side of a mahogany pedestal card table. They were near a tall, mullioned window flanked by thick drapes, which overlooked the Virginia countryside. This club-like room, known as the Library, was in an enormous stone house that the NSA had taken over decades ago. It was used as a retreat as well as for formal dinners for the generals and directors of the organization. Its lower depths, however, were used for other purposes.

When they had ordered drinks and light refreshments, and were alone again, LaValle said, "Do we have a line on Bourne yet?"

"Yes and no." Kendall crossed one leg over the other, arranging the crease in his trousers. "As per our previous briefing, he came onto the grid at six thirty-seven last night, passing through Immigration at Dulles. He was booked on a Lufthansa flight to Moscow. Had he showed we could've put McNally onto the flight."

"Bourne's far too clever for that," LaValle grumbled. "He knows we're after him now. The element of surprise has been neutralized, dammit."

"We managed to discover that he boarded a NextGen Energy Solutions corporate jet."

Like a hunting dog on alert, Lavalle's head came up. "Really? Explain."

"An executive by the name of Moira Trevor was on it."

"What is she to Bourne?"

"A question we're trying to answer," Kendall said unhappily. He hated disappointing his boss. "In the meantime, we obtained a copy of the flight plan. The destination was Munich. Shall I activate a point man there?"

"Don't waste your time." LaValle waved a hand. "My money's on Moscow. That's where he meant to go, that's where he's going."

"I'll get right on it." Kendall opened his cell phone.

"I want Anthony Prowess."

"He's in Afghanistan."

"Then pull him the fuck out," LaValle said shortly. "Get him on a military chopper. I want him on the ground in Moscow by the time Bourne gets there."

Kendall nodded, punched in a special encrypted number, and typed the coded text message to Prowess.

LaValle smiled at the approaching waiter. "Thank you, Willard," he said as the man snapped out a starched white tablecloth, arranged the glasses of whiskey, small plates of nibbles, and cutlery on the table, then departed as silently as he'd come.

LaValle stared at the food. "It seems we've backed the wrong horse."

General Kendall knew he meant Rob Batt. "Soraya Moore witnessed the debacle. She's put two and two together in short order. Batt told us he knew about Hart's meet with Bourne because he was in her office when Bourne's call came in. Other than the Moore woman, who else is she likely to have told? No one. That'll lead Hart right back to the deputy director."

"Hang him out to dry."

Picking up his glass, Kendall said. "Time for Plan B."

LaValle stared into the chestnut liquid. "I always thank God for Plan B, Richard. Always."

Their glasses clinked together. They drank in studied silence while LaValle ruminated. When, half an hour later, they'd drained their whiskeys and new ones were in their hands, LaValle said, "On the subject of Soraya Moore, I do believe it's time to bring her in for a chat."

"Private?"

"Oh, yes." LaValle added a dollop of water his whiskey, releasing its complex scent. "Bring her here."

Fifteen

T ELL ME about Jason Bourne."

Harun Iliev, in an American Nike jogging suit identical to the one worn by his commander, Semion Icoupov, rounded the turn of the natural ice-skating rink in the heart of Grindelwald village. Harun had spent more than a decade as Icoupov's second in command. As a boy he'd been adopted by Icoupov's father, Farid, after his parents had drowned when a ferry taking them from Istanbul to Odessa had capsized. Harun, at the age of four, was visiting his grandmother there. The news of the deaths of her daughter and son-in-law sent her into cardiac arrest. She died almost instantly—which everyone involved felt was a blessing, for she lacked both the strength and the stamina to care for a four-year-old. Farid Icoupov stepped in, because Harun's father had worked for him; the two were close.

"There's no easy answer," Harun said now, "principally because there's no one answer. Some swear he's an agent of the American CI, others claim he's an international assassin for hire. Clearly he can't be both. What is indisputable is that he was responsible for foiling the plot to gas the attendees of the International Anti-Terrorist Conference in

Reykjavik three years ago and, last year, the very real nuclear threat to Washington, DC, posed by Dujja, the terrorist group that was run by the two Wahhib brothers, Fadi and Karim al-Jamil. Rumor has it Bourne killed them both."

"Impressive, if true. But just the fact that no one can get a handle on him is of extreme interest." Icoupov's arms chugged up and down in perfect rhythm to his gliding back and forth. His cheeks were apple red and he smiled warmly at the children skating on either side of them, laughing when they laughed, giving encouragement when one of them fell. "And how did such a man get involved with Our Friend?"

"Through the university in Georgetown," Harun said. He was a slender man with the look of an accountant, which wasn't helped by his sallow skin and the way his olive-pit eyes were sunk deep in his skull. Ice-skating did not come naturally to him as it did to Icoupov. "Besides killing people, it seems Bourne is something of a genius at linguistics."

"Is he now?"

Even though they'd skated for more than forty minutes, Icoupov wasn't breathing hard. Harun knew he was just getting warmed up. They were in spectacular country. The resort of Grindelwald was just under a hundred miles southeast of Bern. Above them towered three of Switzerland's most famous mountains—Jungfrau, Mönch, and Eiger—glittering white with snow and ice.

"It seems that Bourne's weak spot is for a mentor. The first was a man named Alexander Conklin, who—"

"I knew Alex," Icoupov said curtly. "It was before your time. Another lifetime, it often seems." He nodded. "Please continue."

"It seems Our Friend has made a play to become his new mentor."

"I must interject here. That seems improbable."

"Then why did Bourne kill Mikhail Tarkanian?"

"Mischa." Icoupov's pace faltered for a moment. "Allah preserve us! Does Leonid Danilovich know?"

"Arkadin is currently out of contact."

"What's his progress?"

"He's come and gone from Sevastopol."

"That's something, anyway." Icoupov shook his head. "We're running out of time."

"Arkadin knows this."

"I want Tarkanian's death kept from him, Harun. Mischa was his best friend; they were closer than brothers. Under no circumstances can he be allowed to be distracted from his present assignment."

A lovely young woman held out her hand as she skated abreast of them. Icoupov took it and for a time was swept away in an ice dance that made him feel as if he were twenty again. When he returned, he resumed their skate around the rink. Something about the easy gliding motion of skating, he'd once told Harun, helped him to think.

"Given what you've told me," Icoupov said at length, "this Jason Bourne may very well cause an unforeseen complication."

"You can be sure Our Friend has recruited Bourne to his cause by telling him that you caused the death of—"

Icoupov shot him a warning look. "I agree. But the question we must answer is how much of the truth he's risked telling Bourne."

"Knowing Our Friend," Harun said, "I would say very little, if at all."

"Yes." Icoupov tapped a gloved forefinger against his lips. "And if this is the case we can use the truth against him, don't you think?"

"If we can get to Bourne," Harun said. "And if we can get him to believe us."

"Oh, he'll believe us. I'll make sure of that." Icoupov executed a perfect spin. "Your new assignment, Harun, is to ensure we get to him before he can do any more damage. We could ill afford to lose our eye in Our Friend's camp. Further deaths are unacceptable."

Munich was full of cold rain. It was a gray city on the best of days, but in this windswept downpour it seemed to hunker down. Like a turtle, it pulled in its head into its concrete shell, turning its back on all visitors.

Bourne and Moira sat inside the cavernous NextGen 747. Bourne was on his cell, making a reservation on the next flight to Moscow.

"I wish I could authorize the plane to take you," Moira said after he'd folded away the phone.

"No, you don't," Bourne said. "You'd like me to stay here by your side."

"I already told you why I think that would be a bad idea." She looked out at the wet tarmac, rainbow-streaked with droplets of fuel and oil. Raindrops trickled down the Perspex window like racing cars in their lanes. "And I find myself not wanting to be here at all."

Bourne opened the file he'd taken from Veronica Hart, turned it around, held it out. "I'd like you to take a look at this."

Moira turned back, put the file on her lap, paged through it. All at once she looked up. "Was it CI that had me under surveillance?" When Bourne nodded, she said, "Well, that's a relief."

"How is it a relief?"

She lifted the file. "This is all disinformation, a setup. Two years ago, when bidding for the Long Beach LNG terminal was at its height, my bosses suspected that AllEn, our chief rival, was monitoring our communications in order to get a handle on the proprietary systems that make our terminal unique. As a favor to me, Martin went to the Old Man for permission to set up a sting. The Old Man agreed, but it was imperative that no one else know about it, so he never told anyone else at CI. It worked. By tracking our cell conversations we discovered that AllEn was, indeed, monitoring the calls."

"I recall the settlement," Bourne said.

"Because of the evidence Martin and I provided, AllEn had no incentive to go to trial."

"NextGen got a mid-eight-figure settlement, right?"

Moira nodded. "And won the rights to build the LNG terminal in Long Beach. That's how I got my promotion to executive vice president."

Bourne took back the file. He, too, was relieved. For him, trust was like an ill-made boat, springing leaks at every turn, threatening at any moment to sink him. He'd ceded part of himself to Moira, but the loss of control was like a knife in his heart.

Moira looked at him rather sadly. "Did you suspect me of being a Mata Hari?"

"It was important to make sure," he said.

Her face closed up. "Sure. I understand." She began to stuff papers into a slim leather briefcase more roughly than was needed. "You thought I'd betrayed Martin and was going to betray you."

"I'm relieved it's not true."

"I'm so very happy to hear that." She shot him an acid stare.

"Moira . . ."

"What?" She pulled hair off her face. "What is it you want to say to me, Jason?"

"I . . . This is hard for me."

She leaned forward, peering at him. "Just tell me."

"I trusted Marie," Bourne said. "I leaned on her, she helped me with my amnesia. She was always there. And then, suddenly, she wasn't."

Moira's voice softened. "I know."

He looked at her at last. "There is no good thing about being alone. But for me it's all a matter of trust."

"I know you think I haven't told you the truth about Martin and me." She took his hands in hers. "We were never lovers, Jason. We were more like brother and sister. We supported each other. Trust didn't come easily to either of us. I think it's important for both of us that I tell you that now."

Bourne understood that she was also talking about the two of them, not her and Martin. He'd trusted so few people in his life: Marie, Alex Conklin, Mo Panov, Martin, Soraya. He saw all the things that had been keeping him from moving on with his life. With so little past, it was difficult letting go of the people he'd known and cared about.

A pang of sorrow shot through him. "Marie is dead. She's in the past now. And my children are far better off with their grandparents. Their life is stable and happy. That's best for them."

He rose, needing to get moving.

Moira, aware he was ill at ease, changed the subject. "Do you know how long you'll be in Moscow?"

"The same amount of time you'll be in Munich, I imagine."

That got a smile out of her. She stood, leaned toward him. "Be well, Jason. Stay safe." She gave him a lingering, loving kiss. "Remember me."

Sixteen

SORAYA MOORE was ushered cordially into the hushed sanctuary of the Library where less than twenty-four hours before, Luther LaValle and General Kendall had had their post-rendition fireside chat. It was Kendall himself who had picked her up, chauffeured her to the NSA safe house deep in the Virginia countryside. Soraya had, of course, never been here.

LaValle, in a midnight-blue chalk-striped suit, blue shirt with white collar and cuffs, a striped tie in the Yale colors, looked like a merchant banker. He rose as Kendall brought her over to the area by the window. There were three chairs grouped around the antique card table.

"Director Moore, having heard so much about you, it's a genuine pleasure to meet you." Smiling broadly, LaValle indicated a chair. "Please."

Soraya saw no point in refusing the invitation. She didn't know whether she was more curious or alarmed by the abrupt summons. She did, however, glance around the room. "Where is Secretary Halliday? General Kendall informed me that the invitation came from him."

"Oh, it did," LaValle said. "Unfortunately, the secretary of defense was called into a meeting in the Oval Office. He phoned me to convey to you his apologies and to insist that we carry on without him."

All of which meant, Soraya knew, that Halliday had never had any intention of attending this little tête-à-tête. She doubted he even knew about it.

"Anyway," LaValle said as Kendall sat in the third chair, "now that you're here you might as well enjoy yourself." He raised his hand, and Willard appeared as if by prestidigitation. "Something to drink, Director? I know as Muslim you're forbidden alcohol, but we have a full range of potions for you to choose from."

"Tea, please," she said directly to Willard. "Ceylon, if you have it."

"Of course, ma'am. Milk? Sugar?"

"Neither, thank you." She'd never formed the British habit.

Willard seemed to bow before he vanished without a sound.

Soraya redirected her attention to the two men. "Now, gentlemen, in what way can I help you?"

"I rather think it's the other way around," General Kendall said.

Soraya cocked her head. "How d'you figure that?"

"Frankly, because of the turmoil at CI," LaValle said, "we think Typhon is working with one hand tied behind its back."

Willard arrived with Soraya's tea, the men's whiskeys. He set the japanned tray down with the cup, glasses, and tea service, then left.

LaValle waited until Soraya had poured her tea before he continued. "It seems to me that Typhon would benefit immensely from taking advantage of all the resources at NSA's disposal. We could even help you expand beyond the scope of CI's reach."

Soraya lifted her cup to her lips, found the fragrant Ceylon tea exquisitely delicious. "It seems that you know more about Typhon than any of us at CI were aware."

LaValle let go with a soft laugh. "Okay, let's stop beating around the bush. We had a mole inside CI. You know who it is now. He made a fatal mistake in going after Jason Bourne and failing."

Veronica Hart had relieved Rob Batt of his position that morning, a fact that must have come to LaValle's attention, especially since his

replacement, Peter Marks, had been one of Hart's most vocal support-
ers from day one. Soraya knew Peter well, had suggested to Hart that
he deserved the promotion.

"Is Batt now working for NSA?"

"Mr. Batt has outlived his usefulness," Kendall said rather stiffly.

Soraya turned her attention to the military man. "A glimpse of your
own fate, don't you think, General?"

Kendall's face closed up like a fist, but following an almost imperceptible shake of LaValle's head he bit back a rejoinder.

"While it's certainly true that life in the intelligence services can be
harsh, even brutal," LaValle interjected, "certain individuals within it
are—shall we say—inoculated against such unfortunate eventualities."

Soraya kept her gaze on Kendall. "I suppose I could be one of those
certain individuals."

"Yes, absolutely." LaValle put one hand over the other on his knee.
"Your knowledge of Muslim thought and custom, your expertise
as Martin Lindros's right hand as he put Typhon together are invaluable."

"You see how it is, General," Soraya said. "One day an invaluable
asset like me is bound to take over your position."

LaValle cleared his throat. "Does that mean you're on board?"

Smiling sweetly, Soraya put her teacup down. "I'll say this for you,
Mr. LaValle, you certainly know how to make lemonade from lemons."

LaValle returned her smile as if it were a tennis serve. "My dear
Director, I do believe you've hit upon one of my specialities."

"What makes you think I'd abandon CI?"

LaValle put a forefinger beside his nose. "My reading of you is that
you're a pragmatic woman. You know better than we do what kind of a
mess CI is in. How long do you think it's going to take the new DCI to
right the ship? What makes you think she even can?" He raised his
finger. "I'm exceedingly interested in your opinion, but before you answer think about how little time we might have before this unknown
terrorist group is going to strike."

Soraya felt as if she'd been rabbit-punched. How in the hell had

NSA gotten wind of the Typhon terrorist intercepts? At the moment, however, that was a moot point. The important thing was how to respond to this breach of security.

Before she could formulate a counter, LaValle said, "I'm curious about one thing, though. Why is it that Director Hart saw fit to keep this intel to herself, rather than bringing in Homeland Security, FBI, and NSA?"

"That was my doing." *I'm in it now*, Soraya thought. *I might as well go all the way.* "Until the incident at the Freer, the intel was sketchy enough that I felt the involvement of other intelligence agencies would only muddy the waters."

"Meaning," Kendall said, glad of the opportunity to get in a dig, "you didn't want us rooting around in your carrot patch."

"This is a serious situation, Director," LaValle said. "In matters of national security—"

"If this Muslim terrorist group—which we now know calls itself the Black Legion—gets wind that we've intercepted their communications we'll be sunk before we even start trying to counter their attack."

"I could have you shit-canned."

"And lose my invaluable expertise?" Soraya shook her head. "I don't think so."

"So what do we have?" Kendall snapped.

"Stalemate." LaValle passed a hand across his brow. "Do you think it would be possible for me to see the Typhon intercepts?" His tone had changed completely. He was now in conciliatory mode. "Believe it or not, we're not the Evil Empire. We actually might be able to be of some assistance."

Soraya considered. "I think that be can arranged."

"Excellent."

"It would have to be Eyes Only."

LaValle agreed at once.

"And in a controlled, highly restricted environment," Soraya added, following up her advantage. "The Typhon offices at CI would be perfect."

LaValle spread his hands. "Why not here?"

Soraya smiled. "I think not."

"Under the current climate I think you can understand why I'd be reluctant to meet you there."

"I take your point." Soraya thought for a moment. "If I did bring the intercepts here I'd have to have someone with me."

LaValle nodded vigorously. "Of course. Whatever makes you feel comfortable." He seemed far more pleased than Kendall, who looked at her as if he had caught sight of her from a battlefield trench.

"Frankly," Soraya said, "none of this makes me feel comfortable." She glanced around the room again.

"The building is swept three times a day for electronic bugs," La-Valle pointed out. "Plus, we have all the most sophisticated surveillance systems, basically a computerized monitoring system that keeps track of the two thousand closed-circuit video cameras installed throughout the facility and grounds, compares them from second to second for any anomalies whatsoever. The DARPA software compares any anomalies against a database of more than a million images, makes real-time decisions in nanoseconds. For instance, a bird in flight would be ignored, a running figure wouldn't. Believe me, you have nothing to worry about."

"Right now, the only thing I worry about," Soraya said, "is you, Mr. LaValle."

"I understand completely." LaValle finished off his whiskey. "That's what this exercise is all about, Director. To engender trust between us. How else could we be expected to work together?"

General Kendall sent Soraya back to the district with one of his drivers. She had him drop her where she'd arranged to meet Kendall, outside what had once been the National Historical Wax Museum on E Street, SW. She waited until the black Ford had been swallowed up in traffic, then she turned away, walked all the way around the block at a normal pace. By the end of her circuit she was certain she was free of tags, NSA or otherwise. At that point, she sent a three-letter text mes-

sage via her cell. Two minutes later, a young man on a motorcycle appeared. He wore jeans, a black leather jacket, a gleaming black helmet
with the smoked faceplate lowered. He slowed, stopped just long
enough for her to climb on behind him. Handing her a helmet, he
waited for her to don it, then he zoomed off down the street.

I have several contacts within DARPA," Deron said. DARPA was an
acronym for the Defense Advanced Research Projects Agency, an arm
of the Department of Defense. "I have a working knowledge of the
software architecture at the heart of the NSA's surveillance system." He
shrugged. "This is one way I keep my edge."

"We gotta find a way around it or through it," Tyrone said.

He was still wearing his black leather jacket. His black helmet was
on a table alongside the one he'd given Soraya for the high-speed trip
here to Deron's house-lab. Soraya had met both Deron and Tyrone
when Bourne had brought her to this nondescript olive-colored house
just off 7th Street, NE.

"You must be joking, right?" Deron, a tall, slim, handsome man with
skin the color of light cocoa, looked from one to the other. "Tell me you're
joking."

"If we were joking we wouldn't be here." Soraya rubbed the heel of
her hand against her temple as she sought to ignore the fierce headache
that had began after her terrifying interview with LaValle and Kendall.

"It's just not possible." Deron put his hands on his hips. "That software is state-of-the-art. And two thousand CCTV cameras! Fuck me."

They sat on canvas chairs in his lab, a double-height room filled with
all manner of monitors, keyboards, electronic systems whose functions
were known only to Deron. Ranged around the wall were a number of
paintings—all masterpieces by Titian, Seurat, Rembrandt, van Gogh.
Water Lilies, Green Reflection, Left Part was Soraya's favorite. That all of
them were painted by Deron in the atelier in the next room had stunned
her the first time she was here. Now they simply filled her with wonder.
How he had reproduced Monet's exact shade of cobalt blue was beyond

her. It was hardly surprising that Bourne used Deron to forge all his ID documents, when in this day and age it was becoming increasingly difficult to do. Many forgers had quit, claiming governments had made their job impossible, but not Deron. It was his stock in trade. Little wonder that he and Bourne were so close. Birds of a feather, Soraya thought.

"What about mirrors?" Tyrone said.

"That would be simplest," Deron said. "But one of the reasons they've installed so many cameras is to give the system multiple views of the same area. That negates mirrors right there."

"Too bad Bourne killed dat fucker Karim al-Jamil. He could probably write a worm t'screw with the DARPA software like he did with the CI database."

Soraya turned to Deron. "Can it be done?" she said. "Could you do it?"

"Hacking's not my thing. I leave that to my old lady."

Soraya didn't know Deron had a girlfriend. "How good is she?"

"Please," Deron snorted.

"Can we talk to her?"

Deron looked dubious. "This is the NSA we're talking about. Those fuckers don't fool around. To be frank, I don't think you ought to be messing with them in the first place."

"Unfortunately, I have no choice," Soraya said.

"They fuckin' wid us," Tyrone said, "and unless we get all medieval on they ass, they gonna walk all over us an' own us forever."

Deron shook his head. "You sure put some interesting notions in this man's head, Soraya. Before you came along he was the best street protection I ever had. Now look at him. Messing with the big boys in the bad world outside the ghetto." He didn't hide the pride he felt for Tyrone, but his voice held a warning, too. "I hope to hell you know what you're getting yourself into, Tyrone. If this thing comes apart in any way you're in the federal slammer till Gabriel comes calling."

Tyrone crossed his arms over his chest, stood his ground.

Deron sighed. "All right, then. We're all adults here." He reached for his cell. "Kiki's upstairs in her lair. She doesn't like to be interrupted, but in this case I think she'll be intrigued." He spoke briefly into the cell, then put it down. Moments later a slim woman with a beautiful African face and deep chocolate skin appeared. She was as tall as Deron, with the upright carriage of proud and ancient royalty.

Her face split into a ferocious grin when she saw Tyrone. "Hey," they said to each other. That one word seemed all that was needed.

"Kiki, this is Soraya," Deron said.

Kiki's smile was wide and dazzling. "My name's actually Esiankiki. I'm Masai. But in America I'm not so formal; everyone calls me Kiki."

The two women touched hands. Kiki's grip was cool and dry. She regarded Soraya out of large coffee-colored eyes. She had the smoothest skin Soraya had ever seen, which she instantly envied. Her hair was very short, marvelously cut like a cap to fit her elongated skull. She wore a brown ankle-length dress that clung provocatively to her slim hips and small breasts.

Deron briefly outlined the problem while he brought up the DARPA software architecture on one of his computer terminals. While Kiki checked it out, he filled her in on the basics. "We need something that can bypass the firewall, and is undetectable."

"The first isn't all that difficult." Kiki's long, delicate fingers were flying over the keyboard as she experimented with the computer code. "The second, I don't know."

"Unfortunately, that's not the end of it." Deron positioned himself so he could peer over her shoulder at the terminal. "This particular software controls two thousand CCTV cameras. Our friends here need to get in and out of the facility without being detected."

Kiki stood up, turned around to face them. "In other words all two thousand cameras have to be covered."

"That's right," Soraya said.

"You don't need a hacker, dear. You need the invisible man."

"But you can make them invisible, Kiki." Deron slid his arm around her slender waist "Can't you?"

"Hmm." Kiki peered again at the code on the terminal. "You know, there looks like there may be a recurring variance I might be able to exploit." She hunkered down on a stool. "I'm going to transfer this upstairs."

Deron winked at Soraya, as if to say, *I told you so*.

Kiki routed a number of files to her computer, which was separate from Deron's. She spun around, slapped her hands on her thighs, and got up. "Okay, then, I'll see you all later."

"How much later?" Soraya said, but Kiki was already taking the stairs three at a time.

Moscow was wreathed in snow when Bourne stepped off the Aeroflot plane at Sheremetyevo. His flight had been delayed forty minutes, the jet circling while the runways were de-iced. He cleared Customs and Immigration and was met by a small, cat-like individual wrapped in a white down coat. Lev Baronov, Professor Specter's contact.

"No luggage, I see," Baronov said in heavily accented English. He was as wiry and hyperactive as a Jack Russell terrier as he elbowed and barked at the small army of gypsy cab drivers vying for a fare. They were a sad-faced lot, plucked from the minorities in the Caucasus, Asians and the like whose ethnicity prevented them from getting a decent job with decent pay in Moscow. "We'll take care of that on the way in to town. You'll need proper clothes for Moscow's winter. It's a balmy minus two Celsius today."

"That would be most helpful," Bourne replied in perfect Russian.

Baronov's bushy eyebrows rose in surprise. "You speak like a native, *gospadin* Bourne."

"I had excellent instructors," Bourne said laconically.

Amid the bustle of the flight terminal, he was studying the flow of passengers, noting those who lingered at a newsagent or outside the duty-free shop, those who didn't move at all. Ever since he emerged into the terminal he'd had the unshakable feeling that he was being watched. Of course there were CCTV cameras all over, but the particular prickling of his scalp that had developed over the years of fieldwork was unerring. Someone had him under surveillance. This fact was both alarming and reassuring—that he'd already picked up a tag meant someone knew he was scheduled to arrive in Moscow. NSA could have scanned the departing flight manifests back at New York and picked up his name from Lufthansa; there'd been no time to take himself off the list. He looked only in short touristic glances because he had no desire to alert his shadow that he was on to him.

"I'm being followed," Bourne said as he sat in Baronov's wheezing Zil. They were on the M10 motorway.

"No problem," Baronov said, as if he was used to being tailed all the time. He didn't even ask who was following Bourne. Bourne thought of the professor's pledge that Baronov wouldn't get in his way.

Bourne paged through the packet Baronov had given him, which included new ID, a key, and the box number to get money out of the safe-deposit vault in the Moskva Bank.

"I need a plan of the bank building," Bourne said.

"No problem." Baronov exited the M10. Bourne was now Fyodor Ilianovich Popov, a midlevel functionary of GazProm, the gargantuan state-run energy conglomerate.

"How well will this ID hold up?" Bourne asked.

"Not to worry." Baronov grinned. "The professor has friends in Gaz-Prom who know how to protect you, Fyodor Ilianovich Popov."

Anthony Prowess had come a long way to keep the ancient Zil in sight and he wasn't about to lose it, no matter what evasive maneuvers the driver took. He'd been waiting at Sheremetyevo for Bourne to come through Immigration. General Kendall had sent a recent surveillance photo of Bourne to his cell. The photo was grainy and two-dimensional because of the long telephoto lens used, but it was a close-up; there was no mistaking Bourne when he arrived.

For Prowess, the next few minutes were crucial. He had no illusions that he could remain unnoticed by Bourne for any length of time; therefore, in the short moments while his subject was still unself-conscious, he needed to drink in every tic and habit, no matter how minuscule or seemingly irrelevant. He knew from bitter experience that these small insights would prove invaluable as the surveillance ground on, especially when it came time to engage the subject and terminate him.

Prowess was no stranger to Moscow. He'd been born here to a British diplomat and his cultural attaché wife. Not until Prowess was fifteen did he understand that his mother's job was a cover. She was, in fact, a spy for MI6, Her Majesty's Secret Service. Four years later Prowess's mother was compromised, and MI6 spirited them out of the country. Because his mother was now a wanted woman, the Prowesses were sent to America, to begin a new life with a new family name. The danger had been ground so deeply into Prowess that he'd actually forgotten what they were once called. He was now simply Anthony Prowess.

As soon as he'd built up qualified academic credits, he applied to the NSA. From the moment he'd discovered that his mother was a spy, that was all he'd wanted to do. No amount of pleading from his parents could dissuade him. Because of his ease with foreign languages and his knowledge of other cultures, the NSA sent him abroad, first to the Horn of Africa to train, then to Afghanistan, where he liaised with the local tribes fighting the Taliban in rough mountain terrain. He was a hard man, no stranger to hardship, or to death. He knew more ways to kill a human being than there were days in the year. Compared with what he'd been through in the past nineteen months, this assignment was going to be a piece of cake.

Seventeen

BOURNE AND BARONOV sped down Volokolamskoye Highway. Crocus City was an enormous high-end mall. Built in 2002, it was a seemingly endless array of glittering boutiques, restaurants, car showrooms, and marble fountains. It was also an excellent place to lose a tail.

While Bourne shopped for suitable clothes, Baronov was busy on his cell phone. There was no point in going to the trouble of losing the tail inside the maze of the mall only to have him pick them up again when they returned to the Zil. Baronov was calling a colleague to come to Crocus City. They'd take his car, and he'd drive the Zil into Moscow.

Bourne paid for his purchases and changed into them. Baronov took him to the Franck Muller Café inside the mall, where they had coffee and sandwiches.

"Tell me about Pyotr's last girlfriend," Bourne said.

"Gala Nematova?" Baronov shrugged. "Not much to tell, really. She's just another one of those pretty girls one sees around all the latest Moscow nightclubs. These women are a ruble a dozen."

"Where would I find her?"

Baronov shrugged. "She'll go where the oligarchs cluster. Really, your guess is as good as mine." He laughed good-naturedly. "For myself, I'm too old for places like that, but I'll be glad to take you on a round-robin tonight."

"All I need is for you to lend me a car."

"Suit yourself, *miya droog*."

A few moments later, Baronov went to the men's room, where he'd agreed to make the switch of car keys with his friend. When he returned he handed Bourne a folded piece of paper on which was the plan for the Moskva Bank building.

They went out a different direction from the way they'd come in, which led them to a parking lot on the other side of the mall. They got into a vintage black Volga four-door sedan that, to Bourne's relief, started up immediately.

"You see? No problem." Baronov laughed jovially. "What would you do without me, *gospadin* Bourne?"

The Frunzenskaya embankment was located southwest of Moscow's inner Garden Ring. Mikhail Tarkanian had said that he could see the pedestrian bridge to Gorky Park from his living room window. He hadn't lied. His apartment was in a building not far from Khlastekov, a restaurant serving excellent Russian food, according to Baronov. With its two-story, square-columned portico and decorative concrete balconies, the building itself was a prime example of the Stalinist Empire style that raped and beat into submission a more pastoral and romantic architectural past.

Bourne instructed Baronov to stay in the Volga until he returned. He went up the stone steps, under the colonnade, and through the glass door. He was in a small vestibule that ended in an inner door, which was locked. On the right wall was a brass panel with rows of bell pushes corresponding to the apartments. Bourne ran his finger down the rows until he found the push with Tarkanian's name. Noting the apartment number, he crossed to the inner door and used a small flexible blade to fool the lock's tumblers into thinking he had a key. The door clicked open, and he went inside.

There was a small arthritic elevator on the left wall. To the right, a rather grand staircase swept up to the first floor. The first three treads were in marble, but these gave way to simple concrete steps that released a kind of talcum-like powder as the porous treads wore away.

Tarkanian's apartment was on the third floor, down a dark corridor, dank with the odors of boiled cabbage and stewed meat. The floor was composed of tiny hexagonal tiles, chipped and worn as the steps leading up.

Bourne found the door without trouble. He put his ear against it, listening for sounds within the apartment. When he heard none, he picked the lock. Turning the glass knob slowly, he pushed open the door a crack. Weak light filtered in past half-drawn curtains framing windows on the right. Behind the smell of disuse was a whiff of a masculine scent—cologne or hair cream. Tarkanian had made it clear he hadn't been back here in years, so who was using his apartment?

Bourne moved silently, cautiously through the rooms. Where he'd expected to find dust, there was none; where he expected the furniture to be covered in sheets, it wasn't. There was food in the refrigerator, though the bread on the counter was growing mold. Still, within the week, someone had been living here. The knobs to all the doors were glass, just like the one on the front door, and some looked wobbly on their brass shafts. There were photos on the wall: high-toned black-and-whites of Gorky Park in different seasons.

Tarkanian's bed was unmade. The covers lay pulled back in unruly waves, as if someone had been startled out of sleep or had made a hasty exit. On the other side of the bed, the door to the bathroom was half closed.

As Bourne stepped around the end of the bed, he noticed a five-by-seven framed photo of a young woman, blond, with a veneer of beauty cultivated by models the world over. He was wondering whether this was Gala Nematova when he caught a blurred movement out of the corner of his eye.

A man hidden behind the bathroom door made a run at Bourne. He was armed with a thick-bladed fisherman's knife, which he jabbed at Bourne point-first. Bourne rolled away, the man followed. He was blue-eyed, blond, and big. There were tattoos on the sides of his neck and the palms of his hands. Mementos of a Russian prison.

The best way to neutralize a knife was to close with your opponent. As the man lunged after him, Bourne turned, grabbed the man by his shirt, slammed his forehead into the bridge of the man's nose. Blood spurted, the man grunted, cursed in guttural Russian, *"Blyad!"*

He drove a fist into Bourne's side, tried to free his hand with the knife. Bourne applied a nerve block at the base of the thumb. The Russian butted Bourne in the sternum, drove him back off the bed, into the half-open bathroom door. The glass knob drilled into Bourne's spine, causing him to arch back. The door swung fully open and he sprawled on the cold tiles. The Russian, regaining use of his hand, pulled out a Stechkin APS 9mm. Bourne kicked him in the shin, so he went down on one knee, then struck him on the side of the face, and the Stechkin went flying across the tiles. The Russian launched a flurry of punches and hand strikes that battered Bourne back against the door before grabbing the Stechkin. Bourne reached up, felt the cool octagon of the glass doorknob. Grinning, the Russian aimed the pistol at Bourne's heart. Wrenching off the knob, Bourne threw it at the center of the Russian's forehead, where it struck full-on. His eyes rolled up and he slumped to the floor.

Bourne gathered up the Stechkin and took a moment to catch his breath. Then he crawled over to the Russian. Of course, he had no conventional ID on him, but that didn't mean Bourne couldn't find out where he'd come from.

Stripping off the big man's jacket and shirt, Bourne took a long look at a constellation of tattoos. On his chest was a tiger, a sign of an enforcer. On his left shoulder was a dagger dripping blood, a sign that he was a killer. But it was the third symbol, a genie emerging from a Middle Eastern lamp, that interested Bourne the most. This was a sign that the Russian had been put in prison for drug-related crimes.

The professor had told Bourne that two of the Russian Mafia families, the Kazanskaya and the Azeri, were vying for sole control of the drug market. *Don't get in their way*, Specter had warned. *If they have any contact with you, I beg you not to engage them. Instead, turn the other cheek. It's the only way to survive there.*

Bourne was about to get up when he saw something on the inside of the Russian's left elbow: a small tattoo of a figure with a man's body and a jackal's head. Anubis, Egyptian god of the underworld. This symbol was supposed to protect the wearer from death, but it had also latterly been appropriated by the Kazanskaya. What was a member of such a powerful Russian *grupperovka* family doing in Tarkanian's apartment? He'd been sent to find him and kill him. Why? That was something Bourne needed to find out.

He looked around the bathroom at the sink with its dripping faucet, pots of eye cream and powder, makeup pencils, the stained mirror. He pulled back the shower curtain, plucked several blond hairs from the drain. They were long; from a woman's head. Gala Nematova's head?

He made his way to the kitchen, opened drawers, pawed through them until he found a blue ballpoint pen. Back in the bathroom, he took one of the eyeliner pencils. Crouching down beside the Russian, he drew a facsimile of the Anubis tattoo on the inside of his left elbow; when he got a line wrong, he rubbed it off. When he was satisfied, he used the blue ballpoint pen to make the final "tattoo." He knew it wouldn't withstand a close inspection, but for a flash of identification he thought it would suffice. At the sink, he delicately rinsed off the makeup pencil, then shot some hair spray over the ink outline to further fix it on his skin.

He checked behind the toilet tank and in it, favorite hiding places for money, documents, or important materials, but found nothing. He was about to leave when his eyes fell again on the mirror. Peering more closely, he could see a trace of red here and there. Lipstick, which had been carefully wiped off, as if someone—possibly the Kazanskaya Russian—had sought to erase it. Why would he do that?

It seemed to Bourne the smears formed a kind of pattern. Taking up a pot of face powder, he blew across the top of it. The petroleum-based powder sought its twin, clung to the ghost image of the petroleum-based lipstick.

When he was done, he put the pot down, took a step backward. He was looking at a scrawled note:

Off to the Kitaysky Lyotchik. Where R U? Gala.

So Gala Nematova, Pyotr's last girlfriend, did live here. Had Pyotr used this apartment while Tarkanian was away?

On his way out, he checked the Russian's pulse. It was slow but steady. The question of why the Kazanskaya sent this prison-hardened assassin to an apartment where Gala Nematova had once lived with Pyotr loomed large in his mind. Was there a connection between Semion Icoupov and the *grupperovka* family?

Taking another long look at Gala Nematova's photo, Bourne slipped out of the apartment as silently as he'd entered it. Out in the hallway he listened for human sounds, but apart from the muted wailing of a baby in an apartment on the second floor, all was still. He descended the stairs and went through the vestibule, where a little girl holding her mother's hand was trying to drag her upstairs. Bourne and the mother exchanged the meaningless smiles of strangers passing each other. Then Bourne was outside, emerging from under the colonnade. Save for an old woman gingerly picking her way through the treacherous snow, no one was about. He slipped into the passenger's seat of the Volga and shut the door behind him.

That was when he saw the blood leaking from Baronov's throat. At the same instant a wire whipped around his neck, digging into his windpipe.

Four times a week after work, Rodney Feir, chief of field support for CI, worked out at a health club a short walk from his house in Fairfax,

Virginia. He spent an hour on the treadmill, another hour weight training, then took a cold shower and headed for the steam room.

This evening General Kendall was waiting for him. Kendall dimly
saw the glass door open, cold air briefly sucked in as tendrils of steam
escaped into the men's locker room. Then Feir's trim, athletic body appeared through the mist.

"Good to see you, Rodney," General Kendall said.

Feir nodded silently, sat down beside Kendall.

Rodney Feir was Plan B, the backup the general had put in place
in the event the plan involving Rob Batt blew up. In fact, Feir had been
easier to land than Batt. Feir was someone who'd drifted into security
work not for any patriotic reason, not because he liked the clandestine
life. He was simply lazy. Not that he didn't do his job, not that he didn't
do it damn well. It was just that government life suited him down to his
black wing-tip shoes. The key fact to remember about him was that
whatever Feir did, he did because it would benefit him. He was, in fact,
an opportunist. He, more than any of the others at CI, could see the
writing on the wall, which is why his conversion to the NSA cause had
been so easy and seamless. With the death of the Old Man, the end of
days had arrived. He had none of Batt's loyalty to contend with.

Still, it didn't do to take anyone for granted, which is why Kendall
met him here occasionally. They would take a steam, then shower, climb
into their civvies, and go to dinner at one of several grungy barbecue
joints Kendall knew in the southeast section of the district.

These places were no more than shacks. They were mainly the pit
out back, where the pitmaster lovingly smoked his cuts of meat—ribs,
brisket, burnt ends, sweet and hot sausages, sometimes a whole hog—
for hours on end. The old, scarred wooden picnic tables, topped with
four or five sauces of varying ingredients and heat, were a kind of after-
thought. Most folk had their meat wrapped up to take out. Not Kendall
and Feir. They sat at a table, eating and drinking beer, while the bones
piled up along with the wadded-up napkins and the slices of white bread
so soft, they disintegrated under a few drops of sauce.

Now and again Feir stopped eating to impart to Kendall some bit of fact or scuttlebutt currently going around the CI offices. Kendall noted these with his steel-trap military mind, occasionally asking questions to help Feir clarify or amplify a point, especially when it came to the movements of Veronica Hart and Soraya Moore.

Afterward, they drove to an old abandoned library for the main event. The Renaissance-style building had been bought at fire sale prices by Drew Davis, a local businessman familiar in SE but otherwise unknown within the district, which was precisely how he liked it. He was one of those people savvy enough to fly under the Metro police radar. Not so simple a matter in SE, because like almost everyone else who lived there he was black. Unlike most of those around him, he had friends in high places. This was mainly due to the place he ran, The Glass Slipper.

To all intents and purposes it was a legit music club, and an extremely successful one to boot, attracting many big-name R&B acts. But in the back was the real business: a high-end cathouse that specialized in women of color. To those in the know, any flavor of color, which in this case meant ethnicity, could be procured at The Glass Slipper. Rates were steep but nobody seemed to mind, partly because Drew Davis paid his girls well.

Kendall had frequented this cathouse since his senior year in college. He'd come with a bunch of well-connected buddies one night as a hoot. Didn't want to but they'd dared him, and he knew how much he'd be ridiculed if he failed to take them up on it. Ironically he stayed, over the years having developed a taste for, as he put it, walking on the wild side. At first he told himself that the attraction was purely physical. Then he realized he liked being there; no one bothered him, no one made fun of him. Later, his continued interest was a reaction to his role as outsider when it came to working with the power junkies like Luther LaValle. Christ, even the fallen Ron Batt had been a member of Skull & Bones at Yale. *Well, The Glass Slipper is my Skull & Bones*, Kendall thought as he was ushered into the back room. This was as clandestine, as outré as things got inside the Beltway. It was Kendall's own little hideaway, a life that was his alone. Not even Luther knew about The Glass Slipper. It felt good to have a secret from LaValle.

Kendall and Feir sat in purple velvet chairs—the color of royalty, as Kendall pointed out—and were treated to a soft parade of women of all sizes and colors. Kendall chose Imani, one of his favorites, Feir a dusky-skinned Eurasian woman who was part Indian.

They retired to spacious rooms, furnished like bedrooms in European villas, with four-poster beds, tons of chintz, velvet, swags, drapes. There Kendall watched as, in one astonishing shimmy, Imani slid out of her chocolate silk spaghetti-strap dress. She wore nothing underneath. The lamplight burnished her dark skin.

Then she opened her arms and, with a deep-felt groan, General Richard P. Kendall melted into the sinuous river of her flawless body.

The moment Bourne felt his air supply cut off, he levered himself up off the front bench seat, arching his back so that he could put first one foot, then the other on the dashboard. Using his legs, he launched himself diagonally into the backseat, so that he landed right behind the ill-fated Baronov. The strangler was forced to turn to his right in order to keep the wire around Bourne's throat. This was an awkward position for him; he now lacked the leverage he had when Bourne was directly in front of him.

Bourne planted the heel of his shoe in the strangler's groin and ground down as hard as he could, but his strength was depleted from the lack of oxygen.

"Die, fucker," the strangler said in a hard-edged Midwestern accent.

White lights danced in his vision, and a blackness was seeping up all around him. It was as if he were looking down a tunnel through the wrong end of a telescope. Nothing looked real; his sense of perspective was skewed. He could see the man, his dark hair, his cruel face, the unmistakable hundred-mile stare of the American soldier in combat. In the back of his mind, he knew the NSA had found him.

Bourne's lapse of concentration allowed the strangler to free himself, jerk the ends of the wire so that it dug deeper into Bourne's throat. Bourne's windpipe was totally cut off. Blood was running down into his collar as the wire bit through his skin. Strange animal noises bubbled up from deep inside him. He blinked away tears and sweat, used his last ounce of strength to jam his thumb into the agent's eye. Keeping up the pressure despite blows to his midsection gained him a temporary respite: The wire slackened. He gasped in a railing breath, and dug deeper with his thumb.

The wire slackened further. He heard the car door open. The strangler's face wrenched away from him, and the car door slammed shut. He heard running feet, dying away. By the time he managed to unwind the wire, to cough and gasp air into his burning lungs, the street was empty. The NSA agent was gone.

Bourne was alone in the Volga with the corpse of Lev Baronov, dizzy, weak, and sick at heart.

Eighteen

I CAN'T SIMPLY contact Haydar," Devra said. "After what happened in Sevastopol they'll know you'll be going after him."

"That being the case," Arkadin said, "the document is long gone."

"Not necessarily." Devra stirred her Turkish coffee, thick as tar. "They chose this backwater because it's so inaccessible. But that works both ways. Chances are Haydar hasn't yet been able to pass the document along."

They were sitting in a tiny dust-blown café in Eskişehir. Even for Turkey this was a backward place, filled with sheep, the smells of pine, dung, and urine, and not much else. A chill wind blew across the mountain pass. There was snow on the north side of the buildings that made up the village, and judging by the lowering clouds more was on its way.

"*Godforsaken* is too good a word for this hellhole," Arkadin said. "For shit's sake, there isn't even a cell phone signal."

"That's funny coming from you." Devra downed her coffee. "You were born in a shithole, weren't you."

Arkadin felt an almost uncontrollable urge to drag her around the back of the rickety structure and beat her. But he held his hand and his rage, husbanding them both for another day when he would gaze down at her as if from a hundred miles away, whisper into her ear, *I have no regard for you. To me, your life is without meaning. If you have any hope of staying alive even a little longer, you'll never again ask where I was born, who my parents were, anything of a personal nature whatsoever.*

As it turned out, among her other talents Marlene was an accomplished hypnotist. She told him she wanted to hypnotize him in order to get at the root of his rage.

"I've heard there are people who can't be hypnotized," Arkadin said. "Is that right?"

"Yes," Marlene said.

It turned out he was one of them.

"You simply will not take suggestion," she said. "Your mind has put up a wall it's impossible to penetrate."

They were sitting in the garden behind Semion Icoupov's villa. Owing to the steep lay of the land it was the size of a postage stamp. They sat on a stone bench beneath the shade afforded by a fig tree, whose dark, soon-to-be-luscious fruit was just beginning to curl the branches downward to the stony earth.

"Well," Arkadin said, "what are we to do?"

"The question is what are *you* going to do, Leonid." She brushed a fragment of leaf off her thigh. She was wearing American designer jeans, an open-necked shirt, sandals on her feet. "The process of examining your past is designed to help you regain control over yourself."

"You mean my homicidal tendencies," he said.

"Why would you choose to say it that way, Leonid?"

He looked deeply into her eyes. "Because it's the truth."

Marlene's eyes grew dark. "Then why are you so reluctant to talk to me about the things I feel will help you?"

"You just want to worm your way inside my head. You think if you know everything about me you can control me."

"You're wrong. This isn't about control, Leonid."

Arkadin laughed. "What is it about then?"

"What it's always been—it's about helping you control yourself."

A light wind tugged at her hair, and she smoothed it back into place. He noticed such things and attached to them psychological meaning. Marlene liked everything just so.

"I was a sad little boy. Then I was an angry little boy. Then I ran away from home. There, does that satisfy you?"

Marlene tilted her head to catch a bit of sunlight that appeared through the tossed leaves of the fig tree. "How is it you went from being sad to being angry?"

"I grew up," Arkadin said.

"You were still a child."

"Only in a manner of speaking."

He studied her for a moment. Her hands were crossed on her lap. She lifted one of them, touched his cheek with her fingertips, traced the line of his jaw until she reached his chin. She turned his face a bit farther toward her. Then she leaned forward. Her lips, when they touched his, were soft. They opened like a flower. The touch of her tongue was like an explosion in his mouth.

Arkadin, damping down the dark eddy of his emotion, smiled winningly. "Doesn't matter. I'm never going back."

"I second that emotion." Devra nodded, then rose. "Let's see if we can get proper lodgings. I don't know about you but I need a shower. Then we'll see about contacting Haydar without anyone knowing."

As she began to turn away, he caught her by the elbow.

"Just a minute."

Her expression was quizzical as she waited for him to continue.

"If you're not my enemy, if you haven't been lying to me, if you want to stay with me, then you'll demonstrate your fidelity."

"I said, yes, I would do what you asked of me."

"That might entail killing the people who are surely guarding Haydar."

She didn't even blink. "Give me the fucking gun."

Veronica Hart lived in an apartment complex in Langley, Virginia. Like so many other complexes in this part of the world, it served as temporary housing for the thousands of federal government workers, including spooks of all stripes, who were often on assignment overseas or in other parts of the country.

Hart had lived in this particular apartment for just over two years. Not that it mattered; since coming to the district seven years ago she'd had nothing but temporary lodgings. By this point she doubted she'd be comfortable settling down and nesting. At least, those were her thoughts as she buzzed Soraya Moore into the lobby. A moment later a discreet knock sounded, and she let the other woman in.

"I'm clean," Soraya said as she shrugged off her coat. "I made sure of that."

Hart hung her coat in the foyer closet, led her into the kitchen. "For breakfast I have cold cereal or"—she opened the refrigerator—"cold Chinese food. Last night's leftovers."

"I'm not one for conventional breakfasts," Soraya said.

"Good. Neither am I."

Hart grabbed an array of cardboard cartons, told Soraya where to find plates, serving spoons, and chopsticks. They moved into the living room, set everything on a glass coffee table between facing sofas.

Hart began opening the cartons. "No pork, right?"

Soraya smiled, pleased that her boss remembered her Muslim strictures. "Thank you."

Hart returned to the kitchen, put up water for tea. "I have Earl Grey or oolong."

"Oolong for me, please."

Hart finished brewing the tea, brought the pot and two small handleless cups back to the living room. The two women settled themselves on opposite sides of the table, sitting cross-legged on the abstract patterned rug. Soraya looked around. There were some basic prints on the wall, the kind you'd expect to find at any midlevel hotel chain. The furniture looked rented, as anonymous as anything else. There were no photos, no sense of Hart's background or family. The only unusual feature was an upright piano.

"My only real possession," Hart said, following Soraya's gaze. "It's a Steinway K-52, better known as a Chippendale hamburg. It's got a sounding board larger than many grand pianos, so it lets out with a helluva sound."

"You play?"

Hart went over, sat down on the stool, began to play Frédéric Chopin's Nocturne in B-Flat Minor. Without missing a beat she segued into Isaac Albéniz's sensuous "Malagueña," and, finally, into a raucous transposition of Jimi Hendrix's "Purple Haze."

Soraya laughed and applauded as Hart rose, came back to sit opposite her.

"My absolute only talent besides intelligence work." Hart opened one of the cartons, spooned out General Tso's chicken. "Careful," she said as she handed it over, "I order it extra hot."

"That's okay by me," Soraya said, digging deep into the carton. "I always wanted to play the piano."

"Actually, I wanted to play electric guitar." Hart licked oyster sauce off her finger as she passed over another carton. "My father wouldn't hear of it. According to him, electric guitar wasn't a 'lady's' instrument."

"Strict, was he?" Soraya said sympathetically.

"You bet. He was a full-bird colonel in the air force. He'd been a fighter pilot back in his salad days. He resented being too old to fly, missed that damn oily-smelling cockpit something fierce. Who could he complain to in the force? So he took his frustration out on me and my mother."

Soraya nodded. "My father is old-school Muslim. Very strict, very rigid. Like many of his generation he's bewildered by the modern world, and that makes him angry. I felt trapped at home. When I left, he said he'd never forgive me."

"Did he?"

Soraya had a faraway look in her eyes. "I see my mom once a month. We go shopping together. I speak to my father once in a while. He's never invited me back home; I've never gone."

Hart put down her chopsticks. "I'm sorry."

"Don't be. It is what it is. Do you still see your father?"

"I do, but he doesn't know who I am. My mother's gone now, which is a blessing. I don't think she could've tolerated seeing him like that."

"It must be hard for you," Soraya said. "The indomitable fighter pilot reduced like that."

"There's a point in life where you have to let go of your parents." Hart resumed eating, though more slowly. "Whoever's lying in that bed isn't my father. He died a long time ago."

Soraya looked down at her food for a moment. Then she said, "Tell me how you knew about the NSA safe house."

"Ah, that." Hart's face brightened. Clearly, she was happy to be on a work topic. "During my time at Black River we were often hired by NSA. This was before they trained and deployed their own home-grown black-ops details. We were good for them because they never had to specify to anyone what we'd been hired to do. It was all 'fieldwork,' priming the battlefield for our troops. No one on Capitol Hill was going to look farther than that."

She dabbed her mouth, sat back. "Anyway, after one particular mission, I caught the short straw. I was the one from my squad who brought the findings back to the NSA. Because it was a black-ops mission, the debriefing took place at the safe house in Virginia. Not in the fine library you were taken to, but in one of the basement-level cubicles—windowless, featureless, just gritty reinforced concrete. It's like a war bunker down there."

"And what did you see?"

"It wasn't what I saw." Hart said. "It was what I heard. The cubicles are soundproof, except for the doors, I assume so the guards in the corridors know what's going on. What I heard was ghastly. The sounds were barely human."

"Did you tell your bosses at Black River?"

"What was the point? They didn't care, and even if they did, what were they going to do? Start a congressional investigation on the basis of sounds I heard? The NSA would have cut them off at the knees, put them out of business in a heartbeat." She shook her head. "No, these boys are businessmen, pure and simple. Their ideology revolves around milking as much money from the government as possible."

"So now we have a chance to do what you couldn't before, what Black River wouldn't do."

"That's right," Hart said. "I want to get photos, videos, absolute proof of what NSA is doing down there so I can present the evidence myself to the president. That's where you and Tyrone come in." She shoved her plate away. "I want Luther LaValle's head on a platter, and by God I'm going to get it."

Nineteen

BECAUSE OF the corpse and all the blood on the seats Bourne was forced to abandon the Volga. Before he did, though, he took Baronov's cell phone, as well as his money. It was freezing. Within the preternatural afternoon winter darkness came the snow, swirling down in ever-heavier curtains. Bourne knew he had to get out of the area as quickly as possible. He took the SIM card out of his phone, put it in Baronov's, then threw his own cell phone down a storm drain. In his new identity as Fyodor Ilianovich Popov he couldn't afford to be in possession of a cell with an American carrier.

He walked, leaning into the wind and snow. After six blocks, huddled in a doorway, he used Baronov's cell phone to call his friend Boris Karpov. The voice at the end of the line grew cold.

"Colonel Karpov is no longer with FSB."

Bourne felt a chill go through him. Russia had not changed so much that lightning-swift dismissals on trumped-up charges were a thing of the past.

"I need to contact him," Bourne said.

"He's now at the Federal Anti-Narcotics Agency." The voice recited a local number before abruptly hanging up.

That explained the attitude, Bourne thought. The Federal Anti-Narcotics Agency was headed up by Viktor Cherkesov. But many believed he was much more than that, a *silovik* running an organization so powerful that some had taken to calling it FSB-2. Recently an internal war between Cherkesov and Nikolai Patrushev, the head of the FSB, the modern-day successor to the notorious KGB, had sprung up within the government. The *silovik* who won that war would probably be the next president of Russia. If Karpov had gone from the FSB to FSB-2, it must be because Cherkesov had gotten the upper hand.

Bourne called the office of the Federal Anti-Narcotics Agency, but he was told that Karpov was away and could not be reached.

For a moment he contemplated calling the man who had picked up Baronov's Zil in the Crocus City parking lot, but he almost immediately thought better of it. He'd already gotten Baronov killed; he didn't want any more deaths on his conscience.

He walked on until he came to a tram stop. He took the first one that appeared out of the gloom. He'd used the scarf he'd bought at the boutique in Crocus City to cover up the mark the wire had made across his throat. The small seepage of blood had dried up as soon as he'd hit the frigid air.

The tram jounced and rattled along its rails. Crammed inside with a stinking, noisy crowd, he felt thoroughly shaken. Not only had he discovered a Kazanskaya assassin waiting in Tarkanian's apartment, but his contact had been murdered by an NSA assassin sent to kill him. His sense of apartness had never been more extreme. Babies cried, men rustled newspapers, women chatted side by side, an old man, big-knuckled hands curled over the head of his walking stick, clandestinely ogled a young girl engrossed in a manga comic. Here was life, bustling all around him, a burbling stream that parted when it came to him, an immovable rock, only to come together when it passed him, flowing on while he remained behind, still and alone.

He thought of Marie, as he always did at times like this. But Marie was gone, and her memory was of little solace to him. He missed his children, and wondered whether this was the David Webb personality bubbling up. An old, familiar despair swept through him, as it hadn't since Alex Conklin had taken him out of the gutter, formed the Bourne identity for him to slip on like a suit of armor. He felt the crushing weight of life on him, a life lived alone, a sad and lonely life that could only end one way.

And then his thoughts turned to Moira, of how impossibly difficult that last meeting with her had been. If she had been a spy, if she had betrayed Martin and meant to do the same with him, what would he have done? Would he have turned her over to Soraya or Veronica Hart?

But she wasn't a spy. He would never have to face that conundrum.

When it came to Moira, his personal feelings were now bound up in his professional duty, inextricably combined. He knew that she loved him and, now, in the face of his despair, he understood that he loved her, as well. When he was with her he felt whole, but in an entirely new way. She wasn't Marie, and he didn't want her to be Marie. She was Moira, and it was Moira he wanted.

By the time he swung off the tram in Moscow Center, the snow had abated to veils of drifting flakes whirled about by stray gusts of wind across the huge open plazas. The city's lights were on against the long winter evening, but the clearing sky turned the temperature bitter. The streets were clogged with gypsy cabbies in their cheap cars manufactured during the Brezhnev years, trundling slowly in bumper-to-bumper lines so as to not miss a fare. They were known in local slang as *bombily*—those who bomb—because of the bowel-loosening speed with which they bombed around the city's streets as soon as they had a passenger.

He went into a cybercafé, paid for fifteen minutes at a computer terminal, typed in Kitaysky Lyotchik. Kitaysky Lyotchik Zhao-Da, the full name—or The Chinese Pilot in its English translation—turned out to be a throbbing *elitny* club at proyezd Lubyansky 25. The Kitai-Gorod metro stop let Bourne out at the end of the block. On one side was a canal, frozen solid; on the other, a row of mixed-use buildings. The Chinese Pilot was easy enough to spot, what with the BMWs, Mercedeses, and Porsche SUVs, as well as the ubiquitous gaggle of *bombily* Zhigs clustered on the street. The crowd behind a velvet rope was being held in check by fierce-looking face-control bullies, so that waiting partygoers spilled drunkenly off the pavement. Bourne went up to the red Cayenne, rapped on the window. When the driver scrolled the window down, Bourne held out three hundred dollars.

"When I come out that door, this is my car, right?"

The driver eyed the money hungrily. "Right you are, sir."

In Moscow, especially, American dollars talked louder than words.

"And if your client comes out in the meantime?"

"He won't," the driver assured Bourne. "He's in the champagne room till four at the earliest."

Another hundred dollars got Bourne past the shouting, unruly mob. Inside, he ate an indifferent meal of an Oriental salad and almond-crusted chicken breast. From his perch along the glowing bar, he watched the Russian *siloviki* come and go with their diamond-studded, mini-skirted, fur-wrapped *dyevochkas*—strictly speaking, young women who had not yet borne a child. This was the new order in Russia. Except Bourne knew that many of the same people were still in power—either ex-KGB *siloviki* or their progeny lined up against the boys from Sokolniki, who came from nothing into sudden wealth. The *siloviki*, derived from the Russian word for "power," were men from the so-called power ministries, including the security services and the military, who had risen during the Putin era. They were the new guard, having overthrown the Yeltsin-period oligarchs. No matter. *Siloviki* or mobster, they were criminals, they'd killed, extorted, maimed, blackmailed; they all had blood on their hands, they were all strangers to remorse.

Bourne scanned the tables for Gala Nematova, was surprised to find half a dozen *dyevs* who might have fit the bill, especially in this low light. It was astonishing to observe firsthand this wheat field of tall, willowy young women, one more striking than the next. There was a prevalent theory, a kind of skewed Darwinism—survival of the prettiest—that explained why there were so many startlingly handsome *dyevochkas* in Russia and Ukraine. If you were a man in his twenties in these countries in 1947 it meant that you'd survived one of the greatest male bloodbaths in human history. These men, being in the vast minority, had their pick of women. Who had they chosen to marry and impregnate? The answer was obvious, hence the acres of *dyevs* partying here and in every other nightclub in Russia.

Out on the dance floor, a crush of gyrating bodies made identification of individuals impossible. Spotting a redheaded *dyev* on her own, Bourne walked over to her, gestured if she wanted to dance. The ear-splitting house music pumped out of a dozen massive speakers made small talk impossible. She nodded, took his hand, and they shoved, elbowed, and squeezed their way into a cramped space on the dance floor. The next twenty minutes could have substituted for a vigorous workout. The dancing was nonstop, as were the colored flashing lights and the chest-vibrating drumming of the high-octane music spewed out by a local band called Tequilajazz.

Over the top of the redhead Bourne caught a glimpse of yet another blond *dyev*. Only this one was different. Grabbing the redhead's hand, Bourne eeled deeper into the gyrating pack of dancers. Perfume, cologne, and sour sweat mixed with the raw tang of hot metal and blazing monster amplifiers.

Still dancing, Bourne maneuvered around until he was certain. The blonde *dyev* dancing with the broad-shouldered mobster was, indeed, Gala Nematova.

It'll never be the same," Dr. Mitten said.

"What the hell does that mean?" Anthony Prowess, sitting in an uncomfortable chair in the NSA safe house just outside Moscow, barked at the ophthalmologist bent over him.

"Mr. Prowess, I don't think you're in the best shape to hear a full diagnosis. Why not wait until the shock—"

"A, I'm not in shock," Prowess lied. "And B, I don't have time to wait." That was true enough: Having lost Bourne's trail, he needed to get back on it ASAP.

Dr. Mitten sighed. He'd been expecting just such a response; in fact, he would've been surprised at anything else. Still, he had a professional responsibility to his patient even if he was on retainer to the NSA.

"What it means," he said, "is that you'll never see out of that eye again. At least, not in any way that'll be useful to you."

Prowess sat with his head back, his damaged eye numbed with drops so the damn ophthalmologist could poke around. "Details, please."

Dr. Mitten was a tall, thin man with narrow shoulders, a wisp of a comb-over, and a neck with a prominent Adam's apple that bobbed comically when he spoke or swallowed. "I believe you'll be able to discern movement, differentiate light from dark."

"That's it?"

"On the other hand," Dr. Mitten said, "when the swelling goes down you may be completely blind in that eye."

"Fine, now I know the worst. Just fix me the hell up so I can get out of here."

"I don't recommend—"

"I don't give a shit what you recommend," Prowess snapped. "Do as I tell you or I'll wring your scrawny little chicken neck."

Dr. Mitten puffed out his checks in indignation, but he knew better than to talk back to an agent. They seemed born with hair-trigger responses to everything, which their training further honed.

As the ophthalmologist worked on his eye, Prowess seethed inside. Not only had he failed to terminate Bourne, he'd allowed Bourne to permanently maim him. He was furious at himself for turning tail and running, even though he knew that when a victim gains the upper hand you have to exit the field as quickly as possible.

Still, Prowess would never forgive himself. It wasn't that the pain had been excruciating—he had an extremely high pain threshold. It wasn't even that Bourne had turned the tables on him—he'd redress that situation shortly. It was his eye. Ever since he was a child, he had a morbid fear of being blind. His father had been blinded in an accidental fall getting off a transit bus, when the impact had detached both his retinas. This was in the days before ophthalmologists could staple retinas back in place. At six years old the horror of watching his father deteriorate from an optimistic, robust man into a bitter, withdrawn nub had imprinted itself forever in his mind. That horror had kicked in the moment Jason Bourne had dug his thumb deep into his eye.

As he sat in the chair, brooding amid the chemical smells emitted by Dr. Mitten's ministrations, Prowess was filled with determination. He promised himself he'd find Jason Bourne, and when he did Bourne would pay for the damage he'd inflicted, he'd pay dearly before Prowess killed him.

Professor Specter was chairing a chancellors' meeting at the university when his private cell phone vibrated. He immediately called a fifteen-minute break, left the room, strode down the hall and outside onto the campus.

When he was clear, he opened his cell, and heard Nemetsov's voice buzzing in his ear. Nemetsov was the man Baronov had called to switch cars with at Crocus City.

"Baronov's dead?" Specter said. "How?"

He listened while Nemetsov described the attack in the car outside Tarkanian's apartment building. "An NSA assassin," Nemetsov concluded. "He was waiting for Bourne, to garrote him as he did Baronov."

"And Jason?"

"Survived. But the assassin escaped as well."

Specter felt a wave of relief wash over him. "Find that NSA man before he finds Jason, and kill him. Is that clear?"

"Perfectly. But shouldn't we also try to make contact with Bourne?"

Specter considered a moment. "No. He's at his best when working alone. He knows Moscow, speaks Russian fluently, and he has our fake IDs. He'll do what must be done."

"You've put your faith in this one man?"

"You don't know him, Nemetsov, otherwise you wouldn't make such a stupid statement. I only wish Jason could be with us permanently."

* * *

When, sweaty and entangled, Gala Nematova and her boy toy left the dance floor, so did Bourne. He watched as the couple made their way to a table where they were greeted by two other men. They all began to guzzle champagne as if it were water. Bourne waited until they'd refilled their flutes, then swaggered over in the style of these new-style gangsters.

Leaning over Gala's companion, he shouted in her ear, "I have an urgent message for you."

"Hey," her companion shouted back with no little belligerence, "who the fuck're you?"

"Wrong question." Glaring at him, Bourne pushed up the sleeve of his jacket just long enough to give him a glimpse of his fake Anubis tattoo.

The man bit his lip and sat back down as Bourne reached over, pulled Gala Nematova away from the table.

"We're going outside to talk."

"Are you crazy?" She tried to squirm away from his grip. "It's freezing out there."

Bourne continued to steer her by her elbow. "We'll talk in my limo."

"Well, that's something." Gala Nematova bared her teeth, clearly unhappy. Her teeth were very white, as if scrubbed to within an inch of their lives. Her eyes were a remote chestnut, large with uptilted corners that revealed the Asian blood in her ancestry.

A frigid wind swept off the canal, blocked only partially by the gridlock of expensive cars and *bombily*. Bourne rapped on the Porsche's door and the driver, recognizing him, unlocked the doors. Bourne and the *dyev* piled in.

Gala, shivering, hugged her inadequately short fur coat around her. Bourne asked the driver to turn up the heat. He complied, sank down in his fur-collared greatcoat.

"I don't care what message you have for me," Gala said sullenly. "Whatever it is, the answer's no."

"Are you sure?" Bourne wondered where she was going with this.

"Sure I'm sure. I've had it with you guys trying to find out where Leonid Danilovich is."

Leonid Danilovich, Bourne said to himself. *There's a name the professor never mentioned*.

"The reason we keep hounding you is he's sure you know." Bourne had no idea what he was saying, but he felt if he kept running with her he'd be able to open her up.

"I don't." Now Gala sounded like a little girl in a snit. "But even if I did I wouldn't rat him out. You can tell Maslov that." She fairly spat out the name of the Kazanskaya's leader, Dimitri Maslov.

Now we're getting somewhere, Bourne thought. But why was Maslov after Leonid Danilovich, and what did any of this have to do with Pyotr's death? He decided to explore this link.

"Why were you and Leonid Danilovich using Tarkanian's apartment?"

Instantly he knew he'd made a mistake. Gala's expression changed dramatically. Her eyes narrowed and she made a sound deep in her throat. "What the hell is this? You already know why we were camped out there."

"Tell me again," Bourne said, improvising desperately. "I've only heard it thirdhand. Maybe something was left out."

"What could be left out? Leonid Danilovich and Tarkanian are the best of friends."

"Is that where you took Pyotr for your late-night trysts?"

"Ah, so that's what this is all about. The Kazanskaya want to know all about Pyotr Zilber, and I know why. Pyotr ordered the murder of Borya Maks, in prison, of all places—High Security Prison Colony 13. Who could do that? Get in there, kill Maks, a Kazanskaya contract killer of great strength and skill, and get out without being seen."

"That's precisely what Maslov wants to know," Bourne said, because it was the safe comment to make.

Gala picked at her nail extensions, realized what she was doing, stopped. "He suspects Leonid Danilovich did it because Leonid is known for such feats. No one else could do that, he's sure."

Time to press her, Bourne decided. "He's right on the money."

Gala shrugged.

"Why are you protecting Leonid?"

"I love him."

"The way you loved Pyotr?"

"Don't be absurd." Gala laughed. "I never loved Pyotr. He was a job Semion Icoupov paid me handsomely for."

"And Pyotr paid for your treachery with his life."

Gala seemed to peer at him in a different light. "Who are you?"

Bourne ignored her question. "During that time where did you meet Icoupov?"

"I never met him. Leonid served as intermediary."

Now Bourne's mind raced to put the building blocks Gala had provided into their proper order. "You know, don't you, that Leonid murdered Pyotr." He didn't of course know that, but given the circumstances it seemed all too likely.

"No." Gala blanched. "That can't be."

"You can see how it must be what happened. Icoupov didn't kill Pyotr himself, surely that much must be clear to you." He observed the fear mounting behind her eyes. "Who else would Icoupov have trusted to do it? Leonid was the only other person to know you were spying on Pyotr for Icoupov."

The truth of what he said was written on Gala's face like a road sign appearing out of the fog. While she was still in shock, Bourne said, "Please tell me Leonid's full name."

"What?"

"Just do as I tell you," Bourne said. "It may be the only way to save him from being killed by the Kazanskaya."

"But *you're* Kazanskaya."

Pushing up his sleeve, Bourne gave her a close-up look at the false tattoo. "A Kazanskaya was waiting for Leonid in Tarkanian's apartment this evening."

"I don't believe you." Her eyes widened. "What were you doing there?"

"Tarkanian's dead," Bourne said. "Now do you want to help the man you say you love?"

"I *do* love Leonid! I don't care what he did."

At that moment, the driver cursed mightily, turned in his seat. "My client's coming."

"Go on," Bourne urged Gala. "Write his name down."

"Something must've happened in the VIP," the driver said. "Shit, he looks pissed. You gotta get outta here now."

Bourne grabbed Gala, opened the street-side door, nearly burying it in the fender of a hurtling *bombily*. He flagged it down with a fistful of rubles, made the transfer from Western luxury to Eastern poverty in one stride. Gala Nematova broke away from him as he was entering the Zhig. He clutched her by the back of her fur coat, but she shrugged it off, began to run. The cabbie stepped on the gas, the stench of diesel fumes foaming up into the interior, choking them so badly Bourne had to crank open a window. As he did so, he saw two men who'd been at her table come out of the club. They looked right and left. One of them spotted Gala's running figure, gestured to the other one, and they took off after her.

"Follow those men!" Bourne shouted to the cabbie.

The cabbie had a flat face with a distinctly Asian caste. He was fat, greasy, and spoke Russian with an abominable accent. Clearly, Russian wasn't his first language. "You're joking, yes?"

Bourne thrust more rubles at him. "I'm joking, no."

The cabbie shrugged, crashed the Zhig into first gear, depressed the gas pedal.

At that moment the two men caught up with Gala.

Twenty

AT PRECISELY that moment, Leonid Danilovich Arkadin and Devra were deciding how to get to Haydar without Devra's people knowing about it.

"Best would be to extract him from his environment," Arkadin said. "But for that we need to know his habitual movements. I don't have time—"

"I know a way," Devra said.

The two of them were sitting side by side on a bed on the ground floor of a small inn. The room wasn't much to look at—just a bed, a chair, a broken-down dresser—but it had its own bathroom, a shower with plenty of hot water, which they'd used one after the other. Best of all, it was warm.

"Haydar's a gambler," she continued. "Almost every evening he's hunkered down in the back room of a local café. He knows the owner, who lets them play without imposing a fee. In fact, once a week he joins them." She glanced at her watch. "He's sure to be there now."

"What good is that? Your people are sure to protect him there."

"Right, that's why we aren't going to go near the place."

* * *

An hour later, they were sitting in their rented car on the side of a two-lane road. All their lights were off. They were freezing. Whatever snow had seemed imminent had passed them by. A half-moon rode in the sky, an Old World lantern revealing wisps of clouds and bluish crusty snowbanks.

"This is the route Haydar takes to and from the game." Devra tilted her watch face so it was illuminated by the moonglow coming off the banked snow. "He should show any minute now."

Arkadin was behind the wheel. "Just point out the car, leave the rest to me." One hand was on the ignition key, the other on the gearshift. "We have to be prepared. He might have an escort."

"If he's got guards they'll be in the same car with him," Devra said. "The roads are so bad it will be extremely difficult to keep him in sight from a trailing vehicle."

"One car," Arkadin said. "All the better."

A moment later the night was momentarily lit by a moving glow below the rise in the road.

"Headlights." Devra tensed. "That's the right direction."

"You'll know his car?"

"I'll know it," she said. "There aren't many cars in the area. Mostly old trucks for carting."

The glow brightened. Then they saw the headlights themselves as the vehicle crested the rise. From the position of the headlights, Arkadin could tell this was a car, not a truck.

"It's him," she said.

"Get out," Arkadin ordered. "Run! Run now!"

Keep moving," Bourne told the cabbie, "in first gear only till I tell you different."

"I don't think—"

But Bourne had already swung open the curbside door, was sprinting toward the two men. One had Gala, the other was turning, raising his hand, perhaps a signal for one of the waiting cars. Bourne chopped his midsection with his two hands, brought his head down to his raised knee. The man's teeth clacked together and he toppled over.

The second man swung Gala around so that she was between him and Bourne. He scrabbled for his gun, but Bourne was too quick. Reaching around Gala, Bourne went for him. He moved to block Bourne and Gala stamped her heel on his instep. That was all the distraction Bourne needed. With a hand around her waist, he pulled her away, delivered a vicious uppercut to the man's throat. Reflexively, he put two hands up, choking and gagging. Bourne delivered two quick blows to his stomach and he, too, hit the pavement.

"Come on!"

Bourne grabbed Gala by the hand, made for the *bombila*, moving slowly along the street with its door open. Bourne swung her inside, climbed in after her, slammed the door shut.

"Take off!" he shouted at the cabbie. "Take off now!"

Shivering with the cold, Gala rolled up the window.

"My name is Yakov," the cabbie said, craning his neck to look at them in the rearview mirror. "You make much excitement for me tonight. Is there more? Where can I take you?"

"Just drive around," Bourne said.

Several blocks on he discovered Gala staring at him.

"You weren't lying to me," she said.

"Neither were you. Clearly, the Kazanskaya think you know where Leonid is."

"Leonid Danilovich Arkadin." She was still trying to catch her breath. "That's his name. It's what you wanted, isn't it?"

"What I want," Bourne said, "is a meeting with Dimitri Maslov."

"The head of the Kazanskaya? You're insane."

"Leonid has been playing with a very bad crowd," Bourne said. "He's put you in harm's way. Unless I can persuade Maslov that you don't know where Arkadin is you'll never be safe."

Shivering, Gala struggled back into her fur jacket. "Why did you save me?" She pulled the jacket tight around her slender frame. "Why are you doing this?"

"Because I can't let Arkadin throw you to the wolves."

"That's not what he's done," she protested.

"What would you call it?"

She opened her mouth, closed it again, bit her lip as if she could find an answer in her pain.

They had reached the inner Garden Road. Traffic whizzed by at dizzying speeds. The cabbie was about to earn his *bombily* name.

"Where to?" he said over his shoulder.

There was silence for a moment. Then Gala leaned forward, gave him an address.

"And where the fuck might that be?" the cabbie asked.

That was another oddity about *bombily*. Since almost none of them were Muscovites, they had no idea where anything was. Unfazed, Gala gave him directions and, with a horrific belching of diesel fumes, they lurched into the madly spinning traffic.

"Since we can't go back to the apartment," Gala said, "we'll crash at my girlfriend's place. I've done it before. She's cool with it."

"Do the Kazanskaya know about her?"

Gala frowned. "I don't think so, no."

"We can't take the chance." Bourne gave the cabbie the address of one of the new American-run hotels near Red Square. "That's the last place they'll think to look for you," he said as the cabbie changed gears and they hurtled through the spangled Moscow night.

Alone in the car, Arkadin fired the ignition and pulled out. He stamped on the gas pedal, accelerating so quickly his head jerked back. Just before he slammed into the right corner of Haydar's car, he switched on his headlights. He could see Haydar's bodyguards in the rear seat. They were in the process of turning around when Arkadin's car made jarring contact. The rear end of Haydar's car slewed to the left, beginning its spin; Arkadin braked sharply, rammed the right back door, staving it in. Haydar, who had been struggling with the wheel, completely lost control of the car. It spun off the road, its front now facing the way it had come. Its rear struck a tree, the bumper broke in two, the trunk collapsed, and there it sat, a crippled animal. Arkadin drove off the road, put his car in park, got out, stalking toward Haydar. His headlights were shining directly into the wrecked car. He could see Haydar behind the wheel, conscious, clearly in shock. Only one of the men in the backseat was visible. His head was thrown back and to one side. There was blood on his face, black and glistening in the harsh light.

Haydar cringed fearfully as Arkadin made for the bodyguards. Both rear doors were so buckled they could not be opened. Using his elbow, Arkadin smashed the near-side rear window and peered in. One man had been caught in Arkadin's broadside hit. He'd been thrown clear across the car, lay half on the lap of the bodyguard still sitting up. Neither one moved.

As Arkadin moved to haul Haydar out from behind the wheel, Devra came hurtling out of the darkness. Haydar's eyes opened wide as he recognized her. She tackled Arkadin, her momentum knocking him off his feet.

Haydar watched in amazement as they rolled over through the snow, now visible, now not in the headlight beams. Haydar could see her striking him, the much larger man fighting back, gradually gaining the upper hand by dint of his superior bulk and strength. Then Devra reared back. Haydar could see a knife in her hand. She drove it down into darkness, stabbing again and again.

When she rose again into the headlight beams he could see her breathing heavily. Her hand was empty. Haydar figured she must have left the knife buried in her adversary. She staggered for a moment with the aftereffects of her struggle. Then she made her way over to him.

Yanking open the car door, she said, "Are you okay?"

He nodded, shrinking away from her. "I was told you'd turned on us, joined the other side."

She laughed. "That's just what I wanted that sonovabitch to think.

He managed to get to Shumenko and Filya. After that I figured the only way to survive was to play along with him until I got a chance to take him down."

Haydar nodded. "This is the final battle. The thought that you'd turned traitor was dispiriting. I know some of us thought your status was earned on your back, in Pyotr's bed. But not me." The shock was coming out of his eyes. The old canny light was returning.

"Where is the package?" she said. "Is it safe?"

"I handed it off to Heinrich this evening —at the card game."

"Has he left for Munich?"

"Why the hell would he stay a minute more than he had to? He hates it here. I assume he was driving to Istanbul for his usual early-evening flight." His eyes narrowed. "Why d'you want to know?"

He gave a little yelp as Arkadin loomed out of the night. Looking from Devra to Arkadin and back again, he said, "What is this? I saw you stab him to death."

"You saw what we wanted you to see." Arkadin handed Devra his gun, and she shot Haydar between the eyes.

She turned back to him, handed him the gun butt-first. There was clear defiance in her voice when she said, "Have I proved myself to you now?"

Bourne checked into the Metropolya Hotel as Fyodor Ilianovich Popov. The night clerk didn't bat an eye at Gala's presence, nor did he ask for her ID. Having Popov's was enough to satisfy hotel policy. The lobby, with its gilt sconces and accents, and glittering crystal chandeliers, looked like something out of the czarist era, the designers thumbing their nose at the architecture of Soviet Brutalism.

They took one of the silk-lined elevators to the seventeenth floor. Bourne opened the door to their room with an electronically coded plastic card. After a thorough visual check, he allowed her to enter. She took off her fur jacket. The act of sitting on the bed rode her mini-skirt farther up her thighs, but she appeared unconcerned.

Leaning forward, elbows on knees, she said, "Thank you for saving me. But to be honest, I don't know what I'll do now."

Bourne pulled out the chair that went with the desk, sat facing her. "The first thing you have to do is tell me whether you know where Arkadin is."

Gala looked down at the carpet between her feet. She rubbed her arms as if she was still cold, though the temperature in the room was warm enough.

"All right," Bourne said, "let's talk about something else. Do you know anything about the Black Legion?"

Her head came up, her brows furrowed. "Now, that's odd you should mention them."

"Why is that?"

"Leonid would speak about them."

"Is Arkadin one of them?"

Gala snorted. "You must be joking! No, he never actually spoke about them to me. I mean, he mentioned them now and again when he was going to see Ivan."

"And who is Ivan?"

"Ivan Volkin. He's an old friend of Leonid's. He used to be in the *grupperovka*. Leonid told me that from time to time the leaders ask him for advice, so he knows all the players. He's a kind of de facto underworld historian now. Anyway, he's the one Leonid would go to."

This interested Bourne. "Can you take me to him?"

"Why not? He's a night owl. Leonid used to visit him very late." Gala searched in her handbag for her cell phone. She scrolled through her phone book, dialed Volkin's number.

After speaking to someone for several minutes, she terminated the connection and nodded. "He'll see us in an hour."

"Good."

She frowned, put away her phone. "If you're thinking that Ivan knows where Leonid is, you're mistaken. Leonid told no one where he was going, not even me."

"You must love this man a great deal."

"I do."

"Does he love you?"

When she turned back to him, her eyes were full of tears. "Yes, he loves me."

"Is that why you took money to spy on Pyotr? Is that why you were partying with that man tonight at The Chinese Pilot?"

"Christ, none of that matters."

Bourne sat forward. "I don't understand. Why doesn't it matter?"

Gala regarded him for a long time. "What's the matter with you? Don't you know anything about love?" A tear overflowed, ran down her cheek. "Whatever I do for money allows me to live. Whatever I do with my body has nothing to do with love. Love is strictly a matter of the heart. My heart belongs to Leonid Danilovich. That's sacred, pure. No one can touch it or defile it."

"Maybe we have different definitions of love," Bourne said.

She shook her head. "You've no right to judge me."

"Of course you're right," Bourne said. "But that wasn't meant as a judgment. I have difficulty understanding love, that's all."

She cocked her head. "Why is that?"

Bourne hesitated before continuing. "I've lost two wives, a daughter, and many friends."

"Have you lost love, too?"

"I have no idea what that means."

"My brother died protecting me." Gala began to shake. "He was all I had. No one would ever love me the way he did. After our parents were killed we were inseparable. He swore he'd make sure nothing bad happened to me. He went to his grave keeping that promise." She sat up straight. Her face was defiant. "Now do you understand?"

Bourne realized that he'd seriously underestimated this *dyev*. Had he done the same with Moira? Despite admitting his feelings for Moira, he'd unconsciously made the decision that no other woman could be as strong, as imperturbable as Marie. In this, he was clearly mistaken. He had this Russian *dyevochka* to thank for the insight.

Gala peered at him now. Her sudden anger seemed to have burned itself out. "You're like Leonid Danilovich in many ways. You no longer will walk off the cliff, you no longer trust in love. Like him, you were damaged in terrible ways. But now, you see, you've made your present as bleak as your past. Your only salvation is to find someone to love."

"I did find someone," Bourne said. "She's dead now."

"Is there no one else?"

Bourne nodded. "Maybe."

"Then you must embrace her, instead of running away." She clasped her hands together. "Embrace love. That's what I would tell Leonid Danilovich if he were here instead of you."

Three blocks away, parked at the curb, Yakov, the cabbie who had dropped Gala and Bourne off, opened his cell phone, pressed a speed-dial digit on the keypad. When he heard the familiar voice, he said, "I dropped them off at the Metropolya not ten minutes ago."

"Keep an eye out for them," the voice said. "If they leave the hotel, tell me. Then follow them."

Yakov gave his assent, drove back around, installed himself opposite the hotel entrance. Then he dialed another number, delivered precisely the same information to another of his clients.

We just missed the package," Devra said as they walked away from the wreck. "We'd better get on the road to Istanbul right away. The next contact, Heinrich, has a good couple of hours' head start."

They drove through the night, negotiating the twists, turns, and switchbacks. The black mountains with their shimmering stoles of snow were their silent, implacable companions. The road was as pockmarked as if they were in a war zone. Once, hitting a patch of black ice, they spun out, but Arkadin didn't lose his head. He turned into the skid, tamped gently on the brakes several times while he threw the car into neutral, then turned the engine off. They came to a stop in the side of a snowdrift.

"I hope Heinrich had the same difficulty," Devra said.

Arkadin restarted the car but couldn't build up enough traction to get them moving. He walked around to the rear while Devra took the wheel. He found nothing useful inside the trunk, so he trudged several paces into the trees, snapped off a handful of substantial branches, which he wedged in front of the right rear tire. He slapped the fender twice and Devra stepped on the gas. The car wheezed and groaned. The tires spun, sending up showers of granular snow. Then the treads found the wood, rolled up onto it and over. The car was free.

Devra moved over as Arkadin took the wheel. Clouds had slid across the moon, steeping the road in dense shadow as they made their way through the mountain pass. There was no traffic; the only illumination for many miles was the car's own headlights. Finally, the moon rose from its cloud bed and the hemmed-in world around them was bathed in an eerie bluish light.

"Times like this when I miss my American," Devra mused, her head against the seat back. "He came from California. I loved especially his stories about surfing. My God, what a weird sport. Only in America, huh? But I used to think how great it would be to live in a land of sunshine, ride endless highways in convertibles, and swim whenever you wanted to."

"The American dream," Arkadin said sourly.

She sighed. "I so wanted him to take me with him when he left."

"My friend Mischa wanted me to take him with me," Arkadin said, "but that was a long time ago."

Devra turned her head toward him. "Where did you go?"

"To America." He laughed shortly. "But not to California. It didn't matter to Mischa; he was crazy about America. That's why I didn't take him. You go to a place to work, you fall in love with it, and now you don't want to work anymore." He paused for a moment, concentrated on navigating through a hairpin switchback. "I didn't tell him that, of course," he continued. "I could never hurt Mischa like that. We both grew up in slums, you know. Fucking hard life, that is. I was beaten up so many times I stopped counting. Then Mischa stepped in. He was bigger than I was, but that wasn't it. He taught me how to use a knife—not just stab, but how to throw it, as well. Then he took me to a guy he knew, skinny little man, but he had no fat on him at all. In the blink of an eye he had me down on my back in so much pain my eyes watered. Christ, I couldn't even breathe. Mischa asked me if I'd like to be able to do that and I said, 'Shit, where do I sign up?'"

The headlights of a truck appeared, coming toward them, a horrific dazzle that momentarily blinded both of them. Arkadin slowed down until the truck lumbered past.

"Mischa's my best friend, my only friend, really," he said. "I don't know what I'd do without him."

"Will I meet him when you take me back to Moscow?"

"He's in America now," Arkadin said. "But I'll take you to his apartment, where I've been staying. It's along the Frunzenskaya embankment. His living room overlooks Gorky Park. The view is very beautiful." He thought fleetingly of Gala, who was still in the apartment. He knew how to get her out; it wouldn't be a problem at all.

"I know I'll love it," Devra said. It was a relief to hear him talk about himself. Encouraged by his talkative mood, she continued, "What work did you do in America?"

And just like that his mood flipped. He braked the car to a halt. "You drive," he said.

Devra had grown used to his mercurial mood swings, but watched him come around the front of the car. She slid over. He slammed the passenger's-side door shut and she put the car in gear, wondering what tender nerve she'd touched.

They continued along the road, heading down the mountainside.

"We'll hit the highway soon enough," she said to break the thickening silence. "I can't wait to crawl into a warm bed."

Inevitably there came a time when Arkadin took the initiative with Marlene. It happened while she was sleeping. He crept down the hall to her door. It was child's play for him to pick the lock with nothing more than the wire that wrapped the cork in the bottle of champagne Icoupov served at dinner. Of course, being a Muslim, Icoupov himself had not partaken of the alcohol, but Arkadin and Marlene had no such restrictions. Arkadin had volunteered to open the champagne and when he did he palmed the wire.

The room smelled of her—of lemons and musk, a combination that set off a stirring below his belly. The moon was full, low on the horizon. It looked as if God were squeezing it between his palms.

Arkadin stood still, listening to her deep even breaths, every once in a while catching the hint of a snore. The bedcovers rustled as she turned onto her right side, away from him. He waited until her breathing settled again before moving to the bed. He climbed, knelt over her. Her face and shoulder were in moonlight, her neck in shadow, so that it appeared to him as if he'd already decapitated her. For some reason, this vision disturbed him. He tried to breathe deeply and easily, but the disturbing vision tightened his chest, made him so dizzy that he almost lost his balance.

And then he felt something hard and cold that in a drawn breath brought him back to himself. Marlene was awake, her head turned, staring at him. In her right hand was a Glock 20 10mm.

"I've got a full magazine," she said.

Which meant she had fourteen more rounds if she missed the kill with her first shot. Not that that was likely. The Glock was one of the most powerful handguns on the market. She wasn't fooling around.

"Back off."

He rolled off the bed and she sat up. Her bare breasts shone whitely in the moonlight. She appeared totally unconcerned with her semi-nudity.

"You weren't asleep."

"I haven't slept since I came here," Marlene said. "I've been anticipating this moment. I've been waiting for you to steal into my room."

She set aside the Glock. "Come to bed. You're safe with me, Leonid Danilovich."

As if mesmerized, he climbed back onto the bed and, like a little child, rested his head against the warm cushion of her breasts while she rocked him tenderly. She lay curled around him, willing her warmth to seep into his cool, marble flesh. Gradually, she felt his heartbeat cease its manic racing. To the steady sound of her heartbeat, he fell into slumber.

Some time later, she woke him with a whisper in his ear. It wasn't difficult; he wanted to be released from his nightmare. He started, staring at her for a long moment, his body rigid. His mouth felt raw from yelling in his sleep. Returning to the present, he recognized her. He felt her arms around him, the protective curl of her body, and to her astonishment and elation he relaxed.

"Nothing can harm you here, Leonid Danilovich," she breathed. "Not even your nightmares."

He stared at her in an odd, unblinking fashion. Anyone else would have been frightened, but not Marlene.

"What made you cry out?" she said.

"There was blood everywhere . . . on the bed."

"Your bed? Were you beaten, Leonid?"

He blinked, and the spell was broken. He turned over, faced away from her, waiting for the ashen light of dawn.

Twenty-One

ON A FINE clear afternoon, with the sun already low in the sky, Tyrone drove Soraya Moore to the NSA safe house nestled within the rolling hills of Virginia. Somewhere, in some anonymous cybercafé in northeast Washington, Kiki was sitting at a public computer terminal, waiting to sow the software virus she'd devised to disable the property's two thousand CCTV surveillance cameras.

"It'll loop the video images back on themselves endlessly," she'd told them. "That was the easy part. In order to make the code a hundred percent invisible it'll work for ten minutes, no more. At that point, it will, in essence, self-destruct, deforming into tiny packets of harmless code the system won't pick up as anomalous."

Everything now depended on timing. Since it was impossible to send an electronic signal from the NSA safe house without it being picked up and tagged as suspicious, they had worked out an external timing scheme, which meant that if anything went wrong—if Tyrone was delayed for any reason—the ten minutes would tick by and the plan would fail. This was the plan's Achilles' heel. Still, it was their only option and they decided to take it.

Besides, Deron had a number of goodies he'd concocted for them after consulting the architectural plans of the building he'd mysteriously conjured up. She had tried to get them herself and struck out; NSA had what she thought was a total lock on the property records.

Just before they stopped at the front gates, Soraya said, "Are you sure you want to go through with this?"

Tyrone nodded, stony-faced. "Let's get on wid it." He was pissed that she'd even thought to ask that question. When he was on the street, if one of his crew dared to question his courage or resolve that would've been the end of him. Tyrone had to keep reminding himself that this wasn't the street. He knew all too well that she'd accepted a huge risk in taking him in off the street—civilizing him, as he sometimes thought of the process when he felt particularly hemmed in by the rules and regulations of white men he knew nothing about.

He glanced at her out of the corner of his eye, wondering if he'd ever have stepped into the white man's world were it not for his love of her. Here was a woman of color—a Muslim, no less—who was working for the Man. Not just the Man, but the Man squared, cubed into infinity, whatever. If she didn't mind doing it, why should he? But his upbringing was about as different from hers as it could get. From what she'd told him her parents had given her everything she needed; he barely had parents, and they either didn't want to give him anything or were incapable of giving it. She had the advantage of a first-class education; he had Deron who, though he'd taught Tyrone many things, was no substitute for white man's education.

What was ironic was that only months ago, he would have sneered at the kind of education she had. But once he'd met her he began to understand how ignorant he really was. He was street-smart, sure—more than she was. But he was intimidated around people who'd graduated high school and college. The more he observed them maneuvering through their world—how they talked, negotiated, interacted with one another—the more he understood just how stunted his life had been. Street smarts and nothing else was just what the doctor ordered for picking your way through the hood, but there was a whole fucking world beyond the hood. Once he realized that, like Deron, he wanted to explore the world beyond the borders of his neighborhood, he knew he'd have to remake himself from the toes up.

All this was on his mind when he saw the imposing stone-and-slate building within the high iron fence. As he knew from the plans he'd memorized at Deron's it was perfectly symmetrical, with four high chimneys, eight gabled rooms. A spiky fistful of antennas, aerials, and satellite dishes was the only anomalous feature.

"You look very handsome in that suit," Soraya said.

"It's fuckin' uncomfortable," he said. "I feel stiff."

"Just like every NSA agent."

He laughed the way a Roman gladiator might as he entered the Colosseum.

"Which is the point," she added. "You've got the tag Deron gave you?"

He patted a place over his heart. "Safe and sound."

Soraya nodded. "Okay, here we go."

He knew there was a chance he'd never come out of that house alive, but he didn't care. Why should he? What had his life amounted to up until now? Shit-all. He'd stood up—just as Deron had—made his choice. That's all a man asks for in this life.

Soraya presented the credentials LaValle had sent her by messenger this morning. Nevertheless, both she and Tyrone were scrutinized by a bookend pair of suits with square jaws and standing orders not to smile. Finally, they passed muster, and were waved through.

As Tyrone drove down the snaking gravel drive Soraya pointed out the terrible gauntlet of surveillance systems an intruder would have to pass in order to infiltrate from beyond the property's borders. This monologue reassured him that they'd already bypassed these risks by being LaValle's guests. Now all they had to do was negotiate the interior of the house. Getting out again was another matter entirely.

He drove up to the portico. Before he could turn off the engine, a valet came to relieve him of the car, yet another square-jawed military type who'd never look right in his civilian suit.

General Kendall, punctual as usual, was at the door to meet them.

He gave Soraya's hand a perfunctory shake, then eyeballed Tyrone as she introduced him.

"Your bodyguard, I presume," Kendall said in a tone someone would use for a rebuke. "But he doesn't look like standard-issue CI material."

"This isn't a standard CI rendezvous," Soraya returned tartly.

Kendall shrugged. Another perfunctory handshake and he turned on his heel, leading them inside the hulking structure. Through the public rooms, gilt-edged, refined, expensive beyond modern-day imagining, along hushed corridors lined with martial paintings, past mullioned windows through which the January sunlight sparked in beams that stretched across the plush blue carpet. Without seeming to, Tyrone took note of every detail, as if he were casing the joint for a high-end robbery, which in fact he was. They passed the door down to the basement levels. It looked precisely as Soraya had drawn it from memory for him and Deron.

They went on another ten yards to the walnut doors leading to the Library. The fireplace contained a roaring blaze, a grouping had been set with four chairs in the same spot where Soraya said she had sat with Kendall and LaValle on her first visit. Willard met them just inside the door.

"Good afternoon, Ms. Moore," he said with his customary half bow. "How very nice to see you again so soon. Would you care for your Ceylon tea?"

"That would be wonderful, thank you."

Tyrone was about to ask for a Coke, but thought better of it. Instead he ordered another Ceylon tea, having not the faintest idea what it tasted like.

"Very good," Willard said, and left them.

"This way," Kendall said unnecessarily, leading them to the grouping of chairs where Luther LaValle was already seated, staring out the mullioned windows at the light gathered to an oval over the western hills.

He must have heard the whisper of their approach, because he rose and turned just as they came up. The maneuver seemed to Soraya artfully rehearsed, and therefore as artificial as LaValle's smile. Dutifully, she introduced Tyrone, and they all sat down together.

LaValle steepled his fingers. "Before we begin, Director, I feel compelled to point out that our own archives department has unearthed some fragmentary history on the Black Legion. Apparently, they did exist during the time of the Third Reich. They were composed of Muslim prisoners of war who were brought back to Germany from the first putsches into the Soviet Union. These Muslims, mainly of Turkish descent from the Caucasus, detested Stalin so much they'd do anything to topple his regime, even becoming Nazis."

LaValle shook his head like a history professor recounting evil days to a class of wide-eyed students. "It's a particularly unpleasant footnote in a thoroughly repugnant decade. But as for the Black Legion itself, there's no evidence whatsoever that it survived the regime that spawned it. Besides which, its benefactor Himmler was a master of propaganda, especially when it came to advancing himself in the eyes of Hitler. Anecdotal evidence suggests that the role of the Black Legion on the Eastern Front was minimal, that it was in fact Himmler's fantastic propaganda machine that gave it the feared reputation it enjoyed, not anything its members themselves did."

He smiled, the sun emerging from behind storm clouds. "Now, in that light, let me take a look at the Typhon intercepts."

Soraya tolerated this rather condescending introduction, meant to discredit the origin of the intercepts before she even handed them over. She allowed indignation and humiliation to pass through her so she could remain calm and focused on her mission. Pulling the slim briefcase onto her lap, she unlocked the coded lock, extracted a red file with a thick black stripe across its upper right-hand corner, marking it as DIRECTOR EYES ONLY—material of the highest security clearance.

Staring LaValle in the face, she handed it over.

"Excuse me, Director." Tyrone held out his hand. "The electronic tape."

"Oh, yes, I forgot," Soraya said. "Mr. LaValle, would you please hand the file to Mr. Elkins."

LaValle checked the file more closely, saw a ribbon of shiny metal sealing the file. "Don't bother. I can peel this back myself."

"Not if you want to read the intercepts," Tyrone said. "Unless the tape is opened with this"—he held up a small plastic implement—"the file will incinerate within seconds."

LaValle nodded his approval of the security measures Soraya had taken.

As he gave the file to Tyrone, Soraya said, "Since our last meeting my people have intercepted more communication from the same entity, which increasingly seems to be the command center."

LaValle frowned. "A command center? That's highly unusual for a terrorist network, which is, by definition, made up of independent cadres."

"That's what makes the intercepts so compelling."

"It also makes them suspect, in my opinion," LaValle said. "Which is why I'm anxious to read them myself."

By this time, Tyrone had slit the metallic security tape, handed the file back. LaValle's gaze dropped as he opened the file and began to read.

At this point Tyrone said, "I need to use the bathroom."

LaValle waved a hand. "Go ahead," he said without looking up.

Kendall watched him as he went up to Willard, who was on his way over with the drinks, to ask for directions. Soraya saw this out of the corner of her eye. If all went well, in the next couple of minutes Tyrone would be standing in front of the door down to the basement at the precise moment Kiki sent the virus to the NSA security system.

Ivan Volkin was a hairy bear of a man, salt-and-pepper hair standing straight up like a madman, a full beard white as snow, small but cheerful eyes the color of a rainstorm. He was slightly bandy-legged, as if he'd been riding a horse all his life. His lined and leathery face lent him a certain dignified aspect, as if in his life he'd earned the respect of many.

He greeted them warmly, welcoming them into an apartment that appeared small because of the stacks of books and periodicals that covered every conceivable horizontal surface, including the kitchen stovetop and his bed.

He led them down a narrow, winding aisle from the vestibule to the living room, made room for them on the sofa by moving three teetering stacks of books.

"Now," he said, standing in front of them, "how can I be of help?"

"I need to know everything you can tell me about the Black Legion."

"And why are you interested in such a tiny footnote to history?" Volkin looked at Bourne with a jaundiced eye. "You don't have the look of a scholar."

"Neither do you," Bourne said.

This produced a spraying laugh from the older man. "No, I suppose not." Volkin wiped his eyes. "Spoken like one soldier to another, eh? Yes." Reaching around behind him, he swung over a ladder-backed chair, straddled it with his arms crossed over the top. "So. What specifically do you want to know?"

"How did they manage to survive into the twenty-first century?"

Volkin's face immediately shut down. "Who told you the Black Legion survives?"

Bourne did not want to use Professor Specter's name. "An unimpeachable source."

"Is that so? Well, that source is wrong."

"Why bother to deny it?" Bourne said.

Volkin rose, went into the kitchen. Bourne could hear the refrigerator door open and close, the light clink of glassware. When Volkin returned, he had an iced bottle of vodka in one hand, three water glasses in the other.

Handing them the glasses, he unscrewed the cap, filled their glasses halfway. When he'd poured for himself, he sat down again, the bottle standing between them on the threadbare carpet.

Volkin raised his glass. "To our health." He emptied his glass in two great gulps. Smacking his lips, he reached down, refilled it. "Listen to me closely. If I were to admit that the Black Legion exists today there would be nothing left of my health to toast."

"How would anyone know?" Bourne said.

"How? I'll tell you how. I tell you what I know, then you go out and act on that information. Where d'you think the shitstorm that ensues is going to land, hmm?" He tapped his barrel chest with his glass, slopping vodka onto his already stained shirt. "Every action has a reaction, my friend, and let me tell you that when it comes to the Black Legion every reaction is fatal for someone."

Since he'd already as much as admitted that the Black Legion had, in fact, survived the defeat of Nazi Germany, Bourne brought the subject around to what really concerned him. "Why would the Kazanskaya be involved?"

"Pardon?"

"In some way I can't yet understand the Kazanskaya are interested in Mikhail Tarkanian. I stumbled across one of their contract killers in his apartment."

Volkin's expression turned sour. "What were you doing in his apartment?"

"Tarkanian's dead," Bourne said.

"What?" Volkin exploded. "I don't believe you."

"I was there when it happened."

"And I tell you it's impossible."

"On the contrary, it's a fact," Bourne said. "His death was a direct result of him being a member of the Black Legion."

Volkin crossed his arms over his chest. He looked like the silverback in the National Zoo. "I see what's happening here. How many ways will you try to get me to talk about the Black Legion?"

"Every way I can," Bourne said. "The Kazanskaya are in some way in league with the Black Legion, which is an alarming prospect."

"I may look as if I have all the answers, but I don't." Volkin stared at him, as if daring Bourne to call him a liar.

Though Bourne was certain that Volkin knew more than he would admit, he also knew it would be a mistake to call him on it. Clearly, this was a man who couldn't be intimidated, so there was no point in trying. Professor Specter had warned him not to get caught up in the *grupperovka* war, but the professor was a long way away from Moscow; his intelligence was only as accurate as his men on the ground here. Instinct told Bourne there was a serious disconnect. So far as he could see there was only one way to get to the truth.

"Tell me how to get a meet with Maslov," he said.

Volkin shook his head. "That would be most unwise. With the Kazanskaya in the middle of a power struggle with the Azeri—"

"Popov is only my cover name," Bourne said. "Actually, I'm a consultant to Viktor Cherkesov"—the head of the Federal Anti-Narcotics Agency, one of the two or three most powerful *siloviks* in Russia.

Volkin pulled back as if stung by Bourne's words. He shot Gala an accusatory glance, as if Bourne were a scorpion she'd brought into his den. Turning back to Bourne he said, "Have you any proof of this?"

"Don't be absurd. However, I can tell you the name of the man I report to: Boris Illyich Karpov."

"Is that so?" Volkin produced a Makarov handgun, placed it on his right knee. "If you're lying . . ." He picked up a cell phone he scavenged miraculously from out of the clutter, and quickly punched in a number. "We have no amateurs here."

After a moment he said into the phone, "Boris Illyich, I have here with me a man who claims to be working for you. I would like to put him on the line, yes?"

With a deadpan face, Volkin handed over the cell.

"Boris," Bourne said, "it's Jason Bourne."

"Jason, my good friend!" Karpov's voice reverberated down the line. "I haven't seen you since Reykjavik."

"It seems like a long time."

"Too long, I tell you!"

"Where have you been?"

"In Timbuktu."

"What were you doing in Mali?" Bourne asked.

"Don't ask, don't tell." Karpov laughed. "I understand you're now working for me."

"That's right."

"My boy, I've longed for this day!" Karpov let go with another booming laugh. "We must toast this moment with vodka, but not tonight, eh? Put that old goat Volkin back on the line. I assume there's something you want from him."

"Correct."

"He hasn't believed a word you've told him. But I'll change that. Please memorize my cell number, then call me when you're alone. Until we speak again, my good friend."

"He wants to talk to you," Bourne said.

"That's understandable." Volkin took the cell from Bourne, put it to his ear. Almost immediately his expression changed. He stared at Bourne, his mouth slightly open. "Yes, Boris Illyich. Yes, of course. I understand."

Volkin broke the connection, stared at Bourne for what seemed a long time. At length, he said, "I'm going to call Dimitri Maslov now. I hope to hell you know what you're doing. Otherwise, this is the last time anyone will see you, either alive or dead."

Twenty-Two

TYRONE WENT immediately into one of the cubicles in the men's room. Fishing out the plastic tag Deron had made for him, he clipped it on the outside of his suit jacket, a suit that looked like the regulation government suits all the other spooks wore here. The tag identified him as Special Agent Damon Riggs, out of the NSA field office in LA. Damon Riggs was real enough. The tag came straight from the NSA HR database.

Tyrone flushed the toilet, emerged from the cubicle, smiled frostily at an NSA agent bent over one of the sinks washing his hands. The agent glanced at Tyrone's tag, said, "You're a long way from home."

"And in the middle of winter, too." Tyrone's voice was strong and firm. "Damn, I miss goin' top-down in Santa Monica."

"I hear you." The agent dried his hands. "Good luck," he said as he left.

Tyrone stared at the closed door for a moment, took a deep breath, let it out slowly. So far, so good. He went out into the hallway, his eyes straight ahead, his stride purposeful. He passed four or five agents. A couple gave his tag a cursory glance, nodded. The others ignored him altogether.

"The trick," Deron had said, "is to look like you belong. Don't hesitate, be purposeful. If you look like you know where you're going, you become part of the scene, no one notices you."

Tyrone reached the door without incident. He went past it as two agents, deep in conversation, passed him. Then, checking both ways, he doubled back. Quickly he took out what seemed to be an ordinary piece of clear tape, laid it on top of the fingerprint reader. Checking his watch, he waited until the second hand touched the 12. Then, holding his breath, he pressed his forefinger onto the tape so that it was flush against the reader. The door opened. He stripped off the tape, slipped inside. The tape contained LaValle's fingerprint, which Tyrone had lifted off the back cover of the file while working the device that slit the security tape. Soraya had engaged LaValle in conversation as a diversion.

At the bottom of the flight of steps, he paused for a moment. No alarm bells were going off, no sound of armed security guards coming his way. Kiki's software program had done its work. Now the rest was up to him.

He moved swiftly and silently down the rough concrete corridor. Buzzing fluorescent strips were the only decoration here, casting a sickly glow. He saw no one, heard nothing beyond the susurrus of machinery.

Snapping on latex gloves he tried each door he came to. Most were locked. The first one that wasn't opened into a small cubicle with a viewing window in one wall. Tyrone had been in enough police precincts to know this was one-way glass. He peered into a room not much larger than the one he was in. He could make out a metal chair bolted to the center of the floor, beneath which was a large drain. Affixed to the right-hand wall was a three-foot-deep trough as long as a man with manacles bolted to each end, above which was coiled a fire hose. Its nozzle looked enormous in the confines of the small room. This, Tyrone knew from photos he'd seen, was a waterboarding tank. He snapped as many photos of it as possible, because there was the proof Soraya needed that the NSA was enacting illegal and inhuman torture.

Tyrone took photos of everything with the ten-megapixel digital mini camera Soraya had given him. Given the huge memory of its smart card, it could record six videos of up to three minutes in duration.

He moved on, knowing he had an extremely limited amount of time. Opening the door an inch at a time, he determined that the corridor was still deserted. He hurried down it, checking all the doors he came to. At length, he found himself in another viewing room. This time, however, he saw a man kneeling beside a table. His arms were drawn back, his bound hands on the table. A black hood had been pulled down over his head. His attitude was of a defeated soldier about to be forced to kiss the feet of his conqueror. Tyrone felt a surge of rage run through him such as he'd never felt before. He couldn't help thinking of the history of his own people, hunted by rival tribes on the east coast of Africa, sold to the white man, brought as slaves back to America. All of this terrible history Deron had made him study, to learn where he came from, to understand what drove the prejudices, the innate hatreds, all the powerful forces inside him.

With an effort he pulled himself together. This is what they'd been hoping for: proof that the NSA was subjecting prisoners to illegal forms of torture. Tyrone took a slew of photos, even a short video before exiting the viewing room.

Once again, he was the only one in the corridor. This concerned him. Surely he would have heard or seen NSA personnel down here. But there was no sign of anyone.

All at once, he felt a prickling at the back of his neck. He turned, retracing his steps at a half run. His heart pounded, his blood rushed in his ears. With every step he took his sense of foreboding increased. Then he broke into a full-out sprint.

Luther LaValle looked up from his reading, said ominously, "What kind of game are you playing, Director?"

Soraya kept herself from starting. "I beg your pardon?"

"I've been through these transmission intercepts you claim come from the Black Legion twice now. Nowhere do I find any reference to that name or, for that matter, any name at all."

Willard appeared, handed General Kendall a folded slip of paper. Kendall read it without any expression. Then he excused himself. Soraya watched him leave the Library with no little trepidation.

To regain her attention, LaValle waved the sheets briefly in the air like a red flag in front of a bull. "Tell me the truth. For all you know, these conversations could be between two sets of eleven-year-olds playing terrorist games."

Soraya could feel herself bristling. "My people assure me they're genuine, Mr. LaValle, and they're the best in the business. If you don't believe that, I can't imagine why you want a piece of Typhon."

LaValle conceded her point, but he wasn't finished with her. "Then how do you know they're from the Black Legion."

"Collateral intelligence."

LaValle sat back in his chair. His drink was left untouched on the table. "Just what the holy hell does *collateral intelligence* mean?"

"Another source, unrelated to the intercepts, has knowledge of an imminent attack on American soil that originates with the Black Legion."

"Who we have no tangible evidence actually exist."

Soraya was growing increasingly uncomfortable. The conversation was veering perilously close to an interrogation. "I brought these intercepts at your behest with the intention of engendering trust between us."

"That's as may be," LaValle said. "But quite frankly these anonymous intercepts, alarming as they seem on the surface, don't do it for me. You're holding something back, Director. I want to know the source of your so-called collateral intel."

"I'm afraid that's impossible. The source is absolutely sacrosanct." Soraya could not tell him that her source was Jason Bourne. "However—" She reached down to her slim attaché case, pulled out several photos, handed them over.

"It's a corpse," LaValle said. "I fail to see the significance—"

"Look at the second photo," Soraya said. "It's a close-up of the inside of the victim's elbow. What do you see?"

"A tattoo of three horses' heads attached to—what is this? It looks like the Nazi SS death's head."

"And so it is." Soraya handed him another photo. "This is the uniform patch of the Black Legion under their leader Heinrich Himmler."

LaValle pursed his lips. Then he put sheets back in the file, returned it to Soraya. He held up the photos. "If you could find this insignia, anyone could. This could be a group that's simply appropriated the Black Legion's sign, like the skinheads in Germany appropriated the swastika. Besides, this isn't proof that the intercepts came from the Black Legion. And even if they did I have a problem, Director. It's the same as yours, I would think. You've told me—also according to your sacrosanct source—that the Black Legion is being fronted by the Eastern Brotherhood. If the NSA acts on this intel, we'll have every flavor of PR nightmare visited on us. The Eastern Brotherhood, as I'm sure you're aware, is exceedingly powerful, especially with the overseas press. We run with this and we're wrong, it's going to cause the president and this country an enormous amount of humiliation, which we can't afford now. Do I make myself clear?"

"Perfectly, Mr. LaValle. But if we ignore it and America is successfully attacked again, then how do we look?"

LaValle scrubbed his face with one hand. "So we're between a rock and hard place."

"Sir, you know as well as I do that action is better than inaction, especially in a volatile situation like this."

LaValle was about to capitulate, Soraya knew it, but here came Willard again, gliding up, silent as a ghost. He bent, whispered something in LaValle's ear.

"Thank you, Willard," Lavalle said, "that will be all." Then he returned his attention to Soraya. "Well, Director, it seems I'm urgently wanted elsewhere." He stood up and smiled down at her, but spoke with a steely tone. "Please join me."

Soraya's heart plummeted. This invitation wasn't a request.

Yakov, the *bombila* driver, who'd been ordered to park across the avenue from the front entrance of the Metropolya Hotel, had been joined forty minutes ago by a man who looked as if he'd been in a fistfight with a meat grinder. Despite efforts to cover it up, his face was swollen, dark as pounded flesh. He wore a silver patch over one eye. He was a surly bastard, Yakov decided, even before the man handed him a fistful of money. He uttered not a word of greeting, but slammed into the backseat, slithered down so even the crown of his head was invisible to anyone glancing casually in.

The atmosphere inside the *bombila* quickly grew so toxic that Yakov was forced to vacate the semi-warmth for the freezing Moscow night. He bought himself some food from a passing Turkish vendor, spent the next half hour eating it, talking to his friend Max, who'd pulled up behind him because Max was a lazy sonovabitch who grasped at any excuse not to work.

Yakov and Max were in the middle of heated speculation that concerned last week's death of a high-level RAB Bank officer, who was discovered tied up, tortured, and asphyxiated in the garage of his own *elitny* dacha. The two of them were wondering why the General Prosecutor's Office and the president's newly formed Investigative Committee were fighting over jurisdiction of the death.

"It's politics, pure and simple," Yakov said.

"*Dirty* politics," Max retorted. "There's nothing pure and simple about *that*."

It was then that Yakov spotted Jason Bourne and the sexy *dyev* getting out of a *bombila* in front of the hotel. When he struck the side of his cab three times with the flat of his hand, he sensed a stirring in the backseat.

"He's here," he said as the rear window rolled down.

* * *

Bourne was about to drop Gala off at the Metropolya Hotel when he looked out the *bombila* window, saw the taxi that had earlier taken him from The Chinese Pilot to the hotel. Yakov, the driver, was leaning against the fender of his dilapidated junkmobile, eating something greasy while talking to the cabbie parked right behind him.

Bourne saw Yakov glance over as he and Gala exited the *bombila*. When they'd gone through the revolving door, Bourne told her to stay put. To his left was the service door used by porters to take guests's luggage in and out of the hotel. Bourne looked out across the street. Yakov stuck his head in the rear window, huddled with a man who'd been hidden in the backseat.

In the elevator, on the way up to their room, he said, "Are you hungry? I'm starved." Harun Iliev, the man Semion Icoupov sent to find Jason Bourne, had expended hours in contentious negotiations and frustrating dead ends, and finally spent a great deal of money in his pursuit. It wasn't coincidence that had led him at last to the *bombila* named Yakov, for Yakov was an ambitious man who knew he'd never get rich driving around Moscow, fending off other *bombily*, pissing them off by cutting in, snatching their fares from under their noses. What could be more lucrative than spying on other people? Especially when your chief client was the American. Yakov had many clients, but none of them knew how to throw around dollars like the Americans. It was their sincere belief that enough money bought you anything. Mostly, they were right. When they weren't, though, it was still costly for them.

Most of Yakov's other clients laughed at the kind of money the Americans threw around. Chiefly, though, he suspected it was because they were jealous. Laughing at what you didn't have and never would was, he supposed, better than letting it depress you.

Icoupov's people were the only ones who paid as well. But they used him far less than the Americans. On the other hand, they had him on retainer. Yakov knew Harun Iliev well, had dealt with him a number of times before, and both liked and trusted him. Besides, they were both

Muslim. Yakov kept his religion a secret in Moscow, especially from the Americans, who, stupidly, would have dropped him like a fake ruble.

Directly after the American attaché contacted him for the job, Yakov had called Harun Iliev. As a consequence, Harun had already inserted himself in the staff of the Metropolya Hotel through a cousin of his, who worked in the kitchen as one of the expediters. He coordinated food orders for the line chefs. The moment he saw the room-service order come down from 1728, Bourne's room, he called Harun.

"We're short-staffed tonight," he said. "Get down here in the next five minutes and I'll make sure you're the one to take the order up to him."

Harun Iliev quickly presented himself to his cousin and was shown to a trolley, neatly covered in starched white linen, laden with covered bowls, platters, plates, silverware, and napkins. Thanking his cousin for this opportunity to get to Jason Bourne, he rolled his trolley to the ser- vice elevator. Someone was already there. Harun took him to be one of the hotel managers until, as they entered the elevator, he turned so Harun caught a fleeting glimpse of his pulped face and the silver patch over one eye.

Harun reached out, pressed the button for the seventeenth floor. The man pressed the button for the eighteenth. The elevator stopped at the fourth floor, where a maid got on with her turn-down cart. She exited a floor later.

The elevator had just passed the fifteenth floor when the man reached over, pulled out the large red EMERGENCY STOP button. Harun turned to question the man's action, but the man fired one bullet from a exceptionally quiet 9mm Welrod equipped with a suppressor. The bullet pierced Harun's forehead, tore through his brain. He was dead before he collapsed to the elevator floor.

Anthony Prowess mopped up what little blood there was with a napkin from the room-service cart. Then he quickly stripped the clothes off his victim, donned the uniform of the Metropolya Hotel. He pushed in the EMERGENCY STOP button again and the elevator continued its ascent to the seventeenth floor. After determining that the hallway was clear, Prowess consulted a map of the floor, dragged the corpse into a utility room, then wheeled the cart around the corner to room 1728.

Why don't you take shower? A long hot," Bourne said.

Gala's expression was mischievous. "If I stink at least it's not as bad as you." She began to slip out of her mini skirt. "Why don't we take one together?"

"Some other time. I have business to attend to."

Her lower lip comically pouted. "God, what could be more boring?"

Bourne laughed as she crossed into the bathroom, closed the door behind her. Soon after, the sound of running water came to him, along with tiny curls of steam. He turned on the TV, watched a dreadful show in Russian with the sound turned up.

There was a knock on the door. Bourne rose from his position on the bed, opened the door. A uniformed waiter in a short jacket and a hat with a bill pulled down over his face pushed a trolley full of food into the room. Bourne signed the bill, the waiter turned to leave. Instantly he whirled, a knife in his hand. In one blurred movement, he drew his arm back. But Bourne was ready. As the waiter threw the knife Bourne raised a domed metal top off a chafing dish, used it as a shield to deflect the knife. With a flick of his wrist, he sent it spinning at the waiter, who ducked out of the way. The edge of the domed top caught his hat, spun it off his head, revealing the puffy face of the man who'd strangled Baronov and tried to kill Bourne, as well.

The attacker drew a Welrod and squeezed off two shots before Bourne shoved the cart into his midsection. He staggered back. Bourne threw himself across the cart, grabbed Prowess by the front of the uniform, then wrestled him to the floor.

Bourne managed to kick away the Welrod. The man attacked with hands and feet, moving Bourne so that he could regain possession of the gun. Bourne could see the patch over the NSA agent's eye, could only surmise the damage he'd inflicted.

The agent feinted one way, then caught Bourne flush on the jaw. Bourne staggered and his attacker was on him with another wire, which he whipped around Bourne's neck. Pulling hard on it, he drew Bourne back to his feet. Bourne staggered against the cart. As it skittered away from him, he grabbed the chafing dish, hurled its contents in the agent's face. The scalding soup struck the attacker like a torch, and he shouted but failed to drop the wire, instead pulling it tighter, jerking Bourne against his chest.

Bourne was on his knees, his back arched. His lungs were screaming for oxygen, his muscles were rapidly losing their strength, and it was becoming increasingly difficult to concentrate. Soon, he knew, he'd pass out.

With his remaining strength, he jabbed his elbow into the agent's crotch. The wire slacked off enough for him to get to his feet. He slammed the back of his head into the agent's face, heard the satisfying thunk as the man's head struck the wall. The wire slackened a bit more, enough for Bourne to pull it from his throat, gasping in air, and reverse their positions, wrapping the wire around Prowess's neck. He fought and kicked like a madman, but Bourne held on, working the wire tighter and tighter, until the agent's body went slack. His head toppled to one side. Bourne didn't slacken the wire until he'd assured himself there was no longer a pulse. Then he let the man slide to the floor.

He was bent over, hands on thighs, taking deep, slow breaths when Gala walked out of the bathroom amid a halo of lavender-scented mist.

"Jesus Christ," she said. Then she turned and vomited all over her bare pink feet.

Twenty-Three

ANY WAY you slice it or dice it," Luther LaValle said, "he's a dead man."

Soraya stared bleakly through the one-way glass at Tyrone, who was standing in a cubicle ominously outfitted with a shallow coffin-like tub that had restraints for wrists and ankles, a fire hose above it. In the center of the room a steel table was bolted down to the bare concrete floor, beneath which was a drain to sluice both water and blood away.

LaValle held up the digital camera. "General Kendall found this on your compatriot." He touched a button, and the photos Tyrone had taken scrolled across the camera's screen. "This smoking gun is enough to convict him of treason."

Soraya couldn't help wondering how many shots of the torture chambers Tyrone had managed to take before he was caught.

"Off with his head," Kendall said, baring his teeth.

Soraya could not rid herself of the sick feeling in her stomach. Of course, Tyrone had been in dangerous situations before, but she was directly responsible for putting him in harm's way. If anything happened to him she knew she'd never be able to forgive herself. What was she thinking involving him in such perilous work? The enormity of her miscalculation was all too clear to her now, when it was too late to do anything about it.

"The real pity," LaValle went on, "is that with very little difficulty we can make a case against you, as well."

Soraya was solely focused on Tyrone, whom she had wronged so terribly.

"This was my idea," she said dully. "Let Tyrone go."

"You mean he was only following orders," General Kendall said. "This isn't Nuremberg. Frankly, there's no viable defense the two of you can put up. His conviction and execution—as well as yours—are a fait accompli."

They took her back to the Library, where Willard, seeing her ashen face, fetched her a fresh pot of Ceylon tea. The three of them sat by the window. The fourth chair, conspicuously empty, was an accusation to Soraya. Her grievous mismanagement of this mission was compounded by the knowledge that she had seriously underestimated LaValle. She'd been lulled by his smug, overaggressive nature into thinking he was the sort of man who'd automatically underestimate her. She was dead wrong.

She fought the constriction in her chest, the panic welling up, the sense that she and Tyrone were trapped in an impossible situation. She used the tea ritual to refocus herself. For the first time in her life she added cream and sugar, and drank the tea as if it were medication or a form of penance.

She was trying to get her brain unfrozen from shock, to get it working normally again. In order to help Tyrone, she knew she needed to get herself out of here. If LaValle meant to charge her as he threatened to do with Tyrone, she'd already be in an adjacent cell. The fact that they'd brought her back to the Library allowed a sliver of light into the darkness that had settled around her. She decided for now to allow this scenario to play out on LaValle's and Kendall's terms.

The moment she set her teacup down, LaValle took up his ax. "As I said before, Director, the real pity is your involvement. I'd hate to lose you as an ally—though, I see now, I never really had you as an ally."

This little speech sounded canned, as if each word had been chewed over by LaValle.

"Frankly," he continued, "in retrospect, I can see that you've lied to me from the first. You never had any intention of switching your allegiance to NSA, did you?" He sighed, as if he were a disciplinary dean addressing a bright but chronically wayward student. "That's why I can't believe that you concocted this scheme on your own."

"If I were a betting man," Kendall said, "I'd wager your orders came from the top."

"Veronica Hart is the real problem here." LaValle spread his hands. "Perhaps through the lens of what's happened here today you can begin to see things as we do."

Soraya didn't need a weatherman to see which way the wind was blowing. Keeping her voice deliberately neutral, she said, "How can I be of service?"

LaValle smiled genially, turned to Kendall, said, "You see, Richard, the director can be of help to us, despite your reservations." He quickly turned back to Soraya, his expression sobering. "The general wants to prosecute you both to the full extent of the law, which I needn't reiterate is very full indeed."

Their good-cop, bad-cop routine would seem clichéd, Soraya thought bitterly, except this was for real. She knew Kendall hated her guts; he'd made no effort to hide his contempt. He was a military man, after all. The possibility of having to report to a female superior was unthinkable, downright risible. He hadn't thought much of Tyrone, either, which made his capture of the younger man that much harder to stomach.

"I understand my position is untenable," she said, despising having to kowtow to this despicable human being.

"Excellent, then we'll start from that point."

LaValle stared up at the ceiling, giving an impersonation of someone trying to decide how to proceed. But she suspected he knew very well what he was doing, every step of the way.

His eyes engaged hers. "The way I see it we have a two-part problem. One concerns your friend down in the hold. The second involves you."

"I'm more concerned with him," Soraya said. "How do I get him out?"

LaValle shifted in his chair. "Let's take your situation first. We can build a circumstantial case against you, but without direct testimony from your friend—"

"Tyrone," Soraya said. "His name is Tyrone Elkins."

To hammer home just whose conversation this was, LaValle quite deliberately ignored her. "Without direct testimony from your friend we won't get far."

"Direct testimony we will get," Kendall said, "as soon as we water-board him."

"No," Soraya said. "You can't."

"Why, because it's illegal?" Kendall chuckled.

Soraya turned to LaValle. "There's another way. You and I both know there is."

LaValle said nothing for a moment, drawing out the tension. "You told me that your source for the attribution of the Typhon intercepts was sacrosanct. Does that decision still stand?"

"If I tell you will you let Tyrone go?"

"No," LaValle said, "but you'll be free to leave."

"What about Tyrone?"

LaValle crossed one leg over another. "Let's take one thing at a time, shall we?"

Soraya nodded. She knew that as long as she was sitting here she had no wiggle room. "My source was Bourne."

LaValle looked startled. "Jason Bourne? Are you kidding me?"

"No, Mr. LaValle. He has knowledge of the Black Legion and that they were being fronted by the Eastern Brotherhood."

"Where the hell did this knowledge come from?"

"He had no time to tell me, even if he had a mind to," she said. "There were too many NSA agents in the vicinity."

"The incident at the Freer," Kendall said.

LaValle held up a hand. "You helped him to escape."

Soraya shook her head. "Actually, he thought I'd turned on him."

"Interesting." LaValle tapped his lip. "Does he still think that?"

Soraya determined it was time for a little defiance, a little lie. "I don't know. Jason has a tendency toward paranoia, so it's possible."

LaValle looked thoughtful. "Maybe we can use that to our ad–vantage."

General Kendall looked disgusted. "So, in other words, this whole story about the Black Legion could be nothing more than a lunatic fantasy."

"Or, more likely, deliberate disinformation," LaValle said.

Soraya shook her head. "Why would he do that?"

"Who knows why he does anything?" LaValle took a slow sip of his whiskey, diluted now by the melted ice cubes. "Let's not forget that Bourne was in a rage when he told you about the Black Legion. By your own admission, he thought you'd betrayed him."

"You have a point." Soraya knew better than to defend Bourne to these people. The more you argued against them, the more entrenched they became in their position. They'd built a case against Jason out of fear and loathing. Not because, as they claimed, he was unstable, but because he simply didn't care about their rules and regulations. Instead of flouting them, something the directors had knowledge of and knew how to handle, he annihilated them.

"Of course I do." LaValle set down his glass. "Let's move on to your friend. The case against him is airtight, open-and-shut, no hope what-soever of appeal or commutation."

"Let him eat cake," Kendall said.

"Marie Antoinette never said that, by the way," Soraya said.

Kendall glared at her, while LaValle continued, "*Let the punishment fit the crime* would be more apropos. Or, in your case, *Let the expiation fit the crime*." He waved the approaching Willard away. "What we're going to need from you, Director, is proof—incontrovertible proof—that your illegal foray into NSA territory was instigated by Veronica Hart."

She knew what he was asking of her. "So, basically, we're talking an exchange of prisoners—Hart for Tyrone."

"You've grasped it entirely," LaValle said, clearly pleased.

"I'll have to think about it."

LaValle nodded. "A reasonable request. I'll have Willard prepare you a meal." He glanced at his watch. "Richard and I have a meeting in fifteen minutes. We'll be back in approximately two hours. You can think over your answer until then."

"No, I need to think this over in another environment," Soraya said.

"Director Moore, given your history of deception that would be a mistake on our part."

"You promised I could leave if I told you my source."

"And so you shall, when you've agreed to my terms." He rose, and with him Kendall. "You and your friend came in here together. Now you're joined at the hip."

Bourne waited until Gala was sufficiently recovered. She dressed, shivering, not once looking at the body of the dead agent.

"I'm sorry you got dragged into this," Bourne said.

"No you're not. Without me you never would've gotten to Ivan." Gala angrily jammed her feet into her shoes. "This is a nightmare," she said, as if to herself. "Any minute I'll wake up in my own bed and none of this will have happened."

Bourne led her toward the door.

Gala shuddered anew as she carefully skirted the body.

"You're hanging out with the wrong crowd."

"Ha, ha, good one," she said, as they made their way down the hall. "That includes you."

A moment later, he signaled her to stop. Kneeling down, he touched his fingertip to a wet spot on the carpet.

"What is it?"

Bourne examined his fingertip. "Blood."

Gala gave a little whimper. "What's it doing out here?"

"Good question," Bourne said as he crept along the hallway. He noted a tiny smear in front of a narrow door. Wrenching it open, he switched on the utility room's light.

"Christ," Gala said.

Inside was a crumpled body with a bullet in its forehead. It was nude, but there was a pile of clothes tossed in a corner, obviously those of the NSA agent. Bourne knelt down, rifled through them, hoping to find some form of ID, to no avail.

"What are you doing?" Gala cried.

Bourne spotted a tiny triangle of dark brown leather sticking out from under the corpse, which was only visible from this low angle. Rolling the corpse on its side, he discovered a wallet. The dead man's ID would prove useful, since Bourne now had none of his own. His assumed identity, which he'd used to check in, was unusable, because the moment the corpse was found in Fyodor Ilianovich Popov's room, there'd be a massive manhunt for him. Bourne reached out, took the wallet.

Then he rose, grabbed Gala's hand, and got them out of there. He insisted they take the service elevator down to the kitchen. From there it was a simple matter to find the rear entrance.

Outside, it had begun to snow again. The wind, slicing in from the square, was icy and bitter. Flagging down a *bombila*, Bourne was about to give the cabbie the address of Gala's friend, then realized that Yakov, the cabbie working for the NSA, knew that address.

"Get in the taxi," Bourne said quietly to Gala, "but be prepared to get out quickly and do exactly as I say."

Soraya didn't need a couple of hours to make up her mind; she didn't even need a couple of minutes.

"All right," she said. "I'll do whatever it takes to get Tyrone out of here."

LaValle turned back to regard her. "Well, now, that kind of capitulation would do my heart good if I didn't know you to be such a duplicitous little bitch.

"Unfortunately," he went on, "in your case, verbal capitulation isn't quite as convincing as it would be in others. That being the case, the general here will make crystal clear to you the consequences of further treachery on your part."

Soraya rose, along with Kendall.

LaValle stopped her with his voice, "Oh, and, Director, when you leave here you'll have until ten tomorrow morning to make your decision. I'll expect you back here then. I hope I've made myself clear."

The general led her out of the Library, down the corridor to the door to the basement. The moment she saw where he was taking her, she said, "No! Don't do this. Please. There's no need."

But Kendall, his back ramrod-straight, ignored her. When she hesitated at the security door, he grasped her firmly by the elbow and, as if she were a child, steered her down the stairs.

In due course, she found herself in the same viewing room. Tyrone was on his knees, his arm behind him, bound hands on the tabletop, which was higher than shoulder level. This position was both extremely painful and humiliating. His torso was forced forward, his shoulder blades back.

Soraya's heart was filled with dread. "Enough," she said. "I get it. You've made your point."

"By no means," General Kendall said.

Soraya could see two shadowy figures moving about the cell. Tyrone had become aware of them, too. He tried to twist around to see what they were up to. One of the men shoved a black hood over his head.

My God, Soraya said to herself. What did the other man have in his hands?

Kendall shoved her hard against the one-way glass. "Where your friend is concerned we're just warming up."

Two minutes later, they began to fill the waterboarding tank. Soraya began to scream.

* * *

Bourne asked the *bombila* driver to pass by the front of the hotel. Everything seemed calm and normal, which meant that the bodies on the seventeenth floor hadn't been discovered yet. But it wouldn't be long before someone went to look for the missing room-service waiter.

He turned his attention across the street, searching for Yakov. He was still outside his car, talking to a fellow driver. Both of them were swinging their arms to keep their circulation going. He pointed out Yakov to Gala, who recognized him. When they'd passed the square, Bourne had the *bombila* pull over.

He turned to Gala. "I want you to go back to Yakov and have him take you to Universitetskaya Ploshchad at Vorobyovy Gory." Bourne was speaking of the top of the only hill in the otherwise flat city, where lovers and university students went to get drunk, make love, and smoke dope while looking out over the city. "Wait there for me and whatever you do, don't get out of the car. Tell the cabbie you're meeting someone there."

"But he's the one who's been spying on us," Gala said.

"Don't worry," Bourne reassured her. "I'll be right behind you."

The view out over Vorobyovy Gory was not so very grand. First, there was the ugly bulk of Luzhniki Stadium in the mid-foreground. Second, there were the spires of the Kremlin, which would hardly inspire even the most ardent lovers. But for all that, at night it was as romantic as Moscow could get.

Bourne, who'd had his *bombila* track the one Gala was in all the way there, was relieved that Yakov had orders only to observe and report back. Anyway, the NSA was interested in Bourne, not a young blond *dyev*.

Arriving at the overlook, Bourne paid the fare he'd agreed to at the beginning of the ride, strode down the sidewalk, and got into the front seat of Yakov's taxi.

"Hey, what's this?" Yakov said. Then he recognized Bourne and made a scramble for the Makarov he kept in a homemade sling under the ratty dash.

Bourne pulled his hand away and held him back against the seat while taking possession of the handgun. He pointed it at Yakov. "Who do you report to?"

Yakov said in a whiny voice, "I challenge you to sit in my seat night after night, driving around the Garden Ring, crawling endlessly down Tverskaya, being cut out of fares by kamikaze *bombily* and make enough to live on."

"I don't care why you pimp yourself out to the NSA," Bourne told him. "I want to know who you report to."

Yakov held up his hand. "Listen, listen, I'm from Bishkek in Kyrgyz-stan. It's not so nice there, who can make a living? So I pack my family and we travel to Russia, the beating heart of the new federation, where the streets are paved with rubles. But when I arrive here I am treated like dirt. People in the street spit on my wife. My children are beaten and called terrible names. And I can't get a job anywhere in this city. 'Moscow for Muscovites,' that is the refrain I hear over and over. So I take to the *bombily* because I have no other choice. But this life, sir, you have no idea how difficult it is. Sometimes after twelve hours I come home with a hundred rubles, sometimes with nothing. I cannot be faulted for taking money the Americans offer.

"Russia is corrupt, but Moscow, it's more than corrupt. There isn't a word for how bad things are here. The government is made up of thugs and criminals. The criminals plunder the natural resources of Russia— oil, natural gas, uranium. Everyone takes, takes, takes so they can have big foreign cars, a different *dyev* for every day of the week, a dacha in Miami Beach. And what's left for us? Potatoes and beets, if we work eighteen hours a day and if we're lucky."

"I have no animosity toward you," Bourne said. "You have a right to earn a living." He handed Yakov a fistful of dollars.

"I see no one, sir. I swear. Just voices on my cell phone. All moneys come to a post office box in—"

Bourne carefully placed the muzzle of the Makarov in Yakov's ear. The cabbie cringed, turned mournful eyes on Bourne.

"Please, please, sir, what have I done?"

"I saw you outside the Metropolya with the man who tried to kill me."

Yakov squealed like a skewered rat. "Kill you? I'm employed merely to watch and report. I have no knowledge about—"

Bourne hit the cabbie. "Stop lying and tell me what I want to know."

"All right, all right." Yakov was shaking with fear. "The American who pays me, his name is Low. Harris Low."

Bourne made him give a detailed description of Low, then he took Yakov's cell phone.

"Get out of the car," he said.

"But sir, I answered all your questions," Yakov protested. "You've taken everything of mine. What more do you want?"

Bourne leaned across him, opened the door, then shoved him out. "This is a popular place. Plenty of *bombily* come and go. You're a rich man now. Use some of the money I gave you to get a ride home."

Sliding behind the wheel he put the Zhig in gear, drove back into the heart of the city.

Harris Low was a dapper man with a pencil mustache. He had the prematurely white hair and ruddy complexion of many blue-blooded families in the American Northeast. That he had spent the last eleven years in Moscow, working for NSA, was a testament to his father, who had trod the same perilous path. Low had idolized his father, had wanted to be like him for as long as he could remember. Like his father, he had the Stars and Stripes tattooed on his soul. He'd been a running back in college, gone through the rigorous physical training to be an NSA field agent, had tracked down terrorists in Afghanistan and the Horn of Africa. He wasn't afraid to engage in hand-to-hand combat or to kill a target. He did it for God and country.

During his eleven years in the capital of Russia, Low had made many friends, some of whom were the sons of his father's friends. Suffice to say he had developed a network of *apparatchiks* and *siloviks* for whom a quid pro quo was the order of the day. Harris held no illusions. To further his country's cause he would scratch anyone's back—if they, in turn, scratched his.

He heard about the murders at the Metropolya Hotel from a friend of his in the General Prosecutor's Office, who'd caught the police squeal. Harris met this individual at the hotel and was consequently one of the first people on the scene.

He had no interest in the corpse in the utility closet, but he immediately recognized Anthony Prowess. Excusing himself from the crime scene, he went into the stairwell off the seventeenth-floor hallway, punched in an overseas number on his cell. A moment later Luther LaValle answered.

"We have a problem," Low said. "Prowess has been rendered inoperative with extreme prejudice."

"That's very disturbing," LaValle said. "We have a rogue operative loose in Moscow who has now murdered one of our own. I think you know what to do."

Low understood. There was no time to bring in another of NSA's wet-work specialists, which meant terminating Bourne was up to him.

"Now that he's killed an American citizen," LaValle said, "I'll bring the Moscow police and the General Prosecutor's Office into the picture. They'll have the same photo of him I'm sending to your cell within the hour."

Low thought a moment. "The question is tracking him. Moscow is way behind the curve in closed-circuit TVs."

"Bourne is going to need money," LaValle said. "He couldn't take enough through Customs when he landed, which means he wouldn't try. He'll have set up a local account at a Moscow bank. Get the locals to help with surveillance pronto."

"Consider it done," Low said.

"And Harris. Don't make the same mistake with Bourne that Prowess did."

Bourne took Gala to her friend's apartment, which was lavish even by American standards. Her friend, Lorraine, was an American of Armenian extraction. Her dark eyes and hair, her olive complexion, all served to increase her exoticism. She hugged and kissed Gala, greeted Bourne warmly, and invited him to stay for a drink or tea.

As he took a tour through the rooms, Gala said, "He's worried about my safety."

"What's happened?" Lorraine asked. "Are you all right?"

"She'll be fine," Bourne said, coming back into the living room. "This'll all blow over in a couple of days." Having satisfied himself of the security of the apartment, he left them with the warning not to open the door for anyone they didn't know.

Ivan Volkin had directed Bourne to go to Novoslobodskaya 20, where the meet with Dimitri Maslov would take place. At first Bourne thought it lucky that the *bombila* he flagged down knew how to find the address, but when he was dropped off he understood. Novoslobodskaya 20 was the address of Motorhome, a new club jammed with young partying Muscovites. Gigantic flat-panel screens above the center island bar showed telecasts of American baseball, basketball, football, English rugby, and World Cup soccer. The floor of the main room was dominated by tables for Russian billiards and American pool. Following Volkin's direction, Bourne headed for the back room, which was fitted out as an Arabian Nights hookah room complete with overlapping carpets, jewel-toned cushions, and, of course, gaily colored brass hookahs being smoked by lounging men and women.

Bourne, stopped at the doorway by two overdeveloped members of club security, told them he was here to see Dimitri Maslov. One of them pointed to a man lounging and smoking a hookah in the far left corner.

"Maslov," Bourne said when he reached the pile of cushions surrounding a low brass table.

"My name is Yevgeny. Maslov isn't here." The man gestured. "Sit down, please."

Bourne hesitated a moment, then sat on a cushion opposite Yevgeny. "Where is he?"

"Did you think it would be so simple? One call and *poof!* he pops into existence like a genie from a lamp?" Yevgeny shook his head, offered Bourne the pipe. "Good shit. Try some."

When Bourne declined, Yevgeny shrugged, took a toke deep into his lungs, held it, then let it out with an audible hiss. "Why do you want to see Maslov?"

"That's between me and him," Bourne said.

Yevgeny shrugged again. "As you like. Maslov is out of the city."

"Then why was I told to come here?"

"To be judged, to see whether you are a serious individual. To see whether Maslov will make the decision to see you."

"Maslov trusts people to make decisions for him?"

"He is a busy man. He has other things on his mind."

"Like how to win the war with the Azeri."

Yevgeny's eyes narrowed. "Perhaps you can see Maslov next week."

"I need to see him now," Bourne said.

Yevgeny shrugged. "As I said, he's out of Moscow. But he may be back tomorrow morning."

"Why don't you ensure it."

"I could," Yevgeny said. "But it will cost you."

"How much?"

"Ten thousand."

"Ten thousand dollars to talk to Dimitri Maslov?"

Yevgeny shook his head. "The American dollar has become too debased. Ten thousand Swiss francs."

Bourne thought a moment. He didn't have that kind of money on him, and certainly not in Swiss francs. However, he had the information Baronov had given him on the safe-deposit box at the Moskva Bank.

The problem was that it was in the name of Fyodor Ilianovich Popov, who was no doubt now wanted for questioning regarding the body of the man in his room at the Metropolya Hotel. There was no help for it, Bourne thought. He'd have to take the chance.

"I'll have the money tomorrow morning," Bourne said.

"That will be satisfactory."

"But I'll give it to Maslov and no one else."

Yevgeny nodded. "Done." He wrote something on a slip of paper, showed it to Bourne. "Please be at this address at noon tomorrow." Then he struck a match, held it to the corner of the paper, which burned steadily until it crumbled into ash.

Semion Icoupov, in his temporary headquarters in Grindelwald, took the news of Harun Iliev's death very hard. He'd been a witness to death many times, but Harun had been like a brother to him. Closer, even, because the two had no sibling baggage to clutter and distort their relationship. Icoupov had relied on Harun for his wise counsel. His was a sad loss indeed.

His thoughts were interrupted by the orchestrated chaos around him. A score of people were staffing computer consoles hooked up to satellite feeds, surveillance networks, public transportation CCTV from major hubs all over the world. They were coming to the final buildup to the Black Legion's attack; every screen had to be scrutinized and analyzed, the faces of suspicious people picked out and run through a nebula of software that could identify individuals. From this, Icoupov's operatives were building a mosaic of the real-time backdrop against which the attack was scheduled to take place.

Icoupov became aware that three of his aides were clustered around his desk. Apparently, they'd been trying to talk to him.

"What is it?" His voice was testy, the better to cover up his grief and inattention.

Ismail, the most senior of his aides, cleared his throat. "We wanted to know who you intend to send after Jason Bourne now that Harun . . ." His voice trailed off.

Icoupov had been contemplating the same question. He'd made a mental list that included any number of people he could send, but he kept eliminating most of them, for one reason or another. But on the second and third run through he began to realize that these reasons were in one way or another trivial. Now, as Ismail asked the question again, he knew.

He looked up into his aides' anxious faces and said. "It's me. I'm going after Bourne myself."

Twenty-Four

IT WAS disturbingly hot in the Alter Botanischer Garten, and as humid as a rain forest. The enormous glass panels were opaque with beads of mist sliding down their faces. Moira, who had already taken off her gloves and long winter coat, now shrugged out of the thick cable-knit sweater that helped protect her from Munich's chill, damp morning, which could penetrate to the bone.

When it came to German cities, she much preferred Berlin to Munich. For one thing, Berlin had for many years been on the cutting edge of popular music. Berlin was where such notable pop icons as David Bowie, Brian Eno, and Lou Reed, among many others, had come to recharge their creative batteries by listening to what musicians far younger than they were creating. For another, it hadn't lost its legacy of the war and its aftermath. Berlin was like a living museum that was reinventing itself with every breath it took.

There was, however, a strictly personal reason why she preferred Berlin. She came for much the same reason Bowie did, to get away from stale habits, to breathe the fresh air of a city unlike those she knew. At an early age Moira became bored with the familiar. Every time she felt compelled to join a group because that was what her friends were doing she sensed she was losing a piece of herself. Gradually, she realized that her friends had ceased to become individuals, devolving into a cliquey "they" she found repellent. The only way to escape was to flee beyond the borders of the United States.

She could have chosen London or Barcelona, as some other college sophomores did, but she was a freak for Bowie and the Velvet Underground, so Berlin it was.

The botanical garden was built in the mid-1800s as an exhibition hall, but eighty years later, after its garden was destroyed by a fire, it gained new life as a public park. Outside, the awful bulk of the prewar Fountain of Neptune cast a shadow across the space through which she strolled.

The array of gorgeous specimens on display inside this glassed-in space only underscored the fact that Munich itself was without verve or spark. It was a plodding city of *untermenchen*, businessmen as gray as the city, and factories belching smoke into the low, angry sky. It was also a focal point of European Muslim activity, which, in one of those classic action–reaction scenarios, made it a hotbed of skinhead neo-Nazis.

Moira glanced at her watch. It was precisely 9:30 AM, and here came Noah, striding toward her. He was cool and efficient, personally opaque, even withholding, but he wasn't a bad sort. She'd have refused him as a handler if he was; she was senior enough to command that respect. And Noah did respect her, she was certain of that.

In many ways Noah reminded her of Johann, the man who'd recruited her while she was at the university. Actually, Johann hadn't contacted her at college; he was far too canny for that. He asked his girlfriend to make the approach, rightly figuring Moira would be more responsive to a fellow female student. Ultimately, Moira had met with Johann, was intrigued by what he had to offer her, and the rest was history. Well, not exactly. She'd never told anyone, including Martin or Bourne, who she really worked for. To do so would have violated her contract with the firm.

She stopped in front of the pinkly intimate blooms of an orchid, speckled like the bridge of a virgin's nose. Berlin had also been the site of her first passionate love affair, the kind that curled your toes, obliterated your focus on responsibility and the future. The affair almost ruined her, principally because it possessed her like a whirlwind and, in the process, she'd lost any sense of herself. She became a sexual instrument on which her lover played. What he wanted, she wanted, and so dissolution.

In the end, it was Johann who had saved her, but the process of separating pleasure from self was immensely painful. Especially because two months afterward her lover died. For a time, her rage at Johann was boundless; curdling their friendship, jeopardizing the trust they'd placed in each other. It was a lesson she never forgot. It was one reason she hadn't allowed herself to fall for Martin, though part of her yearned for his touch. Jason Bourne was another story entirely, for she had once again been overtaken by the whirlwind. But this time, she wasn't diminished. Partly, that was because she was mature now and knew better. Mainly, though, it was because Bourne asked nothing of her. He sought neither to lead nor to dominate her. Everything with him was clean and open. She moved on to another orchid, this one dark as night, with a tiny lantern of yellow hidden in its center. It was ironic, she thought, that despite his own issues, she had never before met a man so in control of himself. She found his self-assurance a compelling aphrodisiac, as well as a powerful antidote to her own innate melancholy.

That was another irony, she thought. If asked, Bourne would surely say that he was a pessimist, but being one herself, she knew an optimist when she met one. Bourne would take on the most impossible situations and somehow find a solution. Only the greatest of optimists could accomplish that.

Hearing soft footfalls, she turned to see Noah, shoulders hunched within a tweed overcoat. Though born in Israel, he could pass for a German now, perhaps because he'd lived in Berlin for so long. He'd been Johann's protégé; the two had been very close. When Johann was killed, it was Noah who took his place.

"Hello, Moira." He had a narrow face below dark hair flecked with premature gray. His long nose and serious mouth belied a keen sense of the absurd. "No Bourne, I see."

"I did my best to get him on board at NextGen."

Noah smiled. "I'm sure you did."

He gestured and they began to walk together. Few people were around this gloomy morning so there was no chance of being overheard.

"But to be honest, from what you told me, it was a long shot."

"I'm not disappointed," Moira said. "I detested the entire experience."

"That's because you have feelings for him."

"What if I do?" Moira said rather more defensively than she expected.

"You tell me." Noah watched her carefully. "There is a consensus among the partners that your emotions are interfering with your work."

"Where the hell is that coming from?" she said.

"I want you to know that I'm on your side." His voice was that of a psychoanalyst calming an increasingly agitated patient. "The problem is you should have come here days ago." They passed a worker tending a swath of African violets. When they were out of her earshot, he continued. "Then you go and bring Bourne with you."

"I told you. I was still trying to recruit him."

"Don't lie to a liar, Moira." He crossed his arms over his chest. When he spoke again, every word had weight. "There is a grave concern that your priorities aren't straight. You have a job to do, and a vitally important one. The firm can't afford to have your attention wandering."

"Are you saying you want to replace me?"

"It's an option that was discussed," he acknowledged.

"Bullshit. At this late stage there's no one who knows the project as well as I do."

"But then another option was requested: withdrawal from the project."

Moira was truly shocked. "You wouldn't."

Noah kept his gaze on her. "The partners have determined that in this instance it would be preferable to withdraw than to fail."

Moira felt her blood rising. "You can't withdraw, Noah. I'm not going to fail."

"I'm afraid that's no longer an option," he said, "because the decision's been made. As of oh seven hundred this morning we've officially notified NextGen that we've withdrawn from the project."

He handed her a packet. "Here is your new assignment. You're required to leave for Damascus this afternoon."

Arkadin and Devra reached the Bosporus Bridge and crossed over into Istanbul just as the sun was rising. Since coming down from the cruel, snow-swept mountains along Turkey's spine they had shed layers of clothes, and now the morning was exceptionally clear and mild. Pleasure yachts and huge tankers alike plowed the Bosporus on their way to various destinations. It felt good to roll down the windows. The air, fresh, moist, tangy with salt and minerals, was a distinct relief after the dry hard winter of the hinterlands.

During the night they'd stopped at every gas station, beaten-down motel, or store that was open—though most were not—in an attempt to find Heinrich, the next courier in Pyotr's network.

When it came time for him to spell her, she moved to the passenger's side, put her head against the door, and fell into a deep sleep, from which emerged a dream. She was a whale, swimming in icy black water. No sun pierced the depths where she swam. Below her was an unfathomable abyss. Ahead of her was a shadowy shape. She didn't know why, but it seemed imperative that she follow that shape, catch up with it, identify it. Was it friend or foe? Every so often she filled her head and throat with sound, which she sent out through the darkness. But she received no reply. There were no other whales around, so what was she chasing, what was she so desperate to find? There was no one to help her. She became frightened. The fright grew and grew . . .

It clung to her as she awoke with a start in the car beside Arkadin.

The grayish predawn light creeping through the landscape rendered every shape unfamiliar and vaguely threatening.

Twenty-five minutes later they were in the seething, clamorous heart of Istanbul.

"Heinrich likes to spend the time before his flight in Kilyos, the beach community in the northern suburbs," Devra said. "Do you know how to get there?"

Arkadin nodded. "I'm familiar with the area."

They wove their way through Sultanahmet, the core of Old Istanbul, then took the Galata Bridge, which spanned the Golden Horn, to Karaköy in the north. In the old days, when Istanbul was known as Constantinople, seat of the Byzantine Empire, Karaköy was the powerful Genoese trading colony known as Galata. As they reached the center of the bridge Devra looked west toward Europe, then east across the Bosporus to Üsküdar and Asia.

They passed into Karaköy, with its fortified Genoese walls and, rising from it, the stone Galata tower with its conical top, one of the monuments that, along with the Topkapi Palace and Blue Mosque, dominated the modern-day city's skyline.

Kilyos lay along the Black Sea coast twenty-two miles north of Istanbul proper. In the summer it was a popular beach resort, packed with people swimming, snacking in the restaurants that lined the beach, shopping for sunglasses and straw hats, sunbathing, or just dreaming. In winter it possessed a sad, vaguely disreputable air, like a dowager sinking into senility. Still, on this sun-splashed morning, under a cloudless cerulean sky, there were figures walking up and down the beach: young couples hand in hand; mothers with young children who ran laughing to the waterline, only to run back, screaming with terror and delight when the surf piled roughly in. An old man sat on a fold-up stool, smoking a crooked hand-rolled cigar that gave off a stench like the smokestack of a tannery.

Arkadin parked the car and got out, stretching his body after the long drive.

"He'll recognize me the moment he sees me," Devra said, staying put. She described Heinrich in detail. Just before Arkadin headed down to the beach, she added, "He likes putting his feet in the water, he says it grounds him."

Down on the beach it was warm enough that some people had taken off their jackets. One middle-aged man had stripped to the waist and sat with knees drawn up, arms locked around them, facing up to the sun like a heliotrope. Kids dug in the sand with yellow plastic Tweety Bird shovels, poured sand into pink plastic Petunia Pig buckets. One pair of lovers had stopped at the shoreline, embracing. They kissed passionately.

Arkadin walked on. Just behind them a man stood in the surf. His trousers were rolled up; his shoes, with socks stuffed into them, had been placed on a high point in the sand not far away. He was staring out at the water, dotted here and there with tankers, tiny as LEGOs, inching along the blue horizon.

Devra's description was not only detailed, it was accurate. The man in the surf was Heinrich.

The Moskva Bank was housed in an enormous, ornate building that would pass for a palace in any other city but was run-of-the-mill by Moscow standards. It occupied a corner of a busy thoroughfare a stone's throw from Red Square. The streets and sidewalks were packed with both Muscovites and tourists.

It was just before 9 AM. Bourne had been walking around the area for the last twenty minutes, checking for surveillance. That he hadn't spotted any didn't mean the bank wasn't being watched. He'd glimpsed a number of police cars cruising the snow-covered streets, more than usual, perhaps.

As he walked along a street close to the bank, he saw another police cruiser, this one with its light flashing. Stepping back into a shop doorway, he watched as it sped by. Halfway down the block it stopped behind a double-parked car. It sat there for a moment, then the two policemen got out of their cruiser, swaggered over to the vehicle.

Bourne took the opportunity to walk down the crowded sidewalk.

People were wrapped and bundled, swaddled like children. Breath came out of their mouths and noses in cloud-like bursts as they hurried along with hunched shoulders and bent backs. As Bourne came abreast of the cruiser, he dipped down and glanced in the window. There he saw his face staring up at him from a tear sheet that had obviously been distributed to every cop in Moscow. According to the accompanying text he was wanted for the murder of an American government official.

Bourne walked quickly in the opposite direction, disappearing around a corner before the cops had a chance to return to their car.

He phoned Gala, who was parked in Yakov's battered Zhig three blocks away awaiting his signal. After his call, she pulled out into traffic, made a right, then another. As they had surmised, it was slow going, the morning traffic sluggish.

She checked her watch, saw she needed to give Bourne another ninety seconds. As she approached the intersection near the bank, she used the time to pick a likely target. A shiny Zil limousine, not a speck of snow on its hood or roof, was heading slowly toward the intersection at right angles to her.

At the appointed time she accelerated forward. The *bombila's* tires, which she and Bourne had checked when they'd returned to Lorraine's, were nearly bald, their treads worn down to a nub. Gala braked much too hard and the Zhig shrieked as the brakes locked, the old tires skidding along the icy street until its grille struck the front fender of the Zil limo.

All traffic came to a screeching halt, horns blared, pedestrians detoured from their appointed rounds, drawn by the spectacle. Within thirty seconds three police cruisers had converged on the site of the accident.

As the chaos mounted, Bourne slipped through the revolving door into the ornate lobby of the Moskva Bank. He immediately crossed the marble floor, passing under one of the three huge gilt chandeliers that hung from the vaulted ceiling high above. The effect of the room was to diminish human size, and the experience was not unlike visiting a dead relative in his marble niche.

There was a low banquette two-thirds of the way across the vast room, behind which sat a row of drones, their heads bent over their work. Before approaching, Bourne checked everyone inside the bank for suspicious behavior. He produced Popov's passport, then wrote down the number of the safe-deposit box on a small pad kept for that specific purpose.

The woman glanced at him, took his passport and the slip of paper, which she ripped off the pad. Locking her drawer, she told Bourne to wait. He watched her walk over to the rank of supervisors and managers, who sat in rows behind identical wooden desks, and present Bourne's documentation. The manager checked the number against his master list of safe-deposit boxes, then he checked the passport. He hesitated, then reached for the phone, but when he noticed Bourne staring at him, he returned to receiver to its cradle. He said something to the woman clerk, then rose and came over to where Bourne stood.

"Mr. Popov." He handed back the passport. "Vasily Legev, at your service." He was an oily Muscovite who continually scrubbed his palms together as if his hands had been somewhere he'd rather not reveal. His smile seemed as genuine as a three-dollar bill.

Opening a door in the banquette, he ushered Bourne through. "It will be my pleasure to escort you to our vault."

He led Bourne to the rear of the room. A discreet door opened onto a hushed carpeted corridor with a row of square columns on either side. Bad reproductions of famous landscape paintings hung on the walls. Bourne could hear the muted sounds of phones ringing, computer operators inputting information or writing letters. The vault was directly ahead, its massive door open; to the left a set of marble stairs swept upward.

Vasily Legev showed Bourne through the circular opening and into the vault. The hinges of the door looked to be two feet long and as thick around as Bourne's biceps. Inside was a rectangular room filled floor-to-ceiling with metal boxes, only the fronts of which could be seen.

They went over to Bourne's box number. There were two locks, two keyholes. Vasily Legev inserted his key in the left-hand lock, Bourne inserted his into the right-hand lock. The two men turned their keys at the same time, and the box was free to be pulled out of its niche. Vasily Legev brought the box to one of a number of small viewing rooms. He set it down on a ledge, nodded to Bourne, then left, pulling the privacy curtain behind him.

Bourne didn't bother sitting. Opening the box, he discovered a great deal of money in American dollars, euros, Swiss francs, and a number of other currencies. He pocketed ten thousand Swiss francs, along with some dollars and euros, before he closed the box, pulled aside the curtain, and emerged into the vault proper.

Vasily Legev was nowhere to be seen, but two plainclothes cops had placed themselves between Bourne and the doorway to the vault. One of them aimed a Makarov handgun at him.

The other, smirking, said, "You will come with us now, *gospadin* Popov."

Arkadin, hands in his pockets, strolled down the crescent beach, past a happily barking dog whose owner had let it off the leash. A young woman pulled her auburn hair off her face and smiled at him as they passed each other.

When he was fairly near Heinrich, Arkadin kicked off his shoes, peeled off his socks, and, rolling up his trousers, picked his way down to the surf line, where the sand turned dark and crusty. He moved at an angle, so that as he ventured into the surf he was within earshot of the courier.

Sensing someone near him, Heinrich turned and, shading his eyes from the sun, nodded at Arkadin before turning away.

Under the pretext of stumbling as the surf rolled in, Arkadin edged closer. "I'm surprised that someone besides me likes the winter surf."

Heinrich seemed not to hear him, continued his contemplation of the horizon.

"I keep wondering what it is that feels so good about the water rushing over my feet and pulling back out."

After a moment, Heinrich glanced at him. "If you don't mind, I'm trying to meditate."

"Meditate on this," Arkadin said, sticking a knife very carefully in his side.

Heinrich's eyes opened wide. He staggered, but Arkadin was there to catch him. They sat down together in the surf, like old friends communing with nature.

Heinrich's mouth made gasping sounds. They reminded Arkadin of a fish hauled out of the water.

"What . . . what?"

Arkadin cradled him with one hand as he searched beneath his poplin jacket with the other. Just as he thought, Heinrich had the package on him, not trusting it to be out of his sight for an instant. He held it in his palm for a moment. It was in a rolled cardboard cylinder. So small for something with that much power.

"A lot of people have died for this," Arkadin said.

"Many more will die before it's over," Heinrich managed to get out. "Who are you?"

"I'm your death," Arkadin said. Plunging the knife in again, he turned it between Heinrich's ribs.

"Ah, ah, ah," Heinrich whispered as his lungs filled with his own blood. His breathing turned shallow, then erratic. Then it ceased altogether.

Arkadin continued to shelter him with a comradely arm. When Heinrich, nothing more than deadweight now, slumped against him, Arkadin held him up as the surf crashed and ebbed around them.

Arkadin stared out at the horizon, as Heinrich had done, certain that beyond the demarcation was nothing save a black abyss, endless and unknowable.

Bourne went willingly with the two plainclothes policemen out of the vault. As they stepped into the corridor, Bourne slammed the edge of his hand down on the cop's wrist, causing the Makarov to drop and slide along the floor. Whirling, Bourne kicked the other cop, who was flung back against the edge of a square column. Bourne grabbed hold of the arm of the first cop. Lifting it, he slammed his elbow into the cop's rib cage, then smashed his hand into the back of his neck. With both cops down, Bourne hurried along the corridor, but another man came sprinting toward him, blocking the way to the front of the bank, a man who fit Yakov's description of Harris Low.

Reversing course, Bourne leapt up the marble staircase, taking the steps three at a time. Racing around the turn, he gained the landing of the second floor. He'd memorized the plans Baronov's friend had procured for him and had planned for an emergency, not trusting to chance that he'd get in and out of the bank without being identified. It was clear Vasily Legev, having recognized *gospadin* Popov, would blow the whistle on him while he was inside the safe-deposit viewing cubicle. As Bourne broke out into the corridor he encountered one of the bank's security men. Grabbing him by the front of his uniform, Bourne jerked him off his feet, swung him around, and hurled him down the stairs at the ascending NSA agent.

Racing down the corridor, reached the door to the fire stairs, opened it, and went through. Like many buildings of its vintage this one had a staircase that rose around an open central core.

Bourne took off up the stairs. He passed the third floor, then the fourth. Behind him, he could hear the fire door bang open, the sound of hurried footsteps on the stairs behind him. His maneuver with the guard had slowed down the agent, but hadn't stopped him.

He was midway to the fifth and top floor when the agent fired on him. Bourne ducked, hearing the *spang!* of the ricochet. He sprinted upward as another shot went past him. Reaching the door to the roof at last, he opened it, and slammed it shut behind him.

Harris Low was furious. With all the personnel at his disposal Bourne was still at large. *That's what you get*, he thought as he raced up the stairwell, *when you leave the details to the Russians*. They were great at

brute force, but when it came to the subtleties of undercover work they
were all but useless. Those two plainclothes officers, for instance. Over
Low's objections they hadn't waited for him, had gone into the vault
after Bourne themselves. Now he was left with mopping up the mess
they'd made.

He came to the door to the roof, turned the handle, and banged it
open with the flat of his shoe. The tarred rooftop, the low winter sky
glowered at him. Walther PPK/S at the ready, he stepped out onto the
roof in a semi-crouch. Without warning, the door slammed shut on
him, driving him back onto the small landing.

Up on the roof, Bourne pulled open the door and dived through. He
struck Low three blows, directed first at the agent's stomach and then
at his right wrist, forcing Low to let go of the gun. The Walther flew
down the stairwell, landing on a step just above the fourth floor.

Low, enraged, drove his fists into Bourne's kidney twice in succession. Bourne collapsed to his knees, and Low kicked him onto his back
then straddled his chest, pinning Bourne's arms. Low gripped Bourne's
throat, squeezing as hard as he could.

Bourne struggled to get his arms free, but he had insufficient leverage. He tried to get a breath, but Low's grip on him was so complete
that he was unable to get any oxygen into his system. He stopped trying
to free his arms and pressed down with the small of his back, providing
a fulcrum for his legs, which he drew up, then extended toward his
head. He brought his calves together, sandwiching Low's head between
them. Low tried to shake them off, violently twisting his shoulders back
and forth, but Bourne held on, increasing his grip. Then, with an enormous effort, Bourne spun them both to the left. Low's head hit against
the wall, and Bourne's arms were free. Unwinding his legs, he slammed
the palms of his hands against Low's ears.

Low shouted in pain, kicked away, and scrambled back down the
stairs. Bourne, on his knees, could see that Low was heading for the
Walther. Bourne rose. Just as Low reached it, Bourne launched himself

down and across the air shaft. He landed on Low, who whipped the Walther's short but thick barrel into Bourne's face. Bourne reared back, and Low bent him over the railing. Four floors of air shaft loomed below, ending in an unforgiving concrete base. As they locked in their struggle, Low slowly, inexorably, brought the muzzle of the Walther to bear on Bourne's face. At the same time, the heel of Bourne's hand was pushing Low's head up.

Low shook loose from Bourne's grip, lunged at him in an effort to pistol-whip him into unconsciousness. Bourne bent his knees. Using Low's own momentum, he slid one arm under the agent's crotch, and lifted him up. Low tried to get a fix on Bourne with the Walther, failed, swung his arm back to deliver another blow with the barrel.

Using all his remaining strength, Bourne hefted him up and over the banister, dumping him down the air shaft. Low plummeted, a tangle of arms and legs, until he hit the bottom.

Bourne turned, went back out onto the roof. As he loped across it, he could hear the familiar rise and fall of police sirens. He wiped blood off his cheek with the back of his hand. Reaching the other side of the roof, he climbed atop the parapet, leapt across the intervening space onto the roof of the adjoining building. He did this twice more until he felt that it was safe for him to return to the street.

Twenty-Five

SORAYA HAD NEVER understood the nature of panic, despite the fact that she grew up with an aunt who was prone to panic attacks. When the attacks came on her aunt said she felt as if someone had put a plastic dry-cleaning bag over her head; she felt as if she were being smothered to death. Soraya would watch her huddled in a chair or curled up on her bed and wonder how on earth she could feel such a thing. There weren't even any plastic dry-cleaning bags allowed in the house. How could a person feel as if she were suffocating when there wasn't anything on her face?

Now she knew.

As she drove out of the NSA safe house without Tyrone, as the high reinforced metal gates swung closed behind her, her hands trembled on the wheel, her heart felt as if it was jumping painfully inside her breast. There was a film of sweat on her upper lip, under her arms, and at the nape of her neck. Worst of all, she couldn't catch her breath. Her mind raced like a rat in a cage. She gasped, sucking ragged gulps of air in to her lungs. She felt, in short, as if she were being smothered to death. Then her stomach rebelled.

As quickly as she was able she pulled to the side of the road, got out, and stumbled into the trees. Falling to her hands and knees, she vomited up the sweet, milky Ceylon tea.

Jason, Tyrone, and Veronica Hart were now all in terrible jeopardy because of rash decisions she'd made. She quailed at the thought. It was one thing to be chief of station in Odessa, quite another to be director. Maybe she'd taken on more than she could handle, maybe she didn't have the steel nerve that was required to make tough choices. Where was her vaunted confidence? It was back there in the NSA interrogation cell with Tyrone.

Somehow she made it to Alexandria, where she parked. She sat in the car bent over, her clammy forehead pressed to the steering wheel. She tried to think coherently, but her brain seemed encased in a block of concrete. At last, she wept bitterly.

She had to call Deron, but she was petrified of his reaction when she told him that she had allowed his protégé to be captured and tortured by the NSA. She had fucked up big time. And she had no idea how to rectify the situation. The choice LaValle had given her—Veronica Hart for Tyrone—was unacceptable.

After a time, she calmed down enough to get out of the car. She moved like a sleepwalker through crowds of people oblivious to her agony. It seemed somehow wrong that the world should spin on as it always had, utterly indifferent and uncaring.

She ducked into a little tea shop, and as she rummaged in her handbag for her cell phone she saw the pack of cigarettes. A cigarette would calm her nerves, but standing out in the chilly street while she smoked would make her feel more of a lost soul. She decided to have a smoke on the way back to her car. Placing her cell phone on the table, she stared down at it as if it were alive. She ordered chamomile tea, which calmed her enough for her to pick up her phone. She punched in Deron's number, but when she heard his voice her tongue clove to the roof of her mouth.

Eventually, she was able to get out her name. Before he could ask her how the mission went she asked to speak with Kiki, Deron's girlfriend. Where that came from, she had no idea. She'd met Kiki only twice. But Kiki was a woman and, instinctively, with an atavistic clannishness, Soraya knew it would be easier to confess to her than to Deron.

When Kiki came on the line, Soraya asked if she could come to the little tea shop in Alexandria. When Kiki asked when, Soraya said, "Now. Please."

The first thing you have to do is stop blaming yourself," Kiki said after Soraya had finished recounting in painful detail what had happened at the NSA safe house. "It's your guilt that's paralyzing you, and believe me you're going to need every last brain cell if we're going to get Tyrone out of that hole."

Soraya looked up from her pallid tea.

Kiki smiled, nodding. In her dark red dress, her hair up in a swirl, hammered-gold earrings depending from her earlobes, she looked more regal, more exotic than ever. She towered over everyone in the tea shop by at least six inches.

"I know I have to tell Deron," Soraya said. "I just don't know what his reaction is going to be."

"His reaction won't be as bad as what you fear," Kiki said. "And after all, Tyrone is a grown man. He knew the risks as well as anyone. It was his choice, Soraya. He could've said no."

Soraya shook her head. "That's just it, I don't think he could, at least not from the way he sees things." She stirred her tea, more to forestall what she knew she had to say. Then she looked up, licked her lips. "See, Tyrone's got a thing for me."

"Doesn't he ever!"

Soraya was taken aback. "You know?"

"Everyone who knows him knows, honey. You just have to look at him when the two of you are together."

Soraya felt her cheeks flush. "I think he would've done anything I asked of him no matter how dangerous, even if he didn't want to."

"But you know he wanted to."

It was true, Soraya thought. He'd been excited. Nervous, but definitely excited. She knew that ever since Deron had taken him under his wing he'd chafed at being cooped up in the hood. He was smarter than that, and Deron knew it. But he had neither the interest nor the aptitude for what Deron did. Then she came along. He'd told her he saw her as his ticket out of the ghetto.

Yet she still had a knot in her chest, a sick feeling in the pit of her stomach. She could not get out of her head the image of Tyrone on his knees, hooded, arms held behind him on the tabletop.

"You just turned pale," Kiki said. "Are you all right?"

Soraya nodded. She wanted to tell Kiki what she had seen, but she couldn't. She sensed that to talk about it would give it a reality so frightening, so powerful it would throw her back into panic.

"Then we ought to go."

Soraya's heart tripped over itself. "No time like the present," she said.

As they went out the door, she pulled out the pack of cigarettes and threw it in a nearby trash can. She didn't need it anymore.

As planned, Gala picked up Bourne in Yakov's *bombila* and together they returned to Lorraine's apartment. It was just past 10 AM; his meet with Maslov wasn't until noon. He needed a shower, a shave, and some rest.

Lorraine was kind enough to provide the necessities for all three. She gave Bourne a set of towels, a disposable razor, and said if he gave her his clothes she'd wash and dry them for him. In the bathroom Bourne stripped, then opened the door enough to hand the dirty clothes to Lorraine.

"After I put these in the wash, Gala and I are going out to get food. Can we bring you anything?"

Bourne thanked her. "Whatever you're having will be fine."

He closed the door, crossed to the shower, turned it on full force.

Opening the medicine cabinet, he took out rubbing alcohol, a gauze pad, surgical tape, and antibiotic cream. Then he went back to the toilet, put the seat cover down, and cleaned his abraded heel. It had taken a lot of abuse and was red and raw looking. Squeezing the cream onto the gauze, he placed it over the wound and taped it up.

Then he took his cell phone off the edge of the sink where he'd placed it when undressing, and dialed the number Boris Karpov had given him.

Would you mind going without me?" Gala said, as Lorraine reached into the hall closet for her fur coat. "All of a sudden I'm not feeling well."

Lorraine walked back to her. "What is it?"

"I don't know." Gala sank onto the white leather sofa. "I'm kind of dizzy."

Lorraine took hold of the back of her head. "Bend over. Put your head between your knees."

Gala did as she was told. Lorraine crossed to the sideboard, took out a bottle of vodka, and poured some into a glass. "Here, take a drink. It'll settle you."

Gala came up as gingerly as a drunk walks. She took the vodka, threw it down her throat so fast she almost choked. But then the fire hit her stomach and the warmth began to spread through her.

"Okay?" Lorraine asked.

"Better."

"All right. I'm going to buy you some hot borscht. You need to get some nourishment into you." She drew on her coat. "Why don't you lie down?"

Once again Gala did as she was told, but after her friend left, she rose. She'd never found the sofa comfortable. Making sure of her balance, she went down the hall. She needed to crash on a proper bed.

As she was passing the bathroom, she heard a sound like talking, but Bourne was in there by himself. Curious, she moved closer, then put her ear to the door. She could hear the rushing of the shower more clearly, but also Bourne's voice. He must be on his cell phone.

She heard him say "Medvedev did what?" He was talking politics to whoever was on the other end of the line. She was about to take her ear away from the door when she heard Bourne say, "It was bad luck with Tarkanian . . . No, no, I killed him . . . I had to, I had no other choice."

Gala pulled away as if she'd touched her ear to a hot iron. For some time, she stood staring at the closed door, then she backed away. Bourne had killed Mischa! *My God*, she said to herself. How could he? And then, thinking of Arkadin, Mischa's best friend, *My God*.

Twenty-Six

DIMITRI MASLOV had the eyes of a rattlesnake, the shoulders of a wrestler, and the hands of a bricklayer. He was, however, dressed like a banker when Bourne met him inside a warehouse that could have doubled as an aircraft hanger. He was wearing a chalk-striped three-piece Savile Row suit, an Egyptian cotton shirt, and a conservative tie. His powerful legs ended in curiously dainty feet, as if they'd been grafted on from another, far smaller body.

"Don't bother telling me your name," he said as he accepted the ten thousand Swiss francs, "as I always assume they're fake."

The warehouse was one among many in this soot-laden industrial area on the outskirts of Moscow, and therefore anonymous. Like its neighbors, it had a front area filled with boxes and crates on neat stacks of wooden pallets piled almost to the ceiling. Parked in one corner was a forklift. Next to it was a bulletin board on which had been tacked overlapping layers of flyers, notices, invoices, advertisements, and announcements. Bare lightbulbs at the ends of metal flex burned like miniature suns.

After Bourne had been expertly patted down for weapons and

wires, he'd been escorted through a door to a tiled bathroom that stank of urine and stale sweat. It contained a trough with water running sluggishly along its bottom and a line of stalls. He was taken to the last stall. Inside, instead of a toilet, was a door. His escort of two burly Russians took him through to what appeared to be a warren of offices, one of which was raised on a steel platform bolted onto the far wall. They climbed the staircase to the door, at which point his escort had left him, presumably to go stand guard.

Maslov was seated behind an ornate desk. He was flanked on either side by two more men, interchangeable with the pair outside. In one corner sat a man with a scar beneath one eye, who would have been unprepossessing save for the flamboyant Hawaiian print shirt he wore. Bourne was aware of another presence behind him, his back against the open door.

"I understand you wanted to see me." Maslov's rattlesnake eyes shone yellow in the harsh light. Then he gestured, holding out his left arm, his hand extended, palm-up, as if he were shoveling dirt away from him. "However, there's someone who insists on seeing you."

In a blur, the figure behind Bourne hurled himself forward. Bourne turned in a half crouch to see the man who'd attacked him at Tarkanian's apartment. He came at Bourne with a knife extended. Too late to deflect it, Bourne sidestepped the thrust, grabbed the man's right wrist with his left hand, using his own momentum to pull him forward so that his face met Bourne's raised elbow flush-on.

He went down. Bourne stepped on the wrist with his shoe until the man let go of the knife, which Bourne took up in his hand. At once the two burly bodyguards drew down on him, pointing their Glocks. Ignoring them, Bourne held the knife in his right palm so the hilt pointed away from him. He extended his arm across the desk to Maslov.

Maslov stared instead at the man in the Hawaiian print shirt, who rose, took the knife from Bourne's palm.

"I am Dimitri Maslov," he said to Bourne.

The big man in the banker's suit rose, nodded deferentially to Maslov, who handed him the knife as he sat down behind the desk.

"Take Evsei out and get him a new nose," Maslov said to no one in particular.

The big man in the banker's suit pulled the dazed Evsei up, dragged him out of the office.

"Close the door," Maslov said, again to no one in particular.

Nevertheless, one of the burly Russian bodyguards crossed to the door, closed it, turned and put his back against it. He shook out a cigarette, lit it.

"Take a seat," Maslov said. Sliding open a drawer, he took out a Mauser, laid it on the desk within easy reach. Only then did his eyes slide up to engage Bourne's again. "My dear friend Vanya tells me that you work for Boris Karpov. He says you claim to have information I can use against certain parties who are trying to muscle in on my territory." His fingers tapped the grips of the Mauser. "However, I would be inexcusably naive to believe that you were willing to part with this information without a price, so let's have it. What do you want?"

"I want to know what your connection is with the Black Legion?"

"Mine? I have none."

"But you've heard of them."

"Of course I've heard of them." Maslov frowned. "Where is this going?"

"You posted your man Evsei in Mikhail Tarkanian's apartment. Tarkanian was a member of the Black Legion."

Maslov held up a hand. "Where the hell did you hear that?"

"He was working against people—friends of mine."

Maslov shrugged. "That might be so—I have no knowledge of it one way or another. But one thing I can tell you is that Tarkanian wasn't Black Legion."

"Then why was Evsei there?"

"Ah, now we get to the root of the matter." Maslov's thumb rubbed against his forefinger and middle finger in the universal gesture. "Show me the quid pro quo, to co-opt what Jerry Maguire says." His mouth grinned, but his yellow eyes remained as remote and malevolent as ever. "Though to tell you the truth I'm doubting very much there's any money at all. I mean to say, why would the Federal Anti-Narcotics Agency want to help me? It's anti-fucking-intuitive."

Bourne finally pulled over a chair, sat down. His mind was rerunning the long conversation he'd had with Boris at Lorraine's apartment, during which Karpov had briefed him on the current political climate in Moscow.

"This has nothing to do with narcotics and everything to do with politics. The Federal Anti-Narcotics Agency is controlled by Cherkesov, who's in the midst of a parallel war to yours—the *silovik* wars," Bourne said. "It seems as if the president has already picked his successor."

"That pisspot Mogilovich." Maslov nodded. "Yeah, so what?"

"Cherkesov doesn't like him, and here's why. Mogilovich used to work for the president in the St. Petersburg city administration way back when. The president put him in charge of the legal department of VM Pulp and Paper. Mogilovich promptly engineered VM's dominance to become Russia's largest and most lucrative pulp and timber company. Now one of America's largest paper companies is buying fifty percent of VM for hundreds of millions of dollars."

During Bourne's discourse Maslov had taken out a penknife, was busy paring grime from under his manicured nails. He did everything but yawn. "All this is part of the public record. What's it to me?"

"What isn't known is that Mogilovich cut himself a deal giving him a sizable portion of VM's shares when the company was privatized through RAB Bank. At the time, questions were raised about Mogilovich's involvement with RAB Bank, but they magically went away. Last year VM bought back the twenty-five percent stake that RAB had taken to ensure the privatization would go through without a hitch. The deal was blessed by the Kremlin."

"Meaning the president." Maslov sat up straight, put away the penknife.

"Right," Bourne said. "Which means that Mogilovich stands to make a king's ransom through the American buy-in, by means the president wouldn't want made public."

"Who knows what the president's own involvement is in the deal?"

Bourne nodded.

"Wait a minute," Maslov said. "Last week a RAB Bank officer was found tied up, tortured, and asphyxiated in his dacha garage. I remember because the General Prosecutor's Office claimed he'd committed suicide. We all got a good laugh out of that one."

"He just happened to be the head of RAB's loan division to the timber industry."

"The man with the smoking gun that could ruin Mogilovich and, by extension, the president," Maslov said.

"My boss tells me this man had access to the smoking gun, but he never actually had it in his possession. His assistant absconded with it days before his assassination, and now can't be found." Bourne hitched his chair forward. "When you find him for us and hand over the papers incriminating Mogilovich, my boss is prepared to end the war between you and the Azeri once and for all in your favor."

"And how the fuck is he going to do that?"

Bourne opened his cell phone, played back the MP3 file Boris had sent to him. It was a conversation between the kingpin of the Azeri and one of his lieutenants ordering the hit on the RAB Bank executive. It was just like the Russian in Boris to hold on to the evidence for leverage, rather than go after the Azeri kingpin right away.

A broad grin broke out across Maslov's face. "Fuck," he said, "now we're talking!"

After a time, Arkadin became aware that Devra was standing over him. Without looking at her, he held up the cylinder he'd taken from Heinrich.

"Come out of the surf," she said, but when Arkadin didn't make a move, she sat down on a crest of sand behind him.

Heinrich was stretched out on his back as if he were a sunbather who'd fallen asleep. The water had washed away all the blood.

After a time, Arkadin moved back, first onto the dark sand, then up behind the waterline to where Devra sat, her legs drawn up, chin on her knees. That was when she noticed that his left foot was missing three toes.

"My God," she said, "what happened to your foot?"

It was the foot that had undone Marlene. The three missing toes on Arkadin's left foot. Marlene made the mistake of asking what had happened.

"An accident," Arkadin said with a practiced smoothness. "During my first term in prison. A stamping machine came apart, and the main cylinder fell on my foot. The toes were crushed, nothing more than pulp. They had to be amputated."

It was a lie, this story, a fanciful tale Arkadin appropriated from a real incident that took place during his first stint in prison. That much, at least, was the truth. A man stole a pack of cigarettes from under Arkadin's bunk. This man worked the stamping machine. Arkadin tampered with the machine so that when the man started it up the next morning the main cylinder dropped on him. The result wasn't pretty; you could hear his screams clear across the compound. In the end, they'd had to take his right leg off at the knee.

From that day forward he was on his guard with Marlene. She was attracted to him, of this he was quite certain. She'd slipped from her objective pedestal, from the job Icoupov had given her. He didn't blame Icoupov. He wanted to tell Icoupov again that he wouldn't harm him, but he knew Icoupov wouldn't believe him. Why should he? He had enough evidence to the contrary to make him suitably nervous. And yet, Arkadin sensed that Icoupov would never turn his back on him. Icoupov would never renege on his pledge to take Arkadin in.

Nevertheless, something had to be done about Marlene. It wasn't simply that she'd seen his left foot; Icoupov had seen it as well. Arkadin knew she suspected the maimed foot was connected with his horrendous nightmares, that it was part of something he couldn't tell her. Even the story Arkadin told her did not fully satisfy her. It might have with someone else, but not Marlene. She hadn't exaggerated when she'd told him that she possessed an uncanny ability to sense what her clients were feeling, and to find a way to help them.

The problem was that she couldn't help Arkadin. No one could. No one was allowed to know what he'd experienced. It was unthinkable.

"Tell me about your mother and father," Marlene said. "And don't repeat the pabulum you fed the shrink who was here before me."

They were out on Lake Lugano. It was a mild summer's day, Marlene was in a two-piece bathing suit, red with large pink polka dots. She wore pink rubber slippers; a visor shaded her face from the sun. Their small motorboat lay to, its anchor dropped. Small swells rocked them now and again as pleasure boats went to and fro across the crystal blue water. The small village of Campione d'Italia rose up the hillside like the frosted tiers of a wedding cake.

Arkadin looked hard at her. It annoyed him that he didn't intimidate her. He intimidated most people; it was how he got along after his parents were gone.

"What, you don't think my mother died badly?"

"I'm interested in your mother before she died," Marlene said airily. "What was she like?"

"Actually, she was just like you."

Marlene gave him a basilisk stare.

"Seriously," he said. "My mother was tough as a fistful of nails. She knew how to stand up to my father."

Marlene seized on this opening. "Why did she have to do that? Was your father abusive?"

Arkadin shrugged. "No more than any other father, I suppose. When he was frustrated at work he took it out on her."

"And you find that normal."

"I don't know what the word *normal* means."

"But you're used to abuse, aren't you?"

"Isn't that called leading the witness, Counselor?"

"What did your father do?"

"He was *consiglieri*—the counselor—to the Kazanskaya, the family of the Moscow *grupperovka* that controls drug trafficking and the sale of foreign cars in the city and surrounding areas." He'd been nothing of the sort. Arkadin's father had been an ironworker, dirt-poor, desperate, and drunk as shit twenty hours a day, just like everyone else in Nizhny Tagil.

"So abuse and violence came naturally to him."

"He wasn't on the streets," Arkadin said, continuing his lie.

She gave him a thin smile. "All right, where do *you* think your bouts of violence come from?"

"If I told you I'd have to kill you."

Marlene laughed. "Come on, Leonid Danilovich. Don't you want to be of use to Mr. Icoupov?"

"Of course I do. I want him to trust me."

"Then tell me."

Arkadin sat for a time. The sun felt good on his forearms. The heat seemed to draw his skin tight over his muscles, making them bulge. He felt the beating of his heart as if it were music. For just a moment, he felt free of his burden, as if it belonged to someone else, a tormented character in a Russian novel, perhaps. Then his past came rushing back like a fist in his gut and he almost vomited.

Very slowly, very deliberately he unlaced his sneakers, took them off. He peeled off his white athletic socks, and there was his left foot with its two toes and three miniature stumps, knotty, as pink as the polka dots on Marlene's bathing suit.

"Here's what happened," he said. "When I was fourteen years old, my mother took a frying pan to the back of my father's head. He'd just come home stone drunk, reeking of another woman. He was sprawled facedown on their bed, snoring peacefully, when *whack!*, she took a heavy cast-iron skillet from its peg on the kitchen wall and, without a word, hit him ten times in the same spot. You can imagine what his skull looked like when she was done."

Marlene sat back. She seemed to have trouble breathing. At length, she said, "This isn't another one of your bullshit stories, is it?"

"No," Arkadin said, "it's not."

"And where were you?"

"Where d'you think I was? Home. I saw the whole thing."

Marlene put a hand to her mouth. "My God."

Having expelled this ball of poison, Arkadin felt an exhilarating sense of freedom, but he knew what had to come next.

"Then what happened?" she said when she had recovered her equilibrium.

Arkadin let out a long breath. "I gagged her, tied her hands behind her, and threw her into the closet in my room."

"And?"

"I walked out of the apartment and never went back."

"How?" There was a look of genuine horror on her face. "How could you do such a thing?"

"I disgust you now, don't I?" He said this not with anger, but with a certain resignation. Why wouldn't she be disgusted by him? If only she knew the whole truth.

"Tell me in more detail about the accident in prison."

Arkadin knew at once that she was trying to find inconsistencies in his story. This was a classic interrogator's technique. She would never know the truth.

"Let's go swimming," he said abruptly. He shed his shorts and T-shirt.

Marlene shook her head. "I'm not in the mood. You go if—"

"Oh, come on."

He pushed her overboard, stood up, dived in after her. He found her under the water, kicking her legs to bring herself to the surface. He wrapped his thighs around her neck, locked his ankles, tightening his grip on her. He rose to the surface, held on to the boat, swung water out of his eyes as she struggled below him. Boats thrummed past. He waved to two young girls, their long hair flying behind them like horses' manes. He wanted to hum a love song, but all he could think of was the theme to *Bridge on the River Kwai*.

After a time, Marlene stopped struggling. He felt her weight below him, swaying gently in the swells. He didn't want to, really he didn't, but unbidden the image of his old apartment resurrected itself in his mind's eye. It was a slum, the filthy crumbling Soviet-era piece of shit building teeming with vermin.

Their poverty didn't stop the older man from banging other women. When one of them became pregnant, she decided to have the baby. He was all for it, he told her. He'd help her in any way he could. But what he really wanted was the child his barren wife could never give him. When Leonid was born, he ripped the baby from the girl's arms, brought Leonid to his wife to raise.

"This is the child I always wanted, but you couldn't give me," he told her.

She raised Arkadin dutifully, without complaint, because where could a barren woman go in Nizhny Tagil? But when her husband wasn't home, she locked the boy in the closet of his room for hours at a time. A blind rage gripped her and wouldn't let her go. She despised this result of her husband's seed, and she felt compelled to punish Leonid because she couldn't punish his father.

It was during one of these long punishments that Arkadin woke to awful pain in his left foot. He wasn't alone in the closet. Half a dozen rats, large as his father's shoe, scuttled back and forth, squealing, teeth gnashing. He managed to kill them, but not before they finished what they'd started. They ate three of his toes.

Twenty-Seven

IT ALL STARTED with Pyotr Zilber," Maslov said. "Or rather his younger brother, Aleksei. Aleksei was a wise guy. He tried to muscle in on one of my sources for foreign cars. A lot of people were killed, including some of my men and my source. For that, I had him killed."

Dimitri Maslov and Bourne were sitting in a glassed-in greenhouse built on the roof of the warehouse where Maslov had his office. They were surrounded by a lush profusion of tropical flowers: speckled orchids, brilliant carmine anthurium, birds-of-paradise, white ginger, heliconia. The air was perfumed with the scents of the pink plumeria and white jasmine. It was so warm and humid, Maslov looked right at home in his bright-hued short-sleeved shirt. Bourne had rolled up his sleeves. There was a table with a bottle of vodka and two glasses. They'd already had their first drink.

"Zilber pulled strings, had my man Borya Maks sent to High Security Prison Colony 13 in Nizhny Tagil. You've heard of it?"

Bourne nodded. Conklin had mentioned the prison several times.

"Then you know it's no picnic in there." Maslov leaned forward, refilled their glasses, handed one to Bourne, took the other himself.

"Despite that, Zilber wasn't satisfied. He hired someone very, very good to infiltrate the prison and kill Maks." Drinking vodka, surrounded by a riot of color, he appeared totally at his ease. "Only one person could accomplish that and get out alive: Leonid Danilovich Arkadin."

The vodka had done Bourne a world of good, returning both warmth and strength to his overtaxed body. There was still a smear of blood on the point of one cheek, dried now, but Maslov had neither looked at it nor commented on it. "Tell me about Arkadin."

Maslov made an animal sound in the back of his throat. "All you need to know is that the sonovabitch killed Pyotr Zilber. God knows why. Then he disappeared off the face of the earth. I had Evsei stake out Mischa Tarkanian's apartment. I was hoping Arkadin would come back there. Instead, you showed up."

"What's Zilber's death to you?" Bourne said. "From what you've told me, there was no love lost between the two of you."

"Hey, I don't have to like a person to do business with him."

"If you wanted to do business with Zilber you shouldn't have had his brother murdered."

"I have my reputation to uphold." Maslov sipped his vodka. "Pyotr knew what kinds of shit his brother was into, but did he stop him? Anyway, the hit was strictly business. Pyotr took it far too personally. Turns out he was almost as reckless as his brother."

There it was again, Bourne thought, the slurs against Pyotr Zilber. What, then, was he doing running a secret network? "What was your business with him?"

"I coveted Pyotr's network. Because of the war with the Azeri, I've been looking for a new, more secure method to move our drugs. Zilber's network was the perfect solution."

Bourne put aside his vodka. "Why would Zilber want anything to do with the Kazanskaya?"

"There you've given away the extent of your ignorance." Maslov eyed him curiously. "Zilber would have wanted money to fund his organization."

"You mean his network."

"I mean precisely what I say." Maslov looked hard and long at Bourne. "Pyotr Zilber was a member of the Black Legion."

Like a sailor who senses an onrushing storm, Devra stopped herself from asking Arkadin again about his maimed foot. There was about him at this moment the same slight tremor of intent of a bowstring pulled back to its maximum. She transferred her gaze from his left foot to the corpse of Heinrich, taking in sunlight that would no longer do him any good. She felt the danger beside her, and she thought of her dream: her pursuit of the unknown creature, her sense of utter desolation, the building of her fear to an unbearable level.

"You've got the package now," she said. "Is it over?"

For a moment, Arkadin said nothing, and she wondered whether she'd left her deflecting question too late, whether he would now turn on her because she had asked about what had happened to that damn foot.

The red rage had gripped Arkadin, shaking him until his teeth rattled in his skull. It would have been so easy to turn to her, smile, and break her neck. So little effort; nothing to it. But something stopped him, something cooled him. It was his own will. He—did—not—want—to—kill—her. Not yet, at least. He liked sitting here on the beach with her, and there were so few things he liked.

"I still have to shut down the rest of the network," he said, at length. "Not that I think it actually matters at this point. Christ, it was put together by an out-of-control commander too young to have learned caution, peopled by drug addicts, inveterate gamblers, weaklings, and those of no faith. It's a wonder the network functioned at all. Surely it would have imploded on its own sooner or later." But what did he know? He was simply a soldier engaged in an invisible war. His was not to reason why.

Pulling out his cell phone, he dialed Icoupov's number.

"Where are you?" his boss said. "There's a lot of background noise."

"I'm at the beach," Arkadin said.

"What? The beach?"

"Kilyos. It's a suburb of Istanbul," Arkadin said.

"I hope you're having a good time while we're in a semi-panic."

Arkadin's demeanor changed instantly. "What happened?"

"The bastard had Harun killed, that's what happened."

He knew how much Harun Iliev meant to Icoupov. Like Mischa meant to him. A rock, someone to keep him from drifting into the abyss of his imagination. "On a happier note," he said, "I have the package."

Icoupov gave a short intake of breath. "Finally! Open it," he commanded. "Tell me if the document is inside."

Arkadin did as he was told, breaking the wax seal, prying open the plastic disk that capped off the cylinder. Inside, tightly rolled sheets of pale blue architectural paper unfurled like sails. There were four in all. Quickly, he scanned them.

Sweat broke out at his hairline. "I'm looking at a set of architectural plans."

"It's the target of the attack."

"The plans," Arkadin said, "are for the Empire State Building in New York City."

Book Three

Twenty-Eight

IT TOOK ten minutes for Bourne to get a decent connection to Professor Specter, then another five for his people to rouse him out of bed. It was 5 AM in Washington. Maslov had gone downstairs to see to business, leaving Bourne alone in the greenhouse to make his calls. Bourne used the time to consider what Maslov had told him. If it was true that Pyotr was a member of the Black Legion, two possibilities arose: One was that Pyotr was running his own operation under the professor's nose. That was ominous enough. The second possibility was far worse, namely that the professor was, himself, a member. But then why had he been attacked by the Black Legion? Bourne himself had seen the tattoo on the arm of the gunman who had accosted Specter, beat him, and hustled him off the street.

At that moment Bourne heard Specter's voice in his ear. "Jason," he said, clearly out of breath, "what's happened?"

Bourne brought him up to date, ending with the information that Pyotr was a member of the Black Legion.

For a long moment, there was silence on the line.

"Professor, are you all right?"

Specter cleared his throat. "I'm fine."

But he didn't sound fine, and as the silence stretched on Bourne strained to catch a hint of his mentor's emotional state.

"Look, I'm sorry about your man Baronov. The killer wasn't Black Legion; he was an NSA agent sent to murder me."

"I appreciate your candor," Specter said. "And while I grieve for Baronov, he knew the risks. Like you, he went into this war with his eyes open."

There was another silence, more awkward than the last one.

Finally, Specter said, "Jason, I'm afraid I've withheld some rather vital information from you. Pyotr Zilber was my son."

"Your son? By why didn't you tell me that in the first place?"

"Fear," the professor said. "I've kept his real identity a secret for so many years it's become habit. I needed to protect Pyotr from his enemies—my enemies—the enemies who were responsible for murdering my wife. I felt the best way to do that was to change his name. So in the summer of his sixth year, Aleksei Specter drowned tragically and Pyotr Zilber came into being. I left him with friends, left everything and came to America, to Washington, to begin my life anew without him. It was the most difficult thing I've ever had to do. But how can a father renounce his son when he can't forget him?"

Bourne knew precisely what he meant. He'd been about to tell the professor what he'd learned about Pyotr and his cast of misfits and fuck-ups, but this didn't seem the right time to bring up more bad news.

"So you helped him?" Bourne guessed. "Secretly."

"Ever so secretly," Specter said. "I couldn't afford to have anyone link us together, I couldn't allow anyone to know my son was still alive. It was the least I could do for him. Jason, I hadn't seen him since he was six years old."

Hearing the naked anguish in Specter's voice, Bourne waited a moment. "What happened?"

"He did a very stupid thing. He decided to take on the Black Legion himself. He spent years infiltrating the organization. He discovered that the Black Legion was planning a major attack inside America, then he spent months worming his way closer to the project. And finally, he had the key to bringing them down: He stole the plans to their target. Since we had to be careful about direct communication, I suggested he use his network for the purpose of getting me information on the Black Legion's movements. This is how he meant to send me the plans."

"Why didn't he simply photograph them and send them to you digitally?"

"He tried that, but it didn't work. The paper the plans are printed on is coated with a substance that makes whatever's printed on it impossible to copy by any means. He had to get me the plans themselves."

"Surely he told you the nature of the plans," Bourne said.

"He was going to," the professor said. "But before he could he was caught, taken to Icoupov's villa, where Arkadin tortured and killed him."

Bourne considered the implications in light of the new information the professor had given him. "Do you think he told them he was your son?"

"I've been concerned about that ever since the kidnapping attempt. I'm afraid Icoupov might know our blood connection."

"You'd better take precautions, Professor."

"I plan to do just that, Jason. I'll be leaving the DC area in just over an hour. Meanwhile, my people have been hard at work. I've gotten word that Icoupov sent Arkadin to fetch the plans from Pyotr's network. He's leaving a trail of bodies in his wake."

"Where is he now?" Bourne said.

"Istanbul, but that won't do you any good," Specter said, "because by the time you get there he'll surely have gone. It's now more imperative than ever that you find him, though, because we have confirmed that he's taken the plans from the courier he murdered in Istanbul, and time is running out before the attack."

"This courier came from where?"

"Munich," the professor said. "He was the last link in the chain before the plans were to be delivered to me."

"From what you tell me, it's clear that Arkadin's mission is twofold," Bourne said. "First, to get the plans; second, to permanently shut down

Pyotr's network by killing its members one by one. Dieter Heinrich, the courier in Munich, is the only one remaining alive."

"Who was Heinrich supposed to deliver the plans to in Munich?"

"Egon Kirsch. Kirsch is my man," Specter said. "I've already alerted him to the danger."

Bourne thought a moment. "Does Arkadin know what Kirsch looks like?"

"No, and neither does the young woman with him. Her name is Devra. She was one of Pyotr's people, but now she's helping Arkadin kill her former colleagues."

"Why would she do that?" Bourne asked.

"I haven't the faintest idea," the professor said. "She was something of a cipher in Sevastopol, where she fell in with Arkadin—no friends, no family, an orphan of the state. So far my people haven't turned up anything useful. In any event, I'm going to pull Kirsch out of Munich."

Bourne's mind was working overtime. "Don't do that. Get him out of his apartment to a safe place somewhere in the city. I'll take the first flight out to Munich. Before I leave here I want all the information on Kirsch's life you can get me—where he was born, raised, his friends, family, schooling, every detail he can give you. I'll study it on the flight over, then meet with him."

"Jason, I don't like the way this conversation is headed," Specter said. "I suspect I know what you're planning. If I'm right, you're going to take Kirsch's place. I forbid it. I won't let you set yourself up as a target for Arkadin. It's far too dangerous."

"It's a little late for second thoughts, Professor," Bourne said. "It's vital I get these plans, you said so yourself. You do your part and I'll do mine."

"Fair enough," Specter said after a moment's hesitation. "But my part includes activating a friend of mine who operates out of Munich."

Bourne didn't like the sound of that. "What do you mean?"

"You've already made it clear that you work alone, Jason, but this man Jens is someone you want at your back. He's intimately familiar with wet work."

A professional killer for hire, Bourne thought. "Thank you, Professor, but no."

"This isn't a request, Jason." Specter's voice held a stern warning not to cross him. "Jens is my condition for you taking Kirsch's place. I won't allow you to walk into this bear trap on your own. My decision is final."

Dimitri Maslov and Boris Karpov embraced like old friends while Bourne stood on, silent. When it came to Russian politics nothing should surprise him, but it was nevertheless astonishing to see a high-ranking colonel in the Federal Anti-Narcotics Agency cordially greeting the kingpin of the Kazanskaya, one of the two most notorious narcotics *grupperovka*.

This bizarre reunion took place in Bar-Dak, near the Leninsky Prospekt. The club had opened for Maslov; hardly surprising, since he owned it. *Bar-Dak* meant both "brothel" and "chaos" in current Russian slang. Bar-Dak was neither, though it did sport a prominent strippers' stage complete with poles and a rather unusual leather swing that looked like a horse's harness.

An open audition for pole dancers was in full swing. The lineup of eye-poppingly-built young blond women snaked around the four walls of the club, which was painted in glossy black enamel. Massive sound speakers, lines of vodka bottles on mirrored shelves, and vintage mirror balls were the major accoutrements.

After the two men were finished slapping each other on the back, Maslov led them across the cavernous room, through a door, and down a wood-paneled hallway. Mixed in with the scent of the cedar was the unmistakable waft of chlorine. It smelled like a health club, and with good reason. They went through a translucent pebbled glass door into a locker room.

"The sauna's just over there," Maslov pointed. "We meet inside in five minutes."

Before Maslov would continue the conversation with Bourne, he insisted on meeting with Boris Karpov. Bourne had thought such a conference unlikely, but when he called Boris, his friend readily agreed. Maslov had given Bourne the name of Bar-Dak, nothing more. Karpov had said only, "I know it. I'll be there in ninety minutes."

Now, stripped down to the buff, white Turkish towels around their loins, the three men reconvened in the steamy confines of the sauna. The small room was lined, like the hallway, in cedar paneling. Slatted wooden benches ran around three walls. In one corner was a heap of heated stones, above which hung a cord.

When Maslov entered, he pulled the cord, showering the rocks with water, which produced clouds of steam that swirled up to the ceiling and down again, engulfing the men as they sat on the benches.

"The colonel has assured me that he will take care of my situation if I take care of his," Maslov said. "Perhaps I should say that I will take care of Cherkesov's problem."

There was a twinkle in his eye as he said this. Stripped of his outsize Hawaiian shirt, he was a small, wiry man with ropy muscles and not an ounce of fat on him. He wore no gold chains around his neck or diamond rings on his fingers. His tattoos were his jewelry; they covered his entire torso. But these were not the crude and often blurred prison tattoos found on so many of his kind. They were among the most elaborate designs Bourne had ever seen: Asian dragons breathing fire, coiling their tails, spreading their wings, grasping with claws outstretched.

"Four years ago I spent six months in Tokyo," Maslov said. "It's the only place to get tattoos. But that's just my opinion."

Boris rocked with laughter. "So that's where you were, you bastard! I scoured all of Russia for your skinny butt."

"In the Ginza," Maslov said, "I hoisted quite a few saki martinis to you and your law enforcement minions. I knew you'd never find me." He made a sweeping gesture. "But that bit of unpleasantness is behind us; the real perpetrator confessed to the murders I was suspected of committing. Now we find ourselves in our own private glasnost."

"I want to know more about Leonid Danilovich Arkadin," Bourne said.

Maslov spread his hands. "Once he was one of us. Then something happened to him, I don't know what. He broke away from the *grupperovka*. People don't do that and survive for long, but Arkadin is in a class by himself. No one dares to touch him. He wraps himself in his reputation for murder and ruthlessness. This is a man—let me tell you—who has no heart. *Yes, Dimitri*, you might say to me, *but isn't that true of most of your kind*? To this I answer, Yes. But Arkadin is also without a soul. This is where he parts company with the others. There is no one else like him, the colonel can back me up on this."

Boris nodded sagely. "Even Cherkesov fears him, our president as well. I personally don't know anyone in either FSB-1 or FSB-2 who'd be willing to take him on, let alone survive. He's like a great white shark, the murderer of killers."

"Aren't you being a bit melodramatic?"

Maslov sat forward, elbows in knees. "Listen, my friend, whatever the hell your real name is, this man Arkadin was born in Nizhny Tagil. Do you know it? No? Let me tell you. This fucking excuse of a city east of here in the southern Ural Mountains is hell on earth. It's filled with smokestacks belching sulfurous fumes from its ironworks. *Poor* is not even a word you can apply to the residents, who swill homemade vodka that's almost pure alcohol and pass out wherever they happen to land. The police, such as they are, are as brutal and sadistic as the citizens. As a gulag is ringed by guard towers, Nizhny Tagil is surrounded by high-security prisons. Since the prison inmates are released without even train fare they settle in the town. You, an American, cannot imagine the brutality, the callousness of the residents of this human sewer. No one but the worst of the crims—as the criminals are called—dares be on the streets after 10 PM."

Maslov wiped the sweat off his cheeks with the back of his hand. "This is the place where Arkadin was born and raised. It was from this cesspit that he made a name for himself by kicking people out of their apartments in old Soviet-era projects and selling them to criminals with a bit of money stolen from regular citizens.

"But whatever happened to Arkadin in Nizhny Tagil in his youth—

and I don't profess to know what that might be—has followed him like a ghoul. Believe me when I tell you that you've never met a man like him. You're better off not."

"I know where he is," Bourne said. "I'm going after him."

"Christ." Maslov shook his head. "You must have a mighty fucking large death wish."

"You don't know my friend here," Boris said.

Maslov eyed Bourne. "I know him as much as I want to, I think." He stood up. "The stench of death is already on him."

Twenty-Nine

THE MAN who stepped off the plane in Munich airport, who dutifully went through Customs and Immigration with all the other passengers from the many flights arriving at more or less the same time, looked nothing like Semion Icoupov. His name was Franz Richter, his passport proclaimed him as a German national, but underneath all the makeup and prosthetics he was Semion Icoupov just the same.

Nevertheless, Icoupov felt naked, exposed to the prying eyes of his enemies, whom he knew were everywhere. They waited patiently for him, like his own death. Ever since boarding the plane he'd been haunted by a sense of impending doom. He hadn't been able to shake it on the flight, he couldn't shake it now. He felt as if he'd come to Munich to stare his own death in the face.

His driver was waiting for him at baggage claim. The man, heavily armed, took the one piece of luggage Icoupov pointed out to him off the chrome carousel, carried it as he led Icoupov through the crowded concourse and out into the dull Munich evening, gray as morning. It wasn't as cold as it had been in Switzerland, but it was wetter, the chill as penetrating as Icoupov's foreboding.

It wasn't fear he felt so much as sorrow. Sorrow that he might not see this battle finished, that his hated nemesis would win, that old grudges would not be settled, that his father's memory would remain sullied, that his murder would remain unavenged.

To be sure, there had been attrition on both sides, he thought as he settled into the backseat of the dove-gray Mercedes. The endgame had begun and already he sensed the checkmate waiting for him not far off. It was difficult but necessary for him to admit that he had been outmaneuvered at every turn. Perhaps he wasn't up to carrying the vision his father had for the Eastern Brotherhood; perhaps the corruption and inversion of ideals had gone too far. Whatever the case, he had lost a great deal of ground to his enemy, and Icoupov had come to the bleak conclusion that he had only one chance to win. His chance rested with Arkadin, the plans for the Black Legion's attack on New York City's Empire State Building, and Jason Bourne. For he realized now that his nemesis was too strong. Without the American's help, he feared his cause was lost.

He stared out the smoked-glass window at the looming skyline of Munich. It gave him a shiver to be back here, where it all began, where the Eastern Brotherhood was saved from Allied war trials following the collapse of the Third Reich.

At that time his father—Farid Icoupov—and Ibrahim Sever were jointly in charge of what was left of the Eastern Legions. Up until the Nazi surrender, Farid, the intellectual, ran the intelligence network that infiltrated the Soviet Union, while Ibrahim, the warrior, commanded the legions that fought on the Eastern Front.

Six months before the Reich's capitulation, the two men met outside Berlin. They saw the end, even if the lunatic Nazi hierarchy was oblivious. So they laid plans for how to ensure their people would survive the war's aftermath. The first thing Ibrahim did was to move his soldiers out of harm's way. By that juncture the Nazi bureaucratic infrastructure had been decimated by Allied bombing, so it was not difficult to redeploy his people into Belgium, Denmark, Greece, and Italy, where they were safe from the reflexive violence of the first wave of invading Allies.

Because Farid and Ibrahim despised Stalin, because they were witness to the massive scale of the atrocities ordered by him, they were in a unique position to understand the Allied fear of communism. Farid argued persuasively that soldiers would be of no use to the Allies, but an intelligence network already inside the Soviet Union would be invaluable. He keenly understood how antithetical communism was to capitalism, that the Americans and the Soviets were allies out of necessity. He felt it inevitable that after the war was over these uncomfortable allies would become bitter enemies.

Ibrahim had no recourse but to agree with his friend's thesis, and indeed this was how it turned out. At every step, Farid and Ibrahim brilliantly outmaneuvered the postwar German agencies in keeping control of their people. As a result, the Eastern Legions not only survived but in fact prospered in postwar Germany.

Farid, however, fairly quickly uncovered a pattern of violence that made him suspicious. German officials who disagreed with his eloquent arguments for continued control were replaced by ones who did. That was odd enough, but then he discovered that those original officials no longer existed. To a one, they had dropped out of sight, never to be seen or heard from again.

Farid bypassed the weakling German bureaucracy and went straight to the Americans with his concerns, but he was unprepared for their response, which was one big shrug. No one, it seemed, cared the least bit about disappeared Germans. They were all too busy defending their slice of Berlin to be bothered.

It was about this time that Ibrahim came to him with the idea of moving the Eastern Legions' headquarters to Munich, out of the way of the increasing antagonism between the Americans and the Soviets. Fed up with the American's disinterest, Farid readily agreed.

They found postwar Munich a bombed-out wreck, seething with immigrant Muslims. Ibrahim wasted no time in recruiting these people into the organization, which by this time had changed its name to the Eastern Brotherhood. For his part, Farid found the American intelligence community in Munich far more receptive to his arguments. Indeed, they were desperate for him and his network. Emboldened, he told them that if they wanted to make a formal arrangement with the Eastern Brotherhood for intelligence from behind the Iron Curtain, they had to look into the disappearances of the list of former German officials he handed them.

It took three months, but at the end of that time he was asked to appear before a man named Brian Folks, whose official title was American attaché of something-or-other. In fact, he was OSS chief of station in Munich, the man who received the intel Farid's network provided him from inside the Soviet Union.

Folks told him that the unofficial investigation Farid asked him to undertake had now been completed. Without another word, he handed over a slim file, sat without comment as Farid read it. The folder contained the photos of each of the German officials on the list Farid had provided. Following each photo was a sheet detailing the findings. All the men were dead. All had been shot in the back of the head. Farid read through this meager material with an increasing sense of frustration. Then he looked up at Folks and said, "Is this it? Is this all there is?"

Folks watched Farid from behind steel-rimmed glasses. "It's all that appears in the report," he said. "But those aren't all the findings." He held out his hand, took the file back. Then he turned, put the sheets one by one through a shredder. When he was finished, he threw the empty folder into the wastebasket, the contents of which were burned every evening at precisely 5 PM.

Following this solemn ritual, he placed his hands on his desk, said to Farid, "The finding of most interest to you is this: Evidence collected indicates conclusively that the murders of these men were committed by Ibrahim Sever."

Tyrone shifted on the bare concrete floor. It was so slippery with his own fluids that one knee went out from under him, splaying him so painfully that he cried out. Of course, no one came to help him; he was alone in the interrogation cell in the basement of the NSA safe house deep in the Virginia countryside. He had to quite literally locate himself in his mind, had to trace the route he and Soraya had taken when they'd driven to the safe house. When? Three days ago? Ten hours? What? The rendition he'd been subjected to had erased any sense of time. The hood over his head threatened to erase his sense of place, so that periodically he had to say to himself: "I'm in an interrogation cell in the basement of the NSA safe house in"—and here he would recite the name of the last town he and Soraya had passed . . . when?

That was the problem, really. His sense of disorientation was so complete, there were periods when he couldn't distinguish up from down. Worse, those periods were becoming both longer and more frequent.

The pain was hardly an issue because he was used to pain, though never this intense or prolonged. It was the disorientation that was worming its way into his brain like a surgeon's drill. It seemed that with each bout he was losing more of himself, as if he were made up of grains of salt or sand trickling away from him. And what would happen when they were all gone? What would he become?

He thought of DJ Tank and the rest of his former crew. He thought of Deron, of Kiki, but none of those tricks worked. They'd slip away like mist and he'd be left to the void into which, he was increasingly sure, he'd disappear. Then he thought of Soraya, conjured her piece by piece, as if he were a sculptor, molding her out of a lump of clay. And he found that as his mind lovingly re-created each minute bit of her, he miraculously stayed intact.

As he struggled back to a position that was tolerably painful, he heard a metallic scrape, and his head came up. Before anything else could transpire, the scents of freshly cooked eggs and bacon came to him, making his mouth water. He'd been fed nothing but plain oatmeal since he was brought here. And at inconsistent times—sometimes one meal right after the other—in order to keep his disorientation absolute.

He heard the scuff of leather soles—two men, his ears told him.

Then General Kendall's voice, saying imperiously, "Set the food on the table, Willard. Right there, thank you. That will be all."

One set of shoe soles clacked across the floor, the sound of the door closing. Silence. Then the screech of a chair being hitched across the concrete. Kendall was sitting down, Tyrone surmised.

"What have we here?" Kendall said, clearly to himself. "Ah, my favorite: eggs over easy, bacon, buttered grits, hot biscuits and gravy." The sound of cutlery being taken up. "You like grits, Tyrone? You like biscuits and gravy?"

Tyrone wasn't too far gone to be incensed. "On'y ting I like betta is watermelon, sah."

"That's a damn fine imitation of one of your brethren, Tyrone." He was obviously talking while eating. "This is damn fine chow. Would you like some?"

Tyrone's stomach growled so loudly he was sure Kendall heard it.

"All you gotta do is tell me everything you and the Moore woman were up to."

"I don't rat anyone out," Tyrone said bitterly.

"Um." The sounds of Kendall swallowing. "That's what they all say in the beginning." He chewed some more. "You do know this is just the beginning, don't you, Tyrone? Sure you do. Just like you know the Moore woman isn't going to save you. She's going to hang you out to dry, sure as I'm sitting here eating the most mouthwatering biscuits I ever had. You know why? Because LaValle gave her a choice: you or Jason Bourne. You know her history with Bourne. She might claim she didn't fuck him but you and I know better."

"She never slept with him," Tyrone said before he could stop himself.

"Sure. She told you that." Munch, munch, munch went Kendall's jaws, shredding the crisp bacon. "What'd you expect her to say?"

The sonovabitch was playing mind games with him, Tyrone knew that for a fact. Trouble was, he wasn't lying. Tyrone knew how Soraya felt about Bourne—it was written all over her face every time she saw him or his name came up. Though she'd said otherwise, the question Kendall had just raised had gnawed at him like an addict at a candy bar.

It was difficult not to envy Bourne with his freedom, his encyclopedic knowledge, his friendship as equals with Deron. But all these things Tyrone dealt with in his own way. It was Soraya's love for Bourne that was so hard to live with.

He heard the scrape of chair legs and then felt the presence of Kendall as he squatted down beside him. It was astonishing, Tyrone thought, how much heat another human being gave off.

"I have to say, Tyrone, you really have taken a beating," Kendall said. "I think you deserve a reward for how well you've held up. Shit, we've had suspects in here who were crying for their mamas after twenty-four hours. Not you, though." The quick *click-clack* of a metal utensil against a china plate. "How about some eggs and bacon? Man, this was some big plate of food, I surely can't finish it myself. So come on. Join me."

As the hood was raised high enough to expose his mouth Tyrone was conflicted. His mind told him to refuse the offer, but his severely shrunken stomach yearned for real food. He could smell the rich flavors of bacon and eggs, felt the food warm as a kiss against his lips.

"Hey, man, what're you waiting for?"

Fuck it, Tyrone said to himself. The tastes of the food exploded inside his mouth. He wanted to moan in pleasure. He wolfed down the first few forkfuls fed to him, then forced himself to chew slowly and methodically, extracting every bit of flavor from the hickory-smoked meat and the rich yolk.

"Tastes good," Kendall said. He must have regained his feet because his voice was above Tyrone when he said, "Tastes real good, doesn't it?"

Tyrone was about to nod his assent when pain exploded in the pit of his stomach. He grunted when it came again. He'd been kicked before, so he knew what Kendall was doing. The third kick landed. He tried to hold on to his food, but the involuntary reaction had begun. A moment later he vomited up all the delicious food Kendall had fed him.

The Munich courier is the last one in the network," Devra said. "His name is Egon Kirsch, but that's all I know. I never met him; no one I know did. Pyotr made sure that link was completely compartmentalized. So far as I know Kirsch dealt directly with Pyotr and no one else."

"Who does Kirsch deliver his intel to?" Arkadin said. "Who's at the other end of the network?"

"I have no idea."

He believed her. "Did Heinrich and Kirsch have a particular meeting place?"

She shook her head.

On the Lufthansa flight from Istanbul to Munich he sat shoulder-to-shoulder with her and wondered what the hell he was doing. She'd given him all the information he was going to get from her. He had the plans; he was on the last lap of his mission. All that remained was to deliver the plans to Icoupov, find Kirsch, and persuade him to lead Arkadin back to the end of the network. Child's play.

Which begged the question of what to do with Devra. He'd already made up his mind to kill her, as he'd killed Marlene and so many others. It was a fait accompli, a fixed point detailed in his mind, a diamond that only needed polishing to sparkle into life. Sitting in the jetliner he heard the quick report from the gun, leaves falling over her dead body, covering her like a blanket.

Devra, who was seated on the aisle, got up, made her way back to the lavatories. Arkadin closed his eyes and was back in the sooty stench of Nizhny Tagil, men with filed teeth and blurry tattoos, women old before their time, bent, swigging homemade vodka from plastic soda bottles, girls with sunken eyes, bereft of a future. And then the mass grave . . .

His eyes popped open. He was having difficulty breathing. Heaving himself to his feet, he followed Devra. She was the last of the passengers waiting. The accordion door on the right opened, an older women bustled out, squeezed by Devra then Arkadin. Devra went into the lavatory, closed the door, and locked it. The OCCUPIED sign came on.

Arkadin walked to the door, stood in front of it for a moment. Then he knocked on it gently.

"Just a minute," her voice came to him.

Leaning his head against the door, he said, "Devra, it's me." And after a short silence, "Open the door."

A moment later, the door folded back. She stood in front of him.

"I want to come in," he said.

Their eyes locked for the space of several heartbeats as each tried to gauge the intent of the other.

Then she backed up against the tiny sink, Arkadin stepped inside, with some difficulty shut the door behind him, and turned the lock.

Thirty

IT'S STATE-OF-THE-ART," Gunter Müller said. "Guaranteed."

Both he and Moira were wearing hard hats as they walked through the series of semi-automated workshops of Kaller Steelworks Gesellschaft, where the coupling link that would receive the LNG tankers as they nosed into the NextGen Long Beach terminal had been manufactured.

Müller, the team leader on the NextGen coupling link project, was a senior vice president of Kaller, a smallish man dressed impeccably in a conservatively cut three-piece chalk-striped suit, expensive shoes, and a tie in black and gold, Munich's colors since the time of the Holy Roman Empire. His skin was bright pink, as if he'd just had his face steam-cleaned, and thick brown hair, graying at the sides. He talked slowly and distinctly in good English, though he was rather endearingly weak with modern American idioms.

At each step he explained the manufacturing process with excruciating detail, great pride. Spread out before them were the design drawings, along with the specs, to which Müller referred time and again.

Moira was listening with only one ear. How her situation had changed now that the Firm was out of the picture, now that NextGen was on its own with the security of its terminal operations in Long Beach, now that she had been reassigned.

But the more things change, she thought, *the more they stay the same*. The moment Noah had handed her the packet for Damascus she knew she wouldn't disengage herself from the Long Beach terminal project. No matter what Noah or his bosses had determined she couldn't leave NextGen or this project in jeopardy. Müller, like everyone else at Kaller and, for that matter, nearly everyone at NextGen, had no idea she worked for the Firm. Only she knew she should be on a flight to Damascus, not here with him. She had a grace period of mere hours before her contact at NextGen would begin to ask questions as to why she was still on the LNG terminal project. By then, she hoped to convince NextGen's president of the wisdom of her disobeying the Firm's orders.

Finally, they reached the loading bay where the sixteen parts of the coupling link were being packed for shipment by air to Long Beach on the NextGen 747 jet that had brought her and Bourne to Munich.

"As specified in the contract, our team of engineers will be accompanying you on the homeward journey." Müller rolled up the drawings, snapped a rubber band around them, and handed them to Moira. "They'll be in charge of putting the coupling link together on site. I have every confidence that all will go smoothly."

"It had better," Moira said. "The LNG tanker is scheduled to dock at the terminal in thirty hours." She shot Müller an unpleasant look. "Not much leeway for your engineers."

"Not to worry, Fraulein Trevor," he said cheerfully. "They're more than up to the task."

"For your company's sake, I sincerely hope so." She stowed the roll under her left arm, preparatory to leaving. "Shall we speak frankly, Herr Müller?"

He smiled. "Always."

"I wouldn't have had to come here at all had it not been for the string of delays that set your manufacturing process back."

Müller's smile seemed immovable. "My dear Fraulein, as I explained to your superiors, the delays were unavoidable—please blame the Chinese for the temporary shortage of steel, and the South Africans for the energy shortages that is forcing the platinum mines to work at half speed." He spread his hands. "We've done the best we could, I assure you." His smile widened. "And now we are at the end of our journey together. The coupling link will be in Long Beach within eighteen hours, and eight hours later it will be in one piece and ready to receive your tanker of liquid natural gas." He stuck out his hand. "All will have a happy ending, yes?"

"Of course it will. Thank you, Herr Müller."

Müller nearly clicked his heels. "The pleasure is all mine, Fraulein."

Moira walked back through the factory with Müller at her side. She said good-bye to him once more at the gates to the factory, walked across the gravel drive to where her chauffeured car sat waiting for her, its precisely engineered German engine purring quietly.

They pulled out of the Kaller Steelworks property, turned left toward the autobahn back to Munich. Five minutes later, her driver said, "There's a car following us, Fraulein."

Turning around, Moira peered out the back window. A small Volkswagen, no more than fifty yards behind them, flashed its headlights.

"Pull over." She pushed aside the hem of her long skirt, took a SIG Sauer out of the holster strapped to her left ankle.

The driver did as he was told, and the car came to a stop on the shoulder of the road. The Volkswagen pulled in behind. Moira sat waiting for something to happen; she was too well trained to get out of the car.

At length, the Volkswagen drove off the shoulder, into the underbrush, where it disappeared from sight. A moment later a man became visible tramping out onto the side of the road. He was tall and narrow, with a pencil mustache and suspenders holding up his trousers. He was in his shirtsleeves, oblivious to the German winter chill. She could see that he had no weapons on him, which, she reasoned, was the point.

When he came abreast of her car, she leaned across the backseat, opened the door for him, and he slipped inside.

"My name is Hauser, Fräulein Trevor. Arthur Hauser." His expression was morose, bitter. "I apologize for the incivility of this impromptu meeting, but I assure you the melodrama is necessary." As if to underscore his words, he glanced back down the road toward the factory, his expression fearful. "I do not have much time so I shall come straight to the point. There is a flaw in the coupling link—not, I hasten to add, in the hardware. That, I assure you, is absolutely sound. But there is a problem with the software. Nothing that will interfere with the operation of the link, no, not at all. It is, rather, a security flaw—a window, if you will. The chances are it might never be discovered, but all the same it's there."

When Hauser glanced again out the back window a car was coming toward them. He clamped his jaws shut, watched as the vehicle passed by, then visibly relaxed as it drove on down the road.

"Herr Müller was not altogether truthful. The delays were caused by this software flaw, nothing else. I should know, since I was part of the software design team. We tried for a patch, but it's been devilishly difficult, and we ran out of time."

"Just how serious is this flaw?" Moira said.

"It depends on whether you're an optimist or a pessimist." Hauser ducked his head, embarrassed. "As I said, it might never be discovered."

Moira glanced out the window for a time, thinking that she shouldn't ask the next question because, as Noah told her in no uncertain terms, the Firm was now out of ensuring the security of NextGen's LNG terminal.

And then she heard herself say, "What if I'm a pessimist?"

Peter Marks found Rodney Feir, chief of field support, in the CI caff, eating a bowl of New England clam chowder. Feir looked up, gestured to Marks to sit. Peter Marks had been elevated to chief of operations after the ill-starred Rob Batt was outed as an NSA rat.

"How's it going?" Feir said.

"How d'you think it's going?" Marks parked himself on the chair opposite Feir. "I've been vetting every one of Batt's contacts for any sign of NSA taint. It's daunting and frustrating work. You?"

"As exhausted as you, I expect." Feir sprinkled oyster crackers into the chowder. "I've been briefing the new DCI on everything from agents in the field to the cleaning firm we've used for the past twenty years."

"D'you think she'll work out?"

Feir knew he had to be careful here. "I'll say this for her: She's a stickler for detail. No stone unturned. She's not leaving anything to chance."

"That's a relief." Marks twiddled a fork between his thumb and fingers. "What we don't need is another crisis. I'd be happy with someone who can right this listing ship."

"My sentiments exactly."

"The reason I'm here," Marks said, "is I'm having a staffing problem. I've lost some people to attrition. Of course, that's inevitable. I thought I'd get some good recruits graduating from the program, but they went to Typhon. I'm in need of a short-term fix."

Feir chewed on a mouthful of gritty clam bits and soft potato cubes. He'd diverted those graduates to Typhon and had been waiting for Marks to come to him ever since. "How can I help?"

"I'd like some of Dick Symes's people to be assigned to my directorate." Dick Symes was the chief of intelligence. "Just temporarily, you understand, until I can get some raw recruits through training and orientation."

"Have you talked to Dick?"

"Why bother? He'll just tell me to go to hell. But you can plead my case to Hart. She's so snowed under that you're the one best suited to get her to listen to me. If she makes the call Dick can yell all he wants, it won't matter."

Feir wiped his lips. "What number of personnel are we talking here, Peter?"

"Eighteen, two dozen tops."

"Not inconsiderable. The DCI is going to want to know what you have in mind."

"I've got a brief detailing it all ready to go," Marks said. "I shoot it to you electronically, you walk it in to her personally."

Feir nodded. "I think that can be arranged."

Relief flooded Marks's face. "Thanks, Rodney."

"Don't mention it." He began to dig into what was left of the chowder. As Marks was about to rise, he said, "Do you by any chance know where Soraya is? She's not in her office and she's not answering her cell."

"Unh-unh." Marks resettled himself. "Why?"

"No reason."

Something in Feir's voice gave him pause. "No reason? Really?"

"Just, you know how office scuttlebutt can be."

"Meaning?"

"You two are tight, aren't you."

"Is that what you heard?"

"Well, yeah." Feir placed his spoon into the empty bowl. "But if it isn't true—"

"I don't know where she is, Rodney." Marks's gaze drifted off. "We never had that kind of thing going."

"Sorry, I didn't mean to pry."

Marks waved away his apology. "Forget it. I have. So what do you want to talk with her about?"

This was what Feir was hoping he'd say. According to the general, he and LaValle required intel on the nuts and bolts of how Typhon worked. "Budgets. She's got so many agents in the field, the DCI wants an accounting of their expenses—which, frankly, hasn't been done since Martin died."

"That's understandable, given what's been going on in here lately."

Feir shrugged deferentially. "I'd do it myself; Soraya's got more on her plate than she can handle, I imagine. Trouble is, I don't even know where the files are." He was going to add: *Do you?* but decided that would be overselling it.

Marks thought a minute. "I might be able to help you there."

How badly does your shoulder hurt?" Devra said.

Arkadin, pressed against her body, his powerful arms around her, said, "I don't know how to answer that. I have an extremely high tolerance for pain."

The airplane's cramped bathroom allowed him to concentrate exclusively on her. It was like being in a coffin together, like being dead, but in a strange afterlife where only they existed.

She smiled up at him as one of his hands traced its way from the small of her back to her neck. His thumb pressed against her jaw, gently tilted her head up while his fingers tightened on the nape of her neck.

He leaned in, his weight arching her torso backward above the sink. He could see the back of her head in the mirror, his face about to eclipse hers. A flame of emotion flickered to life, illuminating the soulless void inside him.

He kissed her.

"Gently," she whispered. "Relax your lips."

Her moist lips opened beneath his, her tongue searched for his, tentatively at first, then with an unmistakable hunger. His lips trembled. He had never felt anything when kissing a woman. In fact, he'd always done his best to avoid it, not knowing what it was for, or why women sought it so relentlessly. An exchange of fluids, that's all it was to him, like a procedure performed in a doctor's office. The best he could say was that it was painless, that it was over quickly.

The electricity that shot through him when his lips met hers stunned him. The sheer pleasure of it astonished him. It hadn't been like this with Marlene; it hadn't been like this with anyone. He did not know what to make of the tremor in his knees. Her sweet, moaning exhalations entered him like silent cries of ecstasy. He swallowed them whole, and wanted more.

Wanting was something Arkadin was unused to. Need was the word that had driven his life up to this moment: He needed to revenge himself on his mother, he needed to escape home, he needed strike out on his own, no matter the course, he needed to bury rivals and enemies, he needed to destroy anyone who got close to his secrets. But want? That was another matter entirely. Devra defined want for him. And it was only when he was certain he no longer needed her that his desire revealed itself. He wanted her.

When he lifted her skirt, probing underneath, her leg drew up. Her fingers nimbly freed him from his clothing. Then he stopped thinking altogether.

Afterward, when they'd returned to their seats, making their way through the line of glaring passengers queued up to use the lavatory, Devra burst into laughter. Arkadin sat watching her. This was another thing unique about her. Anyone else would have asked, Was that your first time? Not her. She wasn't interested in prying his lid open, peering inside to see what made him tick. She had no need to know. Because he was someone who had always needed something, he couldn't tolerate that trait in anyone else.

He was aware of her next to him in a way he was unable to understand. It was as if he could feel her heartbeat, the rush of blood through her body, a body that seemed frail to him, even though he knew how tough she could be, after all she'd suffered. How easily her bones could be broken, how easily a knife slipped through her ribs might pierce her heart, how easily a bullet could shatter her skull. These thoughts sent him into a rage, and he shifted closer to her, as if she were in need of protection—which, when it came to her former allies, she most certainly was. He knew then that he'd do everything in his power to kill anyone who sought to do her harm.

Feeling him edge closer, she turned and smiled. "You know some-thing, Leonid, for the first time in my life I feel safe. All that prickly shit I give off is something I learned early on to keep people away."

"You learned to be tough like your mother."

She shook her head. "That's the really shitty part. My mother had this tough shell, yeah, but it was skin-deep. Beneath it, she was a mass of fears."

Devra put her head against the headrest as she continued, "In fact, the most vivid thing I remember about my mother was her fear. It came off her like a stink. Even after she'd bathed, I smelled it. Of course, for a long time I didn't know what it was, and maybe I was the only one who smelled it, I don't know.

"Anyway, she used to tell me an old Ukrainian folktale. It was about the Nine Levels of Hell. What was she thinking? Was she trying to frighten me or lessen her own fear by sharing it with me? I don't know. In any case, this is what she told me. There is one heaven, but there are nine levels of hell where, depending on the severity of your sins, you're sent when you die.

"The first, the least bad, is the one familiar to everyone, where you roast in flames. The second is where you're alone on the summit of a mountain. Every night you freeze solid, slowly and horribly, only to thaw out in the morning, when the process begins all over again. The third is a place of blinding light; the fourth of pitch blackness. The fifth is a place of icy winds that cut you, quite literally, like a knife. In the sixth, you're pierced by arrows. In the seventh, you're slowly buried by an army of ants. In the eighth, you're crucified.

"But it was the ninth level that terrified my mother the most. There, you lived among wild beasts that gorged themselves on human hearts."

The cruelty of telling this to a child wasn't lost on Arkadin. He was absolutely certain that if his mother had been Ukrainian she'd have told him the same folktale.

"I used to laugh at her story—or at least I tried to," Devra said. "I struggled against believing such nonsense. But that was before a num-ber of those levels of hell were visited on us."

Arkadin felt her presence inside him all the more deeply. The sense of wanting to protect her seemed to bounce around inside him, increasing exponentially as his brain tried to come to terms with what the feeling meant. Had he at last stumbled across something big enough, bright enough, strong enough to put his demons to rest?

After Marlene's death, Icoupov had seen the writing on the wall. He'd stopped trying to peer into Arkadin's past. Instead he'd shipped him off to America to be rehabilitated. "Reprogrammed," Icoupov had called it. Arkadin had spent eighteen months in the Washington, DC, area going through a unique experimental program devised and run by a friend of Icoupov's. Arkadin had emerged changed in many ways, though his past—his shadows, his demons—remained intact. How he wished the program had erased all memory of it! But that wasn't the nature of the program. Icoupov no longer cared about Arkadin's past, what concerned him was his future, and for that the program was ideal.

He fell asleep thinking about the program, but he dreamed he was back in Nizhny Tagil. He never dreamed about the program; in the program he felt safe. His dreams weren't about safety; they were about being pushed from great heights.

Late at night, a subterranean bar called Crespi was the only option when he wanted to get a drink in Nizhny Tagil. It was a reeking place, filled with tattooed men in tracksuits, gold chains around their necks, short-skirted women so heavily made up they looked like store mannequins. Behind their raccoon eyes were vacant pits where their souls had been.

It was in Crespi where Arkadin at age thirteen was first beaten to a pulp by four burly men with pig eyes and Neanderthal brows. And it was to Crespi that Arkadin, after nursing his wounds, returned three months later and blew the men's brains all over the walls. When another crim tried to snatch his gun away, Arkadin shot him point-blank in the face. That sight stopped anyone else in the bar from approaching him. It also gained him a reputation, which helped him to amass a mini real estate empire.

But in that city of smelted iron and hissing slag success had its own particular consequences. For Arkadin, it was coming to the attention of Stas Kuzin, one of the local crime bosses. Kuzin found Arkadin one night, four years later, having a bare-knuckle brawl with a giant lout whom Arkadin called out on a bet, for the prize of one beer.

Having demolished the giant, Arkadin grabbed his free beer, swigged half of it down, and, turning, confronted Stas Kuzin. Arkadin knew him immediately; everyone in Nizhny Tagil did. He had a thick black pelt of hair that came down in a horizontal slash to within an inch of his eyebrows. His head sat on his shoulders like a marble on a stone wall. His jaw had been broken and reconstructed so badly—probably in prison—that he spoke with a peculiar hissing sound, like a serpent. Sometimes what he said was all but unintelligible.

On either side of Kuzin were two ghoulish-looking men with sunken eyes and crude tattoos of dogs on the backs of their hands, which marked them as forever bound to their master.

"Let's talk," this monstrosity said to Arkadin, jerking his tiny head toward a table.

The men who'd been occupying the table rose as one when Kuzin approached, fleeing to the other side of the bar. Kuzin hooked his shoe around a chair leg, dragged it around, and sat down. Disconcertingly, he kept his hands in his lap, as if at any moment he'd draw down on Arkadin and shoot him dead.

He began talking, but it took the seventeen-year-old Arkadin some minutes before he could make heads or tails of what Kuzin was saying. It was like listening to a drowning man going under for the third time. At length, he realized that Kuzin was proposing a merger of sorts: half Arkadin's stake in real estate for 10 percent of Kuzin's operation.

And just what was Stas Kuzin's operation? No one would speak about it openly, but there was no lack of rumors on the subject. Everything from running spent nuclear fuel rods for the big boys over in Moscow to white slave trading, drug trafficking, and prostitution was

laid at Kuzin's doorstep. For his own part, Arkadin tended to dismiss
the more outlandish speculation in favor of what he very well knew
would make Kuzin money in Nizhny Tagil, namely, prostitution and
drugs. Every man in the city had to get laid, and if they had any money
at all, drugs were far preferable to beer and bathtub vodka.

Once again, want never appeared on Arkadin's horizon, only need.
He needed to do more than survive in this city of permasoot, violence,
and black lung disease. He had come as far as he could on his own. He
made enough to sustain himself here, but not enough to break away to
Moscow where he needed to go to grab life's richest opportunities. Outside, the rings of hell rose up: brick smokestacks, vigorously belching
particle-laden smoke, iron guard towers of the brutal prison *zonas*, bristling with assault rifles, powerful spotlights, and bellowing sirens.

In here he was locked inside his own brutal *zona* with Stas Kuzin.
Arkadin gave the only sensible answer. He said yes, and so entered the
ninth level of hell.

Thirty-One

WHILE ON LINE for passport control in Munich, Bourne phoned Specter, who assured him everything was in readiness. Moments later he came in range of the first set of the airport's CCTV cameras. Instantly his image was picked up by the software employed at Semion Icoupov's headquarters, and before he'd finished his call to the professor he'd been identified.

At once Icoupov was called, who ordered his people stationed in Munich to move from standby to action, thus alerting both the airport personnel and the Immigration people under Icoupov's control. The man directing the incoming passengers to the different cordoned-off lanes leading to the Immigration booths received a photo of Bourne on his computer screen just in time to indicate Bourne should go to booth 3.

The Immigration officer manning booth 3 listened to the voice coming through the electronic device in his ear. When the man identified to him as Jason Bourne handed over his passport the officer asked him the usual questions—"How long do you intend to remain in Germany? Is your visit business or pleasure?"—while paging through the passport. He moved it away from the window, passed the photo under a humming purple light. As he did so, he pressed a small metallic disk the thickness of a human nail into the inside back cover of the passport. Then he closed the booklet, smoothed its front and back covers, and handed it back to Bourne.

"Have a pleasant stay in Munich," he said without a trace of emotion or interest. He was already looking beyond Bourne to the next passenger in line.

As in Sheremetyevo, Bourne had the sense that he was under physical surveillance. He changed taxis twice when he arrived at the seething center of the city. In Marienplatz, a large open square from which the historic Marian column ascended, he walked past medieval cathedrals, through flocks of pigeons, lost himself within the crowds of guided tours, gawping at the sugar-icing architecture and the looming twin domes of the Frauenkirche, cathedral of the archbishop of Munich-Freising, the symbol of the city.

He inserted himself in a tour group gathered around a government building in which was inset the city's official shield, depicting a monk with hands spread wide. The tour leader was telling her charges that the German name, *München,* stemmed from an Old High German word meaning "monks." In 1158 or thereabouts, the current duke of Saxony and Bavaria built a bridge over the Isar River, connecting the saltworks, for which the growing city would soon become famous, with a settlement of Benedictine monks. He installed a tollbooth on the bridge, which became a vital link in the Salt Route in and out of the high Bavarian plains on which Munich was built, and a mint in which to house his profits. The modern-day mercantile city was not so far removed from its medieval beginnings.

When Bourne was certain he wasn't being shadowed, he slipped away from the group and boarded a taxi, which dropped him off six blocks from the Wittelsbach Palace.

According to the professor, Kirsch said he'd rather meet Bourne in a public setting. He chose the State Museum for Egyptian Art on Hofgartenstrasse, which was housed within the massive rococo facade of the Wittelsbach Palace. Bourne took a full circuit of the streets around the palace, checking once more for tags, but he couldn't recall being in Munich before. He didn't have that eerie sense of déjà vu that meant he had returned to a place he couldn't remember. Therefore, he knew local tags would have the advantage of terrain. There might be a dozen places to hide around the palace that he didn't know about.

Shrugging, he entered the museum. The metal detector was staffed by a pair of armed security guards, who were also setting aside backpacks and picking through handbags. On either side of the vestibule was a pair of basalt statues of the Egyptian god Horus—a falcon with a disk of the sun on his forehead—and his mother, Isis. Instead of walking directly to the exhibits, Bourne turned, stood behind the statue of Horus, watching for ten minutes as people came and went. He noted everyone between twenty-five and fifty, memorizing their faces. There were seventeen in all.

He then made his way past a female armed guard, into the exhibition halls, where he found Kirsch precisely where he told Specter he'd be, scrutinizing an ancient carving of a lion's head. He recognized Kirsch from the photo Specter had sent him, a snapshot of the two men standing together on the university campus. The professor's courier was a wiry little man with a shiny bald skull and black eyebrows as thick as caterpillars. He had pale blue eyes that darted this way and that as if on gimbals.

Bourne went past him, ostensibly looking at several sarcophagi while using his peripheral vision to check for any of the seventeen people who'd entered the museum after him. When no one presented themselves, he retraced his steps.

Kirsch did not turn as Bourne came up beside him, but said, "I know it sounds ridiculous, but doesn't this sculpture remind you of something?"

"The Pink Panther," Bourne said, both because it was the proper code response, and because the sculpture did look astonishingly like the modern-day cartoon icon.

Kirsch nodded. "Glad you made it without incident." He handed over the keys to his apartment, the code for the front door, and detailed directions to it from the museum. He looked relieved, as if he were handing over his burdensome life rather than his home.

"There are some features of my apartment I want to talk to you about."

As Kirsch spoke they moved on to a granite sculpture of the kneeling Senenmut, from the time of the Eighteenth Dynasty.

"The ancient Egyptians knew how to live," Kirsch observed. "They weren't afraid of death. To them, it was just another journey, not to be undertaken lightly, but still they knew there was something waiting for them after life." He put his hand out, as if to touch the statue or perhaps to absorb some of its potency. "Look at this statue. Life still glows within it, thousands of years later. For centuries the Egyptians had no equal."

"Until they were conquered by the Romans."

"And yet," Kirsch said, "it was the Romans who were changed by the Egyptians. A century after the Ptolemys and Julius Caesar ruled from Alexandria, it was Isis, the Egyptian goddess of revenge and rebellion, who was worshipped throughout the Roman Empire. In fact, it's all too likely that the early Christian Church founders, unable to do away with her or her followers, transmogrified her, stripped her of her war-like nature, and made from her the perfectly peaceful Virgin Mary."

"Leonid Arkadin could use a little less Isis and a lot more Virgin Mary," Bourne mused.

Kirsch raised his eyebrows. "What do you know of this man?"

"I know a lot of dangerous people are terrified of him."

"With good reason," Kirsch said. "The man's a homicidal maniac. He was born and raised in Nizhny Tagil, a hotbed of homicidal maniacs."

"So I've heard," Bourne nodded.

"And there he would have stayed had it not been for Tarkanian."

Bourne's ears pricked up. He'd assumed that Maslov had put his man in Tarkanian's apartment because that's where Gala was living. "Wait a minute, what does Tarkanian have to do with Arkadin?"

"Everything. Without Mischa Tarkanian, Arkadin would never have escaped Nizhny Tagil. It was Tarkanian who brought him to Moscow."

"Are they both members of the Black Legion?"

"So I've been given to understand," Kirsch said. "But I'm only an artist; the clandestine life has given me an ulcer. If I didn't need the money—I'm a singularly unsuccessful artist, I'm afraid—I never would have stayed in this long. This was to be my last favor for Specter." His eyes continued to dart to the left and right. "Now that Arkadin has murdered Dieter Heinrich, *last favor* has taken on a new and terrifying meaning."

Bourne was now on full alert. Specter had assumed that Tarkanian was Black Legion, and Kirsch just confirmed it. But Maslov had denied Tarkanian's affiliation with the terrorist group. Someone was lying.

Bourne was about to ask Kirsch about the discrepancy when out of the corner of his eye he spotted one of the men who'd come into the museum just after he had. The man had paused for a moment in the vestibule, as if orienting himself, then strode purposefully off into the exhibition hall.

Because the man was close enough to overhear them in the museum's hushed atmosphere, Bourne took Kirsch's arm. "Come this way," he said, leading the German contact into another room, which was dominated by a calcite statue of twins from the Eighth Dynasty. It was chipped, time-worn, dating from 2390 BC.

Pushing Kirsch behind the statue, Bourne stood like a sentinel, watching the other man's movements. The man glanced up, saw that Bourne and Kirsch were no longer at the statue of Senenmut, and looked casually around.

"Stay here," Bourne whispered to Kirsch.

"What is it?" There was a slight quaver in Kirsch's voice, but he looked stalwart enough. "Is Arkadin here?"

"Whatever happens," Bourne warned him, "stay put. You'll be safe until I come get you."

As Bourne moved around the far side of the Egyptian twins, the man entered the gallery. Bourne walked to the side opening and into the room beyond. The man, sauntering nonchalantly, took a quick look around and, as if seeing nothing of interest, followed Bourne.

This gallery held a number of high display cases but was dominated by a five-thousand-year-old stone statue of a woman with half her head sheared off. The antiquity was staggering, but Bourne had no time to appreciate it. Perhaps because it was toward the rear of the museum, the room was deserted, save for Bourne and the man, who was standing between Bourne and the one way in or out of the gallery.

Bourne placed himself behind a two-sided display case with a board in the center on which were hung small artifacts—sacred blue scarabs and gold jewelry. Because of a center gap in the board, Bourne could see the man, but the man remained unaware of his position.

Standing completely still, Bourne waited until the man began to come around the right side of the display case. Bourne moved quickly to his right, around the opposite side of the case, and rushed the man.

He shoved him against the wall, but the man maintained his balance. As he took up a defensive posture he pulled a ceramic knife from a sheath under his armpit, swung it back and forth to keep Bourne at bay.

Bourne feinted right, moved left in a semi-crouch. As he did so, he swung his right arm against the hand wielding the knife. His left hand grabbed the man by his throat. As the man tried to drive his knee into Bourne's belly, Bourne twisted to partially deflect the blow. In so doing, he lost his block on the knife hand and now the blade swept in toward the side of his neck. Bourne stopped it just before it struck, and there they stood, locked together in a kind of stalemate.

"Bourne," the man finally got out. "My name is Jens. I work for Dominic Specter."

"Prove it," Bourne said.

"You're here meeting with Egon Kirsch, so you can take his place when Leonid Arkadin comes looking for him."

Bourne let up on his grip of Jens's neck. "Put away your knife."

Jens did as Bourne asked, and Bourne let go of him completely.

"Now where's Kirsch? I need to get him out of here and safely on a plane back to Washington."

Bourne led him back into the adjoining gallery, to the statue of the twins.

"Kirsch, the gallery's clear. You can come out now."

When the contact didn't appear, Bourne stepped behind the statue. Kirsch was there all right, crumpled on the floor, a bullet hole in the back of his head.

Semion Icoupov watched the receiver attuned to the electronic bug in Bourne's passport. As they approached the area of the Egyptian museum, he told the driver of his car to slow down. A keen sense of anticipation coursed through him: He'd decided to take Bourne by gunpoint into his car. It seemed the best way now to get him to listen to what Icoupov had to tell him.

At that moment his cell phone sounded with the ringtone he'd assigned to Arkadin's number, and while on the lookout for Bourne he put the phone to his ear.

"I'm in Munich," Arkadin said in his ear. "I rented a car, and I'm driving in from the airport."

"Good. I've got an electronic tag on Jason Bourne, the man Our Friend has sent to retrieve the plans."

"Where is he? I'll take care of him," Arkadin said in his typical blunt way.

"No, no, I don't want him killed. I'll take care of Bourne. In the meantime, stay mobile. I'll be in touch shortly."

Bourne, kneeling down beside Kirsch, examined the dead body.

"There's a metal detector out front," Jens said. "How the hell could someone bring a gun in here? Plus, there was no noise."

Bourne turned Kirsch's head so the back of it caught the light. "See here." He pointed to the entry wound. "And here. There's no exit wound, which there would have been with a shot fired at close range." He stood up. "Whoever killed him used a suppressor." He went out of the gallery with a purposeful stride. "And whoever killed him works here as a guard; the museum's security personnel are armed."

"There are three of them," Jens said, keeping pace behind Bourne.

"Right. Two on the metal detector, one roaming the galleries."

In the vestibule, the two guards were at their station beside the metal detector. Bourne went up to one of them, said, "I lost my cell phone somewhere in the museum and the guard in the second gallery said she'd help me locate it, but now I can't find her."

"Petra," the guard said. "Yeah, she just took off for her lunch break."

Bourne and Jens went through the front door, down the steps onto the sidewalk, where they looked left and right. Bourne saw a uniformed female figure walking fast down the block to their right, and he and Jens took off after her.

She disappeared around a corner, and the two men sprinted after her. As they neared the corner Bourne became aware of a sleek Mercedes sedan as it came abreast of them.

Icoupov was appalled to discover Bourne exiting the museum in the company of Franz Jens. Jens's appearance told him that his enemy wasn't leaving anything to chance. Jens's job was to keep Icoupov's people away from Bourne, so that Bourne had a clear shot at retrieving the attack plans. A certain dread gripped Icoupov. If Bourne was successful all was lost; his enemy would have won. He couldn't allow that to happen.

Leaning forward in the backseat, he drew a Luger.

"Pick up speed," he told the driver.

Bracing himself against the door frame, he waited until the last instant before depressing the button that slid the window down. He took aim at the running figure of Jens, but Jens sensed him, slowed as he turned. With Bourne now safely three paces ahead, Icoupov squeezed off two shots in succession.

Jens slipped to one knee, skidded off the sidewalk as he went down. Icoupov fired a third shot, just to be sure Jens didn't survive the attack, then he slid the window up.

"Go!" he said to the driver.

The Mercedes shot forward, down the street, screeching away from the bloody body tangled in the gutter.

Thirty-Two

ROB BATT sat in his car, a pair of night-vision binoculars to his eyes, chewing over the recent past as if it were a piece of gum that had lost its flavor.

From the time that Batt had been called into Veronica Hart's office and confronted with his treacherous actions against CI, he'd gone numb. At the moment, he'd felt nothing for himself. Rather, his enmity toward Hart had morphed into pity. Or maybe, he had thought, he pitied himself. Like a novice, he'd stepped into a bear trap; he'd trusted people who never should have been trusted. LaValle and Halliday were going to have their way, he had absolutely no doubt of it. Filled with self-disgust, he'd begun his long night of drinking.

It wasn't until the morning after that Batt, waking up with the father of all hangovers, realized that there was something he could do about it. He thought about that for some time, while he swallowed aspirins for his pounding head, chasing them down with a glass of water and angostura bitters to calm his rebellious stomach.

It was then that the plan formed in his mind, unfolding like a flower to the rays of the sun. He was going to get his revenge for the humiliation LaValle and Kendall had caused him, and the real beauty part was this: If his scheme worked, if he brought them down, he'd resuscitate his own career, which was on life support.

Now, sitting behind the wheel of a rented car, he swept the street across from the Pentagon, on the lookout for General Kendall. Batt was canny enough to know better than to go after LaValle, because LaValle was too smart to make a mistake. The same, however, couldn't be said for the general. If Batt had learned one thing from his abortive association with the two it was that Kendall was a weak link. He was too tied to LaValle, too slavish in his attitude. He needed someone to tell him what to do. The desire to please was what made followers vulnerable; they made mistakes their leaders didn't.

He suddenly saw life the way it must appear to Jason Bourne. He knew the work that Bourne had done for Martin Lindros in Reykjavik and knew that Bourne had put himself on the line to find Lindros and bring him home. But like most of his former co-workers, Batt had conveniently dismissed Bourne's actions as collateral happenstance, choosing to stick to the common wisdom that Bourne was an out-of-control paranoid who needed to be stopped before he committed some heinous act that would disgrace CI. And yet, people in CI had had no compunction about using him when all else failed, coercing him into playing as their pawn. But at last he, Batt, was no one's pawn.

He saw General Kendall exit a side door of the building and, huddled in his trench-coat, hurry across the lot to his car. He kept the general in his sights as he put one hand on the keys he'd already inserted in the ignition. At the precise moment Kendall leaned his right shoulder forward to start his engine, Batt flipped his own ignition, so Kendall didn't hear another car start when his did.

As the general pulled out of the lot, Batt set aside the night glasses and put his car in gear. The night seemed quiet and still, but maybe that was simply a reflection of Batt's mood. He was a sentinel of the night, after all. He'd been trained by the Old Man himself; he'd always been proud of that fact. After his downfall, though, he realized that it was this pride that had distorted his thinking and his decision making.

It was his pride that made him rebel against Veronica Hart, not because of anything she said or did—he hadn't even given her the chance—but because he'd been passed over. Pride was his weakness, one that La-Valle had recognized and exploited. Twenty–twenty hindsight was a bitch, he thought as he followed Kendall toward the Fairfax area, but at least it provided the humility he needed to see how far he'd strayed from his sworn duties at CI.

He kept well back of the general's car, varying his distance and his lane the better to avoid detection. He doubted that Kendall would consider that he might be followed, but it paid to be cautious. Batt was determined to atone for the sin he'd committed against his own organization, against the memory of the Old Man.

Kendall turned in at an anonymous modern-looking building whose entire ground floor was taken up by the In-Tune health club. Batt observed the general park, take out a small gym bag, and enter the club. Nothing useful so far, but Batt had long ago learned to be patient. On stakeouts it seemed nothing came quickly or easily.

And then, because he had nothing better to do until Kendall reappeared, Batt stared at the IN-TUNE sign while he bit hunks off a Snickers bar. Why did that sign seem familiar? He knew he had never been inside, had never, in fact, been in this part of Fairfax. Maybe it was the name: *In-Tune*. Yes, he thought, it sounded maddeningly familiar, but for the life of him he couldn't think of why.

Fifty minutes had passed since Kendall had gone in; time to train his night glasses on the entrance. He watched people of all description and build come in and out. Most were solitary figures; occasionally two women came out talking, once a couple emerged, headed in tandem for their car.

Another fifteen minutes passed and still no Kendall. Batt had taken the glasses away from his eyes to give them a rest when he saw the gym door swung open. Fitting the binoculars back to his eyes he saw Rodney Feir step out into the night. *Are you kidding me?* Batt thought.

Feir ran his hand through his damp hair. And that's when Batt remembered why the name *In-Tune* was so familiar. All CI directors were required to post their whereabouts after hours so if they were needed the duty officer could calculate how long it would take them to get back to headquarters.

Watching Feir walk over and get into his car, Batt bit his lip. Of course it might be sheer coincidence that General Kendall used the same health club as Feir, but Batt knew that in his trade there was no such thing as coincidence.

His suspicion was borne out when Feir did not fire up his car, but sat silent and still behind the wheel. He was waiting for something, but what? Maybe, Batt thought, it was someone.

Ten minutes later, General Kendall emerged from the club. He looked neither to the right nor the left, but went immediately to his car, started it up, and began to back out of his space. Before he'd exited the lot, Feir started his car. Kendall turned right out of the lot and Feir followed.

Excitement flared in Batt's chest. *Game on!* he thought.

After the first two shots struck Jens, Bourne turned back toward him, but the third shot fired into Jens's head made him change his mind. He ran down the street, knowing the other man was dead, there was nothing he could do for him. He had to assume that Arkadin had followed Jens to the museum and had been lying in wait.

Turning the same corner as the museum guard, Bourne saw that she had hesitated, half turned to the sound of the shots. Then, seeing Bourne coming after her, she took off. She darted into an alley. Bourne, following, saw her vault up a corrugated steel fence, beyond which was a cleared building site bristling with heavy machinery. She grabbed hold of the top of the fence, levered herself up and over.

Bourne scaled the fence after her, jumping down onto the packed earth and concrete rubble on the other side. He saw her duck behind the mud-spattered flank of a bulldozer, and ran toward her. She swung up into the cab, slid behind the wheel, and fumbled with the ignition.

Bourne was quite close when the engine rumbled to life. Throwing the bulldozer into reverse, she backed up directly at him. She'd chosen a clumsy vehicle, and he leapt to one side, reached for a handhold, and swung up. The bulldozer lurched, the gears grinding as she struggled to shove it into first, but Bourne was already inside the cab.

She tried to draw her gun, but she was also trying to guide the bulldozer, and Bourne easily slapped the weapon away. It fell to the foot well, where he kicked it away from her. Then he reached over, turned off the engine. The moment he did that, the woman covered her face with her hands and burst into tears.

This is your mess," Deron said.

Soraya nodded. "I know it is."

"You came to us—Kiki and me."

"I take full responsibility."

"I think in this case," Deron said, "we have to share the responsibility. We could've said no, but we didn't. Now all of us—not just Tyrone and Jason—are in serious jeopardy."

They were sitting in the den of Deron's house, a cozy room with a wraparound sofa that faced a stone fireplace and, above it, a large plasma TV. Drinks were set out on a low wooden table, but nobody had touched them. Deron and Soraya sat facing each other. Kiki was curled up in the corner like a cat.

"Tyrone's already totally fucked," Soraya said. "I saw what they're doing to him."

"Hold on." Deron sat forward. "There's a difference between perception and reality. Don't let them skullfuck you. They're not going to risk damaging Tyrone; he's their only leverage to coerce you to bring Jason to them."

Soraya, once again finding fear scattering her thoughts, reached over and poured herself a scotch. Rolling it around in the glass, she inhaled its complex aroma, which called to mind heather and butterscotch. She recalled Jason telling her how sights, scents, idioms, or tones of voice could trigger his hidden memories.

She took a sip of the scotch, felt it ignite a stream of fire down to her stomach. She wanted to be anywhere but here now; she wanted another life; but this was the life she'd chosen, these were the decisions she'd made. There was no help for it—she could not abandon her friends; she had to keep them safe. How to do that was the vexing question.

Deron was right about LaValle and Kendall. Taking her back down to the interrogation room was a psychological ploy. What they'd showed her was minimal, now that she thought about it. They were counting on her to imagine the worst, to let those thoughts prey on her until she gave in, called Jason so they could take him into custody and, like a show dog, present him to the president as proof that, having accomplished what numerous CI initiatives could not, LaValle deserved to take over and run CI.

She took another sip of scotch, aware that Deron and Kiki were silent, patiently waiting for her to work through the mistake she'd made and, coming through the other side, put it behind her. But she had to take the initiative, to formulate a plan of counterattack. That was what Deron meant when he said, *This is your mess.*

"The thing to do," she said, slowly and carefully, "is to beat LaValle at his own game."

"And how do you propose to do that?" Deron said.

Soraya stared down at the dregs of her scotch. That was just it, she had no idea.

The silence stretched out, growing thicker and more deadly by the second. At last, Kiki uncurled herself, stood up, and said, "I for one have had enough of this gloom and doom. Sitting around feeling angry and frustrated isn't helping Tyrone and it isn't helping us find a solution. I'm going out to have a good time at my friend's club." She looked from Soraya to Deron and back again. "So who's going to join me?"

The high–low wail of the police sirens came to Bourne as he sat beside the museum guard in the bulldozer. Up close, she looked younger than he had imagined. Her blond hair, which had been pulled back in a severe bun, had come loose. It flowed down around her pale face. Her eyes were large and liquid—red around the rims now from crying. There was something about them that made him think she'd been born sad.

"Take off your jacket," he said.

"What?" The guard appeared totally confused.

Without saying anything, Bourne helped her off with her jacket. Pushing up the sleeves of her shirt, he checked the insides of her elbows, but found no Black Legion tattoo. Naked fear had joined the sadness in her eyes.

"What's your name?" he said softly.

"Petra-Alexandra Eichen," she said in a quavery voice. "But everyone calls me Petra." She wiped at her eyes, and gave him a sideways look. "Are you going to kill me now?"

The police sirens were very loud, and Bourne had a desire to get as far away from them as possible.

"Why would I do that?"

"Because I . . ." Her voice faltered and she choked, it seemed, on her own words, or on an emotion welling up. "I shot your friend."

"Why did you do that?"

"For money," she said. "I need money."

Bourne believed her. She didn't act like a professional; she didn't talk like one, either. "Who paid you?"

Fear distorted her expression, magnified her eyes until they seemed to goggle at him. "I . . . I can't tell you. He made me promise, he said he'd kill me if I opened my mouth."

Bourne heard raised voices, using the clipped jargon endemic to police the world over. They'd started their dragnet. He retrieved her gun, a Walther P22, the small caliber being the only option for a silent kill in an enclosed space, even with a suppressor.

"Where's the suppressor?"

"I threw it down a storm drain," she said, "as I was instructed to do."

"Continuing to follow orders isn't going to help. The people who hired you are going to kill you anyway," he said as he dragged her down from the bulldozer. "You're in way over your head."

She gave a little moan and tried to break away from him.

He grabbed her. "If you want, I'll let you go straight to the cops. They'll be here any minute."

Her mouth worked, but nothing intelligible came out.

Voices came to him, more distinct now. The police were on the other side of the corrugated wall. He pulled her in the opposite direction. "Do you know another way out of here?"

Petra nodded, pointing. She and Bourne ran diagonally across the yard, dodging heavy equipment as they picked their way through the rubble and around deep holes in the earth. Without turning around, Bourne could tell that the cops had entered the far side of the yard. He pushed Petra's head down as he himself bent over to keep them both from being spotted. Beyond a crane, a crew chief's trailer was set up on concrete blocks. Temporary electric lines were strung into it from just above the tin roof.

Petra threw herself headlong under the trailer, and Bourne followed. The blocks set the trailer just high enough for them to worm their way on their bellies to the far side, where Bourne saw that a gap had been cut in the chain-link fence.

Crawling through the gap, they found themselves in a quiet alley filled with industrial-size garbage bins and a Dumpster filled with broken tiles, jagged blocks of terrazzo, and pieces of twisted metal, no doubt from whatever buildings had once stood in the now empty space behind them.

"This way," Petra whispered as she took them out of the alley and down a residential street. Around the corner, she went to a car and opened it with a set of keys.

"Give me the keys," Bourne said. "They'll be looking for you."

He caught them in midair, and they both got in. A block away they passed a cruising police car. The sudden tension caused Petra's hands to tremble in her lap.

"We're going right past them," Bourne said. "Don't look at them."

Nothing further passed between them until Bourne said, "They've turned around. They're coming after us."

Thirty-Three

I'M GOING to drop you off somewhere," Arkadin said. "I don't want you in the middle of whatever's going to come."

Devra, in the passenger's seat of the rented BMW, shot him a skeptical look. "That doesn't sound like you at all."

"No? Who does it sound like?"

"We still have to get Egon Kirsch."

Arkadin turned a corner. They were in the center of the city, a place filled with old cathedrals and palaces. The place looked like something out of Grimm's Fairy Tales.

"There's been a complication," he said. "The opposition's king has entered the chess match. His name is Jason Bourne and he's here in Munich."

"All the more reason why I should stay with you." Devra checked the action on one of the two Lugers that Arkadin had picked up from one of Icoupov's local agents. "A crossfire has many benefits."

Arkadin laughed. "There's no lack of fire to you."

That was another thing that drew him to her—she wasn't afraid of the male fire burning in her belly. But he had promised her—and himself—that he would protect her. It had been a very long time since he'd said that to anyone, and even though he'd sworn never to make that promise again, he'd done just that. And strange to say, he felt good about it; in fact, there was a sense now when he was around her that he'd stepped out of the shadows he'd been born into, that had been tattooed into his flesh by so many violent incidents. For the first time in his life he felt as if he could take pleasure in the sun on his face, in the wind lifting Devra's hair behind her like a mane, that he could walk down the street with her and not feel as if he was living in another dimension, that he hadn't just arrived here from another planet.

As they stopped at a red light, he glanced at her. Sunlight was streaming into the interior, turning her face the palest shade of pink. At that precise moment he felt something rush out of him and into her, and she turned as if she felt it, too, and she smiled at him.

The light turned green and he accelerated through the cross street. His cell phone buzzed. A glance down at the number of the incoming call told him that Gala was calling. He didn't answer; he had no wish to talk to her now, or ever, for that matter.

Three minutes later, he received a text message. It read: MISCHA DEAD. KILLED BY JASON BOURNE.

Having followed Rodney Feir and General Kendall over the Key Bridge into Washington proper, Rob Batt made sure his long-lens SLR Nikon was fully loaded with fast film. He shot a series of digital photos with a compact camera, but these were only for reference, because they could be Photoshopped in a heartbeat. To forestall any suspicion that the images might be manipulated, he'd present the undeveloped roll of film to . . . well, this was his real problem. For a legitimate reason he was persona non grata at CI. It was astonishing how quickly years-long associations vanished. But now he realized he'd mistaken the camaraderie he'd developed with what had been his fellow directors for friendship. As far as they were concerned he no longer existed, so going to them with any alleged evidence that the NSA had turned yet another CI officer would be either ignored or laughed at. Trying to approach Veronica Hart was similarly out of the question. Assuming he could ever get to her—which he doubted—speaking to her now would be like groveling. Batt had never groveled in his life, and he wasn't going to now.

Then he laughed out loud at how easy it was to become self-deluded. Why should any of his former colleagues want anything to do with him? He'd betrayed them, abandoned them for the enemy. If he were in their shoes—and how he wished he were!—he'd feel the same venomous animosity toward someone who'd sold him out, which was why he'd embarked on this mission to destroy LaValle and Kendall. They'd sold him out—hung him out to dry as soon as it suited their purposes. The moment he came on board, they'd taken control of Typhon away from him.

Venomous animosity. That was an excellent phrase, he thought, one that precisely defined his feelings toward LaValle and Kendall. He knew, deep down, that hating them was the same as hating himself. But he couldn't hate himself; that was self-defeating. At this very moment he couldn't believe he'd sunk so low as to defect to the NSA. He'd gone through his line of thinking over and over, and now it seemed to him as if someone else, some stranger, had made that decision. It hadn't been him, it couldn't have been him, ergo, LaValle and Kendall had made him do it. For that they had to pay the ultimate price.

The two men were on the move again, and Batt headed out after them. After a ten-minute drive, the two cars ahead of him pulled into the crowded parking lot of The Glass Slipper. As Batt passed by, Feir and Kendall got out of their respective cars and went inside. Batt drove around the block, parked on a side street. Reaching into the glove compartment, he took out a tiny Leica camera, the kind used by the Old Man in his youthful days of surveillance. It was the old spy standby, as dependable as it was easy to conceal. Batt loaded it with fast film, put it in the breast pocket of his shirt along with the digital camera, and got out of the car.

The night was filled with a gritty wind. Refuse spiraled up from the gutter, only to come to rest in a different place. Jamming his hands in his coat pockets, Batt hurried down the block and into The Glass Slipper. A slide guitarist was up on stage, wailing the blues, warming up for the feature act, a high-powered band with several hit CDs under its belt.

He'd heard about the club by reputation only. He knew, for instance, that it was owned by Drew Davis, primarily because Davis was a larger-than-life character who continually inserted himself into the political and economic affairs of African Americans in the district. Thanks to his influence, homeless shelters had become safer places for their residents, halfway houses had been built; he made it a point to hire ex-cons. He was so cannily public about these hirings that the ex-cons had no choice but to make the most of their second chances.

What Batt didn't know about was the Slipper's back room, so he was puzzled when, after a full circuit of the space, plus an expedition to the men's room, he could find no trace of either Feir or the general.

Fearing that they'd slipped out the back, he returned to the parking lot, only to find their cars where they'd left them. Back in the Slipper, he took another trip through the crowd, figuring he must have missed them somehow. Still, there was no sign, but as he neared the rear of the space he spotted someone talking to a muscled black man the approximate size of a refrigerator. After a small bout of jawing, Mr. Muscle opened a door Batt hadn't noticed before, and the man slipped through. Guessing this was where Feir and Kendall must have gone, Batt edged his way toward Mr. Muscle and the door.

It was then that he saw Soraya walk through the front door.

Bourne almost stripped the car's gears trying to outrun the police car on their tail.

"Take it easy," Petra said, "or you'll tear my poor car apart."

He wished he'd taken a longer look at the map of the city. A street blocked off with wooden sawhorses flashed by on their left. The paving had been torn up, leaving the heavily pitted and cracked underlayer, the worst parts of which were in the process of being excavated.

"Hold on tight," Bourne said as he reversed, then turned into the street and drove the car through the sawhorses, cracking one and scattering the others. The car hit the underlayer, jounced down the street at what seemed a reckless speed. It felt as if the vehicle were being machine-gunned by a pile driver. Bourne's teeth rattled in his head, and Petra struggled to keep from crying out.

Behind them, the police car was having even more difficulty keeping to a straight path. It jerked back and forth to avoid the deepest of the holes gouged in the roadbed. Putting on another burst of speed, Bourne was able to lengthen the distance between them. But then he glanced ahead. A cement truck was parked crosswise at the other end of the street. If they kept going there was no way to avoid crashing into it.

Bourne kept the speed on as the cement truck loomed larger and larger. The police car was coming up fast behind them.

"What are you doing?" Petra screamed. "Are you out of your fucking mind?"

At that moment, Bourne threw the car into neutral, stepped on the brake. He immediately changed into reverse, took his foot off the brake, and pressed the gas pedal to the floor. The car shuddered, its engine screaming. Then the transmission locked into place, and the car flew backward. The police car came on, its driver frozen in shock. Bourne swerved around it as the vehicle raced forward into the side of the cement truck.

Bourne wasn't even looking. He was busy steering the car back down the street in reverse. Blasting past the shattered sawhorses, he turned, braked, put the car into first, and drove off.

W hat the hell are you doing here?" Noah said. "You should be on your way to Damascus."

"I'm due to take off in four hours." Moira put her hands in her pockets so he wouldn't see that they were curled into fists. "You haven't answered my question."

Noah sighed. "It doesn't make any difference."

Her laugh had a bitter taste to it. "Why am I not surprised?"

"Because," Noah said, "you've been with Black River long enough to know how we operate."

They were walking down Kaufingerstrasse in the center of Munich, a heavily trafficked area just off the Marienplatz. Turning in at the sign for the Augustiner Bierkeller, they entered a long, dim cathedral-like space that smelled powerfully of beer and boiled wurst. The hubbub of noise was just right for masking a private conversation. Crossing the red flagstone floor, they chose a table in one of the rooms, sat on wooden benches. The person closest to them was an old man sucking on a pipe while he leisurely read the paper.

Moira and Noah both ordered a Hefeweizen, a wheat beer still clouded with unfiltered yeast, from a waitress dressed in the regional Dirndlkleid, a long, wide skirt and low-cut blouse. She had an apron around her waist, along with a decorative purse.

"Noah," Moira said when the beers had been served, "I don't hold any illusions about why we do what we do, but how do you expect me to ignore this intel I got right from the source?"

Noah took a long draw of his Hefeweizen, fastidiously wiped his lips before answering. Then he began to tick off points on his fingers. "First, this man Hauser told you that the flaw in the software is virtually unde-tectable. Second, what he told you isn't verifiable. He might simply be a disgruntled employee trying to get revenge on Kaller Steelworks. Have you considered that possibility?"

"We could run our own tests on the software."

"No time. There's less than two days before the LNG tanker is scheduled to dock at the terminal." He continued ticking off points. "Third, we couldn't do anything without alerting NextGen, who would then turn around and confront Kaller Steelworks, which would put us in the middle of a nasty situation. And, fourth and finally, what part of the sentence *We've officially notified NextGen that we've withdrawn from the project* do you not understand?"

Moira sat back for a moment and took a deep breath. "This is solid intel, Noah. It could lead to the situation we were most worried about: a terrorist attack. How can you—"

"You've already taken several steps over the line, Moira," Noah said sharply. "Get your tail on that plane and your head into your new assignment, or you're through at Black River."

It's better for the moment that we don't meet," Icoupov said.

Arkadin was seething, barely holding down his rage, and only then because Devra, canny witch that she was, dug her fingernails into the palm of his hand. She understood him; no questions, no probing, no trying to pick over his past like a vulture.

"What about the plans?" He and Devra were sitting in a miserable, smoke-filled bar, in a run-down part of the city.

"I'll pick them up from you now." Icoupov's voice sounded thin and far away over the cell phone, even though there could be only a mile or two separating them. "I'm following Bourne. I'm going after him myself."

Arkadin didn't want to hear it. "I thought that was my job."

"Your job is essentially over. You have the plans and you've terminated Pyotr's network."

"All except Egon Kirsch."

"Kirsch has already been disposed of," Icoupov said.

"I'm the one who terminates the targets. I'll give you the plans and then take care of Bourne."

"I told you, Leonid Danilovich, I don't want Bourne terminated."

Arkadin made an anguished animal sound under his breath. *But Bourne has to be terminated*, he thought. Devra dug her claws deeper into his flesh, so that he could smell the sweet, coppery scent of his own blood. *And I have to do it. He murdered Mischa.*

"Are you listening to me?" Icoupov said sharply.

Arkadin stirred within his web of rage. "Yes, sir, always. However, I must insist that you tell me where you'll be when you accost Bourne. This is security, for your own safety. I won't stand helplessly by while something unforseen happens to you."

"Agreed," Icoupov said after a moment's hesitation. "At the moment, he's on the move, so I have time to get the plans from you." He gave Arkadin an address. "I'll be there in fifteen minutes."

"It'll take me a bit longer," Arkadin said.

"Within the half hour then. The moment I know where I'll be intercepting Bourne, you'll know. Does that satisfy you, Leonid Danilovich?"

"Completely."

Arkadin folded away his phone, disentangled himself from Devra, and went up to the bar. "A double Oban on rocks."

The bartender, a huge man with tattooed arms, squinted at him. "What's an Oban?"

"It's a single-malt scotch, you moron."

The bartender, polishing an old-fashioned glass, grunted. "What does this look like, the prince's palace? We don't have single-malt anything."

Arkadin reached over, snatched the glass out of the bartender's hands, and smashed it bottom-first into his nose. Then, as blood started to gush, he hauled the dazed man over the bar top and proceeded to beat him to a pulp.

I can't go back to Munich," Petra said. "Not for a while, anyway. That's what he told me."

"Why would you jeopardize your job to kill someone?" Bourne said.

"Please!" She glanced at him. "A hamster couldn't live on what they paid me in that shithole."

She was behind the wheel, driving on the autobahn. They had already passed the outskirts of the city. Bourne didn't mind; he needed to stay out of Munich himself until the furor over Egon Kirsch's death died down. The authorities would find someone else's ID on Kirsch, and though Bourne had no doubt they'd eventually find out his real identity, he hoped by that time to have retrieved the plans from Arkadin and be flying back to Washington. In the meantime the police would be searching for him as a witness to the murders of both Kirsch and Jens.

"Sooner or later," Bourne said, "you're going to have to tell me who hired you."

Petra said nothing, but her hands trembled on the wheel, an aftermath of their harrowing chase.

"Where are we going?" Bourne said. He wanted to keep her engaged
in conversation. He felt that she needed to connect with him on some
personal level in order to open up. He had to get her to tell him who had
ordered her to kill Egon Kirsch. That might answer the question of
whether he was connected to the man who'd gunned down Jens.

"Home," she said. "A place I never wanted to go back to."

"Why is that?"

"I was born in Munich because my mother traveled there to give
birth to me, but I'm from Dachau." She meant the town, of course, after
which the adjacent Nazi concentration camp had been named. "No
parent wants *Dachau* to appear on their child's birth certificate, so when
their time comes the women check into a Munich hospital." Hardly
surprising: Almost two hundred thousand people were exterminated
during the camp's life, the longest of the war, since it was the first built,
becoming the prototype for all the other KZ camps.

The town itself, situated along the Amper River, lay some twelve
miles northwest of Munich. It was unexpectedly bucolic, with its narrow
cobbled streets, old-fashioned street lamps, and quiet tree-lined lanes.

When Bourne observed that most of the people they passed looked
contented enough, Petra laughed unpleasantly. "They go around in a
permanent fog, hating that their little town has such a murderous burden to carry."

She drove through the center of Dachau, then turned north until
they reached what once had been the village of Etzenhausen. There,
on a desolate hill known at the Leitenberg, was a graveyard, lonely and
utterly deserted. They got out of the car, walked past the stone stela
with the sculpted Star of David. The stone was scarred, furry with blue
lichen; the overhanging firs and hemlocks blocked out the sky even on
such a bright midwinter afternoon.

As they walked slowly among the gravestones, she said, "This is the
KZ-Friedhof, the concentration camp cemetery. Through most of
Dachau's life, the corpses of the Jews were piled up and burned in ovens,

but toward the end when the camp ran out of coal, the Nazis had to do something with the corpses, so they brought them up here." She spread her arms wide. "This is all the memorial the Jewish victims got."

Bourne had been in many cemeteries before, and had found them peculiarly peaceful. Not KZ-Friedhof, where a sensation of constant movement, ceaseless murmuring made his skin crawl. The place was alive, howling in its restless silence. He paused, squatted down, and ran his fingertips over the words engraved on a headstone. They were so eroded it was impossible to read them.

"Did you ever think that the man you shot today might have been a Jew?" he said.

She turned on him sharply. "I told you I needed the money. I did it out of necessity."

Bourne looked around them. "That's what the Nazis said when they buried their last victims here."

A flash of anger momentarily burned away the sadness in her eyes. "I hate you."

"Not nearly as much as you hate yourself." He rose, handed her back her gun. "Here, why don't you shoot yourself and end it all?"

She took the gun, aimed it at him. "Why don't I just shoot you?"

"Killing me will only make matters worse for you. Besides . . ." Bourne opened up one palm to show her the bullets he'd taken out of her weapon.

With a disgusted sound, Petra holstered her gun. Her face and hands looked greenish in what light filtered through the evergreens.

"You can make amends for what you did today," Bourne said. "Tell me who hired you."

Petra eyed him skeptically. "I won't give you the money, if that's what you're angling for."

"I have no interest in your money," Bourne said. "But I think the man you shot was going to tell me something I needed to know. I suspect that's why you were hired to kill him."

Some of the skepticism leached out of her face. "Really?"

Bourne nodded.

"I didn't *want* to kill him," she said. "You understand that."

"You walked up to him, put the gun to his head, and pulled the trigger."

Petra looked away, at nothing in particular. "I don't want to think about it."

"Then you're no better than anyone else in Dachau."

Tears spilled over, she covered her face with her hands, and her shoulders shook. The sounds she made were like those Bourne had heard on Leitenberg.

At length, Petra's crying jag was spent. Wiping her reddened eyes with the backs of her hands, she said, "I wanted to be a poet, you know? I always equated being a poet with being a revolutionary. I, a German, wanted to change the world or, at least, do something to change the way the world saw us, to do something to scoop that core of guilt out of us."

"You should have become an exorcist."

It was a joke, but such was her mood that she found nothing funny in it. "That would be perfect, wouldn't it?" She looked at him with eyes still filled with tears. "Is it so naive to want to change the world?"

"*Impractical* might be a better word."

She cocked her head. "You're a cynic, aren't you?" When he didn't answer, she went on. "I don't think it's naive to believe that words—that what you write—can change things."

"Why aren't you writing then," he said, "instead of shooting people for money? That's no way to earn a living."

She was silent for so long, he wondered whether she'd heard him.

At last, she said, "Fuck it, I was hired by a man named Spangler Wald—he's just past being a boy, really, no more than twenty-one or -two. I'd seen him around the pubs; we had coffee together once or twice. He said he was attending the university, majoring in entropic economics, whatever that is."

"I don't think anyone can major in entropic economics," Bourne said.

"Figures." Petra was still sniffling. "I have to get my bullshit meter recalibrated." She shrugged. "I never was good with people; I'm better off communing with the dead."

Bourne said, "You can't take on the grief and rage of so many people without being buried alive."

She looked off at the rows of crumbling headstones. "What else can I do? They're forgotten now. Here's where the truth lies. If you omit the truth, isn't that worse than a lie?"

When he didn't answer, she gave a quick twitch of her shoulders and turned around. "Now that you've been here, I want to show you what the tourists see."

She led him back to her car, drove down the deserted hill to the official Dachau memorial.

There was a pall over what was left of the camp buildings, as if the noxious emissions of the coal-fired incinerators still rose and fell on the thermals, like carrion birds still searching for the dead. An ironwork sculpture, a harrowing interpretation of skeletal prisoners made to resemble the barbed wire that had imprisoned them, greeted them as they drove in. Inside what had once been the main administrative building was a mock-up of the cells, display cases of shoes and other inexpressibly sad items, all that was left of the inmates.

"These signs," Petra said. "Do you see any mention of how many Jews were tortured and lost their lives there? 'One hundred and ninety-three thousand *people* lost their lives here,' the signs say. There's no expiation in this. We're still hiding from ourselves; we're still a land of Jew-haters, no matter how often we try to stifle the impulse with righteous anger, as if we have a right to be the aggrieved ones."

Bourne might have told her that nothing in life is as simple as that, except he deemed it better to let her fury burn itself out. Clearly, she couldn't vent these views to anyone else.

She took him on a tour of the ovens, which seemed sinister even so many years after their use. They seemed alive, appeared to shimmer, to be part of an alternate universe overflowing with unspeakable horror. At length, they passed out of the crematorium and arrived at a long room, the walls of which were covered with letters, some written by prisoners, others by families desperate for news of their loved ones, as well as other notes, drawings, and more formal letters of inquiry. All were in German; none had been translated into other languages.

Bourne read them all. The aftermath of despair, atrocities, and death hung in these rooms, unable to escape. There was a different kind of silence here than the one on the Leitenberg. He was aware of the soft scuff of shoe soles, the whisper of sneakers as tourists dragged themselves from one exhibit to another. It was as if the accumulated inhumanity stifled the ability to speak, or perhaps it was that words—any words—were both inadequate and superfluous.

They moved slowly down the room. He could see Petra's lips move as she read letter after letter. Near the end of the wall, one caught his eye, quickened his pulse. A sheet of paper, obviously stationery, contained a handwritten text complaining that the author had developed what he claimed was a gas far more effective than Zyklon-B, but that no one at Dachau administration had seen fit to answer him. Possibly that was because the gas was never used at Dachau. However, what interested Bourne far more was that the stationery was imprinted with the wheel of three horses' heads joined in the center by the SS death's head.

Petra came up beside him, now her brows knitted together in a frown. "That's damn familiar."

He turned to her. "What do you mean?"

"There was someone I used to know—Old Pelz. He said he lived in town, but I think he was homeless. He'd come down to the Dachau air raid shelter to sleep, especially in winter." She pushed a stray lock of hair behind one ear. "He used to babble all the time, you know how crazy people do, as if he was talking to someone else. I remember him showing me a patch with that same insignia. He was talking about something called the Black Legion."

Bourne's pulse began to pound. "What did he say?"

She shrugged.

"You hate the Nazis so much," he said, "I wonder if you know that some things they gave birth to still exist."

"Yeah, sure, like the skinheads."

He pointed at the insignia. "The Black Legion still exists, it's still a danger, even more so than when Old Pelz knew it."

Petra shook her head. "He talked on and on. I never knew whether he was speaking to me or to himself ."

"Can you take me to him?"

"Sure, but who knows whether he's still alive. He drank like a fish."

Ten minutes later Petra drove down Augsburgerstrasse, heading for the foot of a hill known as Karlsburg. "Fucking ironic," she said bitterly, "that the one place I despise the most is now the safest place for me."

She pulled into the lot outside the St. Jakob parish church. Its octagonal baroque tower could be seen throughout the town. Next door was Hörhammer's department store. "You see there at the side of Hörhammer's," she said as they clambered out of the car, "those steps lead down to the huge air raid bunker built into the hill, but you can't get in that way."

Leading him up the steps into St. Jakob, she led him across the Renaissance interior, past the choir. Adjacent to the sacristy was an unobtrusive dark wooden door, behind which lay a flight of stone stairs curving down to the crypt, which was surprisingly small, considering the size of the church above it.

But as Petra quickly showed him, there was a reason for the size: Beyond it lay a labyrinth of rooms and corridors.

"The bunker," she said, flicking on a string of bare lightbulbs affixed to the stone wall on their right. "Here is where my grandparents fled when your country bombed the shit out of the unofficial capital of the Third Reich." She was speaking of Munich, but Dachau was close enough to feel the brunt of the American air force raids.

"If you hate your country so much," Bourne said, "why don't you leave?"

"Because," Petra said, "I also love it. It's the mystery of being German—proud but self-hating." She shrugged. "What can you do? You play the hand fate deals you."

Bourne knew how that felt. He looked around. "You're familiar with this place?"

She sighed heavily, as if her fury had left her spent. "When I was a child my parents took me to Sunday Mass every week. They're God-fearing people What a joke! Didn't God turn his face away from this place years ago?

"Anyway, one Sunday I was so bored I snuck away. In those days, I was obsessed with death. Can you blame me? I grew up with the stench of it in my nostrils." She looked up at him. "Can you believe that I'm the only one I know who ever visited the memorial? Do you think my parents ever did? My brothers, my aunts and uncles, my classmates? Please! They don't even want to admit it exists."

Seemingly weary again. "So I came down here to commune with the dead, but I didn't see enough of them, so I pushed on and what did I find? Dachau's bunker."

She put her hand on the wall, moved it along the rough-cut stone as caressingly as if it were a lover's flank. "This became my place, my own private world. I was only happy underground, in the company of the one hundred and ninety-three thousand dead. I felt them. I believed that the soul of each and every one of them was trapped here. It was so unfair, I thought. I spent my time trying to figure out how to free them."

"I think the only way to do that," Bourne said, "is to free yourself."

She gestured. "Old Pelz's crash pad is this way."

As they picked their way along a tunnel, she said, "It's not too far. He liked to be near the crypt. He thought a couple of those old folks were his friends. He'd sit and talk to them for hours, drinking away, just as if they were alive and he could see them. Who knows? Maybe he could. Stranger things have happened."

After a short time, the tunnel opened out into a series of rooms. The odors of whiskey and stale sweat came to them.

"It's the third room on the left," Petra said.

But before they reached it, the doorway was filled with a hulking body topped by a head like a bowling ball with hair standing up like the quills of a porcupine. Old Pelz's mad eyes looked them over.

"Who goes there?" His voice was as thick a fog.

"It's me, Herr Pelz. Petra Eichen."

But Old Pelz was looking in horror at the gun on her hip. "The fuck it is!" Hefting a shotgun, he yelled, "Nazi sympathizers!" and fired.

Thirty-Four

SORAYA ENTERED The Glass Slipper behind Kiki and ahead of Deron. Kiki had called ahead, and no sooner were they all inside than the owner, Drew Davis, came waddling over like Scrooge McDuck. He was a grizzled old man with white hair that stood on end as if it were shocked to see he was still alive. He had an animated face with mischievous eyes, a nose like a wad of chewed-up gum, and a broad smile honed to perfection on TV ops and stumping for local politicos, as well as his good works throughout the poorer neighborhoods of the district. But he possessed a warmth that was genuine. He had a way of looking at you when you spoke with him that made you feel he was listening to you alone.

He embraced Kiki while she kissed him on both cheeks and called him "Papa." Later, after the introductions, when they were seated at a prime table that Drew Davis had reserved for them, after the champagne and goodies had been served, Kiki explained her relationship with him.

"When I was a little girl, our tribe was swept by a drought so severe that many of the elderly and newborn grew sick and died. After a time, a small group of white people arrived to help us. They told us they were from an organization that would send us money each month, after they'd set up their program in our village. They had brought water, but of course there wasn't enough.

"After they left, thinking of broken promises, we fell into despair, but true to their word water came, then the rains came until we didn't need their water anymore, but they never left. Their money went for medicines and schooling. Every month I, along with all the other children, got letters from our sponsor—the person sending the money.

"When I was old enough, I started writing back to Drew and we struck up a correspondence. Years later, when I wanted to go on to higher learning, he arranged for me to travel to Cape Town to go to school, then he sponsored me for real, bringing me to the States for college and university. He never asked for anything in return, except that I do well in school. He's like my second father."

They drank champagne and watched the pole dancing—which, much to Soraya's surprise, seemed more artful, less crass than she had imagined. But there were more surgically enhanced body parts in that one room than she'd ever seen. For the life of her she couldn't figure out why a woman would want breasts that looked and acted like balloons.

She continued to drink her champagne, all too aware that she was taking tiny, overly dainty sips. She'd like nothing better than to take Kiki's advice, forget about her problems for a couple of hours, kick back, get drunk, let herself go. The only trouble was, she knew it would never happen. She was too controlled, too closed in. *What I ought to do*, she thought morosely as she watched a redhead with gravity-defying breasts and hips that seemed unattached to the rest of her, *is get smashed, pull off my top, and do some pole dancing myself*. Then she laughed at the absurdity of the notion. She'd never been that kind of person, even when it might have been age-appropriate. She had always been the good girl—cool, calculating to the point of overanalysis. She glanced over at Kiki, whose magnificent face was lit up not only by the colored strobe lights but also by a fiercely experienced joy. Wasn't the good girl's life drained of color, of flavor? Soraya asked herself.

This thought depressed her even more, but it was just the prelude, because a moment later she looked up to see Rob Batt. *What the what?* she thought. He'd seen her, all right, and was making a beeline right at her.

Soraya excused herself, rose, and walked in the other direction, toward the ladies' room. Somehow Batt managed to snake his way to a position in front of her. She turned on her heel, threaded her way around the tables. Batt, running up the waiters' aisle from the kitchen, caught up with her.

"Soraya, I need to talk to you."

She shook him off, kept going, out the front door. In the parking lot she heard him running after her. A light sleet was falling, but the wind had failed entirely, the precipitation coming straight down, melting on her shoulders and bare head.

She didn't know why she'd come out here; Kiki had driven them from Deron's house, so she had no car to get into. Maybe she'd been disgusted by the sight of a man she'd liked and trusted, a man who'd betrayed that trust, who'd defected to the dark side, as she privately called LaValle's NSA because she could no longer bear to utter the words *National Security Agency* without feeling sick to her stomach. The NSA had come to stand for everything that had gone wrong in America over the last number of years—the power grabs, the sense felt by some inside the Beltway that they were entitled to do anything and everything, laws of democracy be damned. It all boiled down to contempt, she thought. These people were so sure they were right, they felt nothing but contempt and perhaps even pity for those who tried to oppose them.

"Soraya, wait! Hold on!"

Batt had caught up with her.

"Get out of here," she said, continuing to walk away.

"But I've got to talk to you."

"The hell you do. We have nothing to talk about."

"It's a matter of national security."

Soraya, shaking her head in disbelief, laughed bitterly and kept on walking.

"Listen, you're my only hope. You're the only one open enough to listen to me."

Rolling her eyes, she turned to face him. "You've got some fucking nerve, Rob. Go back and lick your new master's boots."

"LaValle sold me out, Soraya, you know that." His eyes were pleading. "Listen, I made a terrible mistake. I thought what I was doing would save CI."

Soraya was so incredulous she almost laughed in his face. "What? You don't expect me to believe that."

"I'm a product of the Old Man. I had no faith in Hart. I—"

"Don't use the Old Man routine with me. If you really were his product you'd never have sold us out. You'd have hung in there, become part of the solution, rather than making the problem worse."

"You didn't hear Secretary Halliday, the guy's like a goddamn force of nature. I got sucked into his orbit. I made a mistake, okay? I admit it."

"There's no excuse for your loss of faith."

Batt held up his hands, palms-outward. "You're absolutely right, but, for God's sake, look at me now. I'm being thoroughly punished, aren't I?"

"I don't know, Rob, you tell me."

"I have no job, no prospect of getting one, either. My friends won't answer my calls, and when I run into them on the street or a restaurant, they act like you did, they turn away. My wife's moved out and taken the kids with her." He ran his hand through his wet hair. "Hell, I've been living out of my car since it happened. I'm a mess, Soraya. What could be a worse punishment?"

Was it a flaw in her character that her heart went out to him? Soraya wondered. But she showed no trace of sympathy, simply stood, silent, waiting for him to continue.

"Listen to me," he pleaded. "Listen—"

"I don't want to listen."

As she began to turn away again, he shoved a digital camera into her hand. "At least take a look at these photos."

Soraya was about to hand it back, then she figured she had nothing to lose. Batt's camera was on, and she pressed the REVIEW button. What she saw was a series of surveillance photos of General Kendall.

"What the hell?" she said.

"That's what I've been doing since I got canned," Batt said. "I've been trying to find a way to bring down LaValle. I figured right away that he might be too tough a nut to crack quickly, but Kendall, well, he's another story."

She looked up into his face, which shone with an inner fervor she'd never seen before. "How d'you figure that?"

"Kendall's restless and bitter, chafing under LaValle's yoke. He wants a bigger piece of the action than either Halliday or LaValle is willing to give him. That desire makes him stupid and vulnerable."

Despite herself, she was intrigued. "What have you found out?"

"More than I could've hoped for." Batt nodded at her. "Keep going."

As Soraya continued to scroll through the photos her heart started to hammer in her chest. She peered closer. "Is that . . . Good God, it's Rodney Feir!"

Batt nodded. "He and Kendall met up at Feir's health club, then they went to dinner, and now they're here."

She looked up at him. "The two of them are here at The Glass Slipper?"

"Those are their cars." Batt pointed. "There's a back room. I don't know what goes on in there, but you don't have to be a rocket scientist to figure it out. General Kendall is a God-fearing family man, goes to church with his family and LaValle's every Sunday like clockwork. He's very active in the church, very visible there."

Soraya saw the light at the end of her own personal tunnel. Here was a way to get both her and Tyrone off the hook. "Two birds with one photo shoot," she said.

"Yeah, only trouble is how to get back there to snap 'em. It's invitation only, I checked."

A slow smile spread across Soraya's face. "Leave that to me."

For what seemed a long time after Kendall had kicked him until he vomited, nothing happened. But then, Tyrone had already taken note that time seemed to have slowed down to an agonizing crawl. A minute was made up of a thousand seconds, an hour consisted of ten thousand minutes, and a day—well, there were simply too many hours in a day to count.

During one of the periods when his hood was taken off, he walked back and forth the narrow width of the room, not wanting to go near the far end with its ominous waterboarding tub.

Somewhere inside him he knew he'd lost track of time, that this slippage was part of the process to wear him down, open him up, and turn him inside out. Moment by moment he felt himself sliding down a slope so slick, so steep that whatever he did to try to hold on to it failed. He was falling into darkness, into a void filled only with himself.

This, too, was calculated. He could imagine one of Kendall's underlings coming up with a mathematical formula for how far a subject should break down each hour of each day he was subject to incarceration.

Ever since he had suggested to Soraya that he might be useful to her he'd been reading up on how to handle himself in the worst situations. There was a trick he'd come across that was useful to him now—he needed to find a place in his mind where he could withdraw when the going got really rough, a place that was inviolable, where he knew he'd be safe no matter what was done to him.

He had that place now, he'd been there several times when the pain of kneeling with his arms locked high behind him became too much even for him. But there was one thing that frightened him: that damn trough on the other side of the room. If they decided to waterboard him he was done. For as far back as he could remember he'd been terrified of drowning. He couldn't swim, couldn't even float. Every time he'd tried to do either he'd choked, had to be hauled from the water like a three-year-old. He'd soon given up, figuring it didn't matter. When was he going to go sailing or even lie on a beach? Never.

But now the water had come to him. That damn trough was waiting, grinning like a whale about to swallow him whole. He was no Jonah, he knew that. That fucking thing wasn't going to spit him out alive.

He looked down, saw that the hand he held out in front of him was trembling. Turning away, he pressed it against the wall, as if the cinder block could absorb his unreasoning terror.

He started as the sound of the door being unlocked ricocheted around the small space. In came one of the NSA zombies, with dead eyes and dead breath. He put down the tray of food and left without even glancing at Tyrone, all part of the second phase of the plan to break him down: make him think he didn't exist.

He went over to the tray. As usual, his food consisted of cold oatmeal. It didn't matter; he was hungry. Taking up the plastic spoon, he took a bite of the cereal. It was gummy, had no taste whatsoever. He almost gagged on the second bite because he was chewing on something other than oatmeal. Aware that his every move was monitored, he bent over, spit out the mouthful. Then he used the fork to paw open a folded piece of paper. There was something written on it. He bent over further to make out the letters.

DON'T GIVE UP, it read.

At first, Tyrone couldn't believe his eyes. Then he read it again. After reading it a third time, he scooped the message up with another bite of oatmeal, chewed it all slowly and methodically, and swallowed.

Then he went over to the stainless-steel toilet, sat down on the edge, and wondered who had written that note and how he could communicate with him. It wasn't until some time later that he realized this one brief message from outside his tiny cell had managed to restore the balance he'd lost. Inside his head, time resolved itself into normal seconds and minutes, and the blood began once again to circulate through his veins.

* * *

Arkadin allowed Devra to drag him out of the bar before he could demolish it completely. Not that he cared about the thuggish patrons who sat in stupefied silence, watching the mayhem he wreaked as if it were a TV show, but he was mindful of the cops who had a significant presence in this trashy neighborhood. During the time they'd been in the bar he'd noticed three police cruisers pass slowly by on the street.

They drove through the sunshine down littered streets. He heard dogs barking, voices shouting. He was grateful for the heat of her hip and shoulder against him. Her presence grounded him, wrestled his rage back down to a manageable level. He hugged her more tightly to him, his mind returning with feverish intensity to his past.

For Arkadin, the ninth level of hell began innocently enough with Stas Kuzin's confirmation that his business came from prostitution and drugs. Easy money, Arkadin thought, immediately lulled into a false sense of security.

At first, his role was as simple as it was clearly defined: He'd provide the space in his buildings to expand Kuzin's brothel empire. This Arkadin did with his usual efficiency. Nothing could have been simpler, and for several months as the rubles rolled in he congratulated himself on making a lucrative business deal. Plus, his association with Kuzin brought him a boatload of perks, from free drinks at the local pubs to free sessions with Kuzin's ever-expanding ring of teenage girls.

But it was this very thing—the young prostitutes—that became Arkadin's slippery slope into hell's lowest level. When he stayed away from the brothels, or made his cursory weekly checkups to ensure the apartments weren't being trashed, it was easy to turn a blind eye on what was really going on. He was mostly too busy counting his money. However, on those occasions when he availed himself of a freebie or two, it was impossible not to notice how young the girls were, how afraid they were, how bruised their thin arms were, how hollow their eyes, and, all too often, how drugged up most of them were. It was like Zombie Nation in there.

All of this might have passed Arkadin by with a minimum of speculation had he not developed a liking for one of them. Yelena was a girl with wide lips, skin as pale as snow, and eyes that burned like a coal fire. She had a quick smile and, unlike some of the other girls, she wasn't prone to bursting into tears for no apparent reason. She laughed at his jokes, she lay with him afterward, her face buried in his chest. He liked the feel of her in his arms. Her warmth seeped into him like fine vodka, and he grew used to how she found just the right position so that the curves of her body meshed perfectly with his. He could fall asleep in her arms, which for him was something of a miracle. He couldn't remember when he'd last slept through the night.

About this time, Kuzin called him into a meeting, told him he was doing so well he wanted to increase his partnership stake with Arkadin.

"Of course, I'll need you to play a more active role," Kuzin said in his semi-intelligible voice. "Business is so good that what I need most now is more girls. That's where you come in."

Kuzin made Arkadin the head of a crew whose sole purpose was to solicit teenage girls from the populace of Nizhny Tagil. This Arkadin did with his usual frightening efficiency. His visits to Yelena's bed were as plentiful but not as idyllic. She had grown afraid, she told him, of the disappearances of some of the girls. One day she saw them; the next they had vanished as if they'd never existed. No one spoke of them, no one answered her questions when she asked where they'd gone. In the main, Arkadin dismissed her fears—after all, the girls were young, weren't they leaving all the time? But Yelena was certain the girls' disappearances had nothing to do with them and everything to do with Stas Kuzin. No matter what he said, her fears did not subside until he promised to protect her, to make sure nothing happened to her.

After six months Kuzin took him aside.

"You're doing a great job." A mixture of vodka and cocaine slurred Kuzin's voice even further. "But I need more."

They were in one of the brothels, which to Arkadin's practiced eye looked oddly underpopulated. "Where are all the girls?" he asked.

Kuzin waved an arm. "Gone, run away, who the fuck knows where? These bitches get a bit of money in their pocket, they're off like rabbits."

Ever the pragmatist, Arkadin said, "I'll take my crew and go find them."

"A waste of time." Kuzin's little head bobbled on his shoulders. "Just find me more."

"It's getting difficult," Arkadin pointed out. "Some of the girls are scared; they don't want to come with us."

"Take them anyway."

Arkadin frowned. "I don't follow you."

"Okay, moron, I'll lay it out for you. Take your fucking crew in the fucking van and snatch the bitches off the street."

"You're talking about kidnapping."

Kuzin laughed. "Fuck me, he gets it!"

"What about the cops."

Kuzin laughed even harder. "The cops are in my pocket. And even if they weren't, d'you think they get paid to work? They don't give a rat's ass."

For the next three weeks Arkadin and his crew worked the night shift, delivering girls to the brothel, whether or not they wanted to come. These girls were sullen, often belligerent, until Kuzin took them into a back room, where none of them ever wanted to go a second time. Kuzin didn't mess with their faces, as that would be bad for business; only their arms and legs were bruised.

Arkadin watched this controlled violence as if through the wrong end of a telescope. He knew it was happening, but he pretended it had nothing to do with him. He continued to count his money, which was now piling up at a more rapid clip. It was his money and Yelena that kept him warm at night. Each time he was with her, he checked her arms and legs for bruises. When he made her promise not to take drugs, she laughed, "Leonid Danilovich, who has money for drugs?"

He smiled at this, knowing what she meant. In fact, she had more money than all the other girls in the brothel combined. He knew this because he was the one who gave it to her.

"Get yourself a new dress, a new pair of shoes," he'd tell her, but frugal girl that she was, she'd merely smile and kiss him on the cheek with great affection. She was right, he realized, not to do anything to call attention to herself.

One night, not long after, Kuzin accosted him as he was leaving Yelena's room.

"I have an urgent problem and I need your help," the freak said.

Arkadin went with him out of the apartment building. A large van was waiting on the street, its engine running. Kuzin climbed into the back, and Arkadin followed. Two of the brothel girls were being guarded by Kuzin's pair of personal ghouls.

"They tried to escape," Kuzin said. "We just caught them."

"They need to be taught a lesson," Arkadin said, because he assumed that was what his partner wanted him to say.

"Too fucking late for that." Kuzin signaled to the driver, and the van took off.

Arkadin settled back on the seat, wondering where they were going. He kept his mouth shut, knowing that if he asked questions now he'd look like a fool. Thirty minutes later the van slowed, turned off onto an unpaved road. For the next several minutes they jounced along a rutted track that must have been very narrow because branches kept scraping against the sides of the van.

At length, they stopped, the doors opened, and everyone clambered out. The night was very dark, illuminated only by the headlights of the van, but in the distance the fire of the smelters was like blood in the sky or, rather, on the undersides of the belching miasma churned out by hundreds of smokestacks. No one saw the sky in Nizhny Tagil, and when it snowed the flakes turned gray or even sometimes black as they passed through the industrial murk.

Arkadin followed along with Kuzin as the two ghouls pushed the girls through the thick, weedy underbrush. The resiny scent of pine perfumed the air so strongly, it almost masked the appalling stench of decomposition.

A hundred yards in the ghouls pulled back on the collars of the girls's coats, reining them in. Kuzin took out his gun and shot one of the girls in the back of the head. She pitched forward into a bed of dead leaves. The other girl screamed, squirming within the ghoul's grasp, desperate to run.

Then Kuzin turned to Arkadin, placed the gun in his hand. "When you pull the trigger," he said, "we become equal partners."

There was something in Kuzin's eyes that at this close range gave Arkadin the shivers. It seemed to him that Kuzin's eyes were smiling in the way the devil smiled, without warmth, without humanity, because the pleasure that animated the smile was of an evil and perverted nature. It was at this precise moment that Arkadin thought of the prisons ringing Nizhny Tagil, because he now knew beyond a shadow of a doubt that he was locked within his own private prison, with no idea if there was a key, let alone how to use it.

The gun—an old Luger with the Nazi swastika imprinted on it— was greasy with Kuzin's excitement. Arkadin raised it to the height of the girl's head. She was whimpering and crying. Arkadin had done many things in his young life, some of them unforgivable, but he'd never shot a girl in cold blood. And yet now, in order to prosper, in order to survive the prison of Nizhny Tagil, this was what he had to do.

He was aware of Kuzin's avid eyes boring into him, red as the fire of Nizhny Tagil's foundries themselves, and then he felt the muzzle of a gun at the nape of his neck and knew that the driver was standing behind him, no doubt on Kuzin's orders.

"Do it," Kuzin said softly, "because one way or another in the next ten seconds someone's going to fire his gun."

Arkadin aimed the Luger. The shout of the report echoed on and on through the deep and forbidding forest, and the girl slid along the leaves, into the pit with her friend.

Thirty-Five

THE SOUND of the bolt being thrown on the 8mm Mauser K98 rifle echoed through the Dachau air raid bunker. That was the end of it, however.

"Damn!" Old Pelz groaned. "I forgot to load the thing!"

Petra took out her handgun, pointed it in the air, and squeezed the trigger. Because the result was the same as what had happened to him, Old Pelz threw down the K98.

"*Scheisse!*" he said, clearly disgusted.

She approached him then. "Herr Pelz," she said gently, "as I said, my name is Petra. Do you remember me?"

The old man stopped muttering, peered at her carefully. "You do look an awful lot like a Petra-Alexandra I once knew."

"Petra-Alexandra." She laughed and kissed him on the cheek. "Yes, yes, that's me!"

He recoiled a little, put a hand on his cheek where she'd planted her lips. Then, skeptical to the end, he looked past her at Bourne. "Who's this Nazi bastard? Did he force you to come here?" His hands curled into fists. "I'll box his ears for him!"

"No, Herr Pelz, this is a friend of mine. He's Russian." She used the name Bourne had given her, which was on the passport Boris Karpov had provided.

"Russians're no better than Nazis in my book," the old man said sourly.

"Actually, I'm an American traveling under a Russian passport." Bourne said this first in English and then in German.

"You speak English very well, for a Russian," Old Pelz said in excellent English. Then he laughed, showing teeth yellowed by time and tobacco. At the sight of an American, he seemed to perk up, as if coming out of a decades-long drowse. This was the way he was, a rabbit being drawn out of a hat, only to withdraw again into the shadows. He wasn't mad, just living both in the drab present and in the vivid past. "I embraced the Americans when they liberated us from tyranny," he continued proudly. "In my time I helped them root out the Nazis and the Nazi sympathizers pretending to be good Germans." He spat out the last words, as if he couldn't stand to have them in his mouth.

"Then what are you doing here?" Bourne said. "Don't you have a home to go to?"

"Sure I do." Old Pelz smacked his lips, as if he could taste the life of his younger self. "In fact, I have a very nice house in Dachau. It's blue and white, with flowers all around a picket fence. A cherry tree stands in back, spreading its wings in summer. The house is rented out to a fine young couple with two strapping children, who send their rent check like clockwork to my nephew in Leipzig. He's a big-shot lawyer, you know."

"Herr Pelz, I don't understand," Petra said. "Why not stay in your own home? This is no place to live."

"The bunker is my health insurance." The old man cocked a canny eye her way. "Do you have any idea what would happen to me if I went back to my house? They'd spirit me away in the night, and that's the last anyone would ever see of me."

"Who would do that to you?" Bourne said.

Pelz seemed to consider his answer, as if he needed to remember the text of a book he'd read in high school. "I told you I was a Nazi hunter, a damn fine one, too. In those days I lived like a king—or, if I'm honest, a duke. Anyway, that's before I got cocky and made my mistake. I decided to go after the Black Legion, and that one intemperate decision was my downfall. Because of them I lost everything, even the trust of the Americans, who at that time needed those damn people more than they needed me.

"The Black Legion kicked me into the gutter like a piece of garbage or a mangy dog. From there it was only a short crawl down here into the bowels of the earth."

"It's the Black Legion I came here to talk to you about," Bourne said. "I'm a hunter, too. The Black Legion isn't a Nazi organization anymore. They've turned into a Muslim terrorist network."

Old Pelz rubbed his grizzled jaw. "I'd say I'm surprised, but I'm not. Those bastards knew how to play all the cards in all the hands—the Germans, the Brits, and, most importantly, the Americans. They toyed with all of 'em after the war. Every Western intelligence service was throwing money at them. The thought of having built-in spies behind the Iron Curtain had them all salivating.

"It didn't take the bastards long to figure out it was the Americans who had the upper hand. Why? 'Cause they had all the money and, unlike the Brits, weren't being tight-fisted with it." He cackled. "But that's the American way, isn't it?"

Not waiting for an answer to a question that was self-evident, he plowed on. "So the Black Legion took up with the American intelligence machine. First off, it wasn't difficult to convince the Yanks that they'd never been Nazis, that their only goal was to fight Stalin. And that was true, as far as it went, but after the war they had other goals in mind. They're Muslims, after all; they never felt comfortable in Western society. They wanted to build for the future, and like a lot of other insurgents they created their power base with American dollars."

He squinted up at Bourne. "You're American, poor bastard. None of these modern-day terrorist networks would've existed without your country's backing. Fucking ironic, that is."

For a time he lapsed into muttering, broke into a song whose lyrics were so melancholy tears welled up in his rheumy eyes.

"Herr Pelz," Bourne said, trying to get the old man to focus. "You were talking about the Black Legion."

"Call me Virgil," Pelz said, nodding as he came out of his fugue state. "That's right, my Christian name is Virgil, and for you, American, I will hold my lamp high enough to throw light on those bastards who ruined my life. Why not? I'm at a stage in my life when I should tell someone, and it might as well be you."

They're in the back," Bev said to Drew Davis. "Both of them." A woman in her midfifties with a thick frame and a quick wit, she was The Glass Slipper's girl wrangler, as she wryly called herself—part disciplinarian, part den mother.

"The main interest is in the general," Davis said, "isn't that right, Kiki?"

Kiki nodded. She was closely flanked by Soraya and Deron, and all of them were clustered in Davis's cramped office up a short flight of stairs from the main room. The pounding of the bass and drums thumped against the walls like the fists of angry giants. The room had the appearance of an attic or a garret, windowless, its walls like a time machine, plastered with photos of Drew Davis with Martin Luther King, Nelson Mandela, four different American presidents, a host of Hollywood stars, and various UN dignitaries and ambassadors from virtually every country in Africa. There was also a series of informal snapshots of him with his arm around a younger Kiki in the Masai Mara, totally unself-conscious, looking like a queen-in-training.

After her talk with Rob Batt in the parking lot, Soraya had returned to her table inside and filled in Kiki and Deron on her plan. The noise from the band on stage made eavesdropping impossible, even by anyone at the next table. Because of her longtime friendship with Drew Davis, it had been up to Kiki to create the spark that would light the fuse. This she did, resulting in this impromptu meeting in Davis's office.

"For me to even contemplate what you're asking, you have to guarantee blanket immunity," Drew Davis said to Soraya. "Plus, leave our names out of it, unless you want to piss me off—which you don't—as well as pissing off half the elected officials in the district."

"You have my word," Soraya said. "We want these two people, that's the beginning and the end of it."

Drew Davis glanced at Kiki, who responded with an almost imperceptible nod.

Now Davis turned to Bev.

"Here's what you can do and what you can't do," Bev said, reacting to her boss's cue. "I won't allow anyone on my ranch who's not there for legitimate purposes—that is, either a patron or a working girl. So forget just barging in there. I do that and tomorrow we have no business left."

She wasn't even looking at Drew Davis, but Soraya saw him nod in assent, and her heart fell. Everything depended on their gaining access to the general while he was in the midst of his frolics. Then she had a thought.

"I'll go in as a working girl," she said.

"No, you won't," Deron said. "You're known to both the general and Feir. One look at you and they'll be spooked."

"They don't know me."

Everyone turned their heads to stare at Kiki.

"Absolutely not," Deron said.

"Ease up there," Kiki said with a laugh. "I'm not going through with anything. I just need access." She mimed taking photos. Then she turned to Bev. "How do I get into the general's private room?"

"You can't. For obvious reasons the private rooms are sacrosanct. Another rule of the house. And both the general and Feir have chosen their partners for the evening." She drummed her fingers against Davis's desktop. "But in the case of the general there *is* one way."

* * *

Virgil Pelz took Bourne and Petra farther into the bunker's main tunnel, to a rough-hewn space that opened out into a circle. There were benches here, a small gas stove, a refrigerator.

"Lucky someone forgot to turn off the electricity," Petra said.

"Lucky my ass." Pelz settled himself on a bench. "My nephew pays a town official under the table to keep the lights on." He offered them whiskey or wine, which they refused. He poured himself a shot of liquor, downed it perhaps to fortify himself or to keep himself from sinking back into the shadows. It was obvious he liked having company, that the stimulation of other humans was bringing him out of himself.

"Most of what I've already told you about the Black Legion is basic history, if you know where to look, but the key to understanding their success in negotiating the dangerous postwar landscape lies in two men: Farid Icoupov and Ibrahim Sever."

"I assume this Icoupov you speak of is Semion Icoupov's father," Bourne said.

Pelz nodded. "Just so."

"And did Ibrahim Sever have a son?"

"He had two," Pelz replied, "but I'm getting ahead of myself." He smacked his lips, glanced at the bottle of whiskey, then decided against another shot.

"Farid and Ibrahim were the best of friends. They grew up together, each the only sons in large families. Possibly, this is what bonded them as children. The bond was strong; it lasted for most of their lives, but Ibrahim Sever was a warrior at heart, Farid Icoupov an intellectual, and the seeds of discontent and mistrust must have been sown early. During the war their shared leadership worked out just fine. Ibrahim was in charge of the Black Legion soldiers on the Eastern Front; Farid put in place and directed the intelligence-gathering network in the Soviet Union.

"It was after the war when the problems began. Stripped of his duties as commandant of the military end, Ibrahim began to fret that his power was eroding." Pelz clucked his tongue against the roof of his mouth. "Listen, American, if you're a student of history you know how the two longtime allies and friends Gaius Julius Caesar and Pompey Magnus became enemies infected by the ambitions, fears, deceptions, and power struggles of those under their respective commands. So it was with these two. In time, Ibrahim convinced himself—no doubt abetted by some of his more militant advisers—that his longtime friend was planning a power grab. Unlike Caesar, who was off in Gaul when Pompey declared war on him, Farid lived in the next house. Ibrahim Sever and his men came in the night and assassinated Farid Icoupov. Three days later Farid's son, Semion, shot Ibrahim to death as he was driving to work. In retaliation, Ibrahim's son, Asher, went after Semion in a Munich nightclub. Asher managed to escape, but in the ensuing hail of gunfire Asher's younger brother was killed."

Pelz scrubbed his face with his hand. "You see how it goes, American? Like an ancient Roman vendetta, an orgy of blood of biblical proportions."

"I know about Semion Icoupov, but not about Sever," Bourne said. "Where's Asher Sever now?"

The old man shrugged his thin shoulders. "Who knows? If Icoupov did, Sever would surely be dead by now."

For a time, Bourne sat silent, thinking about the Black Legion's attack on the professor, thinking about all the little anomalies that had been piling up in his mind: the oddity of Pyotr's network of decadents and incompetents, the professor saying it was his idea to have the stolen plans delivered to him via the network, and the question of whether Mischa Tarkanian—and Arkadin himself—was Black Legion. At last, he said, "Virgil, I need to ask you several questions."

"Yes, American." Pelz's eyes looked as bright and eager as a robin's.

Still, Bourne hesitated. Revealing anything of his mission or its background to a stranger violated every instinct, every lesson he'd been taught, and yet he could see no other alternative. "I came to Munich because a friend of mine—a mentor, really—asked me to go after the Black Legion, first because they're planning an attack against my country, and second because their leader, Semion Icoupov, ordered his son, Pyotr, killed."

Pelz looked up, a curious expression on his face. "Asher Sever gathered his power base, which he'd inherited from his father—a powerful intelligence-gathering network strewn across Asia and Europe—and ousted Semion. Icoupov hasn't been running the Black Legion for decades. If he had, I doubt whether I'd still be down here. Unlike Asher Sever, Icoupov was a man you could reason with."

"Are you saying that you've met both Semion Icoupov and Asher Sever?" Bourne said.

"That's right," Pelz said, nodding. "Why?"

Bourne had gone cold as he contemplated the unthinkable. Could the professor have been lying to him all the time? But if so—if he was in fact a member of the Black Legion—why in the world would he entrust the delivery of the attack plans to Pyotr's shaky network? Surely he would have known how unreliable its members were. Nothing seemed to make sense.

Knowing he had to solve this problem one step at a time, he took out his cell phone, scrolled through the photos, brought up the one the professor had sent of Egon Kirsch. He looked at the two men in the photo, then handed the phone to Pelz.

"Virgil, do you recognize either of these men?"

Pelz squinted, then stood and walked nearer to one of the bare lightbulbs. "No." He shook his head, then, after a moment's further scrutiny, his forefinger jabbed at the photo. "I don't know, because he looks so different . . ." He returned to where Bourne sat, turned the phone so they could both see the photo, and tapped the figure of Professor Specter. ". . . but, damn, I'd swear this one is Asher Sever."

Thirty-Six

PETER MARKS, chief of operations, was with Veronica Hart in her office, poring over reams of personnel data sheets, when they came for her. Luther LaValle, accompanied by a pair of federal marshals, had swept through CI security, armed with their warrant. Hart had only the briefest of warnings—a phone call from the first set of security guards downstairs—that her professional world was imploding. No time to get out of the way of the falling debris.

She barely had time to tell Marks, then stand up to face her accusers before the three men entered her office and presented her with the federal warrant.

"Veronica Rose Hart," the senior of the stone-faced federal marshals intoned, "you are hereby placed under arrest for conspiring with one Jason Bourne, a rogue agent, for purposes that violate the regulations of Central Intelligence."

"On what evidence?" Hart said.

"NSA surveillance photos of you in the courtyard of the Freer handing a packet to Jason Bourne," the marshal said in the same zombie voice.

Marks, who was also on his feet, said, "This is insane. You can't really believe—"

"Shut it, Mr. Marks," Luther LaValle said with no fear of contradiction. "One more word out of you and I'll have you put under formal investigation."

Marks was about to reply when a sharp look from the DCI forced him to bite back his words. His jaws clamped shut, but the fury in his eyes was unmistakable.

Hart came around the desk, and the junior marshal cuffed her hands behind her back.

"Is that really necessary?" Marks said.

LaValle pointed at him wordlessly. As they marched Hart from her office, she said, "Take over, Peter. You're acting DCI now."

LaValle grinned. "Not for long, if I have anything to say about it."

After they'd gone, Marks collapsed into his chair. Finding that his hands were trembling, he clasped them together, as if in prayer. His heart was pounding so hard he found it difficult to think. He jumped up, walked over to the window behind the DCI's desk, stood staring out at the Washington night. All the monuments were lit up, all the streets and avenues were filled with traffic. Everything was as it should be, and yet nothing looked familiar. He felt as if he'd entered an alternate universe. He couldn't have been witness to what just happened, NSA couldn't be about to absorb CI into its gigantic corpus. But then he turned around to find the office empty and the full horror of seeing the DCI frog-marched out in handcuffs swept over him, made his legs weak, so that he sought out the big chair behind the desk and sat in it.

Then the implications of where he sat, and why, sank in. He picked up the phone and dialed Stu Gold, CI's lead counsel.

"Sit tight. I'll be right over," Gold told him in his usual no-nonsense voice. Did nothing faze him?

Then Marks began to make a series of calls. It was going to be a long and harrowing night.

* * *

Rodney Feir was having the time of his life. As he accompanied Afrique into one of the rooms in the back of The Glass Slipper, he felt as if he were on top of the world. In fact, popping a Viagra, he decided to ask her to do a number of things he'd never tried before. *Why the hell not*? he asked himself.

While he was undressing he thought of the information on Typhon's field agents Peter Marks had sent him via interoffice mail. Feir had deliberately told Marks he didn't want it sent electronically because it was too insecure. The info was folded into the inside pocket of his coat, ready to give to General Kendall before they left The Glass Slipper tonight. He could have handed it over while they were at dinner, but he'd felt, all things considered, that a champagne toast after all their treats had been consumed was the proper way to cap off the night.

Afrique was already on the bed, spread languidly, her large eyes half closed, but she got right down to business as soon as Feir joined her. He tried to keep his mind on the proceedings, but seeing as how his body was totally in it, there wasn't much point. He preferred dwelling on the things that made him truly happy, like getting the better of Peter Marks. When he was growing up it was people like Marks—and, for that matter, Batt—who'd had it all over him, brainiacs with brawn, in other words, who'd made his life miserable. They were the ones who had the cool circle of friends, who got all the great-looking girls, who rode in cars while he was still tooling around on a scooter. He was the nerd, the chubby—fat, really—kid who was made the butt of all their jokes, who was pushed around and ostracized, who, despite his high IQ, was so tongue-tied he could never stick up for himself.

He'd joined CI as a glorified pencil pusher, and, yes, he'd worked his way up the professional ladder, but not into fieldwork or counterintelligence. No, he was chief of field support, which meant that he was in charge of gathering and distributing the paperwork generated by the very CI personnel he longed to be like. His office was the central hub of supply and demand, and there were days when he could convince himself that it was the nerve center of CI. But most of the time he saw himself for what he really was—someone who kept pushing electronic lists, data entry forms, directorate requests, allocation tables, budget spreadsheets, personnel assignment profiles, matériel lading bills, a veritable landslide of paperwork whizzing through the CI intranet. A monitor of information, in other words, a master of nothing.

He was enveloped in pleasure, a warm, viscous friction spreading outward from his groin into his torso and limbs. He closed his eyes and sighed.

At first, being an anonymous cog in the CI machine suited him, but as the years passed, as he rose in the hierarchy, only the Old Man understood his worth, for it was the Old Man who promoted him, time after time. But no one else—certainly none of the other directors—said a word to him until they needed something. Then a request came flying through CI cyberspace as quick as you could say, *I need it yesterday*. If he got them what they wanted yesterday, he heard nothing, not even a nod of thanks in the hallway, but should there be any delay at all, no matter the reason, they'd land on him like woodpeckers on a tree full of insects. He'd never hear the end of their pestering until they got what they wanted, and then silence again. It seemed sadly ironic to him that even in an insider's paradise like CI he was on the outside.

It was humiliating to be one of those stereotypical Americans who time and again got sand kicked in his face. How he hated himself for being a living, breathing cliché. It was these evenings spent with General Kendall that gave his life color and meaning, the clandestine meetings in the health club sauna, the dinners at local barbecue joints in SE, and then the delicious chocolate nightcaps at The Glass Slipper, where he was for once the insider instead of having his nose pressed to someone else's window. Knowing that he couldn't be transformed he had to settle for losing himself in Afrique's bed at The Glass Slipper.

General Kendall, smoking a cigar in the corral, the colloquial name for the parlor room where the girls were paraded for the benefit of the patrons, was enjoying himself immensely. If he was thinking of his boss at all, it was of the heart attack this scene he was enacting would cause LaValle. As for his family, they were the farthest thing from his mind. Unlike Feir, who always went for the same girl, Kendall was a man of diverse tastes when it came to the women of The Glass Slipper, and why not? He had virtually no choice in any other areas of his life. If not here, where?

He sat on the purple velvet sofa, one arm thrown along the back, watching through slitted eyes the slow parade of flesh. He had already made his choice; the girl was in her room, undressing, but when Bev had come to him, suggesting that he might want something a bit more special—another girl to create a threesome—he hadn't hesitated. He'd been just about to make his choice when he saw someone. She was impossibly tall, with skin like the darkest cocoa, and was so regal in her beauty that he broke out into a sweat.

He caught Bev's eye and she came over. Bev was attuned to his desires. "I want her," he said to Bev, pointing at the regal beauty.

"I'm afraid Kiki's not available," she said.

This answer made Kendall want her all the more. Venal witch; she knew him too well. He produced five hundred-dollar bills. "How about now?" he said.

Bev, true to form, pocketed the money. "Leave it to me," she said.

The general watched her pick her way through the girls to where Kiki was standing, somewhat apart from the others. While he observed the conversation his heart began to beat in his chest like a war drum. He was sweating so much he was obliged to wipe his palms on the purple velvet of the sofa arm. If she said no, what would he do? But she wasn't saying no, she was looking across the corral at him, with a smile that raised his temperature a couple of degrees. Jesus, he wanted her!

As if in a trance, he saw her coming across the room toward him, her hips swaying, that maddening half smile on her face. He stood up, with some difficulty, he noted. He felt like a seventeen-year-old virgin. Kiki held out her hand and he took it, terrified that she'd be repulsed if it was damp, but nothing interfered with that half smile.

There was something intensely pleasurable about allowing her to lead him past all the other girls, enjoying the looks of envy on their faces.

"Which room are you in?" Kiki murmured in a voice like honey.

Kendall, inhaling her spicy, musky scent, could not find his voice. He pointed, and again she led him as if he were on a leash until they were standing in front of the door.

"Are you sure you want two girls tonight?" She brushed her hip against his. "I'm more than enough for any man I've been with."

The general felt a delicious shiver travel down the length of his spine, lodge itself like a heated arrow between his thighs. Reaching out, he opened the door. Lena writhed on the bed, naked. He heard the door close behind him. Without thinking, he undressed himself, then he stepped out of the puddle of his clothes, took Kiki's hand, padded over to the bed. He knelt on it, she let go of his hand, and he fell on Lena.

He felt Kiki's hands on his shoulders, and, groaning, he lost himself within Lena's lush body. The pleasure built along with the anticipation of Kiki's long, lithe body pressed against his glistening back.

It took him some time to become aware that the quick flashes of light weren't a result of the quickened firing of nerve endings behind his eyes. Drugged with sex and desire, he was slow to turn his head directly into another battery of flashes. Even then, negative images dancing behind his retinas, his fogged brain couldn't quite piece together what was happening, and his body continued to move rhythmically against Lena's pliant flesh.

Then the camera flashed again, he belatedly raised his hand to shield his eyes, and there was stark reality staring him in the face. Kiki, still dressed, continued to take shots of him and Lena.

"Smile, General," she said in that sensual, honeyed voice. "There's nothing else you can do."

I've got too much anger inside me," Petra said. "It's like one of those flesh-eating diseases you read about."

"Dachau is toxic for you, so is Munich now," Bourne said. "You've got to go away."

She moved to the left-hand lane of the autobahn, put on some real speed. They were on their way back to Munich in the car Pelz's nephew had bought for him under the nephew's name. The police might still be looking for both of them, but their only lead was Petra's Munich apartment, and neither of them had any intention of going anywhere near it. As long as she didn't get out of the car, Bourne felt it was relatively safe for her to drive him back into the city.

"Where would I go?" she said.

"Leave Germany altogether."

She laughed, but it wasn't a pleasant sound. "Turn tail and run, you mean."

"Why would you see it that way?"

"Because I'm German; because I belong here."

"The Munich police are looking for you," he said.

"And if they find me, then I'll do my time for killing your friend." She flashed her headlights so a slower car could get out of her way. "Meanwhile I have money. I can live."

"But what will you do?"

She gave him a lopsided smile. "I'm going to take care of Virgil. He needs drying out; he needs a friend." Nearing the city, she changed lanes so she could exit when she needed to. "The cops won't find me," she said with an odd kind of certainty, "because I'm taking him far away from here. Virgil and me, we'll be two outlaws learning a whole new way of life."

Egon Kirsch lived in the northern district of Schwabing, known as the young intellectual quarter because of the mass of university students that flooded its streets, cafés, and bars.

As they came abreast of Schwabing's main plaza, Petra pulled over. "When I was younger I used to hang out here with my friends. We were all militants, then, agitating for change, and we felt connected to this place because it was from here that the Freiheitsaktion Bayer, one of the most famed resistance groups, commandeered Radio Munich near the end of the war. They broadcast messages to the populace to seize and arrest all local Nazi leaders, and to signal their rejection of the regime by waving white sheets out of their windows—an action that was punishable by death, by the way. And they managed to save a large number of civilian lives as the American army swept in."

"At last we find something in Munich that even you can be proud of," Bourne said.

"I suppose so." Petra laughed, almost sadly. "But I among all of my friends was the only one who stayed a revolutionary. The others are corporate functionaries or Hausfraus now. They lead sad, gray lives. I see them sometimes, trudging to and from work. I walk by them; they don't even look up. In the end, they all disappointed me."

Kirsch's apartment was on the top floor of a beautiful house of stone-colored stucco, arched windows, and a terra-cotta tile roof. Between two of his windows was a niche holding a stone statue of the Virgin Mary cradling the baby Jesus.

Petra pulled into the curb in front of the building. "I wish you well, American," she said, deliberately using Virgil Pelz's phrasing. "Thank you . . . for everything."

"You may not believe it, but we helped each other," Bourne said as he got out of the car. "Good luck, Petra."

When she'd driven off, he turned, went up the steps to the building, and used the code Kirsch had given him to open the front door. The interior was neat and spotlessly clean. The wood-paneled hallway gleamed with a recent waxing. Bourne climbed the carved wooden staircase to the top floor. Using Kirsch's key, he let himself in. Though the apartment itself was light and airy, with many windows overlooking the street, it was steeped in a deep silence, as if it existed on the bottom of the sea. There was no TV, no computer. Bookcases lined one entire wall of the living room, holding volumes by Nietzsche, Kant, Descartes, Heidegger, Leibniz, and Machiavelli. There were also books by many of the great mathematicians, biographers, fiction writers, and economists. The other walls were covered with Kirsch's framed and matted line drawings, so detailed and intricate that at first glance they seemed to be architectural plans, but then suddenly they came into focus and Bourne realized the drawings were abstracts. Like all good art, they seemed to move back and forth from reality to an imagined dream world where anything was possible.

After taking a brief tour of all the rooms, he settled down in a chair behind Kirsch's desk. He thought long and hard about the professor. Was he Dominic Specter, the nemesis of the Black Legion, as he claimed to be, or was he, in fact, Asher Sever, the leader of the Black Legion? If he was Sever, he'd staged the attack on himself—an elaborate scheme that had cost a number of lives. Could the professor be guilty of such an irrational act? If he was the leader of the Black Legion, certainly. The second question Bourne had been asking himself was why the professor would entrust the stolen plans to Pyotr's thoroughly undependable network. But there was another enigma: If the professor was Sever, why was he so anxious to get those plans? Wouldn't he already have them? These two questions went around and around in Bourne's head without producing a satisfactory solution. Nothing about the situation he found himself in appeared to make sense, which meant that a vital part of the picture was missing. And yet he had the nagging suspicion that, like Egon Kirsch's drawings, he was being shown two separate realities—if only he could decipher which was real and which one was false.

At length, he turned his mind to something that had been bothering him ever since the incident at the Egyptian Museum. He knew that Franz Jens had been the only one to follow him into the museum, so how on earth did Arkadin know where he was? Arkadin had to have been the one to kill Jens. He also must have given the order to kill Egon Kirsch, but, again, how did he know where Kirsch was?

The answers to both questions were firmly rooted in time and place. He hadn't been tailed to the museum, then . . . As a chill spread through him, Bourne went very still. With no physical tail, there had to be an electronic tail somewhere on his person. But how had it been put there? Someone could have brushed up against him in the airport. He rose, slowly undressed. As he did so, he went through every item of clothing, looking for an electronic tag. Finding nothing, he dressed, sat again in the chair, deep in thought.

With his eidetic memory, he went through every step of his journey from Moscow to Munich. When he recalled the German Immigration officer, he realized that his passport had been out of his possession for close to half a minute. Taking it out of his breast pocket, he began to leaf through it, checking each page both by sight and by touch. On the inside of the back cover, stuck in the fold of the binding, he found the tiny transmitter.

Thirty-Seven

Hஹ**OW WONDERFUL** it is to breathe the good night air,"
Veronica Hart said as she stood on the pavement just outside the
Pentagon.

"Diesel fumes and all," Stu Gold said.

"I knew LaValle's charges wouldn't stick," she said as they crossed
to his car. "They're patently trumped up."

"I wouldn't begin celebrating just yet," the attorney said. "LaValle's
put me on notice that he's going to take those surveillance photos of you
and Bourne to the president tomorrow for an executive order to have you
removed."

"Come on, Stu, those were private conversations between Martin
Lindros and a civilian, Moira Trevor. There's nothing in them. LaValle's
banking on hot air."

"He's got the secretary of defense," Gold said. "Under the circumstances that alone is enough to make trouble for you."

The wind was whipping up and Hart caught her hair, pushed it
off her face. "Coming into CI and marching me out in cuffs . . . La-
Valle made a big mistake grandstanding like that." She turned, looked

back at the headquarters of the NSA in which she'd been incarcerated for three hours until the moment Gold showed up with his order from a federal judge for her temporary release. "He'll pay for humiliating me."

"Veronica, don't do anything rash." Gold opened the car door, ushered her inside. "Knowing LaValle as I do it's more than likely that he wants you to go off half-cocked. That's how fatal mistakes are made."

He went around the front of the car, got behind the wheel, and they drove off.

"We can't let him get away with this, Stu. Unless we stop him he's going to hijack CI right out from under us." She watched the Virginia night turn into the district night as they crossed the Arlington Memorial Bridge. The Lincoln Memorial rose up before them. "I made a pledge when I signed on."

"Like all DCIs."

"No, I'm talking about a personal pledge." She very much wanted to see Lincoln sitting on his chair, contemplating all the unknowns that lay before every human being. She asked Gold to make a stop there. "I never told anyone this, Stu, but the day I officially became DCI I went to the Old Man's grave. Have you ever been to the Arlington National Cemetery? It's a sobering place, but in its own way a joyous place as well. So many heroes, so much courage, the bedrock of our freedom, Stu, every one of us."

They'd come to the memorial. They both got out, walked up to the majestic floodlit granite statue, stood gazing up into Lincoln's stern, wise face. Someone had left a bouquet of flowers at his feet, withered heads nodding in the wind.

"I stayed at the Old Man's grave for a long time," Hart continued in a faraway voice. "I swear I could feel him, I swear I felt something stir against me, then inside me." Her gaze swung around to fix on the attorney. "There's a long, exemplary legacy at CI, Stu. I swore then, and I'm swearing now, that I won't let anything or anyone damage that legacy." She took a breath. "So whatever it takes."

Gold returned her stare without flinching. "Do you know what you're asking?"

"Yes, I believe I do."

At last, he said, "All right, Veronica, it's your call. Whatever it takes."

Feeling invigorated and invulnerable after his workout, Rodney Feir met General Kendall in the champagne room, reserved for those VIPs who had consummated the evening's pleasures and wanted to linger, with or without their girls. Of course time spent in there was far more expensive with the girls than without.

The champagne room was decorated like a Middle Eastern pasha's den. The two men lazed on voluminous pillows while being served the bubbly of their choice. This was where Feir planned to hand over the intel on Typhon's field agents. But first he wanted to luxuriate in the pure pleasure provided in the back rooms of The Glass Slipper. After all, the moment he set foot outside, the real world would come crashing in on him with all its annoyances, petty humiliations, drudgery, and the piquancy of fear that preceded every move he made to advance La-Valle's position vis-à-vis CI.

Kendall, his cell phone at his right hand, sat rather stiffly, as befitted a military man. Feir thought he must be slightly uncomfortable in such lush surroundings. The men chatted for a time, sipping their champagne, exchanging theories about steroids and baseball, about the chances of the Redskins making the play-offs next year, the gyrations of the stock market, anything but politics.

After a time, when the bottle of champagne was nearly exhausted, Kendall looked at his watch. "What d'you have for me?"

This was the moment Feir had been keenly anticipating. He couldn't wait to see the look on the general's face when he caught a glimpse of the intel. Reaching into the pocket in the lining of his coat, he brought out the packet. A low-tech hard copy was the safest way to smuggle data out of the CI building, since security systems were in place to monitor the comings and goings of any device with a hard drive large enough to hold substantial data files.

A smile broke out across Feir's face. "The whole enchilada. Every last detail on the Typhon agents across the globe." He held up the packet. "Now let's talk about what I get in return."

"What do you want?" Kendall said without much enthusiasm. "A higher grade? More control?"

"I want respect," Feir said. "I want LaValle to respect me the way you do."

A curious smile curled the general's lips. "I can't speak for Luther, but I'll see what I can do."

As he leaned forward to take the intel, Feir was wondering why he was so solemn—no, worse than solemn, he was downright glum. Feir was on the point of asking him about it when a tall, elegant black woman began snapping a series of photos.

"What the hell?" he said, through the blinding string of flashes.

When his vision cleared, he saw Soraya Moore standing beside them. She had the packet of intel in her hand.

"This isn't a good night for you, Rodney." She picked up the general's cell phone, thumbed it on, and there was the conversation between the general and Feir recorded and regurgitated so everyone could hear his treachery for themselves. "No, I would have to say that all things considered it's the end of the line."

I'm not afraid to die," Devra said, "if that's what you're worried about."

"I'm not worried," Arkadin said. "What makes you think I'm worried?"

She bit into the chocolate ice cream he'd bought her. "You've got that deep vertical indentation between your eyes."

She wanted ice cream even though it was the middle of winter. Maybe it was the chocolate she wanted, he thought. Not that it mattered; pleasing her in little ways was strangely satisfying—as if in pleasing her he was also pleasing himself, although that seemed like an impossibility to him.

"I'm not worried," he said. "I'm thoroughly pissed off."

"Because your boss told you to stay away from Bourne."

"I'm not going to stay away from Bourne."

"You'll piss off your boss."

"There comes a time," Arkadin said, walking faster.

They were in the center of Munich; he wanted to be in a central location when Icoupov told him where he was meeting Bourne in order to get there as quickly as possible.

"I'm not afraid to die," Devra repeated, "the only thing is, though, what do you do when you no longer have memories?"

Arkadin shot her a look. "What?"

"When you look at a dead person what do you see?" She took another bite of ice cream between her teeth, leaving little indentations in what was left of the scoop. "Nothing, right? Not a damn thing. Life has flown the coop, and with it all the memories that have been built up over the years." She looked at him. "At that moment, you cease to be human, so what are you?"

"Who gives a shit?" Arkadin said. "It'll be a fucking relief to be without memories."

Soraya presented herself at the NSA safe house just before 10 AM, so that by the time she cleared the various levels of security, she was being ushered into the Library precisely on time.

"Breakfast, madam?" Willard asked as he escorted her across the plush carpet.

"I believe I will, today," she said. "A fines herbes omelet would be nice. Do you have a baguette?"

"We do, indeed, madam."

"Fine." She shifted the evidence damning General Kendall from one hand to the other. "And a pot of Ceylon tea, Willard. Thank you."

She walked the rest of the way to where Luther LaValle sat, drinking his morning cup of coffee. He stared out the window, casting a jaundiced eye on the early spring. It was so warm the fireplace held only cold, white ash.

He did not turn when she sat down. She placed the evidence file on her lap, then said without preamble, "I've come to take Tyrone home."

LaValle ignored her. "There's nothing on your Black Legion; there's no unusual terrorist activities inside the US. We've come up blank."

"Did you hear what I said? I've come for Tyrone."

"That's not going to happen," LaValle said.

Soraya brought out Kendall's cell phone, played back the conversation he'd had with Rodney Feir in the champagne room of The Glass Slipper.

"*Every last detail on the Typhon agents across the globe,*" came Feir's voice. "*Now let's talk about what I get in return.*"

General Kendall: "*What do you want? A higher grade? More control?*"

Feir: "*I want respect. I want LaValle to respect me the way you do.*"

"Who cares?" LaValle's head swung around. His eyes were dark and glassy. "That's Feir's problem, not mine."

"Maybe so." Soraya slid the file across the table toward him. "However, this is very much your problem."

LaValle stared at her for a moment. His eyes were now full of venom. Without lowering his gaze, he reached out, flipped open the file. There he saw photo after photo of General Kendall, naked as sin, caught in the midst of having intercourse with a young black woman.

"How is that going to look for the career officer and devout Christian family man when the story comes out?"

Willard arrived with her breakfast, snapping down a starched white tablecloth, setting the china and silverware in a precise pattern in front of her. When he was finished, he turned to LaValle. "Anything for you, sir?"

LaValle shooed him away with a curt flick of his hand. For a time, he did nothing more than leaf through the photos again. Then he took out a cell phone, placed it on the table, and pushed it toward her.

"Call Bourne," he said.

Soraya froze with a forkful of omelet halfway to her mouth. "I beg your pardon?"

"I know he's in Munich, our substation there picked him up on their CCTV monitoring of the airport. I have men in place to take him into custody. All that's needed now is for you to set the trap."

She laughed as she set down her fork. "You're dreaming, LaValle. I have you, not the other way around. If these photos become public, your right-hand man will be ruined both professionally and personally. You and I both know you're not going to allow that to happen."

LaValle gathered up the photos, slid them back into the envelope. Then he took out a pen, wrote a name and address on the front of the envelope. When Willard glided over at his beckoning, LaValle said, "Please have these scanned and sent electronically to *The Drudge Report*. Then have a courier deliver them to *The Washington Post* as soon as possible."

"Very good, sir." Willard tucked the envelope under his arm, vanished into another part of the Library.

Then LaValle took out his cell phone, dialed a local number. "Gus, this is Luther LaValle. Fine, fine. How's Ginnie? Good, give her my love. The kids, as well . . . Listen, Gus, I have a situation here. Evidence has come to light regarding General Kendall, that's right, he's been the target of an internal investigation for some months now. Effective immediately, he's been terminated from my command, from the NSA in toto. Well, you'll see, I'm having the photos messengered over to you even as we speak. Of course it's an exclusive, Gus. Frankly, I'm shocked, truly shocked. You will be, too, when you see these photos . . . I'll have an official statement over to you within forty minutes. Yes, of course. No need to thank me, Gus, I always think of you first."

Soraya watched this performance with a sick feeling in the pit of her stomach that grew from an icy ball into an iceberg of disbelief.

"How could you?" she said when LaValle finished his call. "Kendall's your second in command, your friend. You and he go to church together with your families every Sunday."

"I have no permanent friends or allies; I only have permanent interests," LaValle said flatly. "You'll be a damn sight better director when you learn that."

She then drew out another set of photos, this one showing Feir handing a packet to General Kendall. "That packet," she said, "details the number and locations of Typhon field personnel."

LaValle's disdainful expression didn't change. "What's that to me?"

For the second time, Soraya struggled to hide her astonishment. "That's your second in command taking possession of classified CI intel."

"On that score you should see to your own people."

"Are you denying that you gave General Kendall orders to cultivate Rodney Feir as a mole?"

"Yes, I am."

Soraya was almost breathless. "I don't believe you."

LaValle produced an icy smile. "I doesn't matter what you believe, Director. Only the facts matter." He flicked the photo away with his fingernail. "Whatever General Kendall did, he did on his own. I have no knowledge of it."

Soraya was wondering how everything could have gone so wrong, when, once again, LaValle pushed the phone across the table.

"Now call Bourne."

She felt as if there were a steel band around her chest; the blood was singing in her ears. *Now what?* she said to herself. *Dear God, what can I do?*

She heard someone with her voice say, "What should I tell him?"

LaValle produced a slip of paper with a time and an address on it. "He needs to go here, at this time. Tell him that you're in Munich, that you have information vital to the Black Legion's attack, that he has to see it for himself."

Soraya's hand was so slick with sweat, she wiped it on her napkin. "He'll be suspicious if I don't call him on my own phone. In fact, he might not answer if I don't, because he won't know it's me."

LaValle nodded, but when she produced her phone, he said, "I'm going to listen to every word you say. If you try to warn him I promise your friend Tyrone will never leave this building alive. Clear?"

She nodded, but did nothing.

Observing her like a frog split open on a dissecting table, LaValle said, "I know you don't want to do this, Director. I know how *badly* you don't want to do this. But you *will* call Bourne and you *will* set the trap for me, because I'm stronger than you are. By that I mean my will. I get what I want, Director, at any cost, but not you—you *care* too much to have a long career in intelligence work. You're doomed and you know it."

Soraya had stopped listening to him after the first few words. Acutely aware that she had vowed to take control of the situation, to somehow turn disaster into victory, she was furiously marshaling her forces. *One step at a time,* she told herself now. *I have to clear my mind of Tyrone, of the failed ploy with Kendall, of my own guilt. I have to think of this call now; how am I going to make the call and keep Jason from being captured?*

It seemed an impossible task, but that kind of thinking was defeatist, totally unhelpful. Still—what was she to do?

"After your call," LaValle said, "you'll stay here, under constant surveillance, until after Bourne is taken into custody."

Uncomfortably aware of his avid eyes on her, she flipped open her phone, and called Jason.

When she heard his voice, she said, "Hi, it's me, Soraya."

Bourne was standing in Egon Kirsch's apartment, staring down at the street when his cell phone rang. He saw Soraya's number come up on the screen, answered the call, and heard her say, "Hi, it's me, Soraya."

"Where are you?"

"Actually, I'm in Munich."

He perched on the arm of an upholstered chair. "Actually? In Munich?"

"That's what I said."

He frowned, hearing echoes in his head from far away. "I'm surprised."

"Not as much as I am. You came up on the CI surveillance grid at the airport."

"There was no help for it."

"I'm sure not. Anyway, I'm not over here on official CI business. We've been continuing to monitor the Black Legion communications, and at last we got a breakthrough."

He stood up. "What is it?"

"The phone's too insecure," she said. "We should meet." She told him the place and the time.

Glancing at his watch, he said, "That's a little over an hour from now."

"Right as rain. I can make it. Can you?"

"I think I can manage," he said. "See you."

He disconnected, went over to the window, leaned on the sash, replaying the conversation word by word in his mind.

He felt the jolt of a dislocation, as if he had moved outside his body, experiencing something that had happened to someone else. His mind, recording a seismic shift in its neurons, was struggling with a memory. Bourne knew he'd had this conversation before, but for the life of him he couldn't remember where or when, or what significance it might have for him now.

He would have continued on with his fruitless search had not the downstairs bell rang. Turning from the window, he went across the living room, pressed the button that released the outer door's lock. The time had finally come when he and Arkadin would meet face-to-face— the assassin of legend, who specialized in killing killers, who had slipped in and out of a Russian high-security prison without anyone being the wiser, who had managed to eliminate Pyotr and his entire network.

There was a knock on the door. He kept away from the spy hole, kept away from the door itself, unlatching it from the side. There was no gunshot, no splintering of the wood and metal. Instead the door opened inward and a dapper man with dark skin and a spade-shaped beard stepped into the apartment.

Bourne said, "Turn around slowly."

The man, hands where Bourne could see them, turned to face him. It was Semion Icoupov.

"Bourne," he said.

Bourne produced his passport, opened it to the inside cover.

Icoupov nodded. "I see. Is this where you kill me at the behest of Dominic Specter?"

"You mean Asher Sever."

"Oh, dear," Icoupov said, "there goes my surprise." He smiled. "I confess I'm shocked. Nevertheless, I congratulate you, Mr. Bourne. You've come by knowledge no one else has. By what means is a complete mystery."

"Let's keep it that way," Bourne said.

"No matter. What's important is that I don't have to waste time trying to convince you that Sever has played you. Since you've already uncovered his lies, we can move on to the next stage."

"What makes you think I'm going to listen to anything you have to say?"

"If you've discovered Sever's lies, then you know the recent history of the Black Legion, you know we were once like brothers, you know how deep the enmity between us runs. We are enemies, Sever and I. There can be only one outcome to our war, you understand me?"

Bourne said nothing.

"I want to help you stop his people from attacking your country, is that clear enough?" He shrugged. "Yes, of course you're right to be skeptical, I would be if I was in your place." He moved his left hand very slowly to the edge of his overcoat, pulled it back to reveal the lining. There was something sticking out of the slit pocket. "Perhaps before anything untoward happens, you should take a look at what I have here."

Bourne leaned in, took the SIG Sauer Icoupov had holstered at his belt. Then he pulled the packet free.

As he was opening it up, Icoupov said, "I went to a great deal of trouble to steal those from my nemesis."

Bourne found himself looking over the architectural plans for the Empire State Building. When he glanced up, he found Icoupov watching him intently. "This is what the Black Legion means to attack. Do you know when?"

"Indeed, I do." Icoupov glanced at his watch. "Precisely thirty-three hours, twenty-six minutes from now."

Thirty-Eight

VERONICA HART was looking at *The Drudge Report* when Stu Gold escorted General Kendall into her office. She was sitting in front of her desk, the monitor turned toward the door so Kendall could get a clear view of the photos of him and the woman from The Glass Slipper.

"That's just one site," she said, waving them to three chairs that had been arranged opposite her. "There are so many others." When her guests were seated, she addressed Kendall. "Whatever is your family going to say, General? Your minister, and the congregation?" Her expression remained neutral; she was careful to keep the gloat out of her voice. "I understand that a goodly number of them aren't fond of African Americans, even as maids and nannies. They prefer the Eastern Europeans—young blond Polish and Russian women. Isn't that right?"

Kendall said nothing, sat with his back ramrod-straight, his hands clasped primly between his knees, as if he were at a court-martial.

Hart wished Soraya were here, but she hadn't returned from the NSA safe house, which was worrying enough; she wasn't answering her cell, either.

"I've suggested that the best thing he can do now is to help us tie LaValle in to the plot to steal CI secrets," Gold said.

Now Hart smiled rather sweetly at Kendall. "And what do you think of that suggestion, General?"

"Recruiting Rodney Feir was entirely my idea," Kendall said woodenly.

Hart sat forward. "You want us to believe you'd embark on such a risky course without informing your superior?"

"After the fiasco with Batt, I had to do something to prove my worth. I felt I had the best chance romancing Feir."

"This is getting us nowhere," Hart said.

Gold stood up. "I agree. The general has made up his mind to fall on his sword for the man who sold him down the river." He moved to the door. "I'm not sure how that computes, but it takes all kinds."

"Is that it?" Kendall looked straight ahead. "Are you done with me?"

"We are," Hart said, "but Rob Batt isn't."

Batt's name got a reaction out of the general. "Batt? What does he have to do with anything? He's out of the picture."

"I don't think so." Hart got up, stood behind his chair. "Batt's had you under surveillance from the moment you ruined his life. Those photos of you and Feir going in and out of the health club, the barbecue joint, and The Glass Slipper were taken by him."

"But that's not all he has." Gold lifted his briefcase meaningfully.

"So," Hart said, "I'm afraid your stay at CI will continue awhile longer."

"How much longer?"

"What do you care?" Hart said. "You no longer have a life to go back to."

While Kendall remained with two armed agents, Hart and Gold went next door, where Rodney Feir was sitting, guarded by another pair of agents.

"Is the general having fun yet?" Feir said as they took seats facing him. "This is a black day for him." He chuckled at his own joke, but no one else did.

"Do you have any idea how serious your situation is?" Gold said.

Feir smiled. "I do believe I have a handle on the situation."

Gold and Hart exchanged a glance; neither could understand Feir's lighthearted attitude.

Gold said, "You're going to jail for a very long time, Mr. Feir."

Feir crossed one leg over the other. "I think not."

"You think wrong," Gold said.

"Rodney, we have you stealing Typhon secrets and handing them over to a ranking member of a rival intelligence organization."

"Please!" Feir said. "I'm fully aware of what I did and that you caught me at it. What I'm saying is none of that matters." He continued to look like the Cheshire Cat, as if he held a royal flush to their four aces.

"Explain yourself," Gold said curtly.

"I fucked up," Feir said. "But I'm not sorry for what I did, only that I got caught."

"That attitude will certainly help your case," Hart said caustically. She was done being manhandled by Luther LaValle and his cohorts.

"I'm not, by nature, prone to being contrite, Director. But like your evidence, my attitude is of no import. I mean to say, if I *were* contrite like Rob Batt, would it make any difference to you?" He shook his head. "So let's not bullshit each other. What I did, how I feel about it is in the past. Let's talk about the future."

"You have no future," Hart said tartly.

"That remains to be seen." Feir kept his maddening smile trained on her. "What I'm proposing is a barter."

Gold was incredulous. "You want to make a deal?"

"Let's call it a fair exchange," Feir said. "You drop all charges against me, give me a generous severance package and a letter of recommendation I can take into the private sector."

"Anything else?" Hart said. "How about a summer house on the Chesapeake and a yacht to go with it?"

"A generous offer," Feir said with a perfectly straight face, "but I'm not a pig, Director."

Gold rose. "This is intolerable behavior."

Feir eyed him. "Don't get your knickers in a twist, counselor. You haven't heard my side of the exchange."

"Not interested." Gold signaled the two agents. "Take him back down to the holding cell."

"I wouldn't do that if I were you." Feir didn't struggle as the agents grabbed hold of either arm and hauled him to his feet. He turned to Hart. "Director, did you ever wonder why Luther LaValle didn't try a run at CI while the Old Man was alive?"

"I didn't have to; I know. The Old Man was too powerful, too well connected."

"True enough, but there's another, more specific reason." Feir looked from one agent to the other.

Hart wanted to wring his neck. "Let him go," she said.

Gold stepped forward. "Director, I strongly recommend—"

"No harm in hearing the man out, Stu." Hart nodded. "Go ahead, Rodney. You have one minute."

"The fact is LaValle tried several times to make a run at CI while the Old Man was in charge. He failed every time, and do you know why?" Feir looked from one to the other, the Cheshire Cat grin back on his face. "Because for years the Old Man has had a deep-cover mole inside the NSA."

Hart goggled at him. "What?"

"This is bullshit," Gold said. "He's blowing smoke up our ass."

"Good guess, counselor, but wrong. I know the identity of the mole."

"How on earth would you know that, Rodney?"

Feir laughed. "Sometimes—not very often, I admit—it pays to be CI's chief file clerk."

"That's hardly what you—"

"That's precisely what I am, Director." A storm cloud of deep-seated anger momentarily shook him. "No fancy title can obscure the fact."

He waved a hand, his flash of rage quickly banked to embers. "But no matter, the point is I see things in CI no one else does. The Old Man had contingencies in place should he be killed, but you know this better than I do, counselor, don't you?"

Gold turned to Hart. "The Old Man left a number of sealed envelopes addressed to different directors in the event of his sudden demise."

"One of those envelopes," Feir said, "the one with the identity of the mole inside NSA, was sent to Rob Batt, which made sense at the time, since Batt was chief of operations. But it never got to Batt, I saw to that."

"You—" Hart was so enraged that she could barely speak.

"I could say that I'd already begun to suspect that Batt was working for the NSA," Feir said, "but that would be a lie."

"So you held on to it, even after I was appointed."

"Leverage, Director. I figured that sooner or later I'd need my Get Out of Jail Free card."

There was the smile that made Hart want to bury her fist in his face. With an effort, she restrained herself. "And meanwhile, you let LaValle trample all over us. Because of you I was led out of my office in handcuffs, because of you the Old Man's legacy is a hair's breadth from being buried."

"Yeah, well, these things happen. What can you do?"

"I'll tell you what I can do," Hart said, signaling the agents, who grabbed Feir again. "I can tell you to go to hell. I can tell you that you'll spend the rest of your life in jail."

Even then, Feir appeared unfazed. "I said I knew who the mole is, Director. Furthermore—and I believe this will be of especial interest you—I know where he's stationed."

Hart was too enraged to care. "Get him out of my sight."

As he was being led to the door, Feir said, "He's inside the NSA safe house."

The DCI felt her heart thumping hard in her chest. Feir's goddamn smile was not only understandable now, it was warranted.

* * *

Thirty-three hours, twenty-six minutes from now. Icoupov's ominous words were still ringing in Bourne's ears when he saw a flicker of movement. He and Icoupov were standing in the foyer, the front door was still open, and a shadow had for a moment stained the opposite wall of the hallway. Someone was out there, shielded by the half-open door.

Bourne, continuing to talk to Icoupov, took the other man by his elbow and moved him back into the living room, across the rug, toward the hallway to the bedrooms and bath. As they passed one of the windows, it exploded inward with the force of a man swinging through. Bourne whirled, the SIG Sauer he'd taken from Icoupov coming to bear on the intruder.

"Put the SIG down," a female voice said from behind him. He turned his head to see that the figure in the hallway—a young pale woman—was aiming a Luger at his head.

"Leonid, what are you doing here?" Icoupov seemed apoplectic. "I gave you express orders—"

"It's Bourne." Arkadin advanced through the welter of glass littering the floor. "It was Bourne who killed Mischa."

"Is this true?" Icoupov turned on Bourne. "You killed Mikhail Tarkanian?"

"He left me no choice," Bourne said.

Devra, her Luger aimed squarely at Bourne's head, said, "Drop the SIG. I won't say it again."

Icoupov reached out toward Bourne. "I'll take it."

"Stay where you are," Arkadin ordered. His own Luger was aimed at Icoupov.

"Leonid, what are you doing?"

Arkadin ignored him. "Do as the lady says, Bourne. Drop the SIG."

Bourne did as he was told. The moment he let go of the gun, Arkadin tossed his Luger aside and leapt at Bourne. Bourne raised a forearm in time to block Arkadin's knee, but he felt the jolt all the way up into his shoulder. They traded punishing blows, clever feints, and defensive blocks. For each move he employed, Arkadin had the perfect counter, and vice versa. When he stared into the Russian's eyes he saw his darkest deeds reflected back at him, all the death and destruction that lay in his wake. In those implacable eyes there was a void blacker than a starless night.

They moved across the living room as Bourne gave way, until they passed under the archway separating the living room from the rest of the apartment. In the kitchen Arkadin grabbed a cleaver, swung it at Bourne. Dodging away from the executioner's lethal arc, Bourne reached for a wooden block that held several carving knives. Arkadin brought the cleaver down on the countertop, missing Bourne's fingers by less than an inch. Now he blocked the way to the knives, swinging the cleaver back and forth like a scythe reaping wheat.

Bourne was near the sink. Snatching a plate out of the dish rack, he hurled it like a Frisbee, forcing Arkadin to duck out of the way. As the plate shattered against the wall behind Arkadin, Bourne withdrew a carving knife like a sword out of its scabbard. Steel clashed against steel, until Bourne used the knife to stab directly at Arkadin's stomach. Arkadin brought the cleaver down precisely at the place where Bourne was gripping the knife, and he had to let go. The knife rang as it hit the floor, then Arkadin rushed Bourne, and the two closed together.

Bourne managed to keep the cleaver away, and at such close quarters it was impossible to swing it back and forth. Realizing it had become a liability, Arkadin dropped it.

For three long minutes they were locked together in a kind of double death grip. Bloody and bruised, neither managed to gain the upper hand. Bourne had never encountered someone of Arkadin's physical and mental skill, someone who was so much like him. Fighting Arkadin was like fighting a mirror image of himself, one he didn't care for. He felt as if he stood on the precipice of something terrible, a chasm filled with endless dread, where no life could survive. He felt Arkadin had reached out to pull him into this abyss, as if to show him the desolation that lurked behind his own eyes, the grisly image of his forgotten past reflected back at him.

With a supreme effort Bourne broke Arkadin's hold, slammed his fist against the Russian's ear. Arkadin recoiled back against a column, and Bourne sprinted out of the kitchen, down the hall. As he did so, he heard the unmistakable sound of someone racking the slide, and he flung himself headlong into the main bedroom. A shot splintered the wooden door frame just over his head.

Scrambling up, he headed straight for Kirsch's closet, even as he heard Arkadin shout to the pale woman to hold her fire. Pushing aside a rack of clothes on hangers, Bourne scrabbled at the plywood panel in the rear wall of the closet, searching for the clips Kirsch had described to him at the museum. Just as he heard Arkadin rush into the bedroom, he turned the clips, removed the panel, and, crouching almost double, stepped through into a world filled to overflowing with shadow.

When Devra turned around after her attempt to wound Bourne, she found herself looking at the muzzle of the SIG Sauer that Icoupov had retrieved from the floor.

"You fool," Icoupov said, "you and your boyfriend are going to fuck everything up."

"What Leonid is doing is his own business," she said.

"That's the nature of the mistake," Icoupov said. "Leonid has no business of his own. Everything he is he owes to me."

She stepped out of the shadows of the hallway into the living room. The Luger at her hip was pointed at Icoupov. "He's quits with you," she said. "His servitude is done."

Icoupov laughed. "Is that what he told you?"

"It's what I told him."

"Then you're a bigger fool than I thought."

They circled each other, wary of the slightest move. Even so, Devra managed an icy smile. "He's changed since he left Moscow. He's a different person."

Icoupov made a dismissive sound in the back of his throat. "The first thing you need to get through your head is that Leonid is incapable of change. I know this better than anyone because I spent so many years trying to make him a better person. I failed. Everyone who tried failed, and do you know why? Because Leonid isn't whole. Somewhere in the days and nights of Nizhny Tagil he was fractured. All the czar's horses and all the czar's men can't put him back together again; the pieces no longer fit." He gestured with the SIG Sauer's barrel. "Get out now, get out while you can, otherwise, I promise you he'll kill you like he killed all the others who tried to get close to him."

"How deluded you are!" Devra spat. "You're like all your kind, corrupted by power. You've spent so many years removed from life on the streets you've created your own reality, one that moves only to the wave of your own hand." She took a step toward him, which prompted a tense response from him. "Think you can kill me before I kill you? I wouldn't count on it." She tossed her head. "Anyway, you have more to lose than I do. I was already half dead when Leonid found me."

"Ah, I see it now," Icoupov nodded, "he's saved you from yourself, he's saved you from the streets, is that it?"

"Leonid is my protector."

"God in heaven, talk about deluded!"

Devra's icy smile widened. "One of us is fatally mistaken. It remains to be seen which one."

The room is filled with mannequins," Egon Kirsch had said when he'd described his studio to Bourne. "I keep the light out with blackout shades because these mannequins are my creation. I built them from the ground up, so to speak. They're my companions, you might say, as well as my creations. In that sense, they can see or, if you like, I *believe* that they have the gift of sight, and what creature can look upon his creator without going mad or blind, or both?"

With the map of the room in his mind, Bourne crept through the studio, avoiding the mannequins so as not to make noise or, as Kirsch might have said, so as not to disturb the process of their birth.

"You think I'm insane," he'd said to Bourne in the museum. "Not that it matters. To all artists—successful or not!—their creations are alive. I'm no different. It's simply that after struggling for years to bring abstractions to life, I've given my work human form."

Hearing a sound, Bourne froze for a moment, then peered around a mannequin's thigh. His eyes had adjusted to the extreme gloom, and he could see movement: Arkadin had found the panel and had come through into the studio after him.

Bourne liked his chances here far better than in Kirsch's apartment. He knew the layout, the darkness would help him, and if he struck quickly, he'd have the advantage of being able to see where Arkadin couldn't.

With that strategy in mind, he moved out from behind the mannequin, picked his way toward the Russian. The studio was like a minefield. There were three mannequins between him and Arkadin, all set at different angles and poses: One was sitting, holding a small painting as if reading a book; another was standing spread-legged, in a classic shooter's pose; the third was running, leaning forward, as if stretching to cross the finish line.

Bourne moved around the runner. Arkadin was crouched down on his hams, wisely staying in one place until his eyes adjusted. It was precisely what Bourne had done when he'd entered the studio moments before.

Once again Bourne was struck by the eerie mirror image that Arkadin represented. There was no pleasure and a great deal of anxiety at the most primitive level in watching yourself do his best to find you and kill you.

Picking up his pace, Bourne negotiated the space to where the mannequin sat, reading his painting. Keenly aware that he was running out of time, Bourne moved stealthily abreast of the shooter. Just as he was about to lunge at Arkadin, his cell phone buzzed, the screen lighting up with Moira's number.

With a silent curse, Bourne sprang. Arkadin, alert for even the tini-

est anomaly, turned defensively toward the sound, and Bourne was met
with a solid wall of muscle, behind which was a murderous will of fiery
intensity. Arkadin swung; Bourne slid backward, between the legs of
the shooter mannequin. As Arkadin came after him he ran right into
the mannequin's hips. Recoiling with a curse, he swung at the mannequin. The blade struck the acrylic skin and lodged in the sheet metal
underneath. Bourne kicked out while Arkadin was trying to pull the
blade free, and made contact with the left side of his chest. Arkadin
tried to roll away. Bourne jammed his shoulder against the back of the
shooter. It was extremely heavy, he put all of his strength into it, and
the mannequin tipped over, trapping Arkadin underneath.

"Your friend gave me no choice," Bourne said. "He would've killed
me if I hadn't stopped him. He was too far away; I had to throw the
knife."

A sound like the crackle of a fire came from Arkadin. It took a moment for Bourne to realize it was laughter. "I'll make you a bet, Bourne.
Before he died, I bet Mischa said you were a dead man."

Bourne was about to answer him when he saw the dim glint of a
SIG Sauer Mosquito in Arkadin's hand. He ducked just before the .22
bullet whizzed over his head.

"He was right."

Bourne twisted away, dodging around the other mannequins, using
them as cover even as Arkadin squeezed off three more rounds. Plaster,
wood, and acrylic shattered near Bourne's left shoulder and ear before
he dived behind Kirsch's worktable. Behind him, he could hear Arkadin's grunts combined with the screech of metal as he worked to free
himself from the fallen shooter.

Bourne knew from Kirsch's description that the front door was to
the left. Scrambling up, he dashed around the corner as Arkadin fired
another shot. A chunk of plaster and lath disintegrated where the .22
impacted the corner. Reaching the door, Bourne unlocked it, pulled it
open, and sprinted out into the hallway. The open door to Kirsch's
apartment loomed to his left.

* * *

No good can come of us training guns on each other," Icoupov said. "Let's try to reason through this situation rationally."

"That's your problem," Devra said. "Life isn't rational; it's fucked-up chaos. It's part of the delusion; power makes you think you can control everything. But you can't, no one can."

"You and Leonid think you know what you're doing, but you're wrong. No one operates in a vacuum. If you kill Bourne it will have terrible repercussions."

"Repercussions for you, not for us. This is what power does: You think in shortcuts. Expediency, political opportunities, corruption without end."

It was at that moment they both heard the gunshots, but only Devra knew they came from Arkadin's Mosquito. She could sense Icoupov's finger tighten around the SIG's trigger, and she went into a semi-crouch because she knew if Bourne appeared rather than Arkadin she would shoot him dead.

The situation had reached a boiling point, and Icoupov was clearly worried. "Devra, I beg you to reconsider. Leonid doesn't know the whole picture. I need Bourne alive. What he did to Mischa was despicable, but personal feelings have no place in this equation. So much planning, so much spilled blood will come to nothing if Leonid kills Bourne. You must let me stop it; I'll give you anything—anything you want."

"Do you think you can buy me? Money means nothing to me. What I want is Leonid," Devra said just as Bourne appeared through the front doorway.

Devra and Icoupov both turned. Devra screamed because she knew, or she thought she knew, that Arkadin was dead, and so she redirected the Luger from Icoupov to Bourne.

Bourne ducked back into the hallway and she fired shot after shot at him as she walked toward the door. Because her focus was entirely concentrated on Bourne, she took her eyes off Icoupov and so missed the crucial movement as he swung the SIG in her direction.

"I warned you," he said as he shot her in the chest.

She fell onto her back.

"Why didn't you listen?" Icoupov said as he shot her again.

Devra made a little sound as her body arched up. Icoupov stood over her.

"How could you let yourself be seduced by such a monster?" he said.

Devra stared up at him with red-rimmed eyes. Blood pumped out of her with every labored beat of her heart. "That's exactly what I asked him about you." Each ragged breath filled her with indescribable pain. "He's not a monster, but if he were you'd be so much worse."

Her hand twitched. Icoupov, caught up in her words, paid no attention until the bullet she fired from her Luger struck his right shoulder. He spun back against the wall. The pain caused him to drop the SIG. Seeing her struggling to fire again, he turned and ran out of the apartment, fleeing down the stairwell and out onto the street.

Thirty-Nine

WILLARD, relaxing in the steward's lounge adjacent to the Library of the NSA safe house, was enjoying his sweet and milky mid-morning cup of coffee while reading *The Washington Post* when his cell phone buzzed. He checked it, saw that it was from his son, Oren. Of course it wasn't actually from Oren, but Willard was the only one who knew that.

He put down the paper, watched as the photo appeared on the phone's screen. It was of two people standing in front of a rural church, its steeple rising up into the top margin of the photo. He had no idea who the people were or where they were, but these things were irrelevant. There were six ciphers in his head; this photo told him which one to use. The two figures plus the steeple meant he was to use cipher three. If, for instance, the two people were in front of an arch, he'd subtract one from two, instead of adding to it. There were other visual cues. A brick building meant divide the number of figures by two; a bridge, multiply by two; and so on.

Willard deleted the photo from his phone, then picked up the third section of the *Post* and began to read the first story on page three. Starting with the third word, he began to decipher the message that was his call to action. As he moved through the article, substituting certain letters for others as the protocol dictated, he felt a profound stirring inside him. He had been the Old Man's eyes and ears inside the NSA for three decades, and the Old Man's sudden death last year had saddened him deeply. Then he had witnessed Luther LaValle's latest run at CI and had waited for his phone to ring, but for months his desire to see another photo fill his screen had been inexplicably unfulfilled. He simply couldn't understand why the new DCI wasn't making use of him. Had he fallen between the cracks; did Veronica Hart not know he existed? It certainly seemed that way, especially after LaValle had trapped Soraya Moore and her compatriot, who was still incarcerated belowdecks, as Willard privately called the rendition cells in the basement. He'd done what he could for the young man named Tyrone, though God knows it was little enough. Yet he knew that even the smallest sign of hope—the knowledge that you weren't alone—was enough to reinvigorate a stalwart heart, and if he was any judge of character, Tyrone had a stalwart heart.

Willard had always wanted to be an actor—for many years Olivier had been his god—but in his wildest dreams he'd never imagined his acting career would be in the political arena. He'd gotten into it by accident, playing a role in his college company, Henry V, to be exact, one of Shakespeare's great tragic politicians. As the Old Man said to him when he'd come backstage to congratulate Willard, Henry's betrayal of Falstaff is political, rather than personal, and ends in success. "How would you like to do that in real life?" the Old Man had asked him. He'd come to Willard's college to recruit for CI; he said he often found his people in the most unlikely places.

Finished with the deciphering, Willard had his immediate instructions, and he thanked the powers that be that he hadn't been tossed aside with the Old Man's trash. He felt like his old friend Henry V, though more than thirty years had passed since he'd trod a theater stage. Once again he was being called on to play his greatest role, one that he wore as effortlessly as a second skin.

He folded the paper away under one arm, took up his cell phone, and went out of the lounge. He still had twenty minutes left on his break, more than enough time to do what was required of him. What he had been ordered to do was find the digital camera Tyrone had on him when he'd been captured. Poking his head into the Library, he satisfied himself that LaValle was still sitting in his accustomed spot, opposite Soraya Moore, then he went down the hall.

Though the Old Man had recruited him, it was Alex Conklin who had trained him. Conklin, the Old Man had told him, was the best at what he did, namely preparing agents to be put into the field. It didn't take him long to learn that though Conklin was renowned inside CI for training wet-work agents, he was also adept at coaching sleeper agents. Willard spent almost a year with Conklin, though never at CI headquarters; he was part of Treadstone, Conklin's project that was so secret even most CI personnel was unaware of its existence. It was of paramount importance that he have no overt association with CI. Because the role the Old Man had planned for him was inside the NSA, his background check had to be able to withstand the most vigorous scrutiny.

All this flashed through Willard's mind as he walked the sacrosanct hallways and corridors of the NSA's safe house. He passed agent after agent and knew that he'd done his job to perfection. He was the indispensable nobody, the person who was always present, whom no one noticed.

He knew where Tyrone's camera was because he'd been there when Kendall and LaValle had spoken about its disposition, but even if he hadn't, he'd have suspected where LaValle had hidden it. He knew, for instance, that it wouldn't have been allowed to leave the safe house, even on LaValle's person, unless the damaging images Tyrone had taken of the rendition cells and the waterboarding tanks had been transferred to the in-house computer server or deleted off the camera's drive. In fact, there was a chance that the images had been deleted, but he doubted it. In the short amount of time the camera had been in the NSA's possession, Kendall was no longer in residence and LaValle had become obsessed with coercing Soraya Moore into giving him Jason Bourne.

He knew all about Bourne; he'd read the Treadstone files, even the ones that no longer existed, having been shredded and then burned when the information they held became too dangerous for Conklin, as well as for CI. He knew there had been far more to Treadstone than even the Old Man knew. That was Conklin's doing; he'd been a man for whom the word *secrecy* was the holy grail. What his ultimate plan for Treadstone had been was anyone's guess.

Inserting his passkey into the lock on LaValle's office door, he punched in the proper electronic code. Willard knew everyone's code— what use would he be as a sleeper agent otherwise? The door opened inward, and he slipped inside, shutting and locking it behind him.

Crossing to LaValle's desk, he opened the drawers one by one, checking for false backs or bottoms. Finding none, he moved on to the bookcase, the sideboard with its hanging files and liquor bottles side by side. He lifted the prints off the walls, searching behind them for a hidden cache, but there was nothing.

He sat on a corner of the desk, contemplated the room, uncon- sciously swinging his leg back and forth while he tried to work out where LaValle had hidden the camera. All at once he heard the sound the heel of his shoe made against the skirt of the desk. Hopping off, he went around, crawled into the kneehole, and rapped on the skirt until he replicated the sound his heel had made. Yes, he was certain now: This part of the skirt was hollow.

Feeling around with his fingertips, he discovered the tiny latch, pushed it aside, and swung open the door. There was Tyrone's camera. He was reaching for it when he heard the scratch of metal on metal.

LaValle was at the door.

Tell me you love me, Leonid Danilovich." Devra smiled up at him as he knelt over her.

"What happened, Devra? What happened?" was all he could say.

He'd extricated himself at last from the sculpture, and would have gone after Bourne—but he'd heard the shots coming from Kirsch's apartment, then the sound of running feet. The living room was spattered with blood. He saw her lying on the floor, the Luger still in her hand. Her shirt was dyed red.

"Leonid Danilovich." She'd called his name when he appeared in her limited field of vision. "I waited for you."

She started to tell him what had happened, but blood bubbles formed at the corners of her mouth and she started to gurgle horribly. Arkadin lifted her head off the floor, cradled it on his thighs. He pushed matted hair off her forehead and cheeks, leaving red streaks like war paint.

She tried to continue, stopped. Her eyes went out of focus and he thought he'd lost her. Then they cleared, her smile returned, and she said, "Do you love me, Leonid?"

He bent down and whispered her in ear. Was it *I love you*? There was so much static in his head, he couldn't hear himself. Did he love her, and, if he did, what would it mean? Did it even matter? He'd promised to protect her and failed. He stared down into her eyes, into her smile, but all he saw was his own past rising up to engulf him once again.

I need more money," Yelena said one night as she lay entangled with him.

"What for? I give you enough as it is."

"I hate it here, it's like a prison, girls are crying all the time, they're beaten, and then they disappear. I used to make friends just to pass the time, to have something to do during the day, but now I don't bother. What's the point? They're gone within a week."

Arkadin had become aware of Kuzin's seemingly insatiable need for more girls. "I don't see how any of this has to do with you needing more money."

"If I can't have friends," Yelena said, "I want drugs."

"I told you, no drugs," Arkadin said as he rolled away from her and sat up.

"If you love me, you'll get me out of here."

"Love?" He turned to stare at her. "Who said anything about love?"

She started to cry. "I want to live with you, Leonid. I want to be with you always."

Feeling something unknown close around his throat, Arkadin stood up, backed away. "Jesus," he said, gathering up his clothes, "where do you get such ideas?"

Leaving her to her pitiful weeping, he went out to procure more girls. Before he reached the front door of the brothel Stas Kuzin intercepted him.

"Yelena's wailing is disturbing the other girls," he said in his hissing way. "It's bad for business."

"She wants to live with me," Arkadin said. "Can you imagine?"

Kuzin laughed, the sound like nails screeching against a blackboard. "I'm wondering what would be worse, the nagging wife wanting to know where you were all night or the caterwauling brats making it impossible to sleep."

They both laughed at the comment, and Arkadin thought nothing more about it. For the next three days he worked steadily, methodically combing Nizhny Tagil for more girls to restock the brothel. At the end of that time he slept for twenty hours, then went straight to Yelena's room. He found another girl, one he'd recently hijacked off the streets, sleeping in Yelena's bed.

"Where's Yelena?" he said, throwing off the covers.

She looked up at him, blinking like a bat in sunlight. "Who's Yelena?" she said in a voice husky with sleep.

Arkadin strode out of the room and into Stas Kuzin's office. The big man sat behind a gray metal desk, talking on the phone, but he beckoned Arkadin to take a seat while he finished his call. Arkadin, preferring to stand, gripped the back of a wooden chair, leaning forward over its ladder back.

At length, Kuzin put down the receiver, said, "What can I do for you, my friend?"

"Where's Yelena?"

"Who?" Kuzin's frown knit his brows together, making him look something like a cyclops. "Oh, yes, the wailer." He smiled. "There's no chance of her bothering you again."

"What does that mean?"

"Why ask a question to which you already know the answer?" Kuzin's phone rang and he answered it. "Hold the fuck on," he said into it. Then he looked up at his partner. "Tonight we'll go to dinner to celebrate your freedom, Leonid Danilovich. We'll make a real night of it, eh?"

Then he returned to his call.

Arkadin felt frozen in time, as if he was now doomed to relive this moment for the rest of his life. Mute, he walked like an automaton out of the office, out of the brothel, out of the building he owned with Kuzin. Without even thinking, he got into his car, drove north into the forest of dripping firs and weeping hemlocks. There was no sun in the sky, the horizon was rimmed with smokestacks. The air was hazed with carbon and sulfur particles, tinged a lurid orange-red, as if everything were on fire.

Arkadin pulled off the road and walked down the rutted track, following the route the van had taken previously. Somewhere along the line he found that he was running as fast as he could through the evergreens, the stench of decay and decomposition billowing up, as if eager to meet him.

He brought himself up abruptly at the edge of the pit. In places, sacks of quicklime had been shaken out in order to aid the decomposition; nevertheless it was impossible to mistake the content. His eyes roved over the bodies until he found her. Yelena was lying in a tangle where she'd landed after being kicked over the side. Several very large rats were picking their way toward her.

Arkadin, staring into the mouth of hell, gave a little cry, the sound a puppy might make if you mistakenly stepped on its paw. Scrambling down the side, he ignored the appalling stench and, through watering eyes, dragged her up the slope, laid her out on the forest floor, the bed of brown needles, soft as her own. Then he trudged back to the car, opened the trunk, and took out a shovel.

He buried her half a mile away from the pit, in a small clearing that was private and peaceful. He carried her over his shoulder the whole way, and by the time he was finished he smelled like death. At that moment, crouched on his hamstrings, his face streaked with sweat and dirt, he doubted whether he'd ever be able to scrub off the stench. If he knew a prayer, he would have said it then, but he knew only obscenities, which he uttered with the fervor of the righteous. But he wasn't righteous; he was damned.

For a businessman there was a decision to be made. Arkadin was no businessman, though, so from that day forward his fate was sealed. He returned to Nizhny Tagil with his two Stechkin handguns fully loaded and extra rounds of ammunition in his breast pockets. Entering the brothel, he shot the two ghouls dead as they stood at guard. Neither had a chance to draw his weapon.

Stas Kuzin appeared in the doorway, gripping a Korovin TK pistol. "Leonid, what the fuck?"

Arkadin shot him once in each knee. Kuzin went down, screaming. As he tried to raise the Korovin, Arkadin trod heavily on his wrist. Kuzin grunted heavily. When he wouldn't let go of the pistol, Arkadin kicked him in the knee. The resulting bellow brought the last of the girls from their respective rooms.

"Get out of here." Arkadin addressed the girls, though his gaze was fixed on Kuzin's monstrous face. "Take whatever money you can find and go back to your families. Tell them about the lime pit north of town."

He heard them scrambling, babbling to one another, then it was quiet.

"Fucking sonovabitch," Kuzin said, staring up at Arkadin.

Arkadin laughed and shot him in the right shoulder. Then, jamming the Stechkins in their holsters, he dragged Kuzin across the floor. He had to push one of the dead ghouls out of the way, but at last he made it down the stairs and out the front door with the moaning Kuzin in tow. In the street one of Kuzin's vans screeched to a halt. Arkadin drew his guns, emptied them into the interior. The car rocked on its shocks, glass shattered, its horn blared as the dead driver fell over onto it. No one got out.

Arkadin dragged Kuzin to his car and dumped him in the backseat. Then he drove out of town to the forest, turning off at the rutted dirt track. At the end of it, he stopped, hauled Kuzin to the edge of the pit.

"Fuck you, Arkadin!" Kuzin shouted. "Fuck—"

Arkadin shot him point-blank in the left shoulder, shattering it and sending Kuzin down into the quicklime pit. He peered over. There was the monster, lying on the corpses.

Kuzin's mouth drooled blood. "Kill me!" he shouted. "D'you think I'm afraid of death? Go on, do it now!"

"It's not for me to kill you, Stas."

"Kill me, I said. For fuck's sake, finish it now!"

Arkadin gestured at the corpses. "You'll die in your victims's arms, hearing their curses echoing in your ears."

"What about all *your* victims?" Kuzin shouted when Arkadin disappeared from view. "You'll die choking on your own blood!"

Arkadin paid him no mind. He was already behind the wheel of his car, backing out of the forest. It had begun to rain, gunmetal-colored drops that fell like bullets out of a colorless sky. A slow booming coming from the smelters starting up sounded like the thunder of cannons signaling the beginning of a war that would surely destroy him unless he found a way out of Nizhny Tagil that wasn't in a body bag.

Forty

WHERE ARE YOU, Jason?" Moira said. "I've been trying to reach you."

"I'm in Munich," he said.

"How wonderful! Thank God you're close by. I need to see you." She seemed slightly out of breath. "Tell me where you are and I'll meet you there."

Bourne switched his cell phone from one ear to the other, the better to check his immediate surroundings. "I'm on my way to the Englischer Garten."

"What are you doing in Schwabing?"

"It's a long story; I'll tell you about it when I see you." Bourne checked his watch. "But I'm due to meet up with Soraya at the Chinese pagoda in ten minutes. She says she has new intel on the Black Legion attack."

"That's odd," Moira said. "So do I."

Bourne crossed the street, hurrying, but still alert for tags.

"I'll meet you," Moira said. "I'm in a car; I can be there in fifteen minutes."

"Not a good idea." He didn't want her involved in a professional rendezvous. "I'll call you as soon as I'm through and we can—" All of a sudden, he realized he was talking to dead air. He dialed Moira's number, but got her voice mail. Damn her, he thought.

He reached the outskirts of the garden, which was twice the size of New York's Central Park. Divided by the Isar River, it was filled with jogging and bicycle paths, meadows, forests, and even hills. Near the crown of one of these was the Chinese pagoda, which was actually a beer garden.

He was naturally thinking of Soraya as he approached the area. It was odd that both she and Moira had intel on the Black Legion. Now he thought back over his phone conversation with her. Something about it had been bothering him, something just out of reach. Every time he strained for it, it seemed to move farther away from him.

His pace was slowed by the hordes of tourists, American diplomats, children with balloons or kites riding the wind. In addition, a rally of teenagers protesting new rulings on curriculum at the university had begun to gather at the pagoda.

He pushed his way forward, past a mother and child, then a large family in Nikes and hideous tracksuits. The child glanced at him and, instinctively, Bourne smiled. Then he turned away, wiped the blood off his face, though it continued to seep through the cuts opened during his fight with Arkadin.

"No, you can't have sausages," the mother said to her son in a strong British accent. "You were sick all night."

"But Mummy," he replied, "I feel right as rain."

Right as rain. Bourne stopped in his tracks, rubbed the heel of his hand against his temple. *Right as rain;* the phrase rattled around in his head like a steel ball in a pachinko machine.

Soraya.

Hi, it's me, Soraya. That's how she'd started off the call

Then she'd said: *Actually, I'm in Munich.*

And just before she'd hung up: *Right as rain. I can make it. Can you?*

Bourne, buffeted by the quickening throngs, felt as if his head were on fire. Something about those phrases. He knew them, and he didn't, how could that be? He shook his head as if to clear it; memories were appearing like knife slashes through a piece of fabric. Light was glimmering . . .

And then he saw Moira. She was hurrying toward the Chinese pagoda from the opposite direction, her expression intent, grim, even. What had happened? What information did she have for him?

He craned his neck, trying to find Soraya in the swirl of the demonstration. That was when he remembered.

Right as rain.

He and Soraya had had this conversation before—where? In Odessa? *Hi, it's me* coming before her name meant that she was under duress. *Actually* coming before a place where she was supposed to be meant that she wasn't there.

Right as rain meant it's a trap.

He looked up and his heart sank. Moira was heading right into it.

When the door opened, Willard froze. He was on his hands and knees hidden from the doorway by the desk's skirt. He heard voices, one of them LaValle's, and held his breath.

"There's nothing to it," LaValle said. "E-mail me the figures and after I'm done with the Moore woman I'll check them."

"Good deal," Patrick, one of LaValle's aides said, "but you'd better get back to the Library, the Moore woman is kicking up a fuss."

LaValle cursed. Willard heard him cross to the desk, shuffle some papers. Perhaps he was looking for a file. LaValle grunted in satisfaction, walked back across the office, and closed the door after him. It was only when Willard heard the grate of the key in the lock that he exhaled.

He fired up the camera, praying that the images hadn't been deleted, and there they were, one after another, evidence that would damn Luther LaValle and his entire NSA administration. Using both the camera and his cell phone, he linked them through the wireless Bluetooth protocol, then transferred the images to his cell. Once that was completed, he navigated to his son's phone number—which wasn't his son's number, though if anyone called it a young man who had standing instructions to pass as his son would answer—and sent the photos in one long burst. Sending them one by one via separate calls would surely cause a red flag on the security server.

At last, Willard sat back and took a deep breath. It was done; the photos were now in the hands of CI, where they'd do the most good, or—if you were Luther LaValle—the most damage. Checking his watch, he pocketed the camera, relatched the door to the hidden compartment, and scrambled out from under the desk.

Four minutes later, his hair freshly combed, his uniform brushed down, and looking very smart, indeed, he placed a Ceylon tea in front of Soraya Moore and a single-malt scotch in front of Luther LaValle. Ms. Moore thanked him; LaValle, staring at her, ignored him as usual.

Moira hadn't seen him, and Bourne couldn't call out to her because in this maelstrom of people his voice wouldn't carry. Blocked in his forward motion, he edged his way back to the periphery, moving to his left in order to circle around to her. He tried her cell again, but she either couldn't hear it or wasn't answering.

It was as he was disengaging the line that he saw the NSA agents. They were moving in concert toward the center of the crowd, and he could only assume that there were others in a tightening circle within which they meant to trap him. They hadn't spotted him yet, but Moira was close to one of the pair in Bourne's view. There was no way to get to her without them spotting him. Nevertheless, he continued to circle through the fringes of the crowd, which had grown so large that many of the young people were shoving one another as they shouted their slogans.

Bourne pushed on, although it seemed to him at a slower and slower pace, as if he were in a dream where the laws of physics were nonexistent. He needed to get to Moira without the agents seeing him;

it was dangerous for her to be looking for him with NSA infiltrating the crowd. Far better for him to get to her first so he could control both their movements.

Finally, as he neared the NSA agents, he could see the reason for the sudden rancor of the crowd. The shoving was being precipitated by a large group of skinheads, some wielding brass knuckles or baseball bats. They had swastikas tattooed on their bulging arms, and when they began to swing at the chanting university students, Bourne made a run for Moira. But as he lunged for her, one of the agents elbowed a skinhead aside and, as he did so, caught a glimpse of Bourne. He whirled, his lips moving as he spoke urgently into the earpiece with which he was wirelessly connected with the other members of what Bourne assumed was an execution team.

He grabbed Moira, but the agent had hold of him, and he began to jerk Bourne back toward him, as if to detain him long enough for the other members of the team to reach them. Bourne struck him flush on the chin with the heel of his hand. The agent's head snapped back, and he collapsed into a group of skinheads, who thought he was attacking them and started beating him.

"Jason, what the hell happened to you?" Moira said as she and Bourne turned, making their way through the throng. "Where's Soraya?"

"She was never here," Bourne said. "This is another NSA trap."

It would have been best to keep to where the garden was most crowded, but that would put them in the center of the trap. Bourne led them around the crowd, hoping to emerge in a place where the agents wouldn't spot them, but now he saw three more outside the mass of the demonstration and knew retreat was impossible. Instead he reversed course, drawing Moira farther into the surging mass of demonstrators.

"What are you doing?" Moira said. "Aren't we headed straight into the trap?"

"Trust me." Instinctively he headed toward one of the flashpoints where the skinheads were clashing with the university students.

They reached the edge of the escalating fight between the two groups of teens. Out of the corner of his eye Bourne saw an NSA agent struggling through the same mass of people. Bourne tried to alter their course, but their way was blocked, and a resurgent wave of students pushed them like flotsam at the tide line. Feeling the new influx of people, the agent turned to fight against it and ran right into Moira.

He barked Bourne's name into the microphone in his earpiece, and Bourne slammed a shoe into the side of his knee. The agent faltered, but managed to counter the chop Bourne directed at his shoulder blade. The agent drew a handgun, and Bourne snatched a baseball bat from a skinhead's grip, struck the agent so hard on the back of his hands that he dropped the handgun.

Then, from behind him, Bourne heard Moira say. "Jason, they're coming!"

The trap was about to snap shut on both of them.

Forty-One

LUTHER LAVALLE waited on tenterhooks for the call from his extraction team leader in Munich. He sat in his customary chair facing the window that looked out over the rolling lawns to the left of the wide gravel drive, which wound through the elms and oaks lining it like sentinels. Having verbally put her in her place after returning from his office, he contrived to ignore Soraya Moore and Willard who, after the second time, had given up asking him if he wanted his single-malt scotch refreshed. He didn't want his single-malt scotch refreshed and he didn't want to hear another word from the Moore woman. What he wanted was his cell phone to ring, for his team leader to tell him that Jason Bourne was in custody. That's all he required of this day; he didn't think it was too much to ask.

Nevertheless, it was true that his nerves were pulled tighter than a drawn bowstring. He found himself wanting to scream, to punch someone; he'd almost launched himself like a missile at Willard when the steward had approached him the last time—he was so damn servile. Beside him, the Moore woman sat, one leg crossed over her knee, sipping her damnable Ceylon tea. How could she be so calm!

He reached over, slapped the cup and saucer out of her hands. They bounced on the thick carpet, along with what was left of the espresso, but they didn't break. He jumped up, stomped the china beneath his heel until it cracked and cracked again. Aware of Soraya staring up at him, he snapped, "What? What are you looking at?"

His cell phone buzzed and he snatched it off the table. His heart lifted, a smile of triumph wreathed his face. But it was a guard at the front gate, not the leader of his extraction team.

"Sir, I'm sorry to bother you," the guard said, "but the director of Central Intelligence is here."

"What?" LaValle fairly shouted his response. He was flooded with bitter disappointment. "Keep her the fuck out!"

"I'm afraid that's not possible, sir."

"Of course it's possible." He moved to the window. "I'm giving you a direct order!"

"She's with a contingent of federal marshals," the guard said. "They're already on their way to the main house."

It was true, LaValle could see the convoy making its way up the drive. He stood, speechless with confusion and fury. How dare the DCI invade his private sanctuary! He'd have her in prison for this outrage!

He started, feeling someone standing next to him. It was Soraya Moore. Her wide lips were curled in an enigmatic smile.

Then she turned to him and said, "I do believe it's the end of days."

The maelstrom closed around Bourne and Moira. What had once been a simple demonstration was now a full-blown melee. He heard screams and shouts, hurled invective, and then, under it all, the familiar high-low wail of police sirens approaching from several different directions. Bourne was quite certain the NSA hit squad had no desire to run afoul of the Munich police; it was therefore running out of time. The agent near Bourne heard the sirens, too, and with his hands clearly still half numb from the bat grabbed Moira around the throat.

"Drop the bat and come with me, Bourne," he said against the rising tide of screams and shouts, "or so help me I'll break her neck like a twig."

Bourne dropped the bat but, as he did so, Moira bit into the agent's hand. Bourne drove his fist into the soft spot just below his sternum then, taking hold of his wrist, he turned over the arm at an awkward angle, and with a sharp blow broke the agent's elbow. The agent groaned, went to his knees.

Bourne dug out his passport and earbud, threw the passport to Moira as he fitted the electronic bud into his ear canal.

"Name," he said.

Moira already had the wallet open. "William K. Saunders."

"This is Saunders," Bourne said, addressing the wireless network. "Bourne and the girl are getting away. They're heading north by northwest past the pagoda."

Then he took her hand. "Biting his hand," he said as they stepped over the fallen agent. "That was quite a professional move."

She laughed. "It did the trick, didn't it?"

They made their way through the mob, heading southeast. Behind them, the NSA agents were shoving their way toward the opposite side of the mass of people. Ahead, a corps of uniformed policemen outfitted in riot gear were trotting along the path, semi-automatics at the ready. They passed Bourne and Moira without a second look.

Moira glanced at her watch. "Let's get to my car as quickly as possible. We have a plane to catch."

Don't give up. Those three words Tyrone had found in his oatmeal were enough to sustain him. Kendall never came back, nor did any other interrogator. In fact, his meals came at regular intervals, the trays filled with real food, which was a blessing because he didn't think he could ever get oatmeal down again.

The periods when the black hood was taken off seemed to him longer and longer in duration, but his sense of time had been shot, so he didn't really know whether or not that was true. In any case, he'd used those periods to walk, do sit-ups, push-ups, and squats, anything to relieve the terrible, bone-deep aching of his arms, shoulders, and neck.

Don't give up. That message might just as well have read *You're not alone* or *Have faith,* so rich were those words, like a millionaire's cache. When he read them he knew both that Soraya hadn't abandoned him and that something inside the building, someone who had access to the basement, was on his side. And that was the moment when the revelation struck him, as if, if he remembered his Bible correctly, he were Paul on the road to Damascus, converted by God's light.

Someone is on my side —not the side of the old Tyrone, who roamed his hood with perfect wrath and retribution, not the Tyrone who'd been saved from life in the gutter by Deron, not even the Tyrone who'd been awed by Soraya. No, once he spontaneously thought *Someone is on my side,* he realized that *my side* meant CI. He had not only moved out of the hood forever, but also stepped out from under Soraya's beautiful shadow. He was his own man now; he'd found his own calling, not as Deron's protector, or his disciple, not as Soraya's adoring assistant. CI was where he wanted to be, in the service of making a difference. His world was no longer defined by himself on one side and the Man on the other. He was no longer fighting what he was becoming.

He looked up. Now to get out of here. But how? His best choice was to try to find a way to communicate with whoever had sent the note. He considered a moment. The note had been hidden in his food, so the logical answer would be to write a note of his own and somehow hide it in his leftovers. Of course, there was no way to be sure that person would find the note, or even know it was there, but it was his only shot and he was determined to take it.

He was looking around for something to use to write when the clanging of the door brought him up short. He turned to face it as it opened. Had Kendall returned for more sadistic playtime? Had the real torturer arrived? He took a fearful glance over his shoulder at the waterboarding tank and his blood turned cold. Then he turned back and saw Soraya standing in the doorway. She was grinning from ear to ear.

"God," she said, "it's good to see you!"

* * *

Iow nice to see you again," Veronica Hart said, "especially under these circumstances."

Luther LaValle had come away from the window; he was standing when the DCI, flanked by federal marshals and a contingent of CI agents, entered the Library. Everyone else in the Library at the time goggled, then at the behest of the marshals beat a hasty retreat. Now he sat ramrod-straight in his chair, facing Hart.

"How dare you," LaValle said now. "This intolerable behavior won't go unpunished. As soon as I inform Secretary of Defense Halliday of your criminal breach of protocol—"

Hart fanned out the photos of the rendition cells in the basement. "You're right, Mr. LaValle, this intolerable behavior won't go unpunished, but I believe it will be Secretary of Defense Halliday who'll be leading the charge to punish you for your criminal protocols."

"I do what I do in the defense of my country," LaValle said stiffly. "When a country is at war extraordinary actions must be undertaken in order to safeguard its borders. It's you and people like you, with your weak-willed leftist leanings, that are to blame, not me." He was livid, his cheeks aflame. "I'm the patriot here. You—you're just an obstructionist. This country will crack and fall if people like you are left to run it. I'm America's only salvation."

"Sit down," Hart said quietly but firmly, "before one of my 'leftist' people knocks you down."

LaValle glared at her for a moment, then slowly sank into the chair.

"Nice to be living in your own private world where you make the rules and you don't give a shit about reality."

"I'm not sorry for what I did. If you're expecting remorse, you're sorely mistaken."

"Frankly," Hart said, "I'm not expecting anything out of you until after you're waterboarded." She waited until all the blood had drained from his face, before she added, "That would be one solution—*your*

solution—but it isn't mine." She shuffled the photos back into their
envelope.

"Who's seen those?" LaValle asked.

The DCI saw him wince when she said, "Everyone who needs to
see them."

"Well, then." He was unbowed, unrepentant. "It's over."

Hart looked past him to the front of the Library. "Not quite yet."
She nodded. "Here come Soraya and Tyrone."

Semion Icoupov sat on the stoop of a building not far from where the
shooting had taken place. His greatcoat hid the blood that had pooled
inside it, so it he didn't draw a crowd, just a curious glance or two from
pedestrians hurrying by. He felt dizzy and nauseated, no doubt from
shock and loss of blood, which meant he wasn't thinking clearly. He
looked around with bloodshot eyes. Where was the car that had brought
him here? He needed to get out of here before Arkadin emerged from
the building and spotted him. He'd taken a tiger from the wild and had
tried to domesticate him, a historic mistake by any measure. How many
times had it been attempted before with always the same result? Tigers
weren't meant to be domesticated; neither was Arkadin. He was what
he was, and would never be anything else: a killing machine of almost
preternatural abilities. Icoupov had recognized the talent and, greedily,
had tried to harness it to his own needs. Now the tiger had turned on
him; he'd had a premonition that he would die in Munich, now he knew
why, now he knew how.

Looking back toward Egon Kirsch's apartment building, he felt a
sudden rush of fear, as if at any moment death would emerge from it,
stalking him down the street. He tried to pull himself together, tried to
rise to his feet, but a horrific pain shot through him, his knees buckled,
and he collapsed back onto the cold stone.

More people passed, now ignoring him altogether. Cars rolled by.
The sky came down, the day darkened as if covered with a shroud. A

sudden gust of wind brought the onset of rain, hard as sleet. He ducked his head between his shoulders, shivered mightily.

And then he heard his name shouted and, turning his head, saw the nightmare figure of Leonid Danilovich Arkadin coming down the steps of Kirsch's building. Now more highly motivated, Icoupov once again tried to get up. He groaned as he gained his feet, but tottered there uncertainly as Arkadin began to run toward him.

At that moment, a black Mercedes sedan pulled up to the sidewalk. The driver hurried out and, taking hold of Icoupov, half carried him across the pavement. Icoupov struggled, but to no avail; he was weak with lost blood, and growing weaker by the moment. The driver opened the rear door, bundled him into the backseat. He pulled an HK 1911 .45 and with it warned Arkadin away, then he hustled back around the front of the Mercedes, slid behind the wheel, and took off.

Icoupov, slumped in the near corner of the backseat, made rhythmic grunts of pain like puffs of smoke from a steam locomotive. He was aware of the soft rocking of the shocks as the car sped through the Munich streets. More slowly came the realization that he wasn't alone in the backseat. He blinked heavily, trying to clear his vision.

"Hello, Semion," a familiar voice said.

And then Icoupov's vision cleared. "You!"

"It's been a long time since we've seen each other, hasn't it?" Dominic Specter said.

The Empire State Building," Moira said as she studied the plans Bourne had managed to scoop up in Kirsch's apartment. "I can't believe I was wrong."

They were parked in a rest stop by the side of the autobahn on the way to the airport.

"What do you mean, wrong?" Bourne said.

She told him what Arthur Hauser, the engineer hired by Kaller Steelworks, had confessed about the flaw in LNG terminal's software.

Bourne thought a moment. "If a terrorist used that flaw to gain control of the software, what could he do?"

"The tanker is so huge and the terminal is so complex that the docking is handled electronically."

"Through the software program."

Moira nodded.

"So he could cause the tanker to crash into the terminal." He turned to her. "Would that set off the tanks of liquid gas?"

"Quite possibly, yes."

Bourne was thinking furiously. "Still, the terrorist would have to know about the flaw, how to exploit it, and how to reconfigure the software."

"It sounds simpler than trying to blow up a major building in Manhattan."

She was right, of course; and because of the questions he'd been pondering he grasped implications of that immediately.

Moira glanced at her watch. "Jason, the NextGen plane with the coupling link is scheduled to take off in thirty minutes." She put the car in gear, nosed out onto the autobahn. "We have to make up our minds before we get to the airport. Do we go to New York or to Long Beach?"

Bourne said, "I've been trying to figure out why both Specter and Icoupov were so hell-bent on retrieving these plans." He stared down at the blueprints as if willing them to speak to him. "The problem," he said slowly and thoughtfully, "is that they were entrusted to Specter's son, Pyotr, who was more interested in girls, drugs, and the Moscow nightlife than he was in his work. As a consequence, his network was peopled by misfits, junkies, and weaklings."

"Why in the world would Specter entrust so important a document to a network like that?"

"That's just the point," Bourne said. "He wouldn't."

Moira glanced at him. "What does that mean? Is the network bogus?"

"Not as far as Pyotr was concerned," Bourne said, "but so far as Specter saw it, yes, everyone who was a part of it was expendable."

"Then the plans are bogus, too."

"No, I think they're real, and that's what Specter was counting on," Bourne said. "But when you consider the situation logically and coolly, which no one does when it comes to the threat of an imminent terrorist attack, the probability of a cell managing to get what it needs into the Empire State Building is very low." He rolled up the plans. "No, I think this was all an elaborate disinformation scheme—leaking communications to Typhon, recruiting me because of my loyalty to Specter. It was all meant to mobilize American security forces on the wrong coast."

"So you think the Black Legion's real target is the LNG terminal in Long Beach."

"Yes," Bourne said, "I do."

Tyrone stood looking down at LaValle. A terrible silence had descended over the Library when he and Soraya had entered. He watched Soraya scoop up LaValle's cell phone from the table.

"Good," she said with an audible sigh of relief. "No one's called. Jason must be safe." She tried him on her cell, but he wasn't answering.

Hart, who had stood up when they'd come over, said, "You look a little the worse for wear, Tyrone."

"Nothing a stint at the CI training school wouldn't cure," he said.

Hart glanced at Soraya before saying, "I think you've earned that right." She smiled. "In your case, I'll forgo the usual warning about how rigorous the training program is, how many recruits drop out in the first two weeks. I know we won't have to be concerned about you dropping out."

"No, ma'am."

"Just call me Director, Tyrone. You've earned that as well."

He nodded, but he couldn't keep his eyes off LaValle.

His interest did not go unnoticed. The DCI said, "Mr. LaValle, I think it only just that Tyrone decide your fate."

"You're out of your mind." LaValle looked apoplectic. "You can't—"

"On the contrary," Hart said, "I can." She turned to Tyrone. "It's entirely up to you, Tyrone. Let the punishment fit the crime."

Tyrone, impaling LaValle in his glare, saw there what he always saw in the eyes of white people who confronted him: a toxic mixture of contempt, aversion, and fear. Once, that would have sent him into a frenzy of rage, but that was because of his own ignorance. Perhaps what he had seen in them was a reflection of what had been on his own face. Not today, not ever again, because during his incarceration he'd finally come to understand what Deron had tried to teach him: that his own ignorance was his worst enemy. Knowledge allowed him to work at changing other people's expectations of him, rather than confronting them with a switchblade or a handgun.

He looked around, saw the look of expectation on Soraya's face. Turning back to LaValle, he said: "I think something public would be in order, something embarrassing enough to work its way up to Secretary of Defense Halliday."

Veronica Hart couldn't help laughing, she laughed until tears came to her eyes, and she heard the Gilbert and Sullivan lines run through her head: *His object all sublime, he will achieve in time—let the punishment fit the crime!*

Forty-Two

I SEEM TO HAVE you at quite a disadvantage, dear Semion." Dominic Specter watched Icoupov as he dealt with the pain of sitting up straight.

"I need to see a doctor." Icoupov was panting like an underpowered engine struggling up a steep grade.

"What you need, dear Semion, is a surgeon," Specter said. "Unfortunately, there's no time for one. I need to get to Long Beach and I can't afford to leave you behind."

"This was my idea, Asher." Having braced his back against the seat, some small amount of color was returning to Icoupov's cheeks.

"So was using Pyotr. What did you call my son? Oh, yes, a useless wart on fate's ass, that was it, wasn't it?"

"He *was* useless, Asher. All he cared about was getting laid and getting high. Did he have a commitment to the cause, did he even know what the word meant? I doubt it, and so do you."

"You killed him, Semion."

"And you had Iliev murdered."

"I thought you'd changed your mind," Sever said. "I assumed you'd sent him after Bourne to expose me, to gain the upper hand by telling him about the Long Beach target. Don't look at me like that. Is it so strange? After all, we've been enemies longer than we've been allies."

"You've become paranoid," Icoupov said, though at the time he had sent his second in command to expose Sever. He'd temporarily lost faith in Sever's plan, had finally felt the risks to all of them were too great. From the beginning, he'd argued with Sever against bringing Bourne into the picture, but had acquiesced to Sever's argument that CI would bring Bourne into play sooner later. "Far better for us to preempt them, to put Bourne in play ourselves," Sever had said, capping his argument, and that had been the end of it, until now.

"We've both become paranoid."

"A sad fact," Icoupov said with a gasp of pain. It was true: Their great strength in working together without anyone in either camp knowing about it was also a weakness. Because their regimes ostensibly opposed each other, because the Black Legion's nemesis was in reality its closest ally, all other potential rivals shied away, leaving the Black Legion to operate without interference. However, the actions both men were sometimes obliged to take for the sake of appearance caused a subconscious erosion of trust between them.

Icoupov could feel that their level of distrust had achieved its highest point yet, and he sought to defuse it. "Pyotr killed himself—and, in fact, I was only defending myself. Did you know he hired Arkadin to kill me? What would you have had me do?"

"There were other options," Sever said, "but your sense of justice is an eye for an eye. For a Muslim you have a great deal of the Jewish Old Testament in you. And now it appears that that very justice is about to be turned on you. Arkadin will kill you, if he can get his hands on you." Sever laughed. "I'm the only one who can save you now. Ironic, isn't it? You kill my son and now I have the power of life and death over you."

"We always had the power of life and death over each other." Icoupov still struggled to gain equality in the conversation. "There were casualties on both sides—regrettable but necessary. The more things change the more they stay the same. Except for Long Beach."

"There's the problem precisely," Sever said. "I've just come from interrogating Arthur Hauser, our man on the inside. As such, he was monitored by my people. Earlier today, he got cold feet; he met with a member of Black River. It took me some time to convince him to talk, but eventually he did. He told this woman—Moira Trevor—about the software flaw."

"So Black River knows."

"If they do," Sever said, "they aren't doing anything about it. Hauser also told me that they withdrew from NextGen; Black River isn't handling their security anymore."

"Who is?"

"It doesn't matter," Sever said. "The point is the tanker is less than a day away from the California coastline. My software engineer is aboard and in place. The question now is whether this Black River operative is going to act on her own."

Icoupov frowned. "Why should she? You know Black River as well as I do, they act as a team."

"True enough, but the Trevor woman should have been on to her next assignment by now; my people tell me that she's still in Munich."

"Maybe she's taking some downtime."

"And maybe," Sever said, "she's going to act on the information Hauser gave her."

They were nearing the airport, and with some difficulty Icoupov pointed. "The only way to find out is to check to see whether she's on the NextGen plane that's transshipping the coupling link to the terminal." He smiled thinly. "You seem surprised that I know so much. I have my spies as well, many of whom you know nothing about." He gasped in pain as he searched beneath his greatcoat. "It was texted to me, but I can't seem to find my cell." He looked around. "It must have fallen out of my pocket when your driver manhandled me into the car."

Sever waved a hand, ignoring the implied rebuke. "Never mind. Hauser gave me all the details, if we can get through security."

"I have people in Immigration you don't know about."

Sever's smile held a measure of the cruelty that was common to both of them. "My dear Semion, you have a use after all."

Arkadin found Icoupov's cell phone in the gutter where it had fallen as Icoupov had been bundled into the Mercedes. Controlling the urge to stomp it into splinters, he opened it to see whom Icoupov had called last, and noticed that the last incoming message was a text. Accessing it, he read the information on a NextGen jet due to take off in twenty minutes. He wondered why that would be important to Icoupov. Part of him wanted to go back to Devra, the same part that had balked at leaving her to go after Icoupov. But Kirsch's building was swarming with cops; the entire block was in the process of being cordoned off, so he didn't look back, tried not to think of her lying twisted on the floor, her blank eyes staring up at him even after she stopped breathing.

Do you love me, Leonid?

How had he answered her? Even now he couldn't remember. Her death was like a dream, something vivid that made no sense. Maybe it was a symbol, but of what he couldn't say.

Do you love me, Leonid?

It didn't matter, but he knew to her it did. He had lied then, surely he'd lied to ease the moments before her death, but the thought that he'd lied to her sent a knife through whatever passed for his heart.

He looked down at the text message and knew this was where he'd find Icoupov. Turning around, he walked back toward the cordoned-off area. Posing as a crime reporter from the *Abendzeitung* newspaper, he boldly accosted one of the junior uniformed police, asking him pointed questions about the shooting, stories of gunfire he'd gleaned from residents of the neighboring buildings. As he suspected, the cop was on guard duty and knew next to nothing. But that wasn't the point; he'd now gotten inside the cordon, leaning against one of the police cars as he conducted his phony and fruitless interview.

At length, the cop was called away, and he dismissed Arkadin, saying the commissioner would be holding a press conference at 16:00, at which time he would be free to ask all the questions he wanted. This left Arkadin alone, leaning against the fender. It didn't take him long to walk around the front of the vehicle, and when the medical examiner's van arrived—creating a perfect diversion—he opened the driver's-side door, ducked in behind the wheel. The keys were already in the ignition. He started the car and drove off. When he reached the autobahn, he put on the siren and drove at top speed toward the airport.

I won't have a problem getting you on board," Moira said as she turned off onto the four-lane approach to the freight terminal. She showed her NextGen ID at the guard booth, then drove on toward the parking lot outside the terminal. During the drive to the airport she'd thought long and hard about whether to tell Jason about whom she really worked for. Revealing that she was with Black River was a direct violation of her contract, and right now she prayed there'd be no reason to tell him.

After passing through security, Customs, and Immigration, they arrived on the tarmac and approached the 747. A set of mobile stairs rose up to the high passenger door, which stood open. On the far side of the plane, the truck from Kaller Steelworks Gesellschaft was parked, along with an airport hoist, which was lifting crated parts of the LNG coupling link into the jet's cargo area. The truck was obviously late, and the loading process was necessarily slow and tedious. Neither Kaller nor NextGen could afford an accident at this late stage.

Moira showed her NextGen ID to one of the crew members standing at the bottom of the stairs. He smiled and nodded, welcoming them aboard. Moira breathed a sigh of relief. Now all that stood between them and the Black Legion attack was the ten-hour flight to Long Beach.

But as they neared the top of the stairs, a figure appeared from the plane's interior. He stood in the doorway, staring down at her.

"Moira," Noah said, "what are you doing here? Why aren't you on your way to Damascus?"

* * *

Manfred Holger, Icoupov's man in Immigration, met them at the checkpoint to the freight terminals, got in the car with them, and they lurched forward. Icoupov had called him using Sever's cell phone. He'd been about to go off duty, but luckily for them had not yet changed out of his uniform.

"There's no problem." Holger spoke in the officious manner that had been drummed into him by his superiors. "All I have to do is check the recent immigration records to see if she's come through the system."

"Not good enough," Icoupov said. "She may be traveling under a pseudonym."

"All right then, I'll go on board and check everyone's passports." Holger was sitting in the front seat. Now he swiveled around to look at Icoupov. "If I find that this woman, Moira Trevor, is on board, what would you have me do?"

"Take her off the plane," Sever said at once.

Holger looked inquiringly at Icoupov, who nodded. Icoupov's face was gray again, and he was having more difficulty keeping the pain at bay.

"Bring her here to us," Sever said.

Holger had taken their diplomatic passports, passed them quickly through security. Now the Mercedes was sitting just off the tarmac. The 747 with the NextGen logo emblazoned on its sides and tail was at rest, still being loaded from the Kaller Steelworks truck. The driver had pulled up so that the truck shielded them from being seen by anyone boarding the plane or already inside it.

Holger nodded, got out of the Mercedes, and walked across the tarmac to the rolling stairs.

Kriminalpolizei," Arkadin said as he stopped the police car at the freight terminal checkpoint. "We have reason to believe a man who killed two people this afternoon has fled here."

The guards waved him past Customs and Immigration without asking for ID; the car itself was proof enough for them. As Arkadin rolled past the parking lot and onto the tarmac, he saw the jet, crates from the NextGen truck being hoisted into the cargo bay, and the black Mercedes idling some distance away from both. Recognizing the car at once, he nosed the police cruiser to a spot directly behind the Mercedes. For a moment, he sat behind the wheel, staring at the Mercedes as if the car itself were his enemy.

He could see the silhouettes of two male figures in the backseat; it wasn't a stretch for him to figure that one of them was Semion Icoupov. He wondered which of the handguns he had with him he should use to kill his former mentor: the SIG Sauer 9mm, the Luger, or the .22 SIG Mosquito. It all depended on what kind of damage he wanted to inflict and to what part of the body. He'd shot Stas Kuzin in the knees, the better to watch him suffer, but this was another time and, especially, another place. The airport was public space; the adjacent passenger terminal was crawling with security personnel. Just because he had been able to get this far as a member of the *kriminalpolizei,* he knew better than to overstep his luck. No, this kill needed to be quick and clean. All he desired was to look into Icoupov's eyes when he died, for him to know who'd ended his life and why.

Unlike the moment of Kuzin's demise, Arkadin was fully aware of this moment, keyed in to the importance of the son overtaking the father, of revenging himself for the psychological and physical advantages an adult takes with a child. That he hadn't, in fact, been a child when Mischa had sent Semion Icoupov to resurrect him never occurred to him. From the moment the two had met, he had always seen Icoupov as a father figure. He'd obeyed him as he would a father, had accepted his judgments, had swallowed whole his worldview, had been faithful to him. And now, for the sins Icoupov had visited on him, he was going to kill him.

* * *

When you didn't show for your scheduled flight, I had a hunch you'd show up here." Noah stared at her, completely ignoring Bourne. "I won't allow you on the plane, Moira. You're no longer a part of this."

"She still works for NextGen, doesn't she?" Bourne said.

"Who is this?" Noah said, keeping his eyes on her.

"My name is Jason Bourne."

A slow smile crept over Noah's face. "Moira, you didn't introduce us." He turned to Bourne, stuck out his hand. "Noah Petersen."

Bourne shook his hand. "Jason Bourne."

Keeping the same sly smile on his face, Noah said, "Do you know she lied to you, that she tried to recruit you to NextGen under false pretenses?"

His eyes flicked toward Moira, but he was disappointed to see neither shock nor outrage on her face.

"Why would she do that?" Bourne said.

"Because," Moira said, "like Noah here, I work for Black River, the private security firm. We were hired by NextGen to oversee security on the LNG terminal."

It was Noah who registered shock. "Moira, that's enough. You're in violation of your contract."

"It doesn't matter, Noah. I quit Black River half an hour ago. I've been made chief of security at NextGen, so in point of fact it's you who isn't welcome aboard this flight."

Noah stood rigid as stone, until Bourne took a step toward him. Then he backed away, descending the flight of rolling stairs. Halfway down, he turned to her. "Pity, Moira. I once had faith in you."

She shook her head. "The pity is that Black River has no conscience."

Noah looked at her for a moment then turned, clattered down the rest of the stairs, and stalked off across the tarmac without seeing the Mercedes or the police car behind it.

* * *

Because it would make the least noise, Arkadin decided on the Mosquito. Hand curled around the grips, he got out of the police car, stalked to the driver's side of the Mercedes. It was the driver—who doubtless doubled as a bodyguard—he had to dispense with first. Keeping his Mosquito out of sight, he rapped on the driver's window with a bare knuckle.

When the driver slid the glass down, Arkadin shoved the Mosquito in his face and pulled the trigger. The driver's head snapped back so hard the cervical vertebrae cracked. Pulling open the door, Arkadin shoved the corpse aside and knelt on the seat, facing the two men in the backseat. He recognized Sever from an old photograph when Icoupov had showed him the face of his enemy. He said, "Wrong time, wrong place," and shot Sever in the chest.

As he slumped over, Arkadin turned his attention to Icoupov. "You didn't think you could escape me, Father, did you?"

Icoupov—who, between the sudden attack and the unendurable pain in his shoulder, was going into delayed shock—said, "Why do you call me father? Your father died a long time ago, Leonid Danilovich."

"No," Arkadin said, "he sits here before me like a wounded bird."

"A wounded bird, yes." With great effort, Icoupov opened his greatcoat, the lining of which was sopping wet with his blood. "Your paramour shot me before I shot her in self-defense."

"This is not a court of law. What matters is that she's dead." Arkadin shoved the muzzle of the Mosquito under Icoupov's chin, and tilted upward. "And you, Father, are still alive."

"I don't understand you." Icoupov swallowed hard. "I never did."

"What was I ever to you, except a means to an end? I killed when you ordered me to. Why? Why did I do that, can you tell me?"

Icoupov said nothing, not knowing what he could say to save himself from judgment day.

"I did it because I was trained to do it," Arkadin said. "That's why you sent me to America, to Washington, not to cure me of my homicidal rages, as you said, but to harness them for your use."

"What of it?" Icoupov finally found his voice. "Of what other use were you? When I found you, you were close to taking your own life. I saved you, you ungrateful shit."

"You saved me so you could condemn me to this life, which, if I am any judge, is no life at all. I see I never really escaped Nizhny Tagil. I never will."

Icoupov smiled, believing he'd gotten the measure of his protégé. "You don't want to kill me, Leonid Danilovich. I'm your only friend. Without me you're nothing."

"Nothing is what I always was," Arkadin said as he pulled the trigger. "Now you're nothing, too."

Then he got out of the Mercedes, walked out on the tarmac to where the NextGen personnel were almost finished off-loading the crates. Without being seen, he climbed onto the hoist. There he hunkered down just beneath the operator's cab, and after the last crate had been stowed aboard, when the NextGen loaders were exiting the cargo hold via the interior stairwell, he leapt aboard the plane, scrambled behind a stack of crates, and sat down, patient as death, while the doors closed, locking him in.

B ourne saw the German official coming and suspected there was something wrong: An Immigration officer had no business interrogating them now. Then he recognized the man's face. He told Moira to get back inside the plane, then stood barring the door as the official mounted the stairs.

"I need to see everyone's passport," the officer said as he approached Bourne.

"Passport checks have already been made, *mein Herr*."

"Nevertheless, another security scan must be made now." The officer held out his hand. "Your passport, please. And then I will check the identity of everyone else aboard."

"You don't recognize me, *mein Herr*?"

"Please." The officer put his hand on the butt of his holstered

Luger. "You are obstructing official government business. Believe me, I will take you into custody unless you show me your passport and then move aside."

"Here's my passport, *mein Herr.*" Bourne opened it to the last page, pointed to a spot on the inside cover. "And here is where you placed an electronic tracking device."

"What accusation is this? You have no proof—"

Bourne produced the broken bug. "I don't believe you're here on official business. I think whoever instructed you to plant this on me is paying you to check these passports." Bourne gripped the officer's elbow. "Let's stroll over to the commandant of Immigration and ask them if they sent you here."

The officer drew himself up stiffly. "I'm not going anywhere with you. I have a job to do."

"So do I."

As Bourne dragged him down the rolling stairs, the officer went for his gun.

Bourne dug his fingers into the nerve bundle just above the man's elbow. "Draw it if you must," Bourne said, "but be prepared for the consequences."

The official's frosty aloofness finally cracked, revealing the fear beneath. His round face was pallid and sweating.

"What do you want of me?" he said as they walked along the tarmac.

"Take me to your real employer."

The officer had one last blast of bravado in him. "You don't really think he's here, do you?"

"As a matter of fact I wasn't sure until you said that. Now I know he is." Bourne shook the official. "Now take me to him."

Defeated, the officer nodded bleakly. No doubt, he was contemplating his immediate future. At a quickened pace, he led Bourne around behind the 747. At that moment, the NextGen truck rumbled to life, heading away from the plane, back the way it had come. That was when Bourne saw the black Mercedes and a police car directly behind it.

"Where did that police car come from?" The officer tore himself away from Bourne and broke into a run toward the parked cars.

Bourne, who saw the driver's-side doors on both vehicles standing open, was at the officer's heels. It was clear as they approached that no one was in the police car, but looking through the Mercedes's door, they saw the driver, slumped over. It looked as if he'd been kicked to the passenger's side of the seat.

Bourne pulled open the rear door, saw Icoupov with the top of his head blown off. Another man had fallen forward against the front seat rests. When Bourne pulled him gently backward, he saw that it was Dominic Specter—or Asher Sever—and everything became clear to him. Beneath the public enmity, the two men were secret allies. This answered many questions, not the least of which was why everyone Bourne had spoken to about the Black Legion had a different opinion about who was a member and who wasn't.

Sever looked small and frail, old beyond his years. He'd been shot in the chest with a .22. Bourne took his pulse, listened to his breathing. He was still alive.

"I'll call for an ambulance," the officer said.

"Do what you have to do," Bourne said as he scooped Sever up. "I'm taking this one with me."

He left the Immigration officer to deal with the mess, crossing the tarmac and mounting the rolling stairs.

"Let's get out of here," he said as he laid Sever down across three seats.

"What happened to him?" Moira said with a gasp. "Is he alive or dead?"

Bourne knelt beside his old mentor. "He's still breathing." As he began to rip off the professor's shirt, he said to Moira. "Get us moving, okay? We need to get out of here now."

Moira nodded. As she went up the aisle, she spoke to one of the flight attendants, who ran for the first-aid kit. The door to the cockpit was still open, and she gave the order for takeoff to the captain and the co-pilot.

Within five minutes the rolling stairs had been removed and the 747 was taxiing to the head of the runway. A moment later the control tower cleared it for takeoff. The brakes were let out, the engines revved up, and, with increasing velocity, the jet hurtled down the runway. Then it lifted off, its wheel retracted, flaps were adjusted, and it soared into a sky filled with the crimson and gold of the setting sun.

Forty-Three

IS HE DEAD?" Sever stared up at Bourne, who was cleaning his chest wound.

"You mean Semion?"

"Yes. Semion. Is he dead?"

"Icoupov and the driver, both."

Bourne held Sever down while the alcohol burned off everything that could cause the wound to suppurate. No organs had been struck, but the injury must be extremely painful.

Bourne applied an antiseptic cream from a tube in the first-aid kit. "Who shot you?"

"Arkadin." Tears of pain rolled down Sever's cheeks. "For some reason, he's gone completely insane. Maybe he was always insane. I thought so anyway. Allah, that hurts!" He took several shallow breaths before he went on. "He came out of nowhere. The driver said, 'A police car has pulled up behind us.' The next thing I know he's rolling down the window and a gun is fired point-blank in his face. Neither Semion nor I had time to think. There was Arkadin inside the car. He shot me, but I'm certain it was Semion he'd come for."

Intuiting what must have happened in Kirsch's apartment, Bourne said, "Icoupov killed his woman, Devra."

Sever squeezed his eyes shut. He was having trouble breathing normally. "So what? Arkadin never cared what happened to his women."

"He cared about this one," Bourne said, applying a bandage.

Sever stared up at Bourne with an expression of disbelief. "The odd thing was, I think I heard him call Semion 'Father.' Semion didn't understand."

"And now he never will."

"Stop your fussing; let me die, dammit!" Sever said crossly. "It doesn't matter now whether I live or die."

Bourne finished up.

"What's done is done. Fate has been sealed; there's nothing you or anyone else can do to change it."

Bourne sat on a seat opposite Sever. He was aware of Moira standing to one side, watching and listening. The professor's betrayal only went to prove that you were never safe when you let personal feelings into your life.

"Jason." Sever's voice was weaker. "I never meant to deceive you."

"Yes, you did, Professor, that's all you know how to do."

"I came to look upon you as a son."

"Like Icoupov looked upon Arkadin."

With an effort, Sever shook his head. "Arkadin is insane. Perhaps they both were, perhaps their shared insanity is what drew them together."

Bourne sat forward, "Let me ask you a question, Professor. Do you think you're sane?"

"Of course I'm sane."

Sever's eyes held steady on Bourne's, a challenge still, at this late stage.

For a moment, Bourne did nothing, then he rose and, together with Moira, walked forward toward the cockpit.

"It's a long flight," she said softly, "and you need your rest."

"We both do."

They sat next to each other, silent for a long time. Occasionally, they heard Sever utter a soft moan. Otherwise, the drone of the engines conspired to lull them to sleep.

It was freezing in the baggage hold, but Arkadin didn't mind. The Nizhny Tagil winters had been brutal. It was during one of those winters that Mischa Tarkanian had found him, hiding out from the remnants of Stas Kuzin's regime. Mischa, hard as a knife blade, had the heart of a poet. He told stories that were beautiful enough to be poems. Arkadin had been enchanted, if such a word could be ascribed to him. Mischa's talent for storytelling had the power to take Arkadin far away from Nizhny Tagil, and when Mischa smuggled him out past the inner ring of smokestacks, past the outer ring of high-security prisons, his stories took Arkadin to places beyond Moscow, to lands beyond Russia. The stories gave Arkadin his first inkling of the world at large.

As he sat now, his back against a crate, knees drawn up to his chest in order to conserve warmth, he had good cause to think of Mischa. Icoupov had paid for killing Devra, now Bourne must pay for killing Mischa. But not just yet, Arkadin brooded, though his blood called out for revenge. If he killed Bourne now, Icoupov's plan would succeed, and he couldn't allow that, otherwise his revenge against him would be incomplete.

Arkadin put his head back against the edge of the crate and closed his eyes. Revenge had become like one of Mischa's poems, its meaning flowering open to surround him with a kind of ethereal beauty, the only form of beauty that registered on him, the only beauty that lasted. It was the glimpse of that promised beauty, the very prospect of it, that allowed him to sit patiently, curled between crates, waiting for his moment of revenge, his moment of inestimable beauty.

* * *

Bourne dreamed of the hell known as Nizhny Tagil as if he'd been born there, and when he awoke he knew Arkadin was near. Opening his eyes, he saw Moira staring at him.

"What do you feel about the professor?" she said, by which he suspected she meant, *What do you feel about me?*

"I think the years of obsession have driven him insane. I don't think he knows good from evil, right from wrong."

"Is that why you didn't ask him why he embarked on this path to destruction?"

"In a way," Bourne said. "Whatever his answer would have been it wouldn't have made sense to us."

"Fanatics never make sense," she said. "That's why they're so difficult to counteract. A rational response, which is always our choice, is rarely effective." She cocked her head. "He betrayed you, Jason. He nurtured your belief in him, and played on it."

"If you climb on a scorpion's back you've got to expect to get stung."

"Don't you have a desire for revenge?"

"Maybe I should I smother him in his sleep, or shoot him to death as Arkadin did to Semion Icoupov. Do you really expect that to make me feel better? I'll exact my revenge by stopping the Black Legion's attack."

"You sound so rational."

"I don't feel rational, Moira."

She took his meaning, and blood rushed to her cheeks. "I may have lied to you, Jason, but I didn't betray you. I could never do that." She engaged his eyes. "There were so many times in the last week when I ached to tell you, but I had a duty to Black River."

"Duty is something I understand, Moira."

"Understanding is one thing, but will you forgive me?"

He put out his hand. "You aren't a scorpion," he said. "It's not in your nature."

She took his hand in hers, brought it up to her mouth, and pressed it to her cheek.

At that moment they heard Sever cry out, and they rose, went down the aisle to where he lay curled on his side like a small child afraid of the dark. Bourne knelt down, drew Sever gently onto his back to keep pressure off the wound.

The professor stared at Bourne, then, as Moira spoke to him, at her.

"Why did you do it?" Moira said. "Why attack the country you'd adopted as your own."

Sever could not catch his breath. He swallowed convulsively. "You'd never understand."

"Why don't you try me?"

Sever closed his eyes, as if to better visualize each word as it emerged from his mouth. "The Muslim sect I belong to, that Semion belonged to, is very old—ancient even. It had its beginnings in North Africa." He paused already out of breath. "Our sect is very strict, we believe in a fundamentalism so devout it cannot be conveyed to infidels by any means. But I can tell you this: We cannot live in the modern world because the modern world violates every one of our laws. Therefore, it must be destroyed.

"Nevertheless . . ." He licked his lips, and Bourne poured out some water, lifted his head, and allowed him to drink his fill. When he was finished, he continued. "I should never have tried to use you, Jason. Over the years there have been many disagreements between Semion and myself—this was the latest, the one that broke the proverbial camel's back. He said you'd be trouble, and he was right. I thought I could manufacture a reality, that I could use you to convince the American security agencies we were going to attack New York City." He emitted a dry, little laugh. "I lost sight of the central tenet of life, that reality can't be controlled, it's too random, too chaotic. So you see it was I who was on a fool's errand, Jason, not you."

"Professor, it's all over," Moira said. "We won't let the tanker dock until we have the software patched."

Sever smiled. "A good idea, but it will avail you nothing. Do you know the damage that much liquid natural gas will do? Five square miles of devastation, thousands killed, America's corrupt, greedy way of life delivered the hammer blow Semion and I have been dreaming of for decades. It's my one great calling in this life. The loss of human life and physical destruction is icing on the cake."

He paused to catch his breath, which was shallower and more ragged than ever. "When the nation's largest port is incinerated, America's economy will go with it. Almost half your imports will dry up. There'll be widespread shortages of goods and food, companies will collapse, the stock exchanges will plummet, wholesale panic will ensue."

"How many of your men are on board?" Bourne said.

Sever smiled weakly. "I love you like a son, Jason."

"You let your own son be killed," Bourne said.

"Sacrificed, Jason. There's a difference."

"Not to him." Bourne returned to his agenda. "How many men, Professor?"

"One, only one."

"One man can't take over the tanker," Moira said.

The smile played around his lips, even as his eyes closed, his consciousness fading. "If man hadn't made machines to do his work . . ."

Moira turned to Bourne. "What does that mean?"

Bourne shook the old man's shoulder, but he'd slipped into deep unconsciousness.

Moira checked his eyes, his forehead, his carotid artery. "Without intravenous antibiotics I doubt he'll make it." She looked at Bourne. "We're near enough New York City now. We could touch down there, have an ambulance waiting—"

"There's no time," Bourne said.

"I know there's no time." Moira took his arm. "But I want to give you the choice."

Bourne stared down at his mentor's face, lined and seamed, far older in sleep, as if it had imploded. "He'll make it on his own, or he won't."

He turned away, Moira at his side, and he said, "Call NextGen. This is what I need."

Forty-Four

THE TANKER *Moon of Hormuz,* plowed through the Pacific no more than an hour out of Long Beach harbor. The captain, a veteran named Sultan, had gotten word that the LNG terminal was online and ready to receive its inaugural shipment of liquid natural gas. With the current state of the world's economies, the LNG had become even more precious; from the time the *Moon of Hormuz* had left Algeria its cargo had increased in value by over 30 percent.

The tanker, twelve stories high and as large as a village, held thirty-three million gallons of LNG cooled to a temperature of −260 degrees. That translated into the energy equivalent of twenty billion gallons of natural gas. The ship required five miles to come to a stop, and because of the shape of its hull and the containers on deck Sultan's view ahead was blocked for three-quarters of a mile. The tanker had been steaming at twenty knots, but three hours ago he'd ordered the engines into reverse. Well within five miles of the terminal, the ship was down to six knots of speed and still decelerating.

Within the five-mile radius to shore his nerves became a jittery flame, the nightmare of Armageddon always with him, because a disaster aboard the *Moon of Hormuz* would be just that. If the tanks spilled into the water, the resulting fire would be five miles in diameter. For another five miles beyond that thermal radiation would burn any human to a crisp.

But those scenarios were just that: nightmares. In ten years there'd never been even a minor incident aboard his ship, and there never would be, if he had anything to say about it. He was just thinking about how fine the weather was, and how much he was going to enjoy his ten days on the beach with a friend in Malibu, when the radio officer handed him a message from NextGen. He was to expect a helicopter in fifteen minutes; he was to give its passengers—Moira Trevor and Jason Bourne—any and all help they requested. That was surprising enough, but he bristled at the last sentence: He was to take orders from them until the *Moon of Hormuz* was safely docked at the terminal.

When the doors to the cargo bay were opened, Arkadin was ready, crouched behind one of the containers. As the airport maintenance team clambered aboard, he edged out, then called from the shadows for one of them to help him. When the man complied, Arkadin broke his neck, dragged him into the deepest shadows of the cargo bay, away from the NextGen containers. He stripped and donned the man's maintenance uniform. Then he stepped over to the work area, keeping the ID tag clipped to it out of full view so that no one could that see that his face didn't match that on the tag. Not that it mattered: These people were here to get the cargo off-loaded and onto the waiting NextGen trucks as quickly as possible. It never occurred to any of them that there might be an imposter among them.

In this way, Arkadin worked his way to the open bay doors, onto the loading lifts with the container. He hopped onto the tarmac as the cargo was being loaded onto the truck, then ducked away beneath the wing. Finding himself alone on the opposite side of the aircraft, he walked away at a brisk, business-like clip. No one challenged him, no one even gave him a second look, because he moved with the authority of someone who belonged there. That was the secret of assuming a different identity, even temporarily—people's eyes either ignored or accepted what looked correct to them.

As he went, he breathed deeply of the clear, salt air, the freshening breeze whipping his pants against his legs. He felt free of all the leashes that had bound him to the earth: Stas Kuzin, Marlene, Gala, Icoupov, they were all gone now. The sea beckoned him and he was coming.

NextGen had its own small terminal on the freight side of the Long Beach airport. Moira had radioed ahead to NextGen headquarters, giving them a heads-up and asking for a helicopter to be ready to take her and Bourne to the tanker.

Arkadin beat Bourne to the NextGen terminal. Hurrying now, he used the badge to open the door to the restricted areas. Out on the tarmac he saw the helicopter right away. The pilot was talking to a maintenance man. The moment they both squatted down, examining one of the runners, Arkadin pulled his cap low on his forehead, walked briskly around to the far side of the helicopter, and made himself busy there.

He saw Bourne and Moira emerge from the NextGen terminal. They paused for a moment and he could hear their argument about whether or not she should come, but they must have had it before, because the fight was hammered out in brief, staccato bursts, like shorthand.

"Face facts, Jason. I work for NextGen; without me you won't get on that copter."

Bourne turned away, and for an instant Arkadin felt a foreboding, as if Bourne had seen him. Then Bourne turned back to Moira, and together they hurried across the tarmac.

Bourne climbed in on the pilot's side, while Moira headed to Arkadin's side of the copter. With a professional smile, he held out a hand, helping her up into the cockpit. He saw the maintenance man about to come across, but waved him off. Looking up at Moira through the curved Perspex door he thought of Devra and felt a lurch in his chest, as if her bleeding head had fallen against him. He waved at Moira, and she lifted her hand in return.

The rotors began to swirl, the maintenance man signaled for Arkadin to come away; Arkadin gave him the thumbs-up sign. Faster and faster the rotors spun, and the copter's frame began to shudder. Just before it lifted off, Arkadin climbed onto the runner and curled himself into a ball as they swung out over the Pacific, buffeted by a stiff onshore wind.

The tanker loomed large in the passengers' vision as the copter sped toward it at top speed. Only one other boat could be seen, a commercial fishing vessel several miles away beyond the security limits imposed by the Coast Guard and Homeland Security. Bourne, who was sitting directly behind the pilot, saw that he was working to keep the copter's pitch at the correct angle.

"Is everything okay?" he shouted over the roar of the rotors.

The pilot pointed to one of the gauges. "There's a small anomaly in the pitch; probably the wind, it's gusting up quite a bit."

But Bourne wasn't so sure. The anomaly was constant, whereas the wind wasn't. He had an intuition what—or, more accurately, who—was causing the problem.

"I think we have a stowaway," Bourne said to the pilot. "Take it in low when you get to the tanker. Skim the tops of the containers."

"What?" The pilot shook his head. "Too dangerous."

"Then I'll take a look myself." Unstrapping himself, Bourne crept toward the door.

"Okay, okay!" the pilot shouted. "Just get back in your seat!"

They were almost at the bow of the tanker now. It was unbelievably big, a city lumbering through the Pacific swells.

"Hang on!" the pilot shouted as he took them down far more quickly than normal. They could see members of the crew racing across the deck, and someone—no doubt the captain—emerged from the wheelhouse near the stern. Someone was shouting to pull up; the tops of the containers were coming at them with frightening speed. Just before they skimmed the top of the nearest container, the copter rocked slightly.

"The anomaly's gone," the pilot said.

"Stay here," Bourne shouted to Moira. "Whatever happens stay on board." Then he gripped the weapon lying astride his knees, opened the door and, as she screamed his name, jumped out of the copter.

He landed after Arkadin, who had already leapt down onto the deck and was scuttling between containers. Crew members rushed toward them both; Bourne had no idea whether one of them was Sever's software engineer, but he raised a hunting crossbow and they stopped in their tracks. Knowing that firing a gun would be tantamount to suicide on a tanker full of liquid natural gas, he'd had Moira ask NextGen to have two crossbows in the copter. How they procured them so quickly was anyone's guess, but a corporation of NextGen's size could get just about anything at a moment's notice.

Behind him, the chopper set down on the part of the foredeck that had been cleared, and cut the engines. Doubled over to avoid the rotors, he opened the copter door and looked up at Moira. "Arkadin is here somewhere. Please stay out of the way."

"I need to report to the captain. I can take care of myself." She, too, was cradling a crossbow. "What does Arkadin want?"

"Me. I killed his friend. It doesn't matter to him that it was in self-defense."

"I can help, Jason. If we work together, two are better than one."

He shook his head. "Not in this case. Besides, you see how slowly the tanker is moving; its screws are in reverse. It's within the five-mile limit. For every foot we travel forward, the danger to thousands of lives and the port of Long Beach itself grows exponentially."

She nodded stiffly, stepped down, and hurried along the deck to where the captain stood, awaiting her orders.

Bourne turned, moving cautiously among the containers, in the direction he'd glimpsed Arkadin heading. Moving along the aisles was like walking down the canyons of Manhattan. Wind howled as it cut across corners, magnified, racing down the aisles as if they were tunnels.

Just before he reached the end of the first set of containers, he heard Arkadin's voice, speaking to him in Russian.

"There isn't much time."

Bourne stood still, trying to determine where the voice was coming from. "What d'you know about it, Arkadin?"

"Why d'you think I'm here?"

"I killed Mischa Tarkanian, now you kill me. Isn't that how you defined it back in Egon Kirsch's apartment?"

"Listen to me, Bourne, if that's what I wanted I could have killed you anytime while you and the woman slept aboard the NextGen 747."

Bourne's blood ran cold. "Why didn't you?"

"Listen to me, Bourne, Semion Icoupov, who saved me, whom I trusted, shot my woman to death."

"Yes, that's why you killed him."

"Do you begrudge me my revenge?"

Bourne said nothing, thinking of what he would do to Arkadin if he hurt Moira.

"You don't have to say anything, Bourne, I already know the answer."

Bourne turned. The voice appeared to have shifted. Where the hell was he hiding?

"But as I said we have little time to find Icoupov's man on board."

"It's Sever's man, actually," Bourne said.

Arkadin laughed. "Do you think that matters? They were in bed together. All the time they posed as bitter enemies they were plotting this disaster. I want to stop it—I *have* to stop it, or my revenge on Icoupov will be incomplete."

"I don't believe you."

"Listen, Bourne, you know we haven't much time. I've avenged myself on the father, but this plan is his child. He and Sever gave birth

to it, fed it, nurtured it through its infancy, through its adolescent growing pains. Now each moment brings this floating supernova closer to
the moment of destruction those two madmen envisioned."

The voice moved again. "Is that what you want, Bourne? Of course
not. Then let's join together to find Sever's man."

Bourne hesitated. He didn't trust Arkadin, and yet he had to trust
him. He examined the situation from all sides and concluded that the
only way to play it was to move forward. "He's a software engineer,"
he said.

Arkadin appeared, climbing down from the top of one of the containers. For a moment, the two men stood facing each other, and once
again Bourne felt the dislocating sensation of looking in a mirror. When
he stared into Arkadin's eyes, he didn't see the madness the professor
spoke of; he saw himself, a heart of darkness and pain beyond understanding.

"Sever told me there was only one man, but he also said we wouldn't
find him, and even if we did it wouldn't matter."

Arkadin frowned, giving him the canny, feral appearance of a wolf.
"What did he mean?"

"I'm not sure." He turned, walking down the deck toward the crew
members who had cleared the space for the copter to land. "What we're
looking for," he said as Arkadin fell into step beside him, "is a tattoo
specific to the Black Legion."

"The wheel of horses with the death's head center." Arkadin nodded. "I've seen it."

"It's on the inside of the elbow."

"We could kill them all." Arkadin laughed. "But I guess that would
offend something inside you."

One by one, the two men examined the arms of the eight crewmen
on deck, but found no tattoo. By the time they reached the wheelhouse,
the tanker was within two miles of the terminal. It was barely moving.
Four tugboats had hove to and were waiting at the one-mile limit to tow
the tanker the rest of the way in.

The captain was a swarthy individual with a face that looked like it had been deeply etched by acid rather than the wind and the sun. "As I was telling Ms. Trevor, there are seven more crewmen, mostly involved in engine room duties. Then there's my first mate here, the communications officer, and the ship's doctor, he's in sick bay, tending to a crewman who fell ill two days out of Algeria. Oh, yes, and the cook."

Bourne and Arkadin glanced at each other. The radioman seemed the logical choice, but when the captain summoned him he, too, was without the Black Legion tattoo. So were the captain and his first mate.

"The engine room," Bourne said.

At his captain's orders, the first mate led them out onto the deck, then down the starboard companionway into the bowels of the ship, reaching the enormous engine room at last. Five men were hard at work, their faces and arms filthy with a coating of grease and grime. As the first mate instructed them, they held out their arms, but as Bourne reached the third in line, the fourth man looked at them beneath half-closed lids before he bolted.

Bourne went after him while Arkadin circled, snaking through the oily city of grinding machinery. He eluded Bourne once but then, rounding a corner, Bourne spotted him near the line of gigantic Hyundai diesel engines, specifically designed to power the world's fleet of LNG tankers. He was trying to furtively shove a small box between the structural struts of the engine, but Arkadin, coming up behind him, grabbed for his wrist. The crewman jerked away, brought the box back toward him, and was about to thumb a button on it when Bourne kicked it out of his hand. The box went flying, and Arkadin dived after it.

"Careful," the crewman said as Bourne grabbed hold of him. He ignored Bourne, was staring at the box Arkadin brought back to them. "You hold the whole world in your hand."

Meanwhile Bourne pushed up his shirtsleeve. The man's arm was smeared with grease, deliberately so, it seemed, because when Bourne took a rag and wiped it off, the Black Legion tattoo appeared on the inside of his left elbow.

The man seemed totally unconcerned. His entire being was focused on the box that Arkadin was holding. "That will blow up everything," he said, and made a lunge toward it. Bourne jerked him back with a stranglehold.

"Let's get him back up to the captain," Bourne said to the first mate. That's when he saw the box up close. He took it out of Arkadin's hand.

"Careful!" the crewman cried. "One slight jar and you'll set it off."

But Bourne wasn't so sure. The crewman was being too vocal with his warnings. Wouldn't he want the ship to blow now that it had been boarded by Sever's enemies? When he turned the box over, he saw that the seam between the bottom and the side was ragged.

"What are you doing? Are you crazy?" The crewman was so agitated that Arkadin slapped him on the side of the head in order to silence him.

Inserting his fingernail into the seam, Bourne pried the box apart. There was nothing inside. It was a dummy.

Moira found it impossible to stay in one place. Her nerves were stretched to the breaking point. The tanker was on the verge of meeting up with the tugboats; they were only a mile from shore. If the tanks went, the devastation to both human life and the country's economy would be catastrophic. She felt useless, a third wheel hanging around while the two men did their hunting.

Exiting the wheelhouse, she went belowdecks, looking for the engine room. Smelling food, she poked her head into the galley. A large Algerian was sitting at the stainless-steel mess table, reading a two-week-old Arabic newspaper.

He looked up, gesturing at the paper. "It gets old the fifteenth time through, but when you're at sea what can you do?"

His burly arms were bare to the shoulders. They bore tattoos of a star, a crescent, and a cross, but not the Black Legion's insignia. Following the directions he gave her, she found the infirmary three decks below. Inside, a slim Muslim was sitting at a small desk built into one of the bulkheads. In the opposite bulkhead were two berths, one of them filled with the patient who had fallen ill. The doctor murmured a traditional Muslim greeting as he turned away from his laptop computer to face her. He frowned deeply when he saw the crossbow in her hands.

"Is that really necessary," he said, "or even wise?"

"I'd like to speak with your patient," Moira said, ignoring him.

"I'm afraid that's impossible." The doctor smiled that smile only doctors can. "He's been sedated."

"What's wrong with him?"

The doctor gestured at the laptop. "I'm still trying to find out. He's been subject to seizures, but so far I can't find the pathology."

"We're near Long Beach, you'll get help then," she said. "I just need to see the insides of his elbows."

The doctor's eyebrows rose. "I beg your pardon?"

"I need to see whether he's got a tattoo."

"They all have tattoos, these sailors." The doctor shrugged. "But go ahead. You won't disturb him."

Moira approached the lower berth, bending over to pull the thin blanket back from the patient's arm. As she did so, the doctor stepped forward and struck her a blow on the back of her head. She fell forward and cracked her jaw on the metal frame of the bunk. The pain pulled her rudely back from a precipice of blackness, and, groaning, she managed to roll over. The copper-sweet taste of blood was in her mouth and she fought against wave after wave of dizziness. Dimly she saw the doctor bent over his laptop, his fingers racing over the keys, and she felt a ball of ice form in her belly.

He's going to kill us all. With this thought reverberating in her head, she grabbed the crossbow off the floor where she'd dropped it. She barely had time to aim, but she was close enough not to have to be accurate. She breathed a prayer as she let fly.

The doctor arched up as the bolt pierced his spine. He staggered backward, toward where Moira sat, braced against the berth frame. His arms extended, his fingers clawing for the keyboard, and Moira rose, swung the crossbow into the back of his head. His blood spattered like rain over her face and hands, the desk, and the laptop's keyboard.

* * *

Bourne found her on the floor of the infirmary, cradling the computer in her lap. When he came in, she looked up at him and said, "I don't know what he did. I'm afraid to shut it off."

"Are you all right?"

She nodded. "The ship's doctor was Sever's man."

"So I see," he said as he stepped over the corpse. "I didn't believe him when he told me he had only one man on board. It would be like him to have a backup."

He knelt down, examined the back of her head. "It's superficial. Did you black out?"

"I don't think so, no."

He took a large gauze pad from the supply cabinet, doused it with alcohol. "Ready?" He placed it against the back of her head, where her hair was plastered down with blood. She moaned a little through gritted teeth.

"Can you hold it in place for a minute?"

She nodded, and gently Bourne lifted the laptop into his arms. There was a software program running, that much was clear. Two radio buttons on the screen were blinking, one yellow, the other red. On the other side of the screen was a green radio button, which wasn't blinking.

Bourne breathed a sigh of relief. "He brought up the program, but you got to him before he could activate it."

"Thank God," she said. "Where Arkadin?"

"I don't know. When the captain told me you'd gone below I took off after you."

"Jason, you don't think . . ."

Putting the computer aside, he helped her to her feet. "Let's get you back up to the captain so you can give him the good news."

There was a fearful look on his face. "And you?"

He handed her the laptop. "Go to the wheelhouse and stay there. And Moira, this time I really mean it."

With the crossbow in one hand, he stepped into the passageway, looked right and left. "All right. Go. Go!"

Arkadin had returned to Nizhny Tagil. Down in the engine room, surrounded by steel and iron, he realized that no matter what had happened to him, no matter where he'd gone, he'd never been able to escape the prison of his youth. Part of him was still in the brothel he and Stas Kuzin had owned, part of him still stalked the nighttime streets, abducting young girls, their pale, fearful faces turned toward him as deer turn toward headlights. But what they'd needed from him he couldn't—or wouldn't—give them. Instead, he'd sent them to their deaths in the quicklime pit Kuzin's regime had dug amid the firs and the weeping hemlocks. Many snows had passed since he'd dragged Yelena from the rats and the quicklime, but the pit remained in his memory, vivid as a blaze of fire. If only he could have his memory wiped clean.

He started at the sound of Stas Kuzin screaming at him. *What about all* your *victims?*

But it was Bourne, descending the steel companionway to the engine room. "It's over, Arkadin. The disaster has been averted."

Arkadin nodded, but inside he knew better: The disaster had already occurred, and it was too late to stop its consequences. As he walked toward Bourne he tried to fix him in his mind, but he seemed to morph, like an image seen through a prism.

When he was within arm's length of him, he said, "Is it true what Sever told Icoupov, that you have no memory beyond a certain point in time?"

Bourne nodded. "It's true. I can't remember most of my life."

Arkadin felt a terrible pain, as if the very fabric of his soul was being torn apart. With an inchoate cry, he flicked open his switchblade, lunged forward, aiming for Bourne's belly.

Turning sideways, Bourne grabbed his wrist, began to turn it in an attempt to get Arkadin to drop the weapon. Arkadin struck out with his other hand, but Bourne blocked it with his forearm. In doing so, the crossbow clattered to the deck. Arkadin kicked it into the shadows.

"It doesn't have to be this way," Bourne said. "There's no reason for us to be enemies."

"There's every reason." Arkadin broke away, tried another attack, which Bourne countered. "Don't you see it? We're the same, you and me. The two of us can't exist in the same world. One of us will kill the other."

Bourne stared into Arkadin's eyes, and even though his words were those of a madmen Bourne saw no madness in them. Only a despair beyond description, and an unyielding will for revenge. In a way, Arkadin was right. Revenge was all he had now, all he lived for. With Tarkanian and Devra gone, the only meaning life had for him lay in avenging their deaths. There was nothing Bourne could say to sway him; that was a rational response to an irrational impulse. It was true, the two of them couldn't exist in the same world.

At that moment Arkadin feinted right with his knife, drove left with his fist, rocking Bourne back onto his heels. At once he stabbed out with the switchblade, burying it in the meat of Bourne's left thigh. Bourne grunted, fought the buckling of his knee, and Arkadin jammed his boot into Bourne's wounded thigh. Blood spurted, and Bourne fell. Arkadin jumped on him, using his fist to pummel Bourne's face when Bourne blocked his knife stabs.

Bourne knew he couldn't take much more of this. Arkadin's desire for revenge had filled him with an inhuman strength. Bourne, fighting for his very life, managed to counterpunch long enough to roll out from under Arkadin. Then he was up and running in an ungainly limp to the companionway.

Arkadin reached up for him as he was half a dozen rungs off the engine room deck. Bourne kicked out with his bad leg, surprising Arkadin, catching him under the chin. As he fell back, Bourne scrambled up the rungs as fast as he could. His left leg was on fire, and he was trailing blood as the wounded muscle was forced to work overtime.

Gaining the next deck, he continued up the companionway, up and

up, until he came to the first level belowdecks, which according to
Moira was where the galley was. Finding it, he raced in, grabbed two
knives and a glass saltshaker. Stuffing the shaker into his pocket, he
wielded the knives as Arkadin loomed in the doorway.

They fought with their knives, but Bourne's unwieldy carving knives
were no match for Arkadin's slender-bladed switchblade, and Bourne
was cut again, this time in the chest. He kicked Arkadin in the face,
dropped his knives in order to wrest the switchblade out of Arkadin's
hand, to no avail. Arkadin stabbed at him again and Bourne nearly suffered a punctured liver. He backed away, then ran out the doorway, up
the last companionway to the open deck.

The tanker was at a near stop. The captain was busy coordinating
the hookups with the tugboats that would bring it the final distance to
the LNG terminal. Bourne couldn't see Moira, which was a blessing.
He didn't want her anywhere near Arkadin.

Bourne, heading for the sanctuary of the container city, was bowled
over as Arkadin leapt on him. Locked together, they rolled over and over
until they fetched up against the port railing. The sea was far below
them, churning against the tanker's hull. One of the tugs signaled with
its horn as it came alongside, and Arkadin stiffened. To him it was the
siren sounding an escape from one of Nizhny Tagil's prisons. He saw
the black skies, tasted the sulfur smoke in his lungs. He saw Stas
Kuzin's monstrous face, felt Marlene's head between his ankles beneath the water, heard the terrible reports when Semion Icoupov shot
Devra.

He screamed like a tiger, pulling Bourne to his feet, pummeling him
over and over until he was bent back over the railing. In that moment,
Bourne knew that he was going to die as he had been born, falling over
the side of a ship, lost in the depth of the sea, and only by the grace of
God being brought in to a fishing boat with their catch. His face was
bloody and swollen, his arms felt like lead weights, he was going over.

Then, at the last instant, he pulled the shaker from his pocket,
broke it against the rail, and threw the salt in Arkadin's eyes. Arkadin
bellowed in shock and pain, his hand flew up reflexively, and Bourne

snatched the switchblade from him. Blinded, Arkadin still fought on, and he grasped the blade. With a superhuman effort, not caring that the edges cut into his fingers, he wrested the switchblade away from Bourne. Bourne heaved him backward. But Arkadin had control of the knife now, he had partial vision back through his tearing eyes, and he ran at Bourne with his head tucked into his shoulders, all his weight and determination behind the charge.

Bourne had one chance. Stepping into the charge, he ignored the knife, grabbed Arkadin by his uniform jacket and, using his own momentum against him, pivoted from the hip as he swung him around and up. Arkadin's thighs struck the railing, his upper body continuing its flight, so that he toppled head-over-heels over the side.

Falling, falling, falling . . . the equivalent of twelve stories, before plunging beneath the waves.

Forty-Five

I NEED A VACATION, "Moira said. "I'm thinking Bali would do me quite well."

She and Bourne were in the NextGen clinic in one of the campus buildings that overlooked the Pacific. The *Moon of Hormuz* had successfully docked at the LNG terminal and the cargo of the highly compressed liquid was being piped from the tanker to onshore containers where it would be slowly warmed, expanding to six hundred times its present volume so it could be used by individual consumers and utility and business power plants. The laptop had been turned over to the NextGen IT depártment, so the software could be parsed and permanently shut down. The grateful CEO of NextGen had just left the clinic, after promoting Moira to president of the security division and offering Bourne a highly lucrative consulting position with the firm. Bourne had phoned Soraya, each of them bringing the other up to date. He'd given her the address of Sever's house, detailing the clandestine operation it housed.

"I wish I knew what a vacation felt like," Bourne said when he'd finished the call.

"Well . . ." Moira smiled at him. "You've only to ask."

Bourne considered for a long time. Vacations were something he'd never contemplated, but if ever there was a time to take one, he thought, this was it. He looked back at her and nodded.

Her smile broadened. "I'll have NextGen make all the arrangements. How long do you want to go for?"

"How long?" Bourne said. "Right now, I'll take forever."

On his way to the airport, Bourne stopped at the Long Beach Memorial Medical Center, where Professor Sever had been admitted. Moira, who had declined to come up with him, was waiting for him in the chauffeured car NextGen had hired for them. They'd put Sever in a private room on the fifth floor. The room was deathly still, except for the respirator. The professor had sunk deeper into a coma and was now unable to breathe on his own. A thick tube emerged from his throat, snaking to the respirator that wheezed like an asthmatic. Other, smaller tubes were needled into Sever's arms. A catheter attached to a plastic bladder hooked to the side of the bed caught his urine. His bluish eyelids were so thin Bourne thought he could see his pupils beneath them.

Standing beside his former mentor he found that he had nothing to say. He wondered why he'd felt compelled to come here. Maybe it was simply to look once more on the face of evil. Arkadin was a killer, pure and simple, but this man had made himself brick by brick into a liar and a deceiver. And yet he looked so frail, so helpless now, it was difficult to believe he was the mastermind of the monstrous plan to incinerate much of Long Beach. Because, as he'd said, his sect couldn't live in the modern world, it was bound to destroy it. Was that the real reason, or had Sever once again lied to him? He'd never know now.

He was abruptly nauseated by being in Sever's presence, but as he turned away a small dapper man came in, allowing the door to close at his back.

"Jason Bourne?" When Bourne nodded, the man said, "My name is Frederick Willard."

"Soraya told me about you," Bourne said. "Well done, Willard."

"Thank you, sir."

"Please don't call me sir."

Willard gave a small, deprecating smile. "Pardon me, my training is so ingrained in me that's all I am now." He glanced over at Sever. "Do you think he'll live?"

"He's alive now," Bourne said, "but I wouldn't call it living."

Willard nodded, though he seemed not at all interested in the disposition of the figure lying in the bed.

"I have a car waiting downstairs," Bourne said.

"As it happens, so do I." Willard smiled, but there was something sad about it. "I know that you worked for Treadstone."

"Not Treadstone," Bourne said, "Alex Conklin."

"I worked for Conklin, too, many years ago. It's one and the same, Mr. Bourne."

Bourne felt impatience now. He was eager to join Moira, to see the sherbet skies of Bali.

"You see, I know all of Treadstone's secrets—all of them. This is something only you and I know, Mr. Bourne."

A nurse came in on her silent white shoes, checked all of Sever's feeds, scribbled on his chart, then left them alone again.

"Mr. Bourne, I thought long and hard about whether I should come here, to tell you . . ." He cleared his throat. "You see, the man you fought on the tanker, the Russian who went overboard."

"Arkadin."

"Leonid Danilovich Arkadin, yes." Willard's eyes met Bourne's, and something inside him winced away. "He was Treadstone."

"What?" Bourne couldn't believe what he was hearing. "Arkadin was Treadstone?"

Willard nodded. "Before you—in fact, he was Conklin's pupil just before you."

"But what happened to him? How did he wind up working for Semion Icoupov?"

"It was Icoupov who sent him to Conklin. They were friends, once upon a time," Willard said. "Conklin was intrigued when Icoupov told him about Arkadin. Treadstone was moving into a new phase by then; Conklin believed Arkadin was perfect for what he had in mind. But Arkadin rebelled. He went rogue, almost killed Conklin before he escaped to Russia."

Bourne was desperately trying to process all this information. At last, he said, "Willard, do you know what Alex had in mind when he created Treadstone?"

"Oh, yes. I told you I know all of Treadstone's secrets. Your mentor, Alex Conklin, was attempting to build the perfect beast."

"The perfect beast? What do you mean?" But Bourne already knew, because he'd seen it when he'd looked into Arkadin's eyes, when he understood that what he was seeing reflected there was himself.

"The ultimate warrior." Willard, one hand on the door handle, smiled now. "That's what you are, Mr. Bourne. That's what Leonid Danilovich Arkadin was—until, that is, he came up against you." He scrutinized Bourne's face, as if searching for a trace of the man who'd trained him to be a consummate covert operative. "In the end, Conklin succeeded, didn't he?"

Bourne felt a chill go through him. "What do you mean?"

"You against Arkadin, it was always meant to be that way." Willard opened the door. "The pity of it is Conklin never lived to see who won. But it's you, Mr. Bourne. It's you."

ABOUT THE AUTHORS

Eric Van Lustbader was born and raised in Greenwich Village. He is the author of over twenty bestselling novels, and his work has been translated into more than twenty languages.

After a successful career in the theatre, Robert Ludlum launched his career as a bestselling writer with *The Scarlatti Inheritance* in 1971, the first of twenty-two consecutive international bestsellers.